THE
OFFICER
SAYS
I Do

JEANETTE MURRAY

sourcebooks
casablanca

Published by Sourcebooks Casablanca, an imprint of Sourcebooks, Inc.
P.O. Box 4410, Naperville, Illinois 60567-4410
(630) 961-3900
Fax: (630) 961-2168
www.sourcebooks.com

Printed and bound in Canada
WC 10 9 8 7 6 5 4 3 2 1

*To my family, for their support
and unwavering faith in me.*

Chapter 1

TIMOTHY O'SHAY WAS POSITIVE OF ONE THING.

He would be dragging his friends' drunken asses out of a ditch before morning if things progressed the same way the rest of the night.

"Twenty!" Dwayne crooned next to him. Whenever D drank, his southern accent only became thicker until it was all twang. If someone wasn't careful, they could easily take Dwayne for an idiot. Big mistake.

"Twenty-one. Sorry, sir," the blackjack dealer said in a monotone voice before sweeping a crestfallen Dwayne's chips away.

Somewhere else in the casino, a siren alerted to a slot machine winner. The sound seemed to rub the loss in Dwayne's face as he scowled more.

"You're going to lose everything you have on the last night in Vegas," Jeremy warned. Not drunk, but plenty buzzed, he seemed to be slowly working his way toward the hammered side of life.

Since Tim had zero intention of using his last night of pre-deployment leave on babysitting their drunk asses—again—he shoved Dwayne until he tumbled out of the chair. "Grab some food to soak up the keg in your stomach. I'm not hauling you around by your shirt collar for what's left of leave."

Tim loved his friends like brothers. Meeting them in The Basic School was the best thing that had happened to him, to all of them. But often their fondness for free-for-all fun led to more problems than good times. Tim's tendency toward moderation and keeping a cool head kept them out of hot water more than once.

"Tim, let me borrow a few more bucks."

"And watch you lose my cash as fast as you lost yours? Hell no." Tim made another modest bet and watched as he broke even with the dealer. Unlike Dwayne and Jeremy, Tim was about to leave Vegas with the exact amount of cash he entered it with. Moderate play and moderate drinking ensured he never played too deep.

Moderate. The story of his life. Hard to shake the "play it safe" feeling when your entire life in the Marines consisted of just that. But then again, if he wasn't willing to play nanny to the two boobs he came with, they'd all be knee-deep in shit.

"Bet your own cash, then. It's our last night," Jeremy reminded him as he doubled down on his next hand.

"I am betting my money, Jer. And I'm doing just fine without a drunken Statler and Waldorf in my ear."

"Statler and who?" Dwayne asked.

"The Muppet hecklers, you idiot," Jeremy shot back.

"Both of you knock it off," Tim started. "I'm not going to—" He cut off, turning his head to follow a woman who passed behind the table, headed toward the slots. She was tall, her head high, and she floated more than walked. A thick mass of chestnut curls rioted down her back, almost covering her bare shoulders.

"Tim. Earth to Timmy." Jeremy waved a hand in front of his face.

Tim slapped it away and snapped, "What?"

"You're daydreaming and the dealer's waiting."

"Oh, sure. Right." Trying to find the brunette again, he shoved some chips out in front without counting. Jeremy whistled and Dwayne muttered a curse, but he didn't take his eyes away from the hunt. She must have slipped down an aisle of slots.

And why did he care? One woman, one night. In the end it amounted to nothing.

"Congratulations, sir."

"Holy shit," Jeremy breathed next to him.

Dwayne slapped his shoulder. "That was some playing, bro."

Huh? Tim looked down and saw that instead of his normal modest bets, he'd shoved almost three hundred dollars in for the hand. And won.

Holy shit indeed. He could have lost three hundred dollars and never even realized it. A cocktail waitress bent over to hand Dwayne the whiskey he'd ordered. Tim grabbed the glass first and tossed the drink back. The burn down his throat only ignited the adrenaline that was blazing low in his gut.

One shot wouldn't kill him. He wouldn't lose control from one shot.

"Do it again," Dwayne encouraged. His friend was starting to sound less sloppy, more like his normal good ole country boy self.

"Are you crazy?" Tim asked. "I could have lost that entire thing!" And why, when the thought should have been a cold wake-up call, did the fear thrill him, just a little?

"That's why it's called gambling," Jeremy pointed out. "Don't be a pussy. Do it again."

"You two are nuts."

Jeremy grabbed his wrist in a tight grip. "If you

lose, I'll pay you back every penny," he muttered in a low voice.

"What the hell has gotten into you?" Tim started to scrape his chips into the palm of his hand. Maybe he could catch up with the hot brunette before she got too far away. Playing all or nothing wasn't his style. Never had been. Measured risks made him a good officer and kept his ass out of trouble.

"Place your bets, gentlemen," the dealer intoned over the clang of another winning alarm bell somewhere in the slots section. Where his anonymous woman had disappeared to. Where he was heading.

"You have spent the entire trip playing nanny. And don't pretend you haven't."

"Someone has to," Tim grumbled. And yeah, it grated just a little that even if he wanted to have fun, it wouldn't be possible. Not with his two friends always being the first to sign up for Party Mascot.

"And we love you for it. But it just occurred to me that while you're babysitting, you're not having as much fun." Jeremy took the glass of Jack and Coke and pushed it in front. When Tim stared at him, he motioned to the glass. Tim took a sip, then a gulp.

"Place your bets." The request was more forceful.

"Hold on," Jeremy shot back, then faced Tim. "Do this. You're my best friend. You need to live. For one fucking night, stop thinking about what can go wrong. We have seven months in Afghanistan to worry about that. Have fun and let go. Don't be a pussy; just go for it."

Let go. It sounded like heaven. And really, if Jeremy was going to pay him back, was it really that much of a risk? For one night, he could act a fool like his friends normally did and worry about the consequences later.

He took all of one second to debate. He stole Dwayne's shot of tequila, ignoring Dwayne's protests, and tossed it back, adding to the burn of whiskey. Then he shoved his pile of chips forward.

"All in."

———⁓———

"Do you hear that?"

Skye McDermott turned to her best friend, Tasha, and asked, "What?"

"That noise. Coming from the tables. Sounds like someone's going to win big," her friend replied.

Skye checked her watch and tried to remember what time the show started. "That happens. It's a casino, after all," she pointed out.

"Do you wanna go watch?" Jessie asked.

Skye watched as she came up broke on the slot and swiveled on the stool. "This is girls' night out. Do you really want to spend it watching some fat, balding CPA have a lucky streak at cards while he pinches the waitresses' butts?"

"Girls' night out. As in the three of us. And two want to go. GNO is a democracy," Tasha said with a smile. "Come on. If it's boring we'll come back."

Skye heaved a sigh but followed in their wake, winding through the rows of slot machines. Just go with the flow. There was likely a reason her friends were so insistent, even if they'd never find out. Fate was weird that way, and like an experienced cardsharp, she didn't always show her hand.

Pulling her hair off her neck for a moment, she gave another sigh—this one of pleasure—as the cool casino air hit her hot skin. The curse of thick curls. She debated pulling it up in a ponytail but didn't bother. She pulled a few strands loose that were caught in her large hoop earrings.

"Can someone remind me why we didn't go elsewhere for our GNO anyway?" Jessie asked. "How much of a night out is it if we hang where we work?"

"We work at Cloud Nine, the restaurant. Just because it's inside the casino doesn't mean we work here on the floor," Skye reminded her. "And it's good to show support for our employer."

"Spoken like a true manager," Tasha teased, then stopped short. With a wide grin splitting her beautiful face, she pointed. "Now tell me. Does that look like a balding CPA?"

Skye glanced around her and saw the blackjack table causing the commotion. A crowd had formed in a semi-circle, completely enamored with the action. And no wonder.

Three men sat at the table meant for eight, but only one was actually playing the game. The one on the left was the largest of the three, his height evident even though they were sitting down. His grin was a bit loopy, as if he was fighting off a good drunk. The one on the right was smaller for sure, more lean than large. He was concentrating hard on the dealer's hands, as if memorizing every move. His body almost quivered with anticipation with each card pulled.

But the man in the middle grabbed her attention and held on tight. Military short, light brown hair, eyes that took in everything, and a mouth that she could watch for hours. He wasn't handsome in an obvious way. And nobody would dare call him pretty. But he was tempting all the same. He looked... relaxed. One arm draped over the back of the tallest one's chair, the other rested on his thigh. No tense energy, no anxiety, as if it was no big deal that he'd just laid down a two-hundred-dollar bet on a ten-dollar table. And he played with reckless abandon. No rhyme or reason. No pattern.

He lost a hand, and his smile quirked to one side as if to say, *Can't win 'em all*. When he won, he grinned like there was no point in playing it cool. He didn't play to the small crowd. In fact, the whooping, cheering horde of people behind him ceased to exist in his world. He was simply having fun for fun's sake. The lack of a plan, the absolute abandon that he played with was more attractive than his pile of chips. His easy laughter was infectious, and she found herself smiling along.

"The guy has absolutely no method to the madness," Jessie said in a murmur. Of the three women, she would be the one to know. Jessie was obsessed with poker and all things related. Skye didn't often gamble. Not with cards, anyway. Her philosophy was that life itself was the big gamble. Everything else sort of paled in comparison.

"I'll take the big sexy one on the left," Tasha said. She was almost rubbing her hands together with glee.

"I want the lean, mean one on the right," Jessie replied. Then without waiting for her, they slipped through the crowd, abandoning Skye behind the dealer.

Those two were man-eaters. Some women might pick a man out of a crowd and only dream of snagging him.

These two made it an actual habit. She watched while they weaved through the tight crowd until they stood behind the shoulder of their designated men.

Skye rolled her eyes. There went the designated girls' night. The poor boys had no chance. Not that they'd mind getting caught. Nobody ever minded getting tangled in Tasha and Jessie's web.

After a moment, she watched Tasha lean over, her breasts close to the big one's face as she shook hands with the table's other two occupants. The tallest, of course, looked like he'd entered heaven. Then her friend nodded her head, and man in the middle glanced up.

The look of instant recognition shook Skye. It was as if an electric shock ran through her from fingertips to toes, and she had to rub her arms to settle the goose bumps that rose. Positive she'd never met the man before in her life, Skye was tempted to check over her shoulder. But instead she couldn't escape the man's gaze. It was intent, focused, like she had a target painted on her forehead and he was ready to take aim.

Something both alarming and somehow serene sounded in a corner of her mind. Like this was a significant moment, to pay attention. Skye never ignored those warnings. Like déjà vu, people all too often dismissed things that they find were important later.

So when the man smiled and motioned for her to join them, it never occurred to Skye to say no.

Fate is never wrong, her mother used to say. It's just waiting for you to catch up. After being dragged to the blackjack tables by her friends, she couldn't ignore that Fate had a reason for her to meet this man.

She slowly made her way through the crowd,

apologizing and weaving until she stood behind the man in the middle, waiting for him to finish his hand.

Jessie grabbed her arm, as if anchoring her there. "Skye. Finally. This is Dwayne, that's Jeremy, and this one with the impressive winning streak is Tim."

Tim turned around, his eyes searching her face. Did he feel that same moment of instant recognition too? Was he trying to place her, make sense of the feeling?

"Skye?" he asked. His deep voice flowed down her spine, gave her the shivers. When was the last time a man's voice—a man's *anything*—gave her such an immediate physical response?

That would have been the week before never.

She shrugged. "It's whimsical, I'm told." Then she grinned when he laughed. She liked his laugh. Quick, full, rich like chocolate.

"So, Whimsical Skye, are you here to be a good luck charm?"

"Looks like you're doing pretty well for yourself without my help," she pointed out.

He shrugged, as if the cash in front of him wasn't the point, and drank half of whatever was in the glass in front of him. "I'm having fun."

Ah, she liked that answer. She liked *him*. "In that case, I'd love to be your good luck charm for fun."

Tim motioned something to the dealer that had the crowd—and his friends—groaning.

"You're giving up? Tim, come on, man!" the one named Jeremy said. "You were on a roll!"

"I think I'm going to roll a different direction," Tim murmured just loud enough for Skye to hear.

She shivered in response. Her night out was turning

into much more than she ever expected. Not that she was complaining. Between relationships, things could be lonely. A little weekend fling might be a nice, uncomplicated way to spice things up for the moment.

Mom was right. Follow the signs, follow Fate. When you least expected it, She dropped something you didn't even realize you needed right in your lap.

Tim pushed his chips forward to the dealer, exchanging them for a smaller, more manageable handful of large denomination chips. Seeing that he was done, the crowd had already dissipated. Vegas tourists had the attention span of a second grader without his ADHD meds. Skye stepped back to give Tim some room, but he grabbed her hand before she got too far away.

"Stay close," he said. It was an order, not a request.

"Are you my designated keeper?" she retorted, though the order gave her another shiver.

"I am tonight," Tim replied. He motioned something to his friends who nodded. Jeremy leaned in to speak in his ear, but Tim shook his head and waved him off. "I'm good." When he glanced down and saw she hadn't moved, he smiled. The look was predatory, pure male satisfaction. "Very good."

With that, he turned on his heel and headed toward the closest cash-out counter. She walked with him, but only because he had an iron grip on her hand and it was either follow or be dragged caveman style.

"We're heading to X-cess!" Tasha called out behind her, naming the popular nightclub also housed within the casino. "Call me if you need me!" When Skye glanced back, all she could see were four blurs moving toward the hotel's largest nightclub.

Abandoned. Tasha and Jessie were in a matchmaking mood tonight. Otherwise they wouldn't have dared leave her alone with a stranger.

Skye stood back a few feet while Tim spoke to the cashier at the window, then a manager. Some papers were thrust at Tim, and he scratched on them with a pen for a few moments and then passed them back. He walked away, slipping what looked like a room card in his pocket.

"Comped room?"

He gave her a strange look. "Yeah. How'd you know?"

"Isn't that how it always works?" she said vaguely. Of course she knew. She was an employee. A one-night stand didn't require she share her life story.

Tim pulled his hand back out of his pocket, the room key still in his hand. Long, tan fingers flipped the card over, rubbed the smooth glossy finish, traced the edges of the plastic. Those fingers—and the not-so-PG images they were creating in her mind—could do some serious damage to her self-control. What little she had.

"Do you believe in following signs?"

Skye's breath caught in her chest. "Yeah. I do." Talk about a big, neon marquee.

Tim nodded silently, still staring at the room key. Was he going to ask her up? That's where this was all heading anyway, right? A night of pleasure before he went back to wherever he came from.

Not that she did that often. Rarely, actually. Skye was more of a relationship person. But she was also a woman, and between boyfriends she never felt like there was much wrong with enjoying herself.

But Tim called to her senses like no other man had

before. And walking away without even seeing if one night was an option would have been almost painful.

"Ever realize that you've been watching life instead of living it?" He looked at her, but his eyes weren't seeing her. Skye would have guessed waving a hand in front of his face wouldn't have fazed him. It was like he mentally left the building.

"Kind of a philosophical question for the first meeting, don't you think?" she teased, hoping for a reaction.

He gave her a grin and she relaxed. "You're right. Screw being philosophical." Before she had a chance to say anything in response, he grabbed her wrist and tugged her around a corner. In the shadow of a potted palm tree, he gently nudged her back against a wall. "Just need to see," he murmured and then his lips were on hers.

The bright casino lights, the buzz of voices, the clanging of bells and wailing of sirens all faded to nothing, as if they'd stepped in a bubble built for two.

Skye wasn't one to lie to herself. She could play the outraged damsel, she could act the indignant uptight woman. But since she was neither, and because it was exactly what she wanted, she only wound her arms around Tim's neck to bring him closer. To encourage.

Not that he needed the encouragement. The man was taking what he wanted whether she agreed or not. His tongue licked the seam of her lips and dove in without waiting for her to catch up.

He tasted like whiskey, and he felt like velvet. Large hands circled her waist and pulled her against him. The outline of his erection was hot against her hip, and she felt powerful. One palm coasted up her ribs until he cupped her breast, then thumbed her nipple through the thin material of her tank top. The other lifted the hem of her shirt up. Just enough to have her gasping, wondering how far he would go. But he only let his thumb rub the skin of her lower stomach. Nothing more.

All smooth and sensual, the kiss wasn't meant to make her knees weak. No, it was meant to strengthen her enough to handle what followed. This wasn't the main course. It was the appetizer.

Thank you. Thank you, Fate, for bringing me this fine specimen.

He murmured something in her ear, but she couldn't hear it.

"What?" she asked. Oh God, was that her voice? It sounded so thin, so vague.

"I said marry me," he said and bit her earlobe.

Marry? Did he just ask—no, tell—her to marry him? *What the hell, Fate?*

"Um…" She tried to form a complete sentence, but her mind was slipping into some hazy alternate universe. A universe where, apparently, the thought of a forever commitment with a complete stranger wasn't enough to send her screaming into the night.

"I have never felt this pull before. And tonight is about living. And we're in Vegas." He took a good nip on her throat and soothed the spot with his tongue. The hand on her breast tugged until her tank neckline lowered. Until his hand was cupping her bra and not her shirt. Oh God, he was going to undress her in the hallway. And she was going to let him.

Skye let her head fall back until it thudded against the wall. Was this what Fate was planning the entire time? Was the fact that she hadn't said no automatically a sign?

"I don't know anything about you," she said weakly. Weakly, as if she was losing power by the second.

"Thirty-one. Never married. Clean bill of health. Captain in the Marine Corps. Twenty-nine Palms. Last name O'Shay." He ended each description with a pinch of her nipple, a twist of the flesh.

She was drowning. That's why her lungs were working double-time to drag air in. No other explanation.

"Not going to share anything?" His other hand scooted up to her bottom rib, taking her shirt with it.

"McDermott," she managed to breathe out. "Twenty-eight. Restaurant manager. Never married."

"Sounds good to me," he said. One knee pried her legs apart until she was riding his thigh. The pressure between her legs was a torment. "Feels better."

On that, she couldn't disagree.

"Well?" he asked against her lips.

Fate is never wrong.

Skye took a deep breath. "Yes."

Fate is just waiting for you to catch up.

Chapter 2

TIM OPENED THE DOOR TO HIS COMPED SUITE WITH A flourish, then caught himself as he almost fell through the door. "Welcome."

The brunette walked in and looked around, dropping her purse on the entry table. Skye. Her name was Skye. How the hell had he gotten her up here? *Think, Tim. Think.*

Blackjack. Palm tree. Car ride. Paperwork. Did he bring paperwork? Did he sign something?

He ran a hand down his face and pressed his thumb and forefinger to his temples. He was losing chunks of time. Damn, why did he keep drinking after he won all that cash?

This is why I don't drink whiskey. This is why I'm always the nanny.

He watched as Skye—what an odd name—surveyed their surroundings. He hadn't been in the suite himself yet. With each step, her hips swayed in that little black skirt she wore and he stopped caring how they got from Point A to Point B.

Kissing Skye. That was something he remembered. Vividly.

She walked over to the L-shaped couch, sat down, and crossed her legs. Her skirt slithered up her thighs, dangerously close to showing him exactly what she was wearing underneath. That was a mystery he was more than willing to look into.

Patting the couch cushion beside her, she said, "Come over here."

He walked over, ignoring the way the room tilted, and plopped down on the couch beside her. Had she followed him up? Or did he invite her? Shit, why couldn't he remember?

"I think we need to get to know each other a little."

He bit back the urge to ask why. That would have been rude. Tim didn't do rude. Unless he was drunk. Fuck, was he drunk? No. If he was drunk he wouldn't be so damn horny. His arm curved around the top of the couch, hand dangling, fingers brushing the soft skin of her shoulder.

She gave a shy smile, like she was embarrassed. "Tell me something about you. I know your name and your age. But that's all."

"What do you want to know?" To take her mind off conversation, he leaned over and placed a kiss on her cheek, then let his lips roam over her jawline.

"Well," she breathed. "What do you do in the Marine Corps?"

Still talking. He scooted until he was facing her and brushed a hand down her arm. She shivered and he smiled against her neck. Working his way down to the place where her shoulder started, he lightly bit the tendons. She gasped, and a hand came up to cup the back of his head. Ah, that was better. He tugged at the hem of her tank, letting the back of his fingers brush against the warm skin of her stomach while they drifted up.

"You… you didn't answer," she said on a sigh.

"Comm. I'm a Comm guy." There. Hopefully that was enough to satisfy her. To ensure her silence, he sealed his mouth over hers.

God, she tasted good, like something light and not entirely tamed. She groaned in his mouth, firing his blood more. He leaned and shifted enough to get a good grip on her hips, then sat back and dragged her over so that she straddled his lap. Letting his hands wander down, he felt the piece of fabric she called a skirt bunched up around the top of her hips, leaving nothing but a scrap of lace between her core and his fingers.

He pulled his head back long enough to yank her tank top off, throwing it behind him. Only he forgot the couch backed up to a wall and the back of his hand bashed against a picture frame and her tank top slithered down to drape around his shoulders.

"Shit," he groaned. Was that the picture frame or his hand he heard crack? Before he could check for damage to either, he glanced up and his mouth watered at the sight in front of him.

See-through black lace cups offered up firm breasts, and he took one pebbled nipple in his mouth. The rasp of fabric and his tongue had her panting, moaning his name.

That was a sound he could get used to. Pain was a long-forgotten sensation.

Quick fingers undid the front hook and he brushed the bra aside and down her arms. He moved his attention to her other breast, sucking and nibbling, inhaling the faint scent of her. Clean, fresh, like she just stepped out of the shower. No cloying, overly sweet, fake scent. He focused on her breasts with the utmost concentration. If he let his mind wander to the nearly-bare heat pressing against his groin, he'd never last. He needed her desperate for him before he even attempted to go further.

Her nails scraped in his short hair, scouring his scalp.

He could feel her galloping heartbeat under his palm as he massaged her other breast. Her hips thrust forward, rubbing her against him, begging for more.

He ran a palm down her stomach. Reaching that layer of lace, he traced one finger down her seam, felt the dampness of her arousal through the lace. He damn near lost it then, knowing how primed and ready she was. But his control was a thing of legend, and he wasn't about to let it go now. He debated for a moment, then took a good hold of the side of her panties and ripped until the fabric split in half.

She gasped and stared at him with wide, wild eyes. She was a goner, and it gave him a fierce sense of satisfaction.

He shoved the fabric aside and let his fingers drift once, twice over her damp lips before pushing one finger deep into her wet heat. She groaned, and he would have sworn her pupils dilated. He smiled against her breast and bit the soft flesh, mostly to hear her breath speed up. He wasn't disappointed.

Another finger added to the first, and her head dropped back. God, she was something.

"Please. Tim, please." Her voice was harsh, like gravel stuck in her throat.

"What do you want?" Would she ask? Was she too embarrassed to ask for an orgasm?

"You." With what looked like great effort, she lifted her head to look directly in his eyes. Her hair was a riot of curls, her eyes were heavy, her mouth swollen. "I want you inside me."

He was beyond denying her—or himself—at that point. He nudged her so that she swung one leg back off. With shaking fingers, he undid the buttons to his jeans and slid them down to his knees, taking his boxers with him. His erection thumped his stomach, and he wondered when the last time he'd been so hard so fast was. With an affectionate slap on the thigh, he pulled her over his lap again. She shrieked and laughed, her core heat cradling his cock.

But when he lifted her up to take him in, she resisted. Looking up, he was surprised to see embarrassment on her face that, seconds ago, had held blind lust.

"What?"

She stared at his lap, then back at him. She chewed on her bottom lip for a moment, then asked, "Protection?"

Shit. How the hell had he forgotten that? Where the fuck was his head? He hadn't made that mistake since he was seventeen. He motioned for her to scoot once more so he could reach into the back pocket of his jeans, still hanging around his knees. Reaching into the wallet, he grabbed the foil packet there and tossed the billfold on the coffee table. But before he could take care of things himself, sly fingers took the packet from him.

Gone was the hint of embarrassment. Now that she didn't have to ask him blatantly stupid questions—like reminding him rule number one of consensual sex— she seemed more at ease. No, not at ease. The slight tilt of her lips as she knelt down on the floor between his legs was one of a temptress who knew exactly what she was doing.

One slender hand peeled his erection away from his stomach. She stroked him, letting her thumb graze the top of his head and spread the moisture that seeped out at her firm touch. She used her teeth to tear open the packet, and in a smooth caress, she rolled the protection over his cock.

When had safe sex ever been so damn sexy?

She stood and gave him a peck on the nose, which had him grinning. Then with a quick zip and a shimmy of her hips, the skirt that had been bunched around her waist fell to the ground with a soft rustle. Keeping her heels on—oh, that was nice—she crawled back onto his lap. Her hands stayed on his shoulders for balance and she rocked against him. Her mouth touched his and he lost all remaining hope of holding off any longer.

Reaching between them, he guided their bodies until he inched inside the beckoning heat. With slow, controlled movements, she slid down until he was fully encased.

Holy mother of Chesty Puller. His head dropped to the back of the couch. She rotated around, and he closed his eyes and bit back a groan. God in heaven that was amazing.

"Feel good?" she asked against his neck. Her teeth grazed his pulse.

"You have no clue how unbelievable that feels."

She chuckled. "I might have an idea. We're kind of in this together. All the way in this."

Her tone was so ominous, he made the effort to look up. For just a moment, her eyes held a serious gleam rather than the sultry promise of earlier. He almost asked what she meant. But then she smiled and rose up on her knees, only to sink down again fully. At that moment, she could have told him she was Mary, Queen of Scots and he wouldn't have cared.

He let her set the pace, and he was thankful that it was a bruising one. Sweat created a sheen over their skin.

Their stomachs stuck together. The pull and give of their bodies created a wet, suctioning noise that was almost more arousing than anything. But the thing that caught his attention most was the intense way she focused on his face. Peppering kisses, gentle caresses, gazing into his eyes. He wasn't sure if she knew it or not, but she was imprinting herself on his brain. He doubted he'd forget the look on her face as she climbed toward release if he lived to be ninety.

She panted his name, but he could barely hear over the buzzing in his ears. His vision started to tunnel. When had that happened before? But he wasn't about to let go of the opportunity to finish with Skye. He reached between them and used his thumb to rub quick circles around her clit.

Explosion. That was the only word to describe her reaction. Her head flew back, hair raining down to almost brush his thighs. She moaned; her nails bit into his shoulder. And her body convulsed around him. The reaction triggered his own orgasm, every moment of release pure bliss.

She dropped her head down onto his shoulder, and all he could think was, *I'm done for. I've never had an orgasm do this to me. Sex can kill.* Then his vision blackened and the world went silent.

Skye woke up to daylight pouring through the window. What the hell? When had she drawn the curtains? She never left those open.

Oh, for the love of Mother Earth.

She shot up in bed, grabbing the sheets to cover her

breasts. Hand impatiently pushing away at hair that flew into her face, she scanned the room.

Bedroom, one of the suites at Celestial Palace. No sign of Tim.

Her husband.

Her knees drew up and she let her forehead drop down to rest on them. What the hell had she done? She let her ideals of Fate walk her into a quickie Vegas wedding. A Vegas wedding. The cliché of all clichés. Where was her head? Where was her common sense?

Where was her husband?

She gingerly pushed the sheets back and crept out of bed, naked as the day she was born. She didn't hear anything. No noise coming from the living room. None from the bathroom. Maybe he snuck out for breakfast?

How he could walk after last night, she wasn't sure. After sharing that mind-blowing orgasm, she was ready to snuggle up and talk. Get to know each other more. See what they had walked into. Make plans for the future.

What an idiot she was.

Instead, Tim had passed out cold. She almost thought he'd died, the way his head tipped back and clonked against the wall. But his breathing had been normal, pulse was steady. Apparently he'd been drunk, and she hadn't even realized it.

How did she miss that? Drinking, she knew that much. But drunk as a skunk? She was a restaurant manager, for cripes' sake. She knew what intoxication looked like. Daily battles were fought with patrons trying for just one more beverage. But she'd either missed every sign he'd given on her quest to follow that conniving bitch Fate, or he was just one of the few who was a light switch. Fine until it flips, then it's game over.

There was no way she would have been able to shift him into the bedroom like that, so she did what she could to clean him up and lie him flat on the couch. The faint sound of his snores followed her as she went to the bedroom to sleep by herself. On her wedding night. With her husband passed out on the couch.

Every bride's dream.

She decided to grab a quick shower while she had the chance. If she was going to face her consequences, she wanted to do it feeling fresh and without morning breath.

A quick shower and blow-dry later, she donned one of the fluffy white robes provided by the hotel. With one hand on the door leading to the living room, she paused. What if he was still asleep? Or waiting for her, ready to ask for an annulment?

Annulment her ass. There was a reason they were married. And she was going to keep it that way.

Skye pressed a hand over her racing heart. *Pull it together. You can do this. Fate led you here for a reason, and you followed willingly. Put on your big girl panties and face the music. Or, well, the Marine.*

She took a deep breath and opened the door. More light poured in from the window, a stark contrast to the dark, seductive cave from last night. Tim wasn't on the couch, but her clothes were. Folded neatly, they sat all alone on the middle cushion, the clutch purse she'd had with her resting on top. On the same cushion where they'd made love the night before.

Her cheeks and neck flushed, though she wasn't sure why. A quick glance to the kitchenette and balcony showed he wasn't in the suite at all. Nor were any of his things. Not his wallet or his watch or anything that showed he even existed anywhere but in her mind. The horrible thought made the bottom of her stomach drop, then double-check her purse.

Yup. Still there. Folded into a tiny square was the marriage license. Signed, dated, and legally binding. She wasn't sure whether the cool relief she felt was because they really were married, or simply because she wasn't crazy, hadn't dreamed the whole thing.

Another few minutes went by as she grabbed a bottle of water, and no sign of him. Probably checking on his friends, or maybe he ran downstairs for breakfast, not wanting to wake her. Kind of sweet, actually. If she'd had a key to the room, she would go down and check herself. But not knowing where to start, she didn't want to leave the room, in case he came back soon.

She dressed in the bathroom and waited, flipping through TV channels. After another twenty minutes, it dawned on her she could check to see if he was downstairs. This was where she worked, after all. And though she was mostly isolated in the restaurant, she knew other employees. Picking up the room phone, she dialed the front desk.

"Hey, this is Skye McDermott. Is Jimmy working today?"

The clerk confirmed and put her on hold. She chewed her lip, not sure how to explain the predicament.

Hey, Jimmy. Skye McDermott. Yeah, so crazy story. Last night I met a guy, got married, and came up to his comped suite to do it like animals. But today he's gone missing. Does the hotel offer any husband-tracking amenities?

"Hey, Skye. What's up?"

Jimmy's easy greeting snapped her out of her wallowing. "Jimmy, hi." Jimmy had been one of her brief forays into inner-Vegas dating. They weren't a match, but more than that, she quickly learned that what happened in Vegas… was everyone else's business. At least when you and your current significant other worked in the same hotel and casino, even in different sections. But if there was one person who could help her, it was Jimmy.

"I'm looking for my… friend. I stayed with him last night, and he's not around anymore. Could you see if he's hanging around downstairs? I don't want to leave the room in case he comes back and we miss each other in the elevators."

"Sure. Name and room number?"

She gave him the info, along with a description of Tim.

Through the connection, she could hear keys being punched. "Uh, Skye. Are you sure he was coming back?"

"What? Why wouldn't he?"

"My records show he checked out of the comped suite about an hour ago. Hold on, let me ask Mandy. Says here she was the one that helped him." Without further warning, he put her on hold.

An hour ago.

He checked out an hour ago and didn't say a word. There was nothing he could have possibly been doing for an hour that would keep him from coming back up to the room.

Skye felt her lungs burn as her breath came in quick, shallow pants. What the hell happened? Did he leave? Was he on the way to get an attorney? Did he even remember that she was there in the bedroom? He'd folded her clothes, surely he knew. Why the hell hadn't he woken her—

"Skye?"

She forced one long breath in and out before answering, "Yeah, Jimmy?"

"Mandy says she remembered. O'Shay checked out, then walked out the front door with two other big guys. Her impression was that he wasn't coming back. You should call his cell; looks like you got your wires crossed."

"Okay. Thanks," she said, voice strangled. Before he could ask her what was wrong, she hung up the phone and choked back a sob.

In the course of twenty-four hours she'd had a girls' night out, met a man that made her body sing, married him, and been abandoned.

What a way to start a marriage.

Chapter 3

TIM TOSSED HIS RUCKSACK INTO THE BOTTOM OF THE BUS AND simply groaned as twelve other bags covered it immediately. That'd be a bitch to find when they got to the airport. Oh well. Nothing he could do about it now.

He climbed onto the bus and took a seat up front with the other officers. After waiting for everyone to board and taking another quick head count, he signaled for the driver to head out. It was a long drive from California to Quantico, Virginia, but that was the plan. Chartered busses would take them across the country, then they would fly the rest of the way to Afghanistan.

Finally, after finishing up the annoying details of his company commander duties, he was able to pop his iPod earbuds in and listen to some music. Best of all, he hoped everyone would get the hint to leave him the fuck alone.

No such luck.

His earbud was ripped out and someone's thick finger flicked him on the side of the head. He turned around to see Dwayne's shit-eating grin, headphone dangling from his hand.

"What?" he growled. "It's been ten minutes. You couldn't possibly have something important to tell me right now."

"Actually, since you're completely caged in with nowhere to go, I was planning on bugging you for details about that hot piece from Vegas. It's been a week."

Jeremy's head popped up from behind the seat, next to Dwayne. A twin grin split his own face. "Yeah. How about it?"

Skye. He didn't want to talk about Skye. And he really didn't want anyone calling her a "piece" of anything.

"Leave it alone," he said, grabbing the earbud back. "I told you everything I planned on telling you on the flight back to Cali. We had a hot night. And I'm still pissed about you guys letting me get that wasted."

Dwayne shrugged massive shoulders, their width only emphasized by his cammies. "Hey. You were in control. And you're a big boy. I'm nobody's mama."

Jeremy gave him a reproving scowl. "You needed to loosen up, Tim. You were completely sober when you made the choice to have some more fun. Don't act like we tricked you."

Tim sighed. It really wasn't Dwayne or Jeremy's fault. He hated when other people brushed off responsibility, so he wouldn't do it himself. But damn, he felt like a fool. And he wasn't even sure how much he had screwed up.

Popping the bud back in his ear, he deliberately turned around and ignored their childish punches on the back of his seat. He wasn't going to give them details about his night with Skye. She didn't deserve that, whether she'd ever know about it or not.

And also, he wasn't sure about a majority of what happened.

He remembered winning at cards, and he especially remembered exactly how much he had won. The amount still astonished him. He recalled having a drink or five. And then he remembered Skye.

Skye with her mile-long legs and adorable smile. With her fresh attitude and fun laugh. He remembered searing kisses behind some tree, he remembered a car ride, some flashy guy who looked like Burt Reynolds clapping him on the back. And he remembered opening the door to the free suite the hotel had given him. Everything else to that moment was either fuzzy or completely blank.

But he remembered her. He remembered how clean she smelled, how soft her breasts were, the way she arched her back when he touched her. The little pants she let out when she begged him to end the slow build and take the plunge.

Yeah. He remembered Skye. And he remembered what a dick he was the next morning, leaving before she woke up. There was no excuse for it. He'd never left without a word in his life. He didn't often have one-nighters. They weren't his style. He was a relationship man and was ready to make a commitment when he found the right woman.

But for some reason, the shame of facing her the next morning, not knowing what he might have said while piss-drunk or how he might have behaved, overwhelmed him. So he checked out, made sure she wouldn't be left with any sort of tab, and took off. And he felt like a jackass for it. He wasn't delusional, didn't expect their one night would go anywhere. But if he had a single clue how to find her to apologize for his behavior, he would.

Someone grabbed his shoulder and shook hard.

He turned around and snapped, "What!"

Jeremy pointed to his knapsack on the seat next to him. "Your phone's ringing, you cranky bastard."

"Oh. Sorry," he mumbled as he reached for his cell in the outer pocket. Not his finest moment in leadership. He checked caller ID and saw his sister was calling. He felt his heart expand and a smile crept onto his lips.

"Hey, Madison. What's up?"

"Are you already gone? I just got off work and I was going to rush over to the battalion parking lot to see you." Her voice was breathless and he smiled at the mental picture of her in scrubs running through the hospital parking lot to her car.

"Stand down, sweetie. We're gone. Took off about twenty minutes ago."

"Oh. Well never mind then." She took a big breath and let it out. "Sorry. I tried to switch shifts but nobody was biting. I know we did the good-bye thing already but—"

"Madison, it's cool. Don't worry about it. I get it. You're a nurse, you're busy saving lives. I'm just glad you're on the same base as me now. When we get home, you'll be right there."

"Literally," she said on a laugh. "Are you sure you're okay with me staying at your townhouse while you're gone?"

"I'd rather have someone there than it sit empty. You can watch over it, take care of the plants, make sure nothing goes wrong or anyone breaks in."

"You don't have any houseplants." She snickered. "They'd commit suicide before going home with you."

"That's true," he admitted. "You know I—" He swatted at the hand grabbing for his cell. "You know how much I hate—cut it out!" He turned and glared daggers at Dwayne.

"Is that your sister?" He gave a sly smile. "Tell her I said hi."

"Cut it out," Jeremy interceded.

"No, I will not tell her hi for you, asshole." He turned back around in his seat. "Mad, you still there?"

"Was that Dwayne?" He could hear the amusement in her voice.

"Yeah, it was Dwayne. Jeremy too. Ignore them, they're giving me a—"

The phone was snatched out of his hands with special ops stealth.

"Hey there, sugar," Dwayne drawled behind him. "How's life treating ya?"

Tim rolled his eyes and scooted until he was sideways on the seat, able to watch his friends behind him and listen in on their side of the phone conversation. He wasn't concerned what either bozo might say to his sister. They'd met his family countless times and thought of Madison like a little sister.

"Yeah? Are you sure you can handle living with this guy? He gets pretty pissy from time to time." Dwayne cocked his head to one side and laughed. "Yeah, I guess you'd know better than most about his moods, huh? All right, well thanks for the luck, sweets. I appreciate it. Mail me some of those cookies you make. The ones covered in cinnamon. Yeah, those. M'kay. Here's Jeremy."

He held out the phone in front of Jeremy, who had a slightly panicked look on his face.

"Here," Dwayne mouthed. "It's just Madison. She wants to say good-bye." When Jeremy looked frozen to the spot—what the hell was that all about?—Dwayne held the phone up to Jeremy's ear and elbowed him in the gut so that he groaned into the receiver.

"Yeah, it's me," he puffed out a second later. "Hey, Madison. What's up?"

Dwayne turned back to Tim. "So do you think the rumors are true?"

Tim snorted. "Which rumors?" Deployments and troop movements were ripe breeding grounds for rumors and hearsay. It was worse than a high school girls' locker room.

"The ones about us having to turn around and come back. Delay the deployment last second, come back, and regroup."

Tim shrugged. "I don't know. You know the drill. When I know, you'll know, unless specifically ordered. It's been mentioned, but nothing is definite."

Dwayne rubbed a hand down his face. "Yeah. This is the part I really hate. We're already on the bus. Can we just fucking go already?"

"Hurry up and wait," Tim said with a smile on his face, quoting a favorite Marine Corps saying.

Jeremy tossed the phone back in his lap. "There. She's still on the line."

Tim heard Jeremy mutter "jackass" to Dwayne before putting the phone back up to his ear.

"Mad? I'm gonna get off here. I'll call you when we get to Quantico and let you know that we're there."

"All right. I love you, you big lug." Her voice sounded watery, like she was choking back tears. Damn, if there was one person on this earth who could inspire him to cry, it was his baby sister.

"Cut that out," he scolded. "You know the deal. I'll be back before you know it. In the meantime, you get a rent-free place to live. Now, don't pass all your cookies to Dwayne. Send some my way, okay?"

"Will do."

"Love you, squirt." He knew she was concentrating too hard on not bawling when she didn't even object to his old childhood nickname for her. "I'll call you soon."

After hanging up the phone, he glanced back and saw both Dwayne and Jeremy engrossed in their own worlds. Dwayne with *Gun Digest* magazine, Jeremy writing in a notebook. He was glad for the chance to slip back into his own private thoughts without the peanut gallery commentary.

But the moment he turned his iPod back on, and closed his eyes, Skye came into focus. Long hair raining down her back, firm thighs clenched around his…

Shit. He was going to have an obvious boner at this rate. Why, of all women, did he have to get stuck on the one that would never even be an option to try with? She lived in Las Vegas, for crissake. He dealt with enough long distance in life, thanks to deployments. Being with a woman who didn't even live with him when he was in the country? Not an option.

Luckily for him, he had several long months to dedicate to forgetting her.

Skye held the scrap of paper in her hand. The corner was smudged and she'd dropped a piece of her grilled cheese on it. But that didn't matter. The address it held was the most important part.

Her husband's address.

It was a nice townhouse, about thirty minutes from base according to the Internet. She could see the appeal. Not a horrible commute, but a decent distance away to separate himself from work. Made sense. The front was painted white, with crisp blue shutters. The lawn was immaculate, shrubs all precisely identical. Very well ordered, put together.

Everything she was not.

She took a deep breath, hiked her bag up her shoulder, and walked up the sidewalk to the front door.

Her palms were sweaty as she reached for the doorbell, and she took a moment to wipe them on her light cotton skirt. Then she glanced down at her outfit. Her skirt fell to her calves, and made a fun swish with every step. The happy coral color made her feel brighter despite the circumstances. She wore sandals that tied around her ankles, and a simple white tank to let the skirt take focus. Her hair, because of the heat, was kept off her neck with a braid, though strands were already escaping. Stupid frizz.

Was this what someone wore to confront their absent husband? Was there such an outfit? She rang the doorbell before she could chicken out, hop back in her car, and head to the hotel and change.

Ten seconds passed, then twenty. She was about to turn and walk away when the door opened. A woman stood there, eying her like she was public enemy number one. Neither said a word, and Skye used the moment to take stock of the gatekeeper.

Short, probably not even five foot three. Her face was free of any makeup, but she was pretty enough without any cosmetic help. Though she'd be prettier if her face wasn't scrunched up into an intimidating frown. Her hair was scraped back into a tight bun, not a stray in sight. Skye's hand went unconsciously to pat her own messy nest of hair.

Though from the neck up the woman was all business, the shoulders down was another story. A baggy navy blue T-shirt with a large gold *N* on the front hung on her frame to almost her knees, paired with stained gray sweatpants that made her look younger than her likely real age. Definitely wearing a male's clothing. Everything about her screamed "I belong here."

Oh God. Was he dating someone else already? Did he have a live-in girlfriend the entire time in Vegas? Horrible thoughts swirled around in her mind, each possibility worse than the one before.

Thanks, Fate.

"Do you need something?" Her voice was crisp and full of authority.

Walk away and say nothing. Walk away. Go. Come back later. "Does Tim live here?"

The woman raised an eyebrow. "I think I'd like to know who was asking."

She took a deep breath, realized it was now or never, and blurted out, "His wife."

"How long are we going to sit around here doing nothing?" Jeremy asked, kicking his bag with the toe of his boot.

Tim just stared at him. "Do I have to give you the same answer again? I told you. We're heading back. They called us back; we knew it was a possibility. So just calm down until we can figure out the bus situation and we'll head back."

"Just want to do something. Anything," Jeremy grumbled.

Tim knew. He understood completely the frustration that Jeremy felt. That bone-deep itching need to be useful. Instead they were stuck in the BOQ at Quantico for another day, waiting to see what kind of mess awaited them at home. It was a rough switch, gearing down from battle-ready to home again. But he didn't make the final call. Their commanding officer didn't make the call either. Everyone had a higher power. God probably had a CO.

His phone rang and he picked it out of his pocket, glad for the distraction from his pissy friend. "O'Shay."

"Tim, hey. Still cooling your heels in Quantico?" his sister asked.

Ah. Madison. Just the distraction he needed. "Yup, still sitting pretty, Mad." Out of the corner of his eye, he saw Jeremy shift his drooping shoulders. Maybe he wanted something to distract him from the inaction as well. "Actually, plans are changing up around here. I'd tell you more but—"

"Yeah, I know. OPSEC. It's all about the operational security. I've heard rumors, though. I can guess. Anyway, glad I caught you. There's a bit of a situation here at the house."

The hairs on the back of his neck stood, and his breath caught. "Situation? What? Are you okay?"

Jeremy moved like lightning, standing beside him, practically breathing down his neck. "What is it?"

"Yeah, no, I'm fine. Sorry. That sounded ominous, didn't it?" She laughed, and he felt the tension drain from his body like an uncorked bottle. He nudged Jeremy back a step and signaled that it was fine. Though he moved out of claustrophobic range, Jeremy's eyes didn't leave the cell, like he was just waiting for the word to jump through the receiver and end up in California to aid his sister. Times like those, when family might be on the line, he knew he had the best friends possible.

"All right, so what's the problem?"

"Well, it's not a problem so much as what I said. Situation. A woman showed up on your doorstep today."

A woman. He was still at square one. "I need something more than that."

"Right, sorry. Does the name Skye McDermott ring a bell for you?"

He almost dropped the phone. Sweet Jesus. His pulse pounded in his ears, his hands were clammy. "Describe her," he rasped, mouth almost too dry to talk. "What does she look like?"

"Um, tall. Way taller than me, which doesn't say much usually. I mean, I know I'm short and all, but she does seem taller than your average—"

"Madison."

"Oh, right. Sorry. Um, brunette. Long, curly hair. In shape. Really cute. Blue-gray eyes."

It was hitting all the right marks. At least, it was hitting all the marks in his foggy memory. What the hell would she have wanted with him? How could she have even tracked him down? He didn't leave anything with his address in the room, he was sure of it. He certainly hadn't talked to her in the week and a half since. So why would she even bother tracking—oh God.

She's pregnant.

"You're pregnant?" his sister shrieked in his ear.

"No!" someone yelled back, voice slightly muffled. Well, fuck. Guess he said that one out loud. Wait—

"Was that Skye? Is she there with you? Is she still at the house?"

"Well, yeah." He could almost see his sister roll her eyes. "You think I'd just kick your wife out on the street?"

"My…" He looked at Jeremy, who had relaxed enough to sit on top of his bed, but was still paying rapt attention. Normally he'd put the blame on his friends for pulling a horrible joke. But this was a little too much, even for their sick and twisted minds.

"All right, can you just back up a bit?"

"Sure," she said, like there was no problem at all. "I got home from my shift, changed, and there was a knock. Skye here was standing on the doorstep. I didn't know what to make of it, but then she told me she was your wife."

No. This wasn't making any sense.

Madison went on without pause. "So I was shocked because, really, why would my brother, one of my best friends in the entire world, go and get married and not tell me? Not to mention your slight anal-retentive problem. Anal-retentive people don't just up and marry strangers in Vegas. I mean, it seemed a little implausible."

That was one word for it.

"So I basically accused her of being a money-grubbing hussy."

"Hussy?" Tim nearly choked on the word. Jeremy's brows raised in surprise. "Uh, squirt, I don't think anyone uses that word anymore."

"Don't call me that. That was my first thought. I mean, why else would someone track your ugly mug down from Vegas?"

"Squirt. The story. It's kinda important."

"No problem. But then she said she had no clue how much you won."

Entirely plausible, since even Tim didn't know how much he'd won until he checked his bank account. Thank God for instant wire transfers.

"Hold on," Madison said suddenly. Muffled words he couldn't quite make out, as if she put her hand over the phone. "She wants me to remind you that you were the one who proposed. Not her. Behind a—behind a what?" Her voice was muted, probably covering the receiver with her fingers. Then she said, "She said you proposed behind a potted palm. Among other things. Apparently the place to be is behind a tree." The dry humor was too obvious to miss. Madison was thoroughly enjoying this.

Tim had a flash of exactly what they'd been doing in the darkened hallway behind the tree. Hot lips, smooth skin... He shifted on the bed and turned away from Jeremy to readjust his cammie pants. "Yeah, moving on."

"Uh huh. So anyway, after hearing that, I figured I needed to get to the bottom of this. So I asked her for some proof. And she produced a license."

A license. A fucking license. How drunk had he been? Where the hell had they gotten a marriage license? And who in God's name would give a marriage license to a drunk ass like him?

Someone who worked in Vegas. Hell, sober people were probably an anomaly in the office.

"But I pointed out—and rightly so—that anyone can forge things these days. Photoshop can do miracle works. Anyway, she wasn't overly pleased with my logic there. I can't really blame her. I mean, I'd probably punch someone if they accused me of something illegal. Luckily she didn't take a swing. But she does have pictures."

"Pictures?"

"Yeah, pictures. Hold on a sec, Skye, I get better reception out here. Help yourself to whatever's in the fridge." He heard a door slide open and shut, and he knew she was out on his back patio. "She had a few pictures on her phone. And a few more that she said came from the actual chapel, came with your package apparently, along with the fake bouquet and her veil." Tim could all but hear the smirk in his sister's voice. "You guys at the clerk's office applying, during the wedding, after the ceremony. It's definitely you, Tim." Her voice took on a misty, watery sound again. "You look happy. Really happy."

Happy? That was one way to describe being so drunk he didn't even know he was getting married. Yeah, he was happy off his ass. But that wasn't what his only sister wanted to hear when confronting him about getting married without the family. "Sorry, Madison."

"Uh huh. Anyway, I just thought you'd want to know. Tim, obviously you were wasted. You don't look it, and anyone who didn't know you well probably wouldn't realize it. But I know you. You wouldn't have kept this from me. Not if you were in your right mind."

"You're right." He sat on the edge of his own bed, rubbing the back of his neck. SNAFU did not begin to describe his life at that very moment.

"She's the real deal, Tim."

"What does that mean?"

Madison blew out a breath. "It means, I don't think

she's a tag chaser or some weirdo with a Marine fetish, or someone who is dead broke and wants a meal ticket and good health insurance. I know I have nothing to go off of, but my instincts say she's legit. Not quite your type, but legit. When she told me the story, it was like she got just as swept away as you did that night, in an honest chain of mistakes."

"I believe it." He trusted his sister's judgment. As a nurse, she saw too many people in every stage of life not to have a pretty decent judge of character. "Wait, what do you mean she wasn't my type?" From his recollection, he'd been attracted to her because she was exactly his type. Beautiful, well-spoken, put together, long legs, big eyes…

"Um, hmm. Did I say that?"

"Yeah. You did. Quit stalling, squirt."

"What do you want me to do about her?"

He blew out a breath. "Did she happen to mention what her plans were when she found me?"

"Not quite. I didn't think it was my place to ask. I know she has a room already at an extended stay motel for now. But as far as the plan, I think that's something you should talk to her about. But not right now. She's tired, and more than a little confused about you not being here. I don't think she realized how soon you were leaving. Besides, this isn't really a convo for the phone."

"I'll call you when I know something, okay? Get her contact info—all of it. The name and address of the motel, permanent address, cell phone, everything you can think of. Knock her over, steal her wallet, and write down her driver's license number if you have to. Just don't let her get away."

"Aye aye, sir," was her only cheeky remark, then there was dead air.

He shut the phone and tossed it on the bed.

"Son of a bitch. What happened?"

Jeremy's remark snapped him out of his plan to wallow in the mess his life was turning into. "Yeah, we'll talk about it later. Let's go talk to the CO, see if there's been a change. I'm finding myself more than a little anxious to shore up plans right now."

Chapter 4

SKYE CAUGHT HERSELF BITING HER THUMBNAIL AND QUICKLY pulled her hand away from her mouth. What she really wanted to do was stand up and pace around the living room, stuff her face into a pillow and scream, or punch her mattress. But she didn't want Madison to think she was five shades of crazy four days after meeting her. So she settled for staring out the window.

"It's okay," Madison said with a smile. She set a tray down on the coffee table with a pitcher of lemonade and two glasses filled with ice. "Things are always delayed with troop movement. Nature of the game." Then, as if it was no big deal that an entire huge batallion-thingie full of Marines was missing, she poured two glasses and sat back to sip on her drink. "Hurry up and wait is a big motto around here. If you stick around, you'll hear it enough."

For a woman who cared about her brother, Madison didn't show much concern about when he'd be returning.

"But he said they'd be back three hours ago."

Madison gave a shrug and sipped her lemonade again. "That's life in the military. Nothing is on time, or at least the time they give you. I'm in the military myself, and we grew up in it. I don't know any other way to be."

"But you're in the Navy," Skye pointed out.

Madison grinned and handed her a frosty glass. "Much to my family's eternal shock and disappointment.

The Marines don't have a medical corps, or I would have been. But when it comes to schedules, the rule is the same across the board." When Skye gave her a questioning look, her shoulders shook with laughter. "The rule is there is no schedule."

Ah. Not sure what to say, she took a sip of lemonade. That was quite a shock to Skye. She'd grown up in a commune of freethinkers, people who were more about doing things when the spirit moved them and less about what the calendar said. If anything, she would have guessed the military to be the exact opposite. But then again, she also doubted the lack of a schedule within the military had much to do with the alignment of the planets or someone's inner chakra speaking and more to do with the uncertainty of war.

"Thank you again for letting me come back each day for an update," she said. "I know this must be very odd for you. You didn't say as much, but I could tell the news was upsetting."

"A little," Madison admitted, placing her glass on the tray with delicacy. She wiped her hands on her jeans and stared out the window.

"I won't be offended," Skye offered. Madison couldn't say anything she hadn't already said to herself. Or her friend Tasha, who gave her the yelling of a lifetime after she'd heard what happened.

Madison glanced back at her, as if trying to decide how far to go. Then she shrugged and spoke. "First of all, we're tight. The whole family is tight, the four of us. There's a decent age gap between myself and my brother—five years, to be exact. But he's always been there for me. When you're the new kid, sometimes the only person on the block to play with for a while is related to you."

"I wish I could relate," Skye said, and she meant it. She'd been "a beautiful accident," as her mother liked to say. But an accident that was never repeated. No siblings for her. But she did have an abundance of other children to run around with on the commune. Siblings under the same sun, her mother told her once, as she dismissed Skye's childish plea for a real brother or sister. It still wasn't the same thing.

"Well, brothers aren't always everything they're cracked up to be," Madison said with a wink. "I endured my fair share of teasing and pranks. But overall, he's the best guy I know. He protected me like a bulldog from the start, always on the lookout for domestic evils. So time to return the favor."

"A domestic evil, huh?" Skye smiled at the thought of being viewed as such. Likely she should have been annoyed, even offended. But she just found it amusing... and a little flattering. She'd been called odd, crazy, a tree-hugging hippie before. But something to be concerned about, that was definitely a new one.

"That came out wrong, didn't it?" Madison asked, not looking at all sorry. "You have to understand, my brother getting married without telling me or my parents? It didn't even seem remotely possible. And besides that, to get married to a woman who is so not..." She trailed off, blushing instead of continuing.

"So not what?"

"Well, just not his usual type."

Skye picked at her baggy cotton drawstring pants. She could easily guess what that meant. She wasn't an idiot.

"You're just easy to talk to, with how laid back you are. And really, I haven't wanted to gag myself once since you got here. You're not super-straightlaced. And thank God for that, because Tim so doesn't need the female version of himself. Worst idea ever. And I can tell you aren't a tag chaser."

"A tag chaser?" These people spoke completely different languages. Skye needed a guidebook and one of those little translation pamphlets you could pick up in customs.

Madison grinned a little. "Women who are obsessed with snatching up a military man. Some sort of fetish, really. The guys wear dog tags. Tag chasers."

"Oh, I get it." She waited for mention of her clothing, but nothing came. Hmm. That wasn't even going to be brought up? Maybe Madison didn't notice fashion much.

Madison chewed on her lip for a moment, then rocked forward, folding her forearms on the table. "Mind if I ask you something?"

"Mmm hmm. I mean no. Ask away."

"What's your plan?"

Skye's heart sped up; her throat clogged a little at the reminder that the future wouldn't always be so easy as lazy afternoon lemonade chats with her fun new sister-in-law. "What do you mean?"

Madison cocked her head to one side, her eyes turning just a little hard. Protective waves rolled off her. "I'm a pretty straight shooter, and I think you are too, though you're trying to be polite about it. I can appreciate that, but seriously, you won't offend me. I'll start with this. I don't think you're stupid. You came out here for something. You obviously knew where to start looking for him. You could have started the divorce proceedings from Vegas." She looked down, then back up again, and her expression softened. "I don't think it's money."

Skye picked invisible lint from her sheer top shirt. Of course she had a plan. But that was between her and Tim. Especially since the plan depended so much on what he was thinking. Was there any nice way of letting Madison know that—

"It's none of my business."

Skye's head snapped up. What—did mind reading capabilities come issued with the uniform?

Madison smiled. "I can tell when someone is dodging." Her head cocked to one side. "Looks like you'll get the chance to tell Tim your plan soon. I hear Dwayne's piece-of-shit backwoods truck now." She jumped up and ran to the window. "Yup, I was right. They're here."

Skye's heart, which had only just started to slow down a bit, skipped several beats before moving double-time. The pulse thundered in her ears, and her hands felt numb. She shook them out and stood up, smoothing down the unseen wrinkles in her pants before following Madison to the front window.

A large, mud-splattered red pickup truck with huge wheels was pulling into the driveway behind Madison's sedan. The sound was almost deafening—or would have been had blood not still been hammering through her eardrums. She saw the passenger door open, someone hop down, then immediately head back to the bed of the truck to haul out bags. His hat and a glare on the living room window blocked any chance at seeing the face. Tossing the bags on the lawn, the man walked to the driver side door and gave the driver a slap on the shoulder through the window. The driver honked the horn once, then backed out. And the man—it had to be Tim—stood with his hands on his hips, looking expectantly toward the front door.

"Sorry, I know you're his wife and all, but you seem like you can't breathe, so I'm gonna take first dibs."

"First dibs on—" Skye started to ask, but Madison was already gone. Out the door, down the sidewalk, and launching herself at Tim. He stumbled back once and caught her, spinning in a circle while her legs dangled.

Well, no time like the present. Skye took one more look at her outfit—one of the most sensible things she owned that wasn't a work uniform—and headed out the door. But she stopped on the sidewalk, feeling like an intruder in a private family moment.

You're a part of that family now too.

But she wasn't. Not really. Not yet.

Soon.

She took one deep breath, prayed her knees would hold her up, and walked up behind Madison, who was still clinging to her brother with a desperation that spoke of her love for him.

His hat had flown off at the sisterly attack, and she could see his face clearly now. And then her lungs compressed again, like a vise in her chest. This was the man she had married. And every single reason for why she had agreed flooded her again. Still handsome, still serious. But at the same time, happy. Happy to see his sister again. Then his eyes blinked open, and she saw a flash of something in them when he noticed her.

The urge to pace the cement walkway was strong, so instead she locked her knees and waited for the moment with Madison to pass. Finally, Madison peeled herself off of Tim and stepped back, wiping tears from her eyes. She gave a sheepish look to Skye.

"Sorry. I know he was only gone a week but… you know. It was supposed to be longer."

At the weepy look in the otherwise-strong woman's eye, Skye felt a little misty herself. But when she caught sight of Tim staring at her, the mushy emotion faded into something much more like panic.

How would he react? Would he give her a hug like his sister? Would he give her a kiss? A handshake? For some stupid reason, how he greeted her seemed like it would set the tone for what was to come.

Apparently the tone was… nothing.

He stared at her, his gaze neither welcoming nor condemning. He shifted his weight forward, then back on his heels again. It was like he couldn't figure out how to respond, what the right thing to say was. The right thing to do.

That makes two of us.

Madison shifted beside Tim, and Skye realized the two of them were staring at each other like a high noon showdown. Okay, so this would be awkward. But what did she expect—him to sweep her off her feet and cart her off to Aruba for a honeymoon?

"Welcome home, I guess. I didn't realize when you said you were deploying that you meant so soon."

He shrugged and bent to pick up a long, olive green bag. "That's the way it works."

Madison picked up a thick briefcase-shaped box

and headed for the front door. Relishing the ability to have something to do with her hands, Skye grabbed a knapsack and slung it over her shoulder, following Madison. She barely made it through the front door before a large hand touched her neck while reaching for the strap. The brush of rough fingertips made her shiver.

"I'll take that." Tim slid the pack off her shoulders and dropped the entire bundle on the tile floor by the door. "I'm just going to leave it here for now."

The three stood in the foyer, a heavy silence settling around them. Nobody seemed to look at anyone else. Should she go? Was this a time for him and his sister to talk? It was their house, anyway. But there was so much she needed to tell him, it was practically bursting out of her. She tamped down the urge to yell out her reason for coming, get it over with like ripping a bandage off.

Definitely not the right impression.

Tim cleared his throat and gave Madison a pointed glance. "Dwayne mentioned drinks at the O Club with Jeremy. Maybe you wanna go check that out, squirt."

Madison rolled her eyes and laughed. "Subtle. Very subtle. But you're right. Drinks with those two sounds perfect." She picked up a purse sitting on the entry table and stood on her tiptoes to give him another kiss on the cheek. "Good to have you back, bro, even for a little while." Before she closed the door behind her, she called out, "Don't call me squirt."

Tim's chuckle rumbled through the nearly empty room. Then he turned toward her, and the amusement evaporated into an intense hunger. Something she could relate to.

She was hungry for him too.

—⁓—

For four days, Tim had planned out exactly what he was going to say. He would apologize profusely for his behavior in Vegas, for getting them into the mess they were in. Yeah, he might have been drunk, but he still should have kept a cool head. And then, like the strategist he was, he outlined exactly how he would fix things, make them better.

His calm, cool, organized plan of attack faded away as he stood there alone with Skye, in his house. He tried to think of his opening sentence, his follow-up statements. Nothing. It was a big, fuzzy blank. Everything but Skye was gone from his mind. She was standing there, in the flesh. The woman he'd been thinking about the entire bus ride across the country. She looked confused and completely out of her element. A contrast from the confident Vegas woman he'd met a few weeks ago. But somehow just as appealing.

"So, um." She fingered the hem of her long shirt, as if afraid or embarrassed to look at him. "How was your trip?"

Was she really going to just stand there and make small talk?

"Good. Long, and proved to be pointless. But can't complain I guess."

She nodded, glancing around like she was looking for inspiration. "Your deployment was canceled, then? Madison was telling me about how sometimes things like that happen. Though she hadn't heard of it happening so soon before you guys left. But that it wasn't out of the question. I guess that's weird to me since nothing in my job would ever be so last-minute. I mean, you get problems all the time and you have to think on your feet in the restaurant business, but then that's true of any… job… I guess…" She lost steam and took a deep breath. And he lost it.

Grabbing her shoulders, he whirled her around until her back hit the wall behind him. A picture rattled on the wall, her hip bumped the entry table, and keys clattered to the floor. He didn't care about that. He cared about her eyes.

Wide, a little shocked, a little wild. But no fear.

He bent his head and did what he'd been dreaming about doing. What had been playing on a God-awful loop in his mind since the day they left Vegas. He kissed her. A testing brush first, but when she didn't haul back and slap him, he tried another. Her lips rose to meet his, and he was lost at holding back. Her hands came up to pull him closer, and she widened her stance to cradle him. Her message was clear.

Take it, it's yours.

And he did.

Teeth clashed as they each moved in desperate strokes to get deeper. He let his fingers tangle in her hair, vaguely remembering the weight of it in his hands before. He definitely remembered the soft skin of her jawline, how her pulse jumped as his tongue flicked over it. There was no forgetting how responsive she was when he ran a hand under the sheer top she wore to cup her breast over the layering tank beneath. How her body arched into his touch. How she moved under him like they were a carefully choreographed duo on the dance floor.

"Tim," she gasped. "Tim, hold on, we need to talk."

"Talk," he muttered into her shoulder. No talking. Why did she always want to talk when they were in these positions?

"Yeah. Talk." She gasped when his teeth scraped along her collarbone. "About our marriage."

A kick to the crotch wouldn't have slowed him down as fast as those three simple words. He let go and took a big step back, breathing heavily. Fuck. How did he forget that? The marriage mix-up. He was trying to find the best way to end this painlessly, and instead he practically attacked her against a wall. Damn.

"Yeah." He screwed his eyes shut and pressed into his eyelids with his thumbs, willing his erection away. The cammies had room, but not that much. "Yeah, marriage. Sorry." He opened his eyes and saw a still-flushed, still-mussed Skye leaning against the table with one hand. The image wasn't doing anything to cool his head, so he turned away and walked toward the living room. "Let's talk in here." She followed without a word.

He got to the room and saw glasses of lemonade. Perfect. He picked one up and took a big gulp, hoping the tangy sweetness would clear out the cotton that seemed to be lining his throat. Just when he wondered whether he should sit on the couch with Skye or not, or what she expected, she did him the favor of choosing the armchair, crossing one leg over the other. He sat on the couch, catty-corner to her spot. Close enough to touch, but he didn't dare.

He waited for her to talk, but instead she sat with

her hands in her lap, staring at them like they held the answer to world hunger. Finally he cleared his throat and decided to give it a shot.

"I need to apologize for being such a dick that night."

The way her head shot up and she stared at him, that wasn't what she expected. He wasn't sure why, but it stung.

"I'm not a teenager anymore. I know better than to run out on a woman and not even say good-bye. Not that I do the one-night thing all that often," he added quickly when her brows drew together. "I just know it's not what a man should do, and I'm sorry."

She nodded. "Thank you. But obviously I didn't chase you down here for an apology."

Understatement of the century. "Right, yeah." He took another drink. "Um, exactly how did you find me anyway? I know the Internet's good and all, but—"

"Friend who works at the hotel." She gave him a smile. "I wouldn't know where to start with the Internet, but I do know someone at the front desk of the hotel. And you filled out a customer form before they gave you the key to the suite. It had your address on it."

"Thought that stuff was private," he grumbled, then saw how one brow raised. "Not that I'm not glad you found out. God, I keep shoving my foot in my mouth, don't I?"

"I think I'll forgive you for odd circumstances," she said with a chuckle. Then she laughed a little harder, and he had a flashback to the casino. Skye smiling at him from across the blackjack table. Breathless behind some tree, in a dark corner while his hand crept up... Okay. That wasn't helping the boner he was fighting off.

He was grateful for her understanding... and her happy attitude. He was wound too tight, like any sudden movement would cause him to snap. But Skye just smiled, slid her feet out of her sandals, and tucked them under her on the chair. God, she was adorable.

"So, um, where do we go from here?"

"That's the million-dollar question, isn't it?" She took a sip of her own glass of lemonade and leaned forward to set it down on the table. Her shirt dipped forward, and he caught a glimpse of the tight tank under the sheer, gauzy fabric of her top.

Focus, man.

He cleared his throat, and hopefully his mind along with it. "Well, I probably don't need to tell you that the night is a little blurry for me. Bits and pieces are there, but not the whole thing. So this is kind of a shock." Yet another understatement.

"Yeah, I got that from Madison. It's funny, though. You never acted drunk. At least, not until you blacked out," she added with a sly smile. "Then it was kind of hard to miss."

He rubbed a hand across the back of his neck. He could feel the heat radiating from his skin. Pure, simple embarrassment mixed with a healthy dose of shame. "I don't drink like that often… basically never. I just—"

She held up a hand. "I work in Vegas. Trust me, you don't have to explain it. And because I can see you're already struggling with this and you're embarrassed, I believe that you don't make a habit of this. So I'll end the misery of wondering and just say that you were a gentleman and didn't do anything obscene or obnoxious." But she blushed as she said it.

What did that mean? When he arched a brow, she just sighed and looked at the fireplace while she mumbled, "You didn't do anything I didn't want."

"Thank God for small miracles," he muttered. "But obviously I made a cake out of myself. How the hell did we get married if I can't even remember it?"

"Short version is you proposed. I accepted. We took a limo to the courthouse and then to a small chapel off the strip, then limo back to the hotel where your suite was waiting. No driving involved, hardly any paperwork." She grinned. "They like to make it easy for couples in Vegas. It's kind of our thing, obviously."

"Our thing." What the hell did that mean? How could she be so nonchalant about the entire thing?

"Yeah, Vegas in general. Tourism, the casino, you know." She waved a hand enthusiastically while she talked. She was a hand-talker, clearly. "People come in for just a short vacation, and then get the wild hair to get married but aren't sure how to make it happen. Vegas, as a whole, makes it easy. It's our stock in trade."

"Our?"

"Oh, I lived there. And worked there. I was a manager at one of the restaurants in the Celestial Palace. Cloud Nine."

"Ah, I see." No, he really didn't. But that wasn't the biggest of his problems. "So we got married. How legal is that?"

She threw her head back and laughed again. He stared at the exposed pulse point, wanted to go back to making her moan while he paid extra attention to her throat.

"It's legal. I have the license. So no worries there."

No worries? He felt like she was talking circles around him. And this time he wasn't even drunk. "Okay, so how do we fix that?"

"Fix what?"

Chapter 5

HE STARED AT HER, WAITING FOR THE "GOTCHA" FACE, OR for her to start laughing again. Or for Ashton Kutcher to bust down his door and tell him he'd been punked. Instead, she stared at him like he was the crazy one. "What do you mean? The marriage. The... the thing. What do we do?"

Her face went carefully blank. "I don't know what you mean. I didn't think there was actually anything to fix, to be honest."

He let that sink in, let her change in demeanor wrap around his mind. Huh. Maybe he was the crazy one. Because if she meant what he thought she meant...

She must have grown impatient with his silence, because she blew out a breath and asked, "Do you believe in Fate?"

He snorted. "No. Not really."

"Okay, how about destiny? Chance? A belief in some invisible string pulling us along a path? People call it different things."

He shook his head. "No. Our future is what we make of it. I've seen too much shit in my life to believe that it's all out of our hands completely. I want to go into war knowing that my future is dependent on the choices I make, not on the whim of some deity or whatever. I control me."

"Well, and I agree. At least to an extent." She folded

her hands in her lap, then looked at them for a moment. Suddenly, she jumped up so fast it was as if there was an eject button under her butt. When he started to stand as well, she waved him down. "No, I just think better on my feet." And with that, she started to pace the floor in front of the fireplace. Her thin top billowed as she made turns in the tight area, her bare feet made no sound on the floor, and her hands were fluttering in front of her. Then she stopped.

"If you don't believe in Fate, then how do you explain this?"

"This what?" He was really starting to lose it. Maybe the AC on the bus was laced with some noxious gas.

"This. Us. Our marriage."

"I explain it as too much alcohol and a misguided desire to let loose for the evening."

She snorted and started to pace again. He sat back and watched, equal parts amused and concerned. He'd never seen someone so animated before, so vibrant. She made thinking exciting. But then again, this wasn't exactly the time for excitement and animation. A serious topic called for calm heads and cool conversation.

Excitement and animation led to a quickie wedding in Vegas. Yeah. They needed more level thinking here.

Suddenly, his mind went back to something she'd said. She'd *lived* in Vegas. She'd *worked* there. Past tense.

"Skye," he said, measuring his tone carefully. "When you said you worked and lived in Las Vegas, was that a tense slip? Do you still live there?"

An about-face had her staring at him with a *Man, you're an idiot* look. "No. If I still lived there, I'd say I live in Vegas. I know English."

"Okay. So where do you live now?"

She tilted her head to one side. "Where do you think?"

He was starting to piece the Skye-shaped puzzle together, one bit at a time. And what he assumed was the finished product both exhilarated and terrified him.

"Maybe you should tell me exactly what you're after here, Skye. Why did you go through all that trouble to find me?"

She walked over and plopped down on the chair again, bouncing once before settling. "I thought it was obvious, but maybe not." She clapped her hands together and sat forward. He blinked and made sure to keep his eyes above her neck.

"You and I are legally married. You don't subscribe to the idea of Fate, but I do. But for whatever reason, you asked me. And I said yes. We got married. And after you left I had a lot of time to think about what that meant."

There was no censure in her voice, no judgment. Even though she'd be justified in giving him hell. Still, Tim internally flinched at the reminder of his own ass-like behavior. Skye didn't seem to notice his own thoughts and kept going.

"Basically, what I'm saying is, there's a reason we're married. And I'm ready to find out what that is."

"In plain English, that means…"

She looked him straight in the eye, all seriousness as she said, "I want to stay married."

His heart skipped, then slowed, then rolled down into his shoe. Holy shit. She was dead serious.

Tim forced himself to breathe and remember his own plan of attack. All the things he had been ready to suggest.

A quiet divorce. Quick annulment. Simple, clean break. A quick roll between the sheets, just for old time's sake.

She wanted none of them. And Tim couldn't quite understand the stab of fierce relief that filled his chest before he remembered the entire reason he'd stopped kissing her in the hallway. The reason they couldn't just do whatever the hell they wanted to.

It wasn't responsible. It wasn't normal. It wasn't the right thing to do.

But first, he needed to work at untangling the mess one knot at a time. "What do you think the reason for our marriage is?"

She threw her hands up in the air and gave a sort of strangled, feral cry to the heavens. "How the hell should I know? That's not for me to understand. At least not yet. But there's a reason. Fate's waiting for us to catch up. And we'll figure it out."

He shook his head. "I told you that's not my thing."

Skye visibly deflated in front of him, like a balloon without the stopper. Just like that, her explosive, dramatic show was over. She gave another sigh, then plopped back down in the chair. Leaning back, she tucked her legs under her in what looked like an impossible position. "Okay, we'll ignore Fate for a second since She makes you uncomfortable." He opened his mouth to argue, but she held up a hand. "Let's just focus on the rational for a second."

Ah, finally they were on his level. "The rational thing is to divorce." He looked at the tray of glasses, for some reason uncomfortable looking at her while he brought it up. "Or get an annulment. Not sure exactly which would be more appropriate in this situation."

"Neither. And let me tell you why." She leaned over and grabbed one of his hands, lacing fingers. He barely stopped himself from jerking back at the jolt. It was like all the pulsating energy she held within her body vibrated down her arm and made his own hand tingle. Pins and needles, like the limb had fallen asleep and was just starting to wake up again.

Or was that another body part?

He met her gaze, saw the little smile in her eyes. "You feel that too. That's why. There's something between us, and even with your death grip on logic and reason, you feel it too." She gave him a quick grin. "I'll be nice, and I won't even make you say it out loud. Maybe we didn't go about it in the most logical manner, at least to you. But I feel like we're supposed to see where this takes us."

She squeezed his hand, then slithered out of his grip. His hand felt empty without her smaller one in it. "We're already married. The deed is done. Which would look worse? A two-week marriage? Or a marriage that just didn't work out down the road, after some time and effort put into it?"

She did have a point. While he didn't relish explaining the quickie wedding to anyone—parents included—an even quicker divorce would be humiliating. "So exactly what are you saying, Skye?"

"I quit my job in Vegas." She paused, as if waiting for him to tell her how crazy that was. But really, at this point, wasn't crazy expected? When he said nothing, she continued. "I'm here. You can't come to me, obviously, so I'm here with you. I figure with my experience I could look for a management position at a hotel or a restaurant. There are enough of them around, it seems. I'm earning my keep, not looking for a handout."

"Never thought you were," he murmured and realized that it was true. As many pathetic stories as there were floating around about female con artists taking advantage of servicemen and cleaning out their bank accounts and homes while they deployed, it never once occurred to him that Skye was one.

"Well, good. Because I'm not," she reiterated fiercely. "I'm here because I believe in this. And you." She ran a hand through her hair, fingers tangling in the long, wavy ends. He had a vague memory of his own hands gripping those silky strands, angling her head so he could access her mouth more deeply with his tongue, giving himself better position to—

"Tim?"

"Yeah?" Shit. One of the most important conversations of his life and he was in the middle of his own wet daydream.

She smiled knowingly. "I could be a bitch and take that 'yeah' as your answer, but I won't. So I ask again… do you want to go out with me?"

"Go out with you." Did they step back in time and hit the seventh grade?

She laughed. "I know, not the most adult way of wording it. But it comes to the same. Do you, for the moment, want to forget we're married and just date? If it doesn't work out, then we're no worse off than if we'd divorced today, except maybe you save some face and I feel like I wasn't going against the plan of Fate. And who knows, maybe we'll surprise ourselves."

She wanted to stay married. And date. It was crazy. It was insane.

And yet he was struggling to bite back the urge to drag her upstairs and whisper yes in her ear… preferably while in the middle of getting her naked.

He drank the Kool-aid. Or rather, lemonade. Where'd he put his new white Nikes again?

Tim thrust the idea of her, pink-skinned and glowing and lying in his bed, out of his mind. "Are we telling people we're married?"

She bit her lip, and he wanted to soothe the mark with his tongue. "That's up to you, I guess. Though I think it makes more sense to tell people than not. They always say the truth comes out eventually, and all that."

"Where are you staying?"

"I have a deal with an extended stay motel, but I thought I'd look at rentals in the area after we were done here." She glanced at the door and said ruefully, "I'd thought Madison might want to come with me. Help me find the nicer areas and—"

"My wife isn't staying at a motel," he bit off, then swore at himself. The caveman routine was not attractive, nor was it going to help him get through this rationally.

She shrugged one shoulder, shifting the fabric of her shirt to drop over the other one, exposing her shoulder. He was thirteen again. That was the only excuse for why that completely innocent slip of skin had him harder than Kevlar.

"You'll stay here."

She raised one brow, as if to say, *Do you know what you're saying?*

But he did. Being in control gave him some sense of normalcy, and he grasped onto it for dear life. "We're going to go get your things from the motel, and you're coming back here. With me."

"But Madison lives here."

"So it's one big party, then. Don't you girls always have sleepovers and stuff?"

She smiled. "Fine. But you don't have to come with me. I can pack myself up."

"How about you get started, and I'll come by to do the heavy lifting?" Before she could argue, he stood, taking her hand and pulling her up with him. In her bare feet, the top of her head reached his chin. She looked up at him, disbelief and skepticism clear in her eyes. Two things he never wanted her—anyone—to feel with him. To wipe them both out of her mind, he pulled her flush to his chest, bent his head, and kissed her with determination.

She resisted for a nanosecond, then melted against him. Her arms crept up around his neck, her hips cradled his erection, and her mouth opened on a sigh. He took the smallest of tastes, not trusting himself with more, then took a step back.

"Grab a head start on packing. I'll catch up soon."

Skye struggled to breathe normally as she packed her things in the sparse, but clean, motel room. She hadn't really relished spending any more time in there than necessary. But at the same time, she wasn't prepared to be so close to Tim on a daily basis.

She tossed her skirts into the open duffle, not caring

if they wrinkled. Someone invented an iron for a reason. With her work clothes from Cloud Nine, she took more care, more out of habit than anything else. Though she had no love for the restricting, monochromatic black pants, white collared shirt, and black vest, she still respected the uniform from her old job. It fit the image the restaurant wanted to uphold, and she wore it with pride.

She threw another gauzy top into the bag and thought about how Tim had stared through her shirt at one point. The memory turned her both hot and cold, causing her skin to feel clammy and her face to feel flushed. Sure, he wanted her. That was both an obvious and delicious fact. But did he want her for more than her body? And why the sudden one-eighty on the trial time period?

Skye realized she'd been twisting a skirt into a knot and deliberately smoothed it out on the bed, then folded it and put it in the bag. She just had to accept that this was another way of Fate lining up things in their favor. So she would move in, and spend time with Tim, and see where it led them.

Skye's cell phone rang and she picked it up absently, still finding things to toss in the suitcase.

"You haven't called in a few days. I was getting worried!"

"Tasha." Skye breathed a sigh of relief and sank down on the bed, crossing her legs under her. The sound of her best friend made her miss home, miss her simple life. Just not enough to turn back around. "What's up?"

"Jessie's here too, on speaker, just to warn you. So has he come back yet? Did you see him? Deets, please."

Skye sighed and ran fingers through her hair, frowning when they got tangled around her shoulders. She pried them out while she spoke. "I saw him today. He finally came home."

There was a silence, very unusual for her friends.

"And after a thoughtful conversation"—and some super-hot making out against a wall—"we're going to give the marriage a shot."

"Yes!"

"No!"

Skye held the phone away from her ringing ear. "Okay, care to share which of you was which?" she called so they could hear her.

"I think this is great." Jessie. The marriage fan. "You deserve happiness. And you liked the guy enough to marry him, so this really just works out for the best!"

"The guy ran out on her on their wedding night. How can that be for the best for anyone?" Tasha now, angry. And blunt. "He doesn't deserve another shot. So sign those annulment papers and hustle your ass back here."

"No can do. I made a commitment, back in Vegas and again today. We're going to try our best. If it doesn't work out, it doesn't work out."

"This isn't like trying out a new car, Skye. It's marriage. In fact, I think you put more effort into researching your cute little hybrid than you did your husband. That's gotta say something, right?"

"Yes. It says something about this man who reached out and grabbed Skye by the throat. And she's open to it." Jessie sighed. "It's all pretty romantic when you think about it."

Tasha snorted.

Skye debated hanging up to see if her two friends would even know she was gone. Obviously they were having more fun talking *about* her than *with* her. Instead, she cleared her throat.

"I have to go. Tim's coming by to help me transport my stuff to his townhouse. And don't say it, Tash. I know you want to. But his sister lives with him too. It's not going to immediately turn into some lovebird's nest. It's a trial period."

Tasha grumbled but said nothing more. Skye ended the phone call quickly, under the pretense of having more to pack. In reality, she was done.

Was Jessie on the right track with the romance angle? Would she and Tim be sitting around in sixty years, telling the funny story to their grandchildren of how Grandma and Grandpa met? Or was the entire thing doomed from the start, as Tasha hinted?

No way to find out but to give it a shot. Maybe Fate meant for them to be married forever. Maybe they were only supposed to be together for a few months. But there might be a million other reasons why she was supposed to be in this place at this time. And she intended to figure it out.

Jeremy sat between a pissed off Dwayne and a somber Madison at the O Club bar. Dwayne was three sheets to the wind and working on a fourth. And Madison was quiet. Too quiet, for a girl who hadn't shut up almost since the day he'd met her.

Yup. Recipe for disaster. He tipped his beer and took another swig, wondering whether it would be an advantage to follow Dwayne into the abyss or a hell of a bad idea. Dwayne took the choice out of his hand by ordering another round for all three of them, then leaned over Jeremy to look Madison in the eye.

"So, are your lips loosened enough yet, sweetheart? Are you going to tell us what the hell is going on with Tim?"

"Loose lips sink ships," Madison said with a smile and a sip of her fresh Jack and Diet Coke. "Tim's business is Tim's business. And I'm not going to bite the hand that gives out the rent-free living. Not that I think that'll last much longer." She leaned her torso over Jeremy to face Dwayne, breast brushing his elbow in an innocent, half-drunken movement, and he froze.

But she didn't notice. Of course. "All I can say is that the woman that he met while in Vegas with you two"—she gestured between himself and Dwight with her glass, ice clinking—"is at the house right now. And they're having a serious discussion, for which I was kicked out."

Dwayne snorted. "Well, this should be interesting. Guess we'll get the scoop tomorrow, when we report back to the battalion." He muttered a curse under his breath and took a long pull of his beer. "Hate this stop-and-go shit. Looks like I'll just be heading back out again though, sans you two."

Jeremy just nodded, not sure what else to say. Deploying without the rest of the battalion was never fun but a necessity at times. Your number was called, you went. At least Dwayne would have his company with him.

Madison stood abruptly, Jeremy and Dwayne lurching to their feet after her out of habit. She scowled at them. "How many times do I have to tell you two to stop that with me? I'm just making a head call." With that she flounced away... as much as someone who was well on her way to Drunktown could flounce. The leers from other Marines that followed her as she shuffled toward the hallway had Jeremy clenching fists.

Dwayne nudged him with his elbow. "You're still standing; go follow her, will ya? If she face-plants and busts that pretty little nose of hers, Tim will never let us hear the end of it."

He wanted to tell Dwayne to follow her if he was so damn concerned, but he'd already turned around and ordered another beer. At this rate, D couldn't hold up a toddler if he had to. Jeremy steeled his senses and headed after the woman who had tormented his mind for the past ten years.

The hallway was empty so he headed toward the rest-rooms. A trio of guys passed by and entered the men's head, then the silence continued. He waited another few moments and was debating the wisdom of knocking on the door and calling out Madison's name when it flew open and she walked right into his chest. On instinct, he grabbed her shoulders, then realized he was pulling her into him rather than steadying her. He humored him-self by taking one deep breath of her scent—whiskey and something fruity, like pears—and leaned her back against the wall. After one giant step away, he studied her in the dim lighting.

Her face was flushed, a few flyaway hairs stuck to her forehead. Instead of the regulation bun he normally saw her with, the brown locks flowed down past her shoulders. No, not brown. Auburn and mahogany and cedar all mixed in a jumble of colors that made him want to bend down and feel how silky they would be against his cheek.

Her eyes were wide, as if she was still caught in surprise. And her lips, which were normally going a mile a minute with her constant friendly chatter, were parted as if caught mouthing the letter *O*. He shoved his hands in his pockets to keep from reaching out, brushing the hairs off her face, tracing her bottom lip with his thumb.

"Everything okay?" he asked, just to break the silence, then inwardly groaned. Now she would think he was asking about her bathroom trip. Casanova, move over. Jeremy Phillips was in the club.

Her eyes widened a fraction more, then crinkled as she chuckled. "Is that why you were about to head into the women's restroom? To check on me?"

Not trusting himself to answer verbally any longer, he shrugged.

Madison glanced around, then grabbed his arm and tugged him toward the end of the hallway. "Come on."

"The bar's back that way," he reminded her, letting the woman drag him along behind. He could have planted his feet and stopped her in a heartbeat, but he had a small problem of never denying Madison what she wanted whenever physically possible.

Or, who knew. Maybe she was about to be sick.

She stopped at the end of the hall, throwing a not-so-subtle look over her shoulder before throwing the door open. Fresh, cool night air greeted them as she led him out and the door shut behind her.

He surveyed their surroundings, which weren't many. A Dumpster, the brick exterior of the O Club itself, and a metal fence. There was no streetlight, nothing but the half-moon to highlight the area. Ambiance was lacking, for sure. But as he started to take mental notes of the spot, thinking it might be a great place for a fictional body dump, Madison pushed his shoulders. Caught off guard, he stumbled back until he smacked against the rough brick wall.

"This has been a long time coming," she said, her voice huskier than it had been only moments earlier.

"What?" He felt like he'd missed an entire conversation between the hallway and the great outdoors. "What are you talking—"

But he didn't get to finish his sentence, as his lips were occupied with something other than talking.

Chapter 6

MADISON PRESSED HER MOUTH TO JEREMY'S, EFFECTIVELY cutting off any hope of finishing his question… and detouring all blood flow to below his belt. Her body slid up against his with violent insistence, one hand fisted in his shirt, the other dragging his head down to make her assault on his senses more complete. She was small, but she was feisty and knew how to make a point. His control was a taut wire, and her every move, every moan, sent that wire vibrating, dangerously close to snapping.

He fought the urge to respond, desperately tried to keep from encouraging her. But he was at a loss at how to defuse the situation. Then the woman he'd spent the last ten years working on forgetting twisted her hips, grinding against his erection and nipped his bottom lip at the same time, and that wire snapped.

Jeremy reached around the small of her back and pulled her against him roughly, letting her feel exactly what her actions had brought him to. Total desperation. His tongue swept in, tasting her in a way he never thought he would, never dreamed was possible. Even his own vibrant imagination couldn't have known how sweet she would feel. Her groan of satisfaction vibrated through them, through the physical connection, and only spurred him on in the worst decision of his life.

Ironic, really, that the worst things always felt so damn good.

She took a nip out of his bottom lip and soothed the sting with a lick.

"God, Jeremy, you kiss even better than I thought you would," she breathed.

That was what sucked him out of the rabbit hole he'd willingly jumped into. Her lips breathing his name. He tore his head back to escape her kisses, but thanks to leaning against the brick wall, it only resulted in intense pain as the back of his head slammed into the hard surface.

"Fuck!" He saw stars and let go of Madison to cradle his throbbing head and doubled over at the waist. His vision tunneled for a moment, bright pinpricks of light floating in the blackness. Light, cool fingers pulled his hands down, and his senses started to come back.

"No, don't stand up yet. You're too tall. Stand still."

"Madison, it's fine. Stop—ow!" He jerked up and stumbled back a step.

"Stop being a baby and get back here." When he didn't move closer, she sighed and rolled her eyes. "I'm a nurse, remember? I do this for a living. It's probably fine, but I just want to check for my peace of mind."

He gently brushed his fingers over the growing bump and looked at them, then held them forward for inspection. "No blood, no broken skin. It's fine." She leaned close, and he took another step back. When she raised her eyebrows in an amused gesture, he felt his temper rise. "Honestly, it's fine."

She threw up her hands in exasperation. "Fine. You're fine. I'm fine. We're all *fine*." Her gaze grew sultry, and she took another step forward, which he countered with another backward step. "So can we get back to being fine together?"

"Uh, no." And cue the awkward conversation. "Listen, Madison. I know you've had a lot to drink and all, so I can just forget it ever happened." Which was a total lie. If he lived to be a hundred and twelve, he'd remember what it felt like to have her taut body pressed up against his in a clear *What are you waiting for?* invitation.

"Forget it ever happened," she repeated slowly.

Christ, this was awful. "Yeah. There's nothing to be embarrassed about."

"Embarrassed." Her eyes had lost their coy seductiveness, her face now a blank canvas. Acid roiled in his gut.

"Right. So, let's just go in and get some coffee, okay?" *Before I toss you against the wall and finish what you started and then hate myself for the rest of my life.*

"Coffee." She shook her head, eyes wide. "I can't believe this. Are you serious?"

He rubbed a hand across his neck. He wasn't sure *what* he was anymore. "I mean, it's just that… we just can't…" He lifted his hands, then let them fall down by his sides helplessly. Where was the shovel? Clearly he wasn't in deep enough yet.

"We can't. Well. We could two minutes ago when you had your hands on my ass," she pointed out smugly.

"I shouldn't have done that. We shouldn't have done that. And now we're going to go back in that bar, have coffee, and move on. Because this"—he waved his arms at the brick wall they'd been leaning up against not five minutes earlier—"didn't happen."

She stared at him a second longer, then turned on her

heel and stalked to the door. After taking a deep breath, he hustled after her. But when he reached around her to open the door, she wrenched it open hard enough to bang him on the shoulder.

"Fuck," he muttered as she walked down the hallway. His shoulder throbbed in time with the dull ache of his head. Maybe if he'd known how painful any intimate experience with Madison would have been, he wouldn't have craved it for so long.

He watched her hips sway as she walked down the hallway toward the bar.

No. He'd still crave it. Like the black widow spider wants his female… even given the inevitable, unfortunate result.

In the bar, he found Madison leaning over Dwayne and giving him a kiss on the cheek before heading toward the exit. He dodged between tables and people to catch up. Just as she pushed on the door, his hand circled her wrist.

"Where do you think you're going?"

She jerked out of his hold and glared at him. "Home. Where I won't be insulted by jackass Marines and their misplaced chivalry."

Ouch.

"You can't drive home. I'm fine to drive; let me take you."

"I think I'd rather climb in the backseat with an entire terrorist cell." She blew a frustrated breath out, shifting hair from her face. "I have cash for a cab, and there's always a line of them outside the O Club at this time of night. You know that."

Jeremy wanted to press, to insist on letting him take

her home. But her eyes said to drop it. Pleaded with him to let her go. And so he did the only fair thing he could think of.

He let her go.

Skye rolled over, reached for the blaring alarm clock, and hit nothing but air. She sat up and squinted at the light pouring in through the window. Why were her curtains not drawn? What the hell? She felt like she'd just fallen asleep. As she glanced to the left bedside table, she noted why she couldn't find the alarm to shut it off.

It wasn't there.

She found the clock on the right nightstand, one she used for her books back home. Who put an alarm clock on the right nightstand? She groaned when her suspicions were confirmed. It was six in the morning. She shoved tangled hair out of her face and tried to run her fingers through it. They made it a whole inch before catching in the knots. Damn curly hair. She yanked her fingers free, biting back a shriek at the pain. At least it woke her up a little bit. Mornings were not her thing. She managed the early evening shift at Cloud Nine, meaning sometimes she went to sleep at two in the morning, but she never had to wake up before noon if she didn't want to. When was the last time she'd seen the ungodly hour of six a.m.?

"You're awake."

The deep voice made her jump, then mentally moan at her appearance. An oversized T-shirt and ratty hair was not exactly the image she wanted to project to anyone, let alone her runaway husband. "Yeah. The alarm went off."

"Sorry." He walked in far enough to click the "off" button, and silence enveloped the bedroom. "I used my cell for an alarm this morning and I forgot I had this set. When we switched bedrooms, it slipped my mind."

He had forced her to take the master bedroom—his bedroom—while he slept in the office on an air mattress. No matter how much she argued, he stood firm. The man was as immobile as a boulder when he wanted to be. But deep inside, she secretly appreciated the man's chivalry.

Somewhere in Texas, her mother was crying out to the goddess Gloria Steinem in horror.

She blinked and let the last of the blurriness from sleep wear off, then took a good look at her husband. He leaned against the doorjamb, imposing and "official-looking" in his uniform.

"They're rolled up," she blurted out, then wanted to crawl under the covers. How stupid could she be? That's how you greet your new husband in the morning?

"What?" He glanced down and back up. "My sleeves? Yeah, we roll them down when we're deployed or in the field. That's why they were down yesterday, since I was still in transit from what was supposed to be a deployment. But since that's not really happening I can roll them back up. Thank God, since it'll be hot. These things trap heat like a solar panel."

"Where's your little hat thingie?"

He tilted his head. "My hat… thingie?"

She waved her hand over her head, like that was going to make the entire question any more clear. "You know. The hat that matches your uniform." Could she feel like any more of a fool?

His lips twitched. "Ah. Right. My… *hat*. It's down-stairs by the front door. They aren't worn inside." He gave her a slow look, not unlike how a tiger might check out his prey. Skye was torn between clutching the sheets over her chest and ripping off her T-shirt in a blatant— and desperate—move of self-promotion. "So what are your plans for the day?"

She glanced at the clock longingly. But it didn't seem like the greatest way to start off the day by admitting she wanted to curl back up and sleep for another four hours. "Explore the area a little bit, I guess." Starting with the townhouse and working her way out.

"Sounds good." He turned, then paused and looked back. "If you need anything, my cell number's on the fridge. But I think today is Madison's day off so when she wakes up, she can help you out with whatever you need." When she nodded, he stared at her for a minute. When she thought he was going to come back toward her, he abruptly left. Though she knew he wore thick boots, he was silent until she heard the front door click shut.

She listened for a few more seconds, the house still and hushed around her, then flopped back down. The pillow puffed and hissed as it deflated beneath her head. Knowing she was alone, she indulged just a moment and turned her face into the cool cotton, absorbing Tim's scent. He'd been ready to strip the bed and put on clean sheets when she said she would handle it. Then had accidentally-on-purpose forgotten to do so, falling asleep with his scent surrounding her.

It would have been nicer had Tim slept next to her, so she could soak up his warmth as well, feel the safe weight of his body around hers while she floated toward that ultimate state of vulnerability with him. But somehow both he and she had come to the unspoken agreement that sleeping in the same bed was off the table. At least for now.

Skye started to drift back to sleep when the mattress dipped. One eye crept open to reveal a grinning Madison, face and front of her shirt damp with perspiration.

"So you're staying." It wasn't a question.

Skye struggled to sit up again, wondering why on Mother Earth these people felt the need to rise with the sun. "Yes. I'm staying. For now. Why are you awake? Tim said it was your day off and it's"—another glance at the clock showed it was half past seven—"still disgustingly early."

"Went for a jog. Lots of empty calories last night."

"Meaning you got drunk." Skye worked in Vegas too long to not know every code known to man for "drinking."

Madison smiled. "Guilty. Anyway, I have a physical fitness test coming up soon so I don't wanna slack. And," she added with a mischievous wink, "I'm not blessed enough to have a svelte figure naturally. I'm girly enough to care what my ass looks like in a pair of jeans."

"Aren't we all," Skye murmured. She drew in a deep breath, opened her mouth… and shut it again. Then thought *Oh, what the hell* and charged ahead. "So this doesn't bother you? That I'm moving in? Starting up with your brother?"

Madison's face scrunched up in an adorable way. "Why should it? My brother's a big boy. He can pick out his women on his own. And you're his wife."

"Don't take this the wrong way, because I'm glad you're not troubled by it. You just came off as very… protective before."

"He's my only brother. And as much as he can be a shithead sometimes, I love him. But my superior people skills tell me that you're not here to mess with his mind or anything else. So if this works out, great. If not, that's his problem. My protection only goes so far. It's just nice to see him taking a chance on something. I'm actually going to go apartment hunting today. Wanna come with?"

"Why?" Madison tilted her head in question, and Skye clarified. "I mean, why are you apartment hunting? I appreciate the invitation, but you don't have to move out. Obviously you know your brother and I aren't… um… yeah." Though sex was a natural and beautiful thing, there were a few instances when it wasn't natural and beautiful to talk about it. Specifically with her new sister-in-law.

Madison leaned her head back and laughed. "Yeah. *Um, yeah* is right. No, I had planned on staying here while Tim was deployed to watch over the place. It was never meant to be a permanent thing. So since he's not leaving in the near future, I need my own space. I'm twenty-six. Living with my big brother got old when I was about ten."

"Ah." More sibling dynamic that she couldn't relate to. Instead she traced the seam of the navy blue bed-spread covering her legs.

"So since I'd be driving all over the place anyway, I thought I'd invite you. Show you around the area a little bit. I'm sure Tim would do it but unlike other jobs, he can't just call in for a personal day. Lots of stuff going down at the battalion today and he has to be there for it."

"I understand," she said gravely, though she didn't understand at all. Family first was the way of life on the commune. It wasn't at all uncommon for a local store to shut down for a week because the owner's child had the flu or just because they needed some quality family time. Or, hell, because the owner didn't like the current alignment of the planets. She had a lot of catching up to do on understanding life in the military. It was like a culture all its own.

At least that she could understand.

Tim sat in his office, thumbs gouging into his eye sockets. Today, of all days, when he just wanted to sit in his office and decompress from the one-eighty his life had just taken, all hell breaks loose. Marines not sure whether they were staying or going, families not sure who to contact about their loved ones, the support battalion that Dwayne's company would be deploying with screaming about not being ready fast enough.

Of course, "fast enough" to them was yesterday. Talk to God about that one, 'cause Tim only had so much pull. And it wasn't as if he had nothing else going on in his life right now. Twenty-hour workdays weren't really an option any longer.

Suddenly there was another woman in his life. Not his sister, and not his mother. But his wife.

Marriage had always been in the back of his mind, something he would get around to one of these days.

Women he'd dated in the past just never worked out. A few turned out to only be interested in hooking up with a man in uniform. Not Tim himself. That stung, but he quickly learned how to weed out the tag chasers. Another woman had been fine with the lifestyle, but then he'd been transferred to another base in another state, and the relationship hadn't withstood the distance.

But the last... the last woman had been perfect. Camille. She'd grown up an Army brat—something they had in common. She understood the lifestyle, was aware of the requirements of a military spouse. Knew the pressure, the potential problems, the whole nine yards. Talked about marrying him. Having babies. His parents adored her, and he was half in love with her himself.

Then he deployed. The emails were frequent, the phone calls cheerful. After a month, the emails were less frequent, the calls more rushed. Then they both stopped. And after he started to worry, debated whether to have someone check up on her and make sure she was okay, he got *The Email*.

He'd been Dear John'ed.

She didn't want the same life her mother had, didn't want the constant pressure, hated the separation, blah blah blah.

The perfect potential military spouse turned out to crave the life of a CPA's wife.

And now he was married to someone who probably wouldn't know the first thing about the military. The pressure, the possible anxiety, the demands on her own time. Hell, she called his cover a "hat thingie," for the love of God. This could easily end in disaster.

His mind flitted back to how Skye looked that

morning. Sleepy, tangled hair, confused, and more than a little grumpy at being woken up at such an hour. In his bed.

Okay, maybe disaster was a bit strong. He shifted a little to accommodate the growing hardness straining the front of his pants. Thank God his uniform blouse was long enough to cover any obvious tentage.

A knock on his door forced him to pull his sorry ass together. "Come in."

Dwayne popped his head in. "There's a lull in my area, and Jeremy's ready to escape too. Wanna grab a bite?"

Sit around his office all afternoon and constantly think about what a clusterfuck his life was, or go have lunch with his best friends and let them take his mind off of everything?

"Let me grab my cover. I'll meet you outside."

A short walk later they stood in front of the O Club.

Dwayne checked his watch. "Thursday. Seafood buffet day."

Jeremy stared at the entrance and shook his head. "I'm not really feeling seafood today. You want to grab a sub from the deli?"

Dwayne gave him the *Are you shitting me?* look. "Dude. Seafood. Buffet."

Jeremy glanced at the front door again. "Just not feeling it today."

"What the hell is your prob—"

"All right, we'll get deli," Tim cut in. If he let them continue, they'd go on all day. "God, it's like living with the Odd Couple," he muttered as he turned on his heel and walked toward the deli shop. "Get seafood for dinner if you want, D."

Ten minutes later, they sat in a booth in the back. Dwayne stared mutinously at his double-Italian sub but didn't open his mouth. Jeremy looked like he wanted to say something, but instead he took a large bite of his sandwich, as if having food in his mouth might keep him from blurting out something stupid.

Tim looked between the two, then sighed. "Yes. I'm married."

"Holy Puller." Dwayne breathed. He sat up, dropped his sullen attitude, and leaned over the table. "So it's true? You seriously got married in Vegas and forgot?"

Tim flicked a pickle at him. "You two saw how much I had to drink. You never should have let me go off by myself in the first place," he accused. Deflection— always the best defense. Even if it was a weak one.

Dwayne settled back and unwrapped his sub. "You looked good to me."

Jeremy nodded, then shook his head. "No, remember the Birthday Ball at TBS? He was shitfaced, but nobody knew it until way later? He played it off like he was stone sober, then he just snapped and we found him swimming in the fountain outside the hotel?"

Dwayne snorted, then threw his head back and laughed. "Oh my God. I totally forgot about that. And besides, I wasn't going to stop you from getting a little tail in Vegas. 'Cause seriously, that's all I thought you were doing. How the hell were we supposed to know Captain Stick would go from having a one-nighter to marrying the girl?"

Captain Stick. Shit, he'd almost forgotten about that nickname. In TBS, when everyone else found creative ways to circumvent some of the more ridiculous rules,

Tim had been adamant about keeping everyone in line—minus that one unfortunate incident with the fountain, which luckily nobody else was witness to. While his restraint might have helped him in school, it didn't win him any friends from his peers. The name Lieutenant Stick-Up-His-Ass was born... Lieutenant Stick for short. Though Dwayne and Jeremy had never jumped on the Stick bandwagon in public, they had continued to use the name privately when they thought he was too rigid.

Like, always.

He watched Jeremy and Dwayne argue the "could haves" and "should haves" of their time in Vegas, then cut in.

"It's done, so there's no point in bitching like girls about it."

Jeremy poked at his sandwich. "What are you gonna tell Blackwater?"

All three men were silent, and Tim felt a cold chill. Shit. For the first time, he thought about what this was going to sound like to his boss.

Dwayne sat back in the bench seat and draped his arm over the top. "You know how nosy he is. You're going to catch shit for not running the wedding by him first."

Tim was losing his appetite. It was lowering to think the man actually thought the Marines needed permission before getting married. "I've never had a CO who actually wanted to be notified before you got married. Have you?" The other two shook their heads. "As if he really deserves a vote on who gets married."

"He thinks he does. And whether he deserves a say on our private lives or not, he thinks he should have one. He's the one who fills out the paperwork for promotions.

Self-important pompous ass," Jeremy muttered and started wrapping his sandwich up.

"Pompous, did you say?" Dwayne's grin was huge. "Quite the word."

"Look it up." He slammed the sandwich back on the table. "Back to the topic. You can save this. Yeah, he'll get pissed about you getting married without telling him." Jer couldn't quite hold back the sneer at the stupidity of it. "But if you tell him you're handling it quietly, that it'll be fixed quickly, then it won't be as bad."

"Fixed?" Dwayne asked.

"Yeah, fixed. Divorce. Or maybe annulment. Whatever. The point is, get started on a solution now. So when you have to explain it to him, then it's done. I'd almost suggest not saying anything at all. But if he did find out by some freak accident, it'd be worse than coming clean now."

Dwayne's jaw dropped, and Tim thanked the Lord he'd already swallowed. "So you're just going to give up that easily?"

Tim figured he could let them in on the real plan, but the fun might just be seeing where this conversation was going to go. He leaned back in his booth seat and crossed his arms. "Why not? It was a drunken decision that I didn't even remember making. Why should I tether myself to the woman for the rest of my life because of a mistake?"

Dwayne shook his head. "Mistake? Dude, you didn't see the way you two were acting in Vegas."

"Are you sure you saw how we were acting? I seem to remember your preoccupation with a certain other leggy lady. Not to mention your own intoxication." Tim smirked.

Dwayne shrugged, not at all embarrassed. "Hey, the leggy chick was hot. But that's not the point." He picked up the other half of his foot long and pointed at Tim with it, bits of lettuce flying across the table. "That woman had you by the balls from the word 'go.' I have never seen you look at someone else like that. And you're just going to throw it all away?" His hands flew up, and a tomato slice plopped on the floor.

"Yes," Jeremy said.

"No," Tim replied at the same time, then they looked at each other.

"You're crazy. You're *insane*. Tim, I know this whole about-face with the deployment is stressful, but you can't really be thinking this. You can't be serious."

"Looks like he is," Dwayne said smugly. "Gotta say, I'm proud of you."

"Thanks, Dad," Tim said dryly.

"How could you possibly be encouraging this? You know how well an almost-non-existent engagement worked out for you in the past," Jeremy accused Dwayne.

Dwayne's face shut down. Shit. Bringing up Dwayne's ex-fiancée, Blair, was a recipe for disaster. A faked pregnancy, a quick engagement, and a nasty split right before things were made legal had definitely not left a good taste in his friend's mouth for future relationships.

"We're not talking about Blair's conniving ass here. We're talking about Skye. She's not saying she's pregnant. She's not asking for money, or a green card, or health insurance. She's asking for a marriage. Right?" Dwayne, ever the optimist—at least where anyone else's love life was concerned—turned questioning eyes toward Tim.

He leaned forward, effectively cutting off the rest of the restaurant from view, and lowered his voice. "Here's the thing. This doesn't leave the table, got it? It gets repeated to nobody. Not your companies, not the CO, not your weekend specials, nobody." He glanced around quickly, making sure no one they knew was in the deli and likely to come over and say hello. With the all clear, he continued. "Skye pulled a few strings in Vegas and found out where I lived. She came down to see me and talk things out, but we had already bugged out. She waited until I got back. She gave up everything in Vegas, including her job, to move down here. And she did all of that because she wants to make this work."

"After knowing you less than twenty-four hours? She's crazy too." Jeremy breathed. "Aren't you supposed to be legally sane to marry?"

Dwayne punched him in the shoulder. "Shut up." He gestured for Tim to continue.

"My original thought was divorce. Or an annulment. I don't know which would have been the right choice. But the fact was, it was going to end."

He paused, wondering how much more to tell them.

Jeremy and Dwayne both leaned forward, and Dwayne insisted, "Well?"

Finally, Tim just shrugged. "We talked. She explained her reasons for wanting it to work out, and I agreed." With some of them, he mentally added. He'd never understand this devotion to the unknown deity of Fate that Skye prescribed to, but his friends didn't need to know that. Jeremy already thought she was a few nuggets short of a Happy Meal. Knowing she believed Fate brought them together would send him over the edge.

"So you're just going to let her walk into your life and take over?" Jeremy sat back, face taut. "I don't believe this. What the hell? She could be a con artist. Or a tag chaser. A crazy psycho, which doesn't sound too far from the truth right now."

Dwayne sat back himself. "I think it'll be fine."

"Have a little faith there, Jer. For the love of God, I'm not some shiny lieutenant straight out of TBS. I know the signs. Skye is different, but in a good way."

"Different how?" Jeremy asked warily.

"Just… different. The fact is the marriage is here to stay. For now. We can reevaluate later if things aren't working out. But when word spreads around the battalion that I'm married all of a sudden, people will want to know info. And they'll head straight to you two. So the official word is that the relationship moved quickly, it's a new marriage, and we're still settling into newlywed life. That's why we're so private about it. That's close enough to the truth to keep it legit, and not so open to invite more questions."

"Given it some thought, huh?" Jeremy shook his head and went back to eating his sub, like he didn't want any part of the plan. Tim knew he'd follow through, though.

Yeah, well, not much to do but think when you're spending all night on a crappy air mattress. "I've thought about it a little. That's the story and we're all sticking to it."

"What will you tell the CO?"

Shit. Though it wasn't a requirement to tell the CO anything about his personal life, it was considered more a professional courtesy. And the fact remained that battalions were about as gossipy as any wives' club. The colonel would find out soon enough. And knowing this particular CO, it could get rough. Colonel Blackwater had some very… strict ideas on family values.

"I'll figure out how to handle it with Colonel Blackwater. I might just have to play that one by ear."

"As long as you're happy," Dwayne said.

"Easy there, Oprah. Wanna talk about our feelings now?" Jeremy sneered.

Damn, he was in a bad mood today. "What's your problem?" Tim asked, grateful for the topic change.

"Fuck off," he mumbled around a mouth full of club sandwich.

"Well, if I may bring this lunch to a happy end," Dwayne said, holding up his plastic cup of soda. "It's not a beer, but we'll fix that later. To our man Tim. First one to bite the bullet." A shit-eating grin spread over his face. "How's it taste?"

Chapter 7

SKYE COULD ONLY STARE AS MADISON DROVE THROUGH THE front gates of Camp Pendleton. She'd never been to a military base before—why would she ever need to?—but for some reason the real deal didn't just come close to her expectations. It blew them away.

Gate guards—Madison called them sentry—stood in front of the opening, checking cars for the proper identification and car registration. Madison flashed her own ID and the guard gave a quick salute, calling out to have a good day as they drove away.

"Do they always salute people?" she asked.

Madison laughed. "Officers they salute. Like Tim and myself."

"Oh." She needed a notepad to write all this down. If this were school, she'd have already failed the pop quiz. "So where are we headed?"

"I just thought we'd drive around base for a bit so you could see the place. It's huge, like a city all itself. And for the most part, self-sustaining. People who live on base don't have to leave for much of anything if they don't want to. Don't feel bad if you can't remember where anything is. It's the second-largest Marine base, period, so it's a good size. But you'll learn your way around fast enough."

Skye glanced around as they drove, trying to memorize landmarks while knowing it was useless. "I can come here on my own?"

"Oh sure," Madison replied, her voice breezy and light. "It's no problem at all. Tim will have to get your military ID all set up and get your car reg… um. Hmm." She trailed off, and Skye looked over to see her new friend blushing furiously.

"What?" When Madison said nothing, Skye rewound the last sentence in her head. "Oh. The ID thing? You're not sure if Tim is ready for all the paperwork. That's okay. I know he told you the deal we have going on. I'm not embarrassed or anything. It is what it is. For now."

Madison's eyes darted over before returning to the road. "You're taking this all really well, the uncertainty of it. For someone who was dead set on staying married, I mean."

Skye shrugged a shoulder and sat back. "I'm dead set on giving it a chance. That's the purpose. That we at least give the marriage the chance to thrive. No sense in getting worked up over this. I'm sure there are other things to worry about. But whether the marriage will end or not isn't one of them."

Madison laughed. "You know, I'm pretty sure that people spend a fortune on marriage counseling to become as Zen as you are about their marriage. And you've been at it for less than a month."

A smile tilted Skye's lips. "Yes, well, I was raised to pick my battles, and pick wisely. Trust me, when I feel the need to fight, it isn't pretty. I suggest you hide, in fact."

"Luckily I'll have a nice little apartment of my own to do that in," Madison said, referring to the rental she'd signed a lease on late that morning.

"I'm glad you'll be close by. I hate that you're moving

out. I feel like I'm shoving you out of the house." And as much as she liked Madison, she truly was torn. Guilt was a large factor, even though Madison had said repeatedly that she would have found another place to stay whether Skye was there or not. But at the same time, she was grateful that she and Tim would have the townhouse to themselves. In order to make a true run at their relationship, they needed their space.

"I would have whether you moved back or not," Madison assured her again. "One O'Shay per house is enough, trust me. Okay, there's the hospital. It's where I work. I'm in the OB wing for now, but they have us on three-week rotations, so I'll be in a new area next week."

"So this is where the Marines are cared for?"

"And dependents. Families," she corrected when Skye gave her a *huh?* face. "Spouses and children are referred to as dependents."

Skye wasn't a fan of that. It seemed like such a… demeaning way to refer to someone's family. "I don't like the thought of being dependent on someone. Seems so… nineteen fifties."

"Just a word. Doesn't have to mean anything," Madison reminded her.

Apparently this was just one of those things Skye needed to get over, since there was no changing it.

"Now if you follow this road straight down, you'll hit the commissary and the exchange. Basically the grocery store and the shopping center. Tax-free shopping. It won't have everything you want, but it usually has the basics and can be way cheaper than shopping in town." She made a left turn at a light instead of driving straight.

"Where are we heading now?"

"Oh, I thought we'd stop by Tim's battalion, see if he's in his office. Maybe say hi to Dwayne. And Jeremy too, I guess." Madison's fingers drummed on the steering wheel. If Skye didn't know better, she'd think her friend was nervous. But that wasn't possible. She'd been here a million times. Maybe just too much bottled energy.

A ball of lead settled heavily in Skye's stomach. She glanced down at the thin blouse and lightweight gypsy skirt she wore to combat the dry heat. Her flip-flops were cute and adorned with jewels, but definitely nothing nice.

Madison, on the other hand, looked easy and simple in a pair of dark jeans, cap-sleeve brown shirt, and brown flats. Suddenly, although the outfit didn't appeal to Skye, it seemed like a much better option. And she felt very out of place.

"Um, are you sure that's a good idea? He might be busy or something."

"Maybe. But we're right here, and if he is busy I can still give you a tour of the building. Though some areas are restricted, a lot of it is just office buildings, so we can roam around."

She opened her mouth to argue but realized it was fruitless. Madison was already pulling into a parking lot filled with cars. The building was long and all-brick, and a tank that looked like it might have been used in World War I was sitting off to the side in a grassy area, roped off with signs stating it was definitely not a toy. After squeezing the car into a spot, they walked inside. Marines passed by, some nodding to Madison. Many gave Skye an assessing glance, like she was an oddity in the day.

Well, at least her shoes were cute.

Madison led her up a flight of stairs to a long hallway, down to the end, and opened the door. The scene could have been any normal outer office in corporate America. Minus the imposing guys in camouflage, that is. Desks sat cubicle-style around the large, open room. Phones rang, people swiveled in chairs, fingers flew over keyboards. A copy machine that sounded like it was on its last leg ran in one corner. It was a beehive of activity.

Bam!

The heavy door slammed behind Skye, and all heads turned their way. It was the dream where you went to high school naked all over again. She had never felt so conspicuous.

"Hey, guys." Madison acted like it was no big deal being stared at by twenty men in uniform. Though being in the military herself, it likely wasn't. "Is my brother around?"

"He left for lunch a bit ago with Robertson and Phillips. Should be back soon," one Marine answered Madison. But his eyes never left Skye. She might have taken the attention as a compliment, if the kid looked old enough to shave. But she was pretty sure attraction wasn't his main reason for the double-glance.

"We'll wait in his office then." And with that, Madison wrapped one hand around Skye's arm and tugged her into a room off to the side.

After shutting the door carefully behind them, Madison sighed. "Sorry, I thought most of them would be at lunch now. Stupid me, forgetting there's another deployment gearing up immediately. I didn't know how to introduce you, so I didn't."

Skye was about to say that was fine when the door opened.

"O'Shay, I need you to—oh. Sorry, ladies. Madison!" A man who looked to be in his late forties stood in the doorway, a smile on his face for Madison. "I didn't know you were here." He took a step in the office, propping the door behind him. "Tim's not around?"

"Afternoon, sir." Though she didn't pop a salute or anything, Madison's posture became stiff, almost rigid. "The PFC said he'd be back soon so I thought we'd wait. Is that all right?"

"Sure is." He looked over at Skye. She could feel his gaze raking over her from head to toe. Observing, judging. She should be used to it by now, really. She must have some sign on her back that said *Peruse at your leisure*. "And who is this young lady?"

A movement in the doorway caught Skye's eye. She turned and, with a combination of relief and dismay, found Tim standing there. His mouth was set in a grim line, eyes shuttered and unreadable.

"Afternoon, sir. This would be my wife."

So much for easing into the marriage slowly.

Colonel Blackwater turned, his face a blank slate. "Wife?"

Tread carefully, man. "Yes, sir. My wife, Skye…" He hesitated, not sure whether to use her own name or his. She hadn't legally changed it, but keeping her own last name might not sound right to a conservative man like the Colonel. So he pushed on. "My wife. Skye, this is my CO, Colonel Blackwater."

The man wasn't an idiot. He might have questions for Tim, but he turned a smiling face to Skye and held out his hand. "Nice to meet you, ma'am. You'll have to excuse my surprise. Apparently Tim was keeping a lid on this one."

The man had no idea.

Skye smiled and nodded, then gave the Colonel a firm handshake. But he could see she was nervous. "Nice to meet you, sir." From Tim's angle, he could see as she reached back to covertly wipe her hands on her flowing, ruffled skirt. Sweating palms. Tim could relate. Then he took a moment to look over her whole outfit.

With her blouse and sandals, and her hair a curling mess, she looked like a wild gypsy come to entertain the troops. He half-expected her to break out a tambourine and start dancing for coins.

And why did that mental image make him want to smile?

"How long have you two been married?"

Skye started to answer, but Tim cut her off. "Newlyweds, sir."

Blackwater gave him a long look, then nodded. "I'll just head back to my office and give you a few minutes alone." The Colonel paused by Tim as he headed out the door. In a low voice only Tim could hear, he warned, "We'll talk about this later," then left.

The silence in the room was deafening. Tim had no clue what to say. He was glad to see Skye, yes. But not here. Not in his office. Not yet anyway. He wasn't even close to ready to make the news of his marriage public knowledge before he had a chance to figure out the angle.

Guess that was just too damn bad.

He wanted to say something, but she looked so miserable. Her hands were clenched around the edge of his desk, and she wouldn't make eye contact. Well, wasn't this marriage just off to a great start.

Madison cleared her throat. "I, uh, found an apartment. I'm moving in over the weekend."

"I'll see if Jeremy and Dwayne can come over to help."

"Oh, don't bother them," she said quickly.

"They'll want to help."

"Great!" Her voice was cheerful. But Tim knew that smile was the one she used every time she wanted to pretend the world was right, but everything was really wrong. What the hell was that all about?

She grabbed Skye's arm and tugged. "Sorry we intruded. I thought we could just slip in really fast and catch you to say hello but..." She shrugged. "Sorry."

"It's okay." He tousled his sister's hair, just to piss her off. He wasn't disappointed. Her face flushed and her mouth set in a stubborn line. "I'll see you when I get home. What do we have in the freezer?"

"I'll get some steaks out."

Skye mumbled something under her breath, and Tim looked over, surprised. Shit. Was dinner something he should be talking to her about? Was she upset? God, being married was hard.

"Um, are steaks okay with you?" He didn't even know if his wife ate meat. Everyone ate meat though, didn't they?

"Uh." She glanced to the side and gave a strangled, "Sure."

Okay. So maybe she wasn't a huge red meat fan. Tim

liked chicken as much as the next guy. "How about bar-beque chicken instead?"

Skye's face paled just a little and she swallowed hard. "Sounds delicious."

Total lie. But she clearly didn't want to talk about it now. His eyes still on Skye's, he motioned with his head toward the hallway. "Madison. Out."

He waited for the door to shut. "What are you doing today?"

She sighed. "We spent the morning looking for a place for Madison. And now I'm going to go put in some résumés at restaurants."

"What? Why?" He stepped back to look at her.

Skye wore a bemused smile. "Because there are no casinos that I could work at," she said, like it was obvious.

"You don't have to work." Did she think she needed to? That he didn't make enough money to support her?

"I want to. I've always worked, and I want to continue. So I'm looking for something related to my old job. I might have to start at the bottom of the food chain, but that's okay."

Tim shook his head. Talk about a one-eighty from expectations. "If that's what you want then."

"It is." She slithered by him, her skirt wrapping around his ankles for a moment. It would be so easy—so damn easy—to toss her up on the desk and flip that skirt up. What would she wear under something like that? Cotton? Satin? Lace?

Nothing?

"Tim. Hello?" Skye waved a hand in front of his face.

His mind snapped back. "Huh?" Okay, maybe it didn't snap back so much as make a slow slide into Idiot Land.

"You were staring at your desk. You just blanked. I was trying to say good-bye."

"Ah. Right." Skye was having an entire conversation and he was stuck in a zone, staring at the spot he'd imagined her ass perched on. Even without touching her, he wasn't safe with her around. "I'll walk you to the car."

"Nope. That's okay. We already interrupted your day enough as it is." Her smile was wide, but her eyes weren't shining like he was used to.

With another quick check to make sure the door was shut, he reached out and pulled Skye to him. The feel of her arms wrapped around his back was heaven. Added bonus, he was completely restricted from trying anything that might or might not have been appropriate, since anyone could come through the door. But God she felt good against him.

He propped his chin on the top of her head. "I'm glad you stopped by." He gave her a quick kiss on the nose before dropping his arms and opening the door. Madison stood on the other side, arms crossed, foot tapping.

"Ya done yet?" she huffed.

"Bug off, squirt. It's your day off. Not like you had something better to do."

"Yeah. Day off. Meaning I have to use today to get all the crap done I don't have time for on the days I'm not off." She grabbed Skye's forearm and started walking toward the outer office door. "We'll see you at home," she called over her shoulder.

"Bye!" Skye yelled as the door to the outer office was shutting behind her.

Tim stood for a moment, watching the two women disappear through the window in the office door.

"Who was that, sir?"

Tim glanced to his left to see PFC Malone staring the same direction, eyes all but bugging out of his head.

He rolled his eyes. "Back to your desk, Marine."

———

"O'Shay, you've always impressed me." Colonel Blackwater leaned back in his chair, elbows resting on the armrest, fingers steepled in front of him. "I've enjoyed our discussions. I've admired your work ethic. And nobody can complain about your attributes. Fourth generation Marine. Top of your class at the Naval Academy. Breezed through TBS."

Tim felt his gut tighten. This sounded very much like it was leading up to a huge "but."

"However—"

Close enough.

"—I am more than a little surprised to find you married." He leaned forward over his desk. "Is this a new development?"

"It's, well…" Tim took a deep breath. He had to remember that he'd done nothing wrong. Unconventional, sure. But wrong? No. "We're newlyweds, sir."

"I haven't seen your wife at any functions yet. Did she not want to attend things while you two were dating?"

"She lived out of state until we married, sir." Total truth.

"I see." Clearly he didn't, given the frown that pulled at the CO's mouth. "Well, I hope she feels comfortable in the battalion. Gets involved. Joins the wives' club. That sort of thing. You know how I feel about spouses plugging into the available resources. And it's my personal opinion that spouse support can be the major difference between a Marine's success or failure in his career."

Tim disagreed with that thought. What did it matter if his wife went to a spouse meeting once a month? Besides, Skye didn't sound much like a joiner to Tim. But now was *really* not the time to bring up her unique perspective on life. "I'll definitely bring it up with her." He could just tack it onto the list of things they had to discuss. Starting with "What's your middle name?"

He nodded sharply. "I hope so. I count on you to be a good example to the younger Marines. And your marriage is a part of that. Setting up good family standards will help solve any possible future problems. I think everyone knows how I feel about family life and its possible consequences in the workplace. A distracted Marine is a dead Marine."

Tim hated that anything in his personal life was considered a requirement for work. Not all commands ran like this. But Blackwater was big on knowing everyone's shit, and a failing family would be seen to him as a major sign of weakness. But instead of telling the CO to mind his own business, he simply said, "Yes, sir." Because what else could you tell your boss?

He'd have liked a little more credit than this. He wasn't a guy to run wild on the weekends, to get speeding tickets every other night, or get tossed in the drunk tank repeatedly. He wasn't filing for bankruptcy or defaulting on child support. He just got married. And maybe it was a little like tooting his own horn, but Tim thought he was a guy who was steady enough in his work that he could make sure a problem at home wouldn't become a major disaster at work.

Apparently the CO held everyone to the same standard.

Tim walked back to his own office with cold sweat pooling in his lower back. He hadn't expected to have to explain his marriage so quickly. Easing in would have been much more welcome.

Guess it was just time to take the plunge and hope the waves didn't knock him on his ass.

Chapter 8

Skye wiped her hands on the dishcloth and surveyed the table set for two. The place was a total bachelor pad, with no napkins—paper or cloth—and she couldn't find anything that remotely resembled a vase in which to put the flowers she'd picked up at a market with Madison earlier, along with a few food items for herself. So she'd settled for a plastic pitcher for the bouquet and set the table with the paper plates and plasticware, with squares of paper towel for napkins. She winced at the waste she could only imagine he'd accumulated up to now.

But as Madison pointed out, she was too busy to care what she ate off of most the time, and Tim was, well, a guy.

He did, however, have a set of steak knives and some of those little corn holders. Skye laughed to herself. Priorities.

While helping Skye find everything in the kitchen, Madison assured her that she had actual matching dishes and silverware, but she'd never unpacked her things when she moved in. Though that turned out to be lucky given the fact that she hadn't stayed in Tim's place long.

Madison, much to Skye's combined disappointment and delight, had cried off for dinner. Skye wasn't buying the "I forgot I promised to meet a coworker" excuse. Madison was playing matchmaker. Skye just couldn't decide if the added pressure was amusing or distressing.

Could someone be a matchmaker if the couple was already matched?

"Squirt? Are you here?"

"It's just me!" Skye called out from the kitchen. "Madison forgot she had something to do so she took off." She opened the fridge and leaned in to find the steaks and veggie kabobs that Madison put in to marinade earlier and backed out, only to bump into something.

"Oh!"

"Easy there." Strong hands circled her waist and steadied her, then one took the dish of steaks from her hand. "I've got this."

"Thank you." Skye turned around and ended up staring at the word "O'Shay" stitched to Tim's uniform. Had he gotten taller since she last saw him? No, her imagination was running away with her. She looked up all the way and asked, "Where's your hat?"

"My hat?" His brows scrunched. "Oh. Right." Tim stepped back and set the dish on the counter. "It's actually called a cover. Any hat that I wear with my uniform is a cover."

"Cover. Right." She seriously needed that notebook to start taking notes. Maybe he wouldn't mind if she stuck Post-its all over the house.

"I'm going to go upstairs and change. Then I'll be back down to start up the grill."

Skye nodded and watched as he left the kitchen. His boots, with their thick soles, should have made some serious noise on the hardwood, but she heard nothing. What she noticed was the way his butt looked in his pants. They were just tight enough to give her a good peep before he turned the corner and was out of sight.

Turning toward the fridge, she opened the door and stuck her head in to cool her flushing face. Her mother would roll her eyes if she knew how unbelievably turned on she was by the sight of a man in camouflage. She could hear the *tisk tisk* now.

"A Marine? They shoot people, dear. That's hardly an exercise in peace. They're walking, talking killing machines."

"Are you truly checking that man out? That's objectifying him just like a man objectifies a poor woman forced to become an exotic dancer for money."

"Why couldn't you have met someone on the commune? A nice pacifist."

Just imagine what she would say if Skye told her she'd *married* the killing machine. In a—gasp!—legally binding ceremony.

"Are you looking for something?"

Bang.

"Ow!" Skye stood back and let the fridge door shut, holding the back of her head where she'd bashed it against the freezer door. She turned to glare at Tim, almost glad for the pain. It cast a nice haze over her lust, allowing her to look at him without blushing. The fact that he'd tossed on a T-shirt and baggy jeans helped too. "Do you use that sneaky tactic on terrorists?"

He gave her a wry grin. "Terrorists usually aren't mumbling to themselves with their heads in the refrigerator. But if I found one in such a situation, sure. What are you looking for?"

"Oh. Um…" She grabbed the bowl of lettuce she'd washed earlier. "Just this."

"Hmm. I'm going to get started at the grill. How do you like your steak done?"

"Uh, same as yours." Did that sound right? He nodded and headed out the back door to the patio, so it must have sounded normal. Oh God. Was she really going to have to eat that? Okay. Sooner or later, she'd have to admit she really didn't eat meat. Why hadn't she said so already? How hard was that? *I'm a pseudo-vegetarian.* There. It's not like she was admitting to leprosy.

Though she had a feeling that he-man out there might very well consider them one and the same.

This isn't going to start off well if you are constantly trying to impress him. That's what people do when they're dating. You're not dating. You're married. So start showing it all. Now.

She watched as he stepped out through the back door and onto the concrete patio to fire up the grill before turning and starting to set the table with foods Madison had assured her were Tim's favorites.

His favorite foods. How he liked his steak cooked. How she didn't want steak at all. Things people found out while they were dating. Things that were basic, didn't require a second thought to a married couple.

They'd just have to figure it out as they went along. And she would have to stop hiding little details just to smooth things over. Skye rolled her shoulders and fought past the dread that tried to claw her down. This wasn't a bad sign. This wasn't the end of the world. They just went out of order a little bit. There had to be a reason for it.

Tim brought the steaks in sooner than she expected. They each filled their cups and sat down silently, as if not sure what to say to each other. Skye reached for her napkin, then halted. Did he pray before meals? She snuck a glance at Tim, who seemed to be staring at his drink cup, at the same impasse she was.

What did Tasha usually call this moment? Right. Awkward turtle.

"Thanks for cooking the meat," she said. Lame. So lame. Then she reached for her own water and took a drink.

The tension leaked out of Tim's body. He settled more solidly into his chair and grabbed his own cup. "No problem. It's the only cooking I really do." He grimaced at his kitchen. "Obviously. Are you much of a cook?"

Skye laughed as she started to cut her salad. "I'm proficient with a microwave. My mother did most of the cooking, and Dad helped out. I just didn't pick up on much while I lived with them, I guess. In college, I ate dorm food. Then in Vegas, I usually took home a to-go box from the restaurant most times I worked and just ate junk the rest of the time."

"Ah. So no four-course meal tomorrow night?" Tim asked, his eyes teasing.

"Probably not, unless you want tofu and veggies with every course," Skye replied, reaching for one of the vegetable kabobs.

The horror on Tim's face was almost comical. "Tofu? You've got to be kidding me."

"Tofu's not so bad, you know. If it's cooked properly, half the time you can't tell."

"If you can't tell the difference, why not eat the real thing?" he asked between bites.

"Well, because some people don't eat meat."

Tim glanced between her plate—which only had salad and the veggies—and the second steak on the platter he'd brought in. "Is that why the steak is still there and not in front of you?"

She smiled sheepishly. "I'm a pseudo-vegetarian."

"A pseudo-vegetarian." Tim looked like she just told him she was actually a robot bent on world domination.

"I'm not über-sensitive. I wear leather. I eat eggs and drink milk. I just don't cook meat, or eat it most of the time. I avoid ordering it in restaurants. But I'm also not so hardcore that I bring my own tofu dish to dinner parties. I'll eat a chicken dish every so often. And when I was younger, I would get a craving so bad that I'd dream about dancing Happy Meals... much to my parents' dismay."

"Who I assume are full-on vegetarians."

"Hardcore, bingo."

"Huh." Tim sat back and chewed another bite of steak for a while. "Well, this is new. I guess that second steak is mine then, right?"

That was it? No questions about why? No mocking or saying that it was weird? "Yeah. That's yours."

"Great." Tim stabbed the other steak and deposited it on his plate, then dug into his salad with gusto. "Gotta say, can't really relate there. I was raised on meat and potatoes. My mom's an amazing cook. She'd give Martha Stewart a run for her money."

Though Skye was positive it wasn't meant to be a jab, it still stung. But she cheerfully asked, "Tell me about your parents."

"Dad was in the Marines," Tim began, talking between bites. "Naval Academy grad like me, total warrior. I think he was my hero before I knew the definition of the word. I wanted to be just like him when I grew up." He chuckled. "I'm sure most boys say that about their dads at some point in their childhood. But I never grew out of it. So I followed in his footsteps. Did the Academy thing, commissioned in the Marines, and went from there. He was a pilot though. So not quite the same. But he was happy."

The pride was so strong in his voice, Skye felt a little choked up. "How about your mom?"

Tim's smile softened. "I used to think she was Superwoman. My dad was gone a lot. Training, deployments, missions, whatever. But she was a rock. She kept things as stable as she could. Always there for sports. Never dropped the ball. Strong woman. Never got overly emotional, never had a breakdown."

Emotional. Didn't that just describe Skye to a T? The inadequacies piled up. Skye mentally pictured shoving each of the imagined shortfalls into a steel box and shutting the lid, then pushing the box off to the side. She was overreacting. "Where do they live?"

"Dad retired and they moved back to Wisconsin. My grandparents live there. Or they do now. Grandpa was a Marine too." The pleasure of carrying on the Marine tradition practically radiated off of him. "What do your parents do?"

Skye stood up, wanting some more ice for her glass. The scrape of Tim's chair startled her.

"What are you doing?"

He looked at her, down at his feet, then back at her again. "Standing?"

"I see that. Did you need something?"

"No, I'm just… I mean that's…" He looked confused. Adorably confused, like a puppy that didn't understand why its owner was displeased with the chewed up shoe it presented. "Men stand when a woman stands. It's how I was raised," he said finally.

"Oh. Huh." She walked to the freezer and grabbed a handful of ice, then reached in the fridge for the filter pitcher.

"Did your dad not do this?"

Skye paused in putting the pitcher back. "Do what? Stand when my mom or I left the table?" She scoffed and walked back. "No. Smacks of inequality." She sat down and dug back in, choosing to ignore the curious look her husband was giving her. But she couldn't ignore his question.

"Inequality how?"

"Just in that it makes the woman appear, I don't know, superior somehow. More worthy of respect. You don't expect me to stand when you leave the table, do you?"

"No." Tim looked offended, and Skye had to laugh. She rubbed his forearm and squeezed.

"And I don't want you to have to do it either."

"But I want to." He looked so lost, completely confused how to work himself out of the mess.

Skye sighed. "I'll just pretend that you're having a leg spasm and had to stand up."

He tilted his head to one side as he picked up his drink cup. "What do your parents do anyway?"

"They own a store." Okay. That wasn't going to cut it. He'd been upfront with her, and she needed to do the same. She wasn't ashamed. So time to air it all out. "Look. Here's the thing."

"Oh, boy," he muttered under his breath.

She ignored that. "My parents are basically what you would call, um, modern-day hippies."

Her husband's mouth dropped open, then snapped shut. He stared at her, eyes wide. "Hippies? Like… hippies? Peace, love, protests, weed?"

"Not weed. My parents don't do drugs. At least, not anymore. What my parents did in their youth before I was born isn't my business." It shouldn't annoy her he had the same stereotype everyone else did… that all hippies were drugged-out potheads. But it did. "But the rest of it, yeah. Basically. They're just pacifists who like causes, like to live as naturally as possible, and without government interference."

Tim's eyes glazed over, and he stared into the distance as if he was still processing. "And so… uh…"

"They live in Texas, on a commune that's in a rural area. They run a health food store that offers mostly organic, all-natural products. And they actually have a very successful Internet business selling organic herbs and spices."

"A commune, huh. Internet business?"

Skye smiled. "Seems a little at odds, doesn't it? My parents are hippies, not idiots. They saw the organic market booming and decided to cash in. They know their food, they know their business. And they do well. They just prefer to do well where they are, with other like-minded folks."

"And you grew up on this commune?"

"Yes. In a house, not a burnt out van that looks like the Mystery Machine van from *Scooby Doo*. Think of the commune as just a rural neighborhood, a little removed from city life."

Tim nodded, but she could tell his head was spinning, trying to take it all in.

Subject change needed. "I didn't cause any problems showing up at work, did I?"

"No. Not at all. If you want to come see me, then come see me."

Relieved, Skye grabbed a few bowls and stood up, patiently ignoring when he stood up as well, and headed to the kitchen to clean. He followed with an armload of plates, which were promptly dumped into the trash.

"Not exactly eco-friendly, but I won't miss washing dishes tonight," she teased. He smiled and she felt better. So the night wasn't a home run. But it was a start.

———

Tim watched as Skye finished rinsing off the last dish, leaving a few to soak for a while. She danced in place while doing the dishes. It was like she had an iPod on shuffle in her head at all times. In her bare feet, she swayed side to side or raised on her toes and back down, always in motion. Her skirt swayed and wrapped around her ankles.

It was a seduction, plain and simple. She was luring him with her own natural way of being, and she had no clue. It was artless, it was effortless. It was Skye. God. No wonder he was so drawn to her from the beginning.

The front of her blouse was wet from splashing water, turning the material almost transparent. She wore a lacy bra that looked like it might be light pink. And he was dying to get the shirt off to double-check.

"Tim."

"Yeah?" He was staring at her chest. Damn. Lifting

his eyes, he caught her wry smile. "Sorry. Zoned out." He did that a lot around her, apparently.

She glanced down, noticed the state of her top, and looked back up. "Uh huh. Zoned. I asked if you needed help with the grill. Outside. The thing you used to cook the steaks? Is anyone in there?" She waved a hand in front of his eyes.

He was watching her lips move. She definitely had tempting lips. Damn, he looked like an idiot. "No. I mean yeah, sorry. I'm just tired. I'll do it now."

She shrugged and wiped down the last of the counter. "Okay."

The temperature had cooled down when Tim stepped back out to clean the grill. Unfortunately, the fresh air did nothing to chill his boiling blood. The woman got under his skin, and he had no clue how. Everything she did seemed natural, second nature. But her unintentional seduction wrapped around his senses and squeezed until he could barely breathe but for wanting her.

Tim applied himself to scrubbing the wire rack down. If he couldn't take his lust out in the bedroom, he'd take it out on the grill.

Wait, why couldn't he apply his lust in the bedroom? She was his wife, wasn't she? They'd already had sex once. What was the problem? He'd left her alone the night before, figuring she might be tired and out of sorts after working out the details of their marriage attempt. But tonight…

Tonight she'd cooked him dinner. Or, well, set it up anyway. She'd set his table and made it look halfway decent with whatever she could find in his house. She'd bought flowers. She was setting up house. Nesting, his mom always called it after every move. Applying herself to the details of what made a house a home.

That had to mean she felt comfortable enough for sex. Right?

God, he hoped so. Otherwise he was going to be taking a very long, cold shower with very unsatisfying results.

Tim glanced down and realized the grill hadn't been this clean since he bought it. That was probably a sign it was time to go in and check on his wife.

His wife.

Just about now he could get used to the sound of that.

Tim finished putting away the grill and its accessories then went into the kitchen to wash his hands. No sign of Skye. He dried his hands and drifted toward the hallway. Low sound emitted from the living room. As he rounded the corner, the soft glow of the television said to look for her there.

Skye was curled up in the big armchair, her knees tucked to her chest, feet peeking out beneath the skirt's hem. Her head lolled to one side, eyes closed, her mouth slightly open. She looked as peaceful as a dreaming child. And he couldn't bring himself to wake her up. Not even with a hard-on that could drive railroad ties.

Tim figured he had two choices. He could either let her sleep in the chair all night and wake up with a crick in her neck. Or he could carry her to bed but risk waking her. Still debating his options, he picked up the remote and turned the TV off. The decision was taken out of his hands when her eyes fluttered open.

"Hey," he said softly, making sure she was entirely awake.

She gave him a sweet smile that had his stomach clenching. "Hey yourself. Is the grill cleaned?"

Polished to a shine, thanks to pent-up sexual tension. "Yup." Hating that he was looming over her, he dropped to his knees in front of the chair. He couldn't resist, so he went with his impulse to brush a hand over her hair. She closed her eyes and turned her head into the caress, all but purring with contentment.

He leaned over and pressed his lips to hers, a testing gesture. She responded, lips moving with his, opening quickly to deepen the kiss. And thank God, since he had no clue how he would manage to take being shot down by his wife with grace and dignity.

Hands speared through her hair; he let Skye be his anchor. Because he was sure he'd drown without someone there to pull him out eventually. His tongue dipped into the recesses of her mouth, tasting and teasing. She gave back, stayed with him with every swirl and flick. Her back arched, pressing her breasts into his chest. Her still-damp shirt had cooled, her nipples pebbling into tight buds, pressing against him. Begging.

Tim worked his way down her jawline, mixing nips with slow kisses. He paused when he reached her rapidly throbbing pulse, letting his tongue feel the intense beat, his confidence growing as he felt how agitated she was. Her body moved restlessly under his, as if holding back and reaching out at the same time.

With one hand he pushed her shirt up, peeling it away where it stuck to skin. Pink. He was right, the bra was pink. And lace. And gorgeously girlish, which only sent his blood into a frenzied rush to escape below his belt buckle. He let his breath warm the skin of her stomach as he pressed kisses from her navel up. Reaching the edge of pink lace, he left it in place and took one tight peak between his teeth.

Skye gasped, and her hands flew to the sides of his head. He waited to see if she'd push him away or pull him closer. But she did neither, leaving him to find his own way. He took another nibble, watched while her head dropped back, her eyes flickered with sparks of heat. He moved to the other breast, rolling her nipple between his teeth. The awkward angle meant he couldn't remove her bra without serious repositioning, and he didn't want to break the moment. But he *could* reach something else.

His hand strayed down to her ankle, following the line of her leg over her bent knee, pushing gently until they fell open, exposing her core. He let his fingertips dance up her thigh, soaking in the restless motion of her body, the way her hands tightened around his head, until he reached the edge of her panties.

More lace. She was a matcher, which surprised the hell out of him. The thought had him smiling against her breast. He tugged gently until he could work one finger under the lace edge.

Skye's legs closed with a snap, trapping his arm between them. Her hands pulled until he released her nipple and looked her in the eye.

Breathing heavily, she managed to pant out, "I probably should have mentioned this before now, but…"

"But. What." The words came out as a growl. He was so close one false move might have him losing his slippery grip on anything resembling control.

She bit her lip and glanced away before looking back

at him. And then he knew. He knew exactly what she was going to say, and the mere thought of it had his legs trembling with exhaustion.

Please, God, do not say it. I am begging You, if You are listening—

"I don't think we should have sex yet."

Chapter 9

TIM'S EYES WIDENED, THEN NARROWED. HE SWALLOWED hard, drawing Skye's eyes to his throat.

"You've got to be shitting me," he said around clenched teeth.

"No, I'm really not. And there's a very logical explanation. If you wouldn't mind, um..." She tapped his elbow, which was all she could reach while her legs were firmly clamped together around his arm and hand.

He looked down, then sighed. With deliberate caution, he let his hand drift down her thigh until it slid out from under her skirt. She shivered automatically. The dirty rat. Though she probably deserved that for letting it get this far. Not that she'd planned it. The man could make her head spin with one kiss. Definitely not convenient for conversation.

"Explain. And make it fast."

She struggled to sit up and pointed to the couch. "Could you sit over there? It's easier to think when you're not so overwhelming." And boy, she could just bite her tongue for that slip.

He gave her a satisfactory—almost predatory—smile before standing up and adjusting the front of his jeans. The bulge was at eye level, impossible to miss. She gulped and looked away. The less temptation the better. She used the time to pull down her shirt and make sure it was covering everything that should be covered. Of course, nothing could disguise the way her nipples stood out through the thin lace and cotton. When she heard the give of the cushions to her left, she looked back.

Tim was lounging in a deceptively casual way, one ankle propped on his other knee, arms spread over the back of the couch. Add in some silky pillows and a few girls in skimpy robes and you'd have an indolent sultan relaxing at home with his harem. But the look in his eyes was anything but relaxed. He was a panther, ready to pounce at a word from her.

Oh, how tempted she was to just give the word...

"I'm ready to hear the amazing theory that you've developed that says we shouldn't have sex yet. You know, us. The married couple who has already had sex once." His tone was wry.

She shifted until she could cross her legs beneath her, adjusting her skirt to cover her knees. Two fingers restlessly traced and worried the hem of her shirt and she forced her hands to lay flat on the armrest. "Do you really want this marriage to work? Be honest." She couldn't look at him when she asked. Too afraid of his face giving away more than his answer.

"I don't half-ass things. Skye. Hey, look at me." She did. "I either go balls to the wall or I don't go at all. I wouldn't have bothered asking you to move in if I thought this was a bad idea. Or a pointless idea, I should say. I don't know what's going to come of this, but I'm trying."

She nodded. "I'm glad to hear that. I want this to work too. And if it doesn't, then I want to make sure we put forth every effort first. There's just something here that Fate has for us."

Tim rolled his eyes at that. "Fate again?"

Anger simmered on the surface, but she fought to keep it down. Three cleansing breaths later, she said, "Yes, Fate. It's what I believe in. It's what I believe led us to this spot. Ignore it all you want, but we're in this position for a reason."

"Please don't get started on that again."

The thin hold she had on her anger snapped. She let out a muted scream from the bottom of her throat, leapt out of the chair, and started to pace, realizing this was in some vague parallel to her conversation with Madison a week earlier.

"No, I will get started on this! If you don't want to call it Fate, then fine. Call it something else to yourself. But at least respect where I'm coming from." She reached the end of the room and whipped around, feeling powerful and in control. The effect was ruined when she had to spit out hair that had flown into her open mouth.

She glanced over and saw Tim fighting a smile. "Not. Amused."

"Do you do this a lot?"

"Do what?"

"Pace like a pissy tiger?"

She continued her pacing, but her anger had abated. "Yes. It helps me work out the tension." When he smiled, she sighed and let the rest of her anger flow from her body. "I want this to work. And sex is going to get in the way."

"Sex can only help, the way I see it," he muttered.

Skye skidded to a halt in front of him. "Care to explain that, soldier?"

One annoying eyebrow winged up. "Number one,

I'm not a soldier. I'm a Marine. Number two, you heard what I said. Doesn't get much more clear than that."

When he didn't elaborate, she grabbed a handful of her hair and gave a sharp tug, letting the pain clear her mind. "How?"

Tim settled back further in the cushions and crossed his arms over his chest, straining the old T-shirt around his shoulders. She could physically see the seams straining. And damn it, she was checking him out again.

"We've already had sex. Plus, we're married. So morally there's really no problem. Besides that, from what I remember, the sex we had was pretty fuc—pretty awesome. Sorry." He gave her a sheepish grin. "As I was saying, sex feels good. Right now, I think feeling good sounds like an excellent way to start off this marriage."

"Sex is all we have, though." Skye flopped back into the chair and propped her feet on the coffee table. "I want you. You want me. There, I said it." She laughed when Tim's eyes widened. "It's the truth. Don't bother denying it. But we can't let that get in the way of working through this marriage. How can we get to know each other, to know whether we fit together—"

"We fit just fine." He smirked and propped his feet next to hers.

She kicked until his feet landed with a thunk on the floor. "Shut up. The fact is, we don't know how compatible we are—don't say it—within the marriage. Removing the haze of lust or the happy pheromones we get from making love will help us focus more on bringing the emotional aspect up. I'm very serious about this. You can laugh at it, but I believe abstaining—for now— will help us grow in the relationship."

Tim was silent, staring at the mantel above the fireplace for what seemed like a lifetime. She glanced up, following his eye line to see him staring at a wooden picture frame holding a smiling family of four. A much younger Tim and Madison, and what was most obviously his parents.

"It's important to me," she added quietly.

Finally he propped his feet up next to hers again and sighed. He looked at the ceiling and called out, "God, are you listening to this? Is this some kind of sick humor?"

"Oh, She has a great sense of humor," Sky teased.

"I'm choosing to ignore that." He ran a hand down his face then looked at her. "I can't believe I'm going to say this, but I get your point. And I guess that we can try it."

Skye smiled. He was reluctant but willing. It was a good sign. Better than she'd had reason to hope for yet.

He placed his hands on his thighs and stood up. "So I guess that means separate bedrooms for now."

"I can take the guest bedroom once Madison moves out."

"Nope." When she started to argue, he held up his hand. "I know this might be hard for you to accept, but *you* need to respect where *I'm* coming from. And this is one of those times that my background trumps all. So you'll take the big bedroom and I'll sleep in the guest room." He shrugged. "Or I will once Madison moves."

"Fine." If he had to give, so would she. She held out a hand to end the negotiations.

Tim stared at it for a moment, then grasped it and pulled until she flew to her feet and landed on his chest.

"I think married couples have a better way to seal a deal, don't they?"

She couldn't get a word out before his lips cruised along hers. Light as a breeze, almost as if it hadn't happened. But when she opened her eyes, he was staring at her with such an intensity she was shocked that's all he did.

"Just remember what we said."

He planted another kiss on her mouth—this time a playful, smacking one—and stepped back. "We said no sex. This is just kissing. Which could lead to sex…" he trailed off hopefully. But when she shook her head, he just sighed. "I figured. Can't blame a guy for trying. Anyway, I can't agree to not kiss my wife. Not gonna happen. So add 'kissing' to the list of things we *can* do. 'Cause, sweetheart," he said while he turned and walked toward the staircase, "if that's all I get, I'm going to take it."

Tim walked up the stairs, leaving the light on for her. She waited until she heard the bathroom door close and the shower turn on—cold, if she had her guess—before she sat down and touched a finger to her lips. And thanked Fate once more for the opportunity in front of her.

———

Tim debated asking the question the next morning. He knew Skye would never ask for it herself. Partly because she wouldn't know what to ask, and partly because she didn't seem to be the sort to rely on others. He respected that about her. But he'd feel like a shit for withholding the opportunity, since he *did* know.

"Do you want an ID card?"

"Hmm?" Skye stood at the stove, making some egg and alfalfa omelet creation she swore was amazing. Tim thought adding hay to a perfectly decent breakfast staple was near criminal, but he politely declined and poured himself a bowl of cereal. Mornings were clearly not her thing, with her sleep-heavy eyes and hair in complete disarray. He wasn't even sure why she woke up so early when she didn't have to. But somehow she was up when he was and had insisted on having breakfast with him.

Her exhausted, just-dragged-myself-from-a-warm-bed look only made him want to drag her back to bed and spend hours tiring her out some more. His muscles were still tense, his nerves taut as a tripwire. Last night's cold shower had done nothing to alleviate the sexual tension he was carrying around.

"An ID card. All dependents carry them. It—"

"I hate that word," she grumbled at the omelet she was flipping.

"It…what? What word?"

"Dependent." She waved her spatula in the air. "Ignore me. Continue."

"Uh, right. The ID card for de—um, spouses gives them access to base stuff. The commissary, exchange, gets you on base, that sort of thing."

"Hum." Her hesitation was obvious. Was the hesitation because of her, or him? She scratched one calf with her opposite foot and didn't turn around. "I think that would be a good idea. If you wouldn't mind. That is, if it won't screw things up for you at work." Skye dared a quick glance over her shoulder before focusing in on the stove again.

She was more observant than he thought. He wondered if she'd picked up on the surprise from Colonel Blackwater the day before. Apparently she had. "No, it won't screw stuff up. It'll just take some paperwork. I guess while we're at it, we should make sure you're signed up for Tricare. Health insurance," he elaborated when she gave him a confused look.

Skye said nothing, just flipped her omelet and patted it with the spatula.

Okay, fine. He could do the talking for two this morning. "And while we're at it, we could get your car registered on base as well. So you don't have to wait for Mad or I to take you." Was he starting to sound desperate? Or was that just his imagination? For a woman who was so concerned about having a nice, healthy marriage, she wasn't exactly making this easy on him.

"That'd be nice," she said absently as she grabbed a plate to slide her breakfast onto.

"I'll try to get out of there early today and come back for you. Will you be around at three?"

"I should be." She cut herself half a grapefruit, poured herself a glass of her own milk she'd bought yesterday—was soy milk really a milk product?—and sat down next to him. "I have some things to do this morning, but afterward I should be good."

He wanted to ask what her plans were that day, where she'd be going. But for some reason he didn't feel like he had the right to ask yet. Stupid, he argued silently, that he didn't feel like he could ask his wife what her plans were for the day. Not when she was being so quiet herself.

He stole quick peeks at Skye from the corner of his eye. But slowly he realized that maybe her lack of conversation skills wasn't so much about her hesitation to get involved in the marriage, but about the fact that she was practically falling asleep in her fruit bowl. Yeah, to say Skye wasn't a morning person would be a vast understatement. He bit back a smile and let the relief soothe his nerves.

He finished his cereal and placed his bowl in the sink. Then, after a moment's thought, he rinsed it out and stuck it in the dishwasher. Normally he did the dishes at the end of the day, but he didn't want Skye thinking he was a slob or thinking she had to pick up after him like a little kid.

God, being married was hard work.

He walked back to the table and kissed her on top of her head. She leaned to one side and looked up at him, all sleepy eyes and a soft half-smile. Then he kissed her sound on the mouth, just because he could.

This part of marriage he could get used to.

"I'll be back around three. Try to be ready so we can knock out as much as we can today."

"Aye aye, Captain," she said and gave a little smart-ass salute.

"That's the Navy, sweetie." But he smiled at the effort. "Have fun today."

As he walked toward the front door, he thought he heard her mumble, "Not likely," but he wasn't sure.

Regret that he couldn't drag her back upstairs for a quick morning nuzzle in bed before he left strained his tentative hold on control. There had to be a better outlet for his frustration than just another cold shower. He grabbed his cover from the entry table and his gym bag, then tripped and almost landed on his face. He glanced down and saw a tangle of shoes, all small and girly and obviously Skye's. Tennis shoes, flip-flops, and sandals were heaped together by the door, begging to be walked over. He shoved them all back into a somewhat tidy pile and headed out the door.

An hour later, he was knocking on Dwayne's door. After hearing the enter command, he poked his head in.

"I'm in the mood to beat the shit out of something. Up for some MCMAP?" Marine Corps Martial Arts Practice. Guaranteed to kick anyone's ass. Hopefully hard enough to dislodge the ever-present physical need for Skye. Maybe if he took enough punches—or gave enough out—he could concentrate on the hurt instead of the burn.

Dwayne tossed his pen on the desk and leaned back in his chair. "That depends. Are you going to put me on medical leave if I go a few rounds with you? I deploy soon. Can't jeopardize that so you can abuse me for your own satisfaction."

Tim blew out a breath. "Fine. I'll go find Jer and see if he wants to spar. Maybe he isn't being a pussy this morning," he added as he started to close the door.

"Damn, man. Below the belt hit and it's not even nine in the morning." Dwayne started putting papers back into a folder and Tim knew he'd scored a spar partner. "What crawled up your ass and died?"

He leaned a shoulder against the door as his friend shut down his computer and left a note for his assistant. "Nothing. Just feeling the urge."

Dwayne grabbed a gym bag and slung it over his shoulder, but Tim shook his head.

"Boots and uts. No gym clothes."

Dwayne sighed and dropped the bag. "Why is it I can't even be comfortable while you kick my ass? Boots and uniforms, seriously?" Then, with a grin, he motioned to head down the hall. "The urge to beat the shit out of something usually comes from frustration of some kind." He stopped to give Tim a comical once-over. "Probably sexual frustration."

"Spare me the Good 'Ole Country psychiatry."

Dwayne laughed, as if his suspicions were confirmed. Tim growled and kept walking.

Dwayne easily caught up at the door. They pushed open at the same time and stepped into the humid air.

"Damn, it's a sauna out here."

The sweat started to roll after three feet. "Good. Let's do this in the yard."

Dwayne looked at him like he was crazy. "You're insane. The gym's three blocks away. And it's got AC."

"I want to work up a sweat." Tim started toward the open grassy area to the side of the battalion building.

"That's what the walk to the gym is for!" Dwayne called after him.

—◆◆◆—

Skye drained her third cup of coffee and made a face. Coffee was never her first option. But the caffeine was more necessary than oxygen. She was tired, her sleep schedule still not adjusted to waking up at the ass-crack of dawn like Tim. But she needed to get used to it. If she hoped to find a job in this area, they'd keep "normal" business hours.

She missed that about Vegas. The flexibility. Restaurants were often open twenty-four seven. If she wanted to work from eleven at night to seven in the morning, she could. And often did.

She stood outside Fletchers, the upscale restaurant, and debated going in. The place was a little more upscale than she was used to. This was no Applebees. But it wasn't crystal glassware either. This was the sort of place you held rehearsal dinners or celebrated graduations. A little bit nicer than average. The sidewalk bistro tables, with their wrought-iron chairs, were a nice, classy touch.

As she walked in, she was glad she wore her old work uniform to pound the pavement. The black pants, white shirt, and vest definitely fit in here. Skye asked for the manager and waited for ten, then twenty minutes by the host stand. She was about to leave when a short man with a nearly bald head in a dark suit and steamed glasses came hustling up.

"Can I help you?"

Skye held out a hand and gave him her best *Trust me, I'm good at this* smile. "I'm hoping it's the other way around, actually. My name is Skye McDermott and I wanted to drop off my résumé for consideration. For management," she clarified.

The short man breathed in and out, looking confused. "Mac Stone. Did you know Angelina?"

"Who?"

"Angelina. Our floor manager who just left. We haven't even advertised the position yet. I haven't had time, too busy covering shifts. I just assumed you… well, never mind. Do you have experience?"

Skye's smile widened. "Oh, a little." She handed him her résumé as he sat down on a padded bench. "I was a floor manager for several years at Cloud Nine, a restaurant in the Celestial Palace hotel and casino in Las Vegas. Along with a bachelors in hospitality management from UNLV."

The man's eyes bulged behind his frames. Or, what she could see of them through the steam on his lenses. "You almost sound overly qualified." He tipped the frames down and peered at her over them. "You aren't gunning for my general manager position, are you?"

Skye laughed. "I actually like being on the floor and working with customers."

"When can you start?"

"Yesterday."

Mac laughed, almost with relieved vigor. "Thank you, God. Follow me back to my office and we can talk further."

She walked behind Mac, observing the restaurant as she did. Low music, minimal, muted décor, and what appeared to be food plated with presentation in mind confirmed her suspicion that the restaurant was definitely a step up from a typical chain. The smell from the kitchen as she walked by was mouthwatering, and she wondered if she'd have time for a bowl of soup before she left.

Mac Stone walked into a small office off the side of the kitchen. Even with the door closed, the aroma of good food followed. The room boasted two desks, both piled high with papers and folders and boxes, and a small window. She could see samples scattered on the floor, order forms tacked to a bulletin board.

Looked like home. Here, in the cramped back office of a restaurant, Skye knew her place. She understood the lingo, the order, the sometimes *lack* of order. The rest of her life might have turned upside down, but this she understood.

"What brought you to the area?"

"Hmm?" Skye ripped her eyes away from the second desk, and from the plans she was already forming in her head for how to organize the chaos. "I'm sorry?"

Mac held up her résumé. "Says here you left your previous position at Cloud Nine about a month ago. What made you leave Vegas?"

"Oh. Lots of life changes." Which might sound like the understatement of the century. But it was the truth.

"Huh." Mac sat back in his chair, the metal squeaking with the movement. "Now that's a new one. Most people I interview here are spouses. You know, military spouses. Looking for work while their husbands are away."

"Oh." Should she say something? Skye knew he couldn't ask her directly if she was married. Not legally. But this was more conversational. And would she look like a liar for not saying anything?

"Some of my best employees have been military spouses. Shame to know they'll eventually pull up stakes and head out. But that's the nature of the beast." Mac's pen flew across the paper as he filled out a form.

Okay, she couldn't ignore it any longer. She would feel wrong otherwise. "Actually, I'm one of them. I married a Marine." Why did that seem more like an admission than a simple statement?

"Well." Mac sat back and laced his fingers over his abdomen. "I appreciate the honesty." After a long pause, Skye wondered if she should just walk back out. But then he continued. "There's still a lot of good here. Just on snap judgment, I like your personality. Your qualifications are nothing to sneeze at either. And frankly, I'm in a serious jam right now with three managers doing the work of four, and not doing it well, I might add. So I need someone soon, yesterday soon. Who knows, maybe you'll be around longer than the usual." He gave her a wink and went back to filling out the form, handing it over after a minute. "Go ahead and finish this, bring your ID tomorrow morning, and we can get the rest filled out."

Skye sat at the second desk, pen in hand, poised to fill out the employment form. But her thoughts strayed back to the conversation. Marines moved often, didn't they? Would she run into this with every move? Having to find a new job, then knowing her employer would be disappointed when she left?

There was so much more to this marriage than she ever could have anticipated.

Fate, you better have a darn good payoff at the end of this road.

Chapter 10

SKYE STEPPED BACK FROM THE BED AND SURVEYED THE FINAL product. Every piece of clothing she'd brought from Vegas was now piled on the bed. Some folded neatly, others in a tangled heap. Jeans, tanks, skirts, shirts, and underwear all with nowhere to go. She stared at the organized chaos until the bright colors melted into one big tie-dyed jumble in front of her and she had to blink a few times. The question was… how did she have so many clothes? They must have been making little clothing babies while they were shoved in her bags.

No, the real question was where could she put it all? Putting her things in the guest bedroom closet wasn't an option, given Madison's things were still in there for the moment. None of the master bedroom drawers were full, but they all had things in them. Same with the double closet. Not even half full. With some rearranging of Tim's clothing and creative stacking, she could fit everything she'd brought into drawers and have room left over for the stuff she had left behind in Vegas. But was that rude to do without asking?

One thing was for sure. She couldn't keep living out of suitcases like a guest. She wasn't a guest, damn it. She was a wife. It might be an unconventional marriage at the moment, but she refused to live a temporary lifestyle. That wasn't positive thinking at all.

And she had a lot to be positive about. Especially

after the morning she'd had. Tim had actually offered up the ID card, the registration, everything. Without a single nudge.

The sound of a car pulling up caught her attention. A few minutes later she heard the front door open and slam shut.

Skye raced down the stairs as she heard the front door close like a little kid whose dad was coming home after a business trip. The back of Tim's head was visible as she turned the corner of the landing. She followed him into the living room, not wanting to startle him. He flopped down on the sofa, and she stepped in front of him.

"Tim, you'll never guess what—what the hell happened to your eye?"

Her husband, who had left that morning hale and hearty, had a massive black eye, which currently appeared to be swollen shut. He let his head drop back and roll to one side, turning his good eye to her. She could then see the dark bruise darkening his jaw from chin to ear.

"Were you mugged?" She sat down next to him and gingerly touched his chin, snatching her hand back when he winced.

"Feels like it." He shifted and groaned. "Definitely had the shit kicked out of me. Which was kind of the point, to be honest."

"What? You mean this was on purpose? Did you just go around asking people to punch you?" Men were so stupid. But didn't they usually play this game with punches to the stomach?

"MCMAP. Marine Corps Martial Arts Practice," he explained when she raised her eyebrows. "A mixture of different martial arts and hand-to-hand combat techniques. More practical than karate in battle, but less disciplined."

"And someone hit you?" She shouldn't feel so outraged. It was a part of his training. Still, they weren't supposed to kill *each other*. They were supposed to kill the bad guys. Counterproductive, anyone?

"I started sparring with Dwayne. My friend," he clarified. "You remember the big hulking giant from Vegas?"

"The one with the honey-coated southern drawl?"

"That's D. We were just working out, burning off some energy. Then a few other guys showed up and it turned into a group exercise. I wasn't concentrating. Let someone get an elbow in, then took a boot to the chin."

"We should go to the doctor. Get back in the car; I'll drive you to that hospital on base." What if he had a concussion?

"I already saw Doc."

That gave her pause. "You went to the doctor already?" Didn't men have to be dragged kicking and screaming to the doctor's office?

"Doc, our battalion corpsman, checked me out. Standard procedure. I was informed I'll live," Tim said dryly.

What if she was overreacting? She silently sighed and rolled her eyes at her own behavior. Tim wasn't a child. Time to be more wifely.

"Do you not have the headache from Hades?" When he closed his eye and nodded, she tapped his shoulder and scooted over. "Lie down."

He cracked his eye back open and looked at her from the side. "Where?"

"Just do it." When he shifted, she angled his shoulders

until his head rested on her lap. He had almost no hair to play with, it was so short on top and all but nonexistent on the sides, but she scratched her fingers over his scalp anyway. His good eye drifted closed and he settled deeper in the couch.

"Feels good," he murmured, turning so she could reach around the back.

"I'm glad." She smoothed fingertips over his face, carefully avoiding the bruised areas. He all but purred at the feeling. From warrior-like tiger to sweet house kitten in thirty seconds flat. "I got a job today. Manager position at Fletchers. Seems like a nice place."

He only hummed in response. Not quite the excitement she had expected for her news, but the man was near-concussed. She'd forgive him.

"Tim," she asked, keeping her voice low and soothing. "Do you think I could have some drawer space for my things?"

"'Course. Whatever you need. We'll go back to base in a minute. Almost forgot about the IDs and stuff," he slurred, turning his face into her until his nose pressed against her stomach. His hot breath spread across her thighs, seeping through the thin skirt.

"Shh. We can do it another day." She paused, waiting for the argument. When it didn't come, she looked down. His face was relaxed, his chest moved in a deep, even rhythm. Out cold.

Should she wake him up? You were supposed to wake up people with head injuries every hour or so, right? That's what they did on TV anyway. But he'd said the doc—no, Doc, the person—took a look at him.

And when did she turn into such a mother hen? She

made the choice to say a quick prayer to whatever healing goddess was on duty and then stood, careful to lift his head and place it back down on a pillow.

He was so peaceful looking, even in his full uniform, minus the hat—cover. Not the stern warrior he normally looked like. She smiled when she saw his boots were still on. If she didn't think he'd wake up, she'd take them off. Or maybe she could manage them after all.

She glanced again at the huge tan boots with tight laces and multiple knots.

Maybe not.

She headed to the kitchen, at a loss with what to do. So she kept herself busy with chopping veggies for a salad. It was a quick and easy dinner, and if she wasn't eating at the restaurant, it was a great quick meal to tide her over—

Wait. Did Marines eat just salad for meals? Of course they ate salad. But that didn't seem like enough to sustain a guy Tim's size with his level of activity. After a workout like he had today, he'd wake up starving.

Skye quickly scanned the fridge for dinner possibilities. Chicken, people put chicken on their salads. But with her having zero idea how to properly cook meat without killing someone, she was mostly at a loss.

Guess it's time to be a good wife and order in. Second night living as a married couple and already I'm ordering food. Good job, Skye.

Skye dragged out some more veggies and began chopping herself a snack. She wasn't being fair to herself. How could anyone expect someone to turn into June Freaking Cleaver overnight? But still, the description that Tim gave of his mother combined with the photographs she'd seen around the house melded in her mind to create some hyper-breed of woman. Super-Mom and Super-Wife all rolled into one. Able to leap tall buildings in a single bound, all while holding a plate of warm cookies fresh from the oven.

Walking back to the living room with a bowl of carrots, she sat in the big chair and watched Tim's chest rise and fall with steady breath. The sight was a comfort. She wanted to drag him upstairs and toss him into the big master bed, curl up by his side, and nap with him. Soothe him back to sleep if he woke up. Take care of him.

She quietly munched on her snack, wondering what her husband really thought of their marriage. Was he just humoring her? Did he see temporary advantages for himself? Or was he in it for the long haul?

Being married was exhausting.

"Careful with that!"

"Squirt, if you can do any better, come on over and give it a whirl," Tim told his sister through a clenched jaw. He juggled the back end of the couch as he walked down the moving van's ramp. How was it her sofa weighed three times what a normal couch would? He wouldn't put it past her to have slipped rocks between the cushions, just for her own personal amusement of watching her brother struggle.

"Why was all your stuff in storage?" Skye asked, carrying a box into the foyer.

"When I first got here, I crashed at the BOQ. Bachelor Officer Quarters," she explained for Skye. "Temporary housing basically, like a hotel. Nowhere to put my stuff.

So I had the movers put it in storage until I could find
an apartment. And when Tim was leaving so soon after
I got here, he asked if I wanted to crash at his townhouse
during the deployment. Since his place is furnished, still
didn't need the furniture."

Jeremy, who was walking backwards through the
front door of Madison's apartment, called, "Hey, where
is this going?"

"I taped a sign on the wall!" she called back. "It's got
an arrow and everything."

"It would kill her to just come in and tell us where it
goes, wouldn't it?" Jer asked Tim across the length of
the couch.

Tim smiled at him. "Don't look at me. I tried to beat
the insolence and sarcasm out of her at a young age, but
our parents stopped me every time."

"Unfortunate," Jer mumbled as they finally maneu-
vered the couch through the door.

Dwayne—thanks to his long-ass arms—was able to
carry the armchair himself. The man was like Babe the
Ox when he put his mind to it. Lucky for them the ox
was still around and not gone. Yet.

They set the couch and chair down in the designated
spot. Tim was tempted for a moment to switch the entire
room around before Mad came back in, just to mess with
her. Once a big brother… But he'd grown out of that
stage in life. Barely.

He and Jeremy dropped onto the couch, resting for a
moment. Dwayne shook his head and went back out for
more stuff.

"Not all of us can be an extreme hybrid between
mountain man and pack mule!" Jeremy yelled at his back.

Dwayne gave a one-finger salute over his shoulder.

"You still pissed we aren't going over and he is?" Tim asked.

"No. Just anxious about what's coming down the pipeline. If we're not deploying now, then when? You know?"

Tim could relate. In the Corps anymore, it wasn't a question of if you would deploy, but when. And how often. "Never thought canceling a deployment would cause more problems than actually going on one."

Jeremy chuckled. "No joke."

Skye floated into the room and plopped down on the chair. Her shorts showed off her long legs, and for once her feet were in tennis shoes instead of sandals or barefoot. Her simple V-neck T-shirt was damp from sweat, a result in equal parts from the activity and the humidity. Her hair, which he was always used to seeing curling and waving in a mass around her face and shoulders, was tied back into a messy knot on the top of her head.

She looked average. Like any other wife he'd met along the way.

Shockingly, Tim found himself mentally redressing her in one of her trademark long, loose skirts and lightweight tops. But he'd keep her barefoot. Barefoot seemed to fit her.

Of course, that would be completely impractical for the afternoon's work.

"So Tim told me you found a job, Skye," Jeremy said.

"Yup. One of the restaurants was hiring. Thanks to my experience—not to mention their current desperation due to a previous manager leaving suddenly—I had a serious leg up. I'm low man on the totem pole, but that's fine. I like that job. Less paperwork, more interaction with the customers."

"Which restaurant is it again?"

"Fletchers, downtown. Pretty nice place. Not exactly white glove service, but close."

"Yeah, I know it. They often cater the birthday ball dinners or dining outs."

"Huh?" Skye looked at Tim for clarification.

He shrugged. "Formal events. I can explain later." He still forgot sometimes how little she knew about the military lifestyle. It wasn't a strike against her. But it was definitely odd having to explain things that he considered second nature at this point in his life. Being raised on military jargon had given him unrealistic expectations, he supposed.

A shriek of laughter had them looking toward the door. Dwayne walked in carrying a box in each arm and Madison on his back. Her arms were wrapped around his neck, legs around his waist. She laughed when he made a quick turn, grappling for a better hold so she didn't slide off.

"Un-fucking-believable," Jeremy muttered.

Tim looked at him. His jaw was hard, his eyes were boring holes into the two clowns. It was a small overreaction to them goofing off. Sure, everyone wanted to get done as soon as possible, but it was too damn hot to not take breaks. A little playing around wasn't that big of a deal.

He glanced at Skye and saw she, too, was watching Jeremy. But her eyes were soft and concerned, like she was watching a lost puppy wander the streets. What the hell was wrong with everyone today?

"So," Madison said, walking into the room and dusting her hands. "We're about three-quarters of the way done unloading. What should we do? Split into two and have half start to put stuff away so the other half has room to unload the rest of the junk? Or keep unloading and do one big pack-in later?"

"Let me guess. You and Dwayne will hang out in the AC and unpack shit while the rest of us do the bitch work in the heat," Jeremy said acidly, getting up and heading to the kitchen. There was silence, and everyone could hear the fridge opening.

Madison pasted a false, overly cheerful smile on her face. "I guess that means Jeremy really wanted to unpack my delicates," she joked.

"I'll talk to him." Tim started to stand up, but Skye beat him to it.

With a hand on his shoulder, she pushed him gently back down. "I need some water. I'll talk while I'm in there." When he looked at her, uncertain of how much to let his new wife interfere with his friends, she smiled. "I'll be gentle, I promise. Why don't you go help your sister unpack the guest room? Take advantage of the cool room for a bit. We can unload more stuff later."

It seemed almost like a test. Like there was a right and a wrong answer to this. But at the same time, he knew she wouldn't be mad if he insisted. She just wanted him to trust her.

He stood up and kissed her forehead. "Okay. Bring me a bottle of water when you're done."

She sighed. "I'm getting you a Nalgene for Christmas," she warned, and he laughed. Skye hated plastic water bottles, claiming they were a serious societal evil. He even had a new water pitcher in his fridge to show for it, along with a set of real glasses.

Let the assimilation begin.

———

"How long have you loved her?"

Jeremy jerked around and stared at her, mouth slightly open. "What?"

Skye paused, making sure she heard three sets of footsteps heading upstairs to the office before repeating, "How long have you loved her?"

Jeremy hesitated, then said, "You're crazy." He tilted the bottle of water and swallowed half in one long swallow.

"I might be," she agreed wryly. Wouldn't have been the first time someone called her crazy over her life choices or beliefs. "Doesn't mean I can't be right. Even the crazies hit a bull's-eye every so often."

He stared at her like she was talking in tongues. Skye assumed he was calculating the odds, mentally figuring what she could handle without spilling her guts to everyone. Finally, he hopped up on the counter and let his head fall back until it hit the cabinet behind. "Forever."

Skye hefted herself onto the counter next to him, and it only took two tries. Feet thumping against the cabinets below, she nudged him with her shoulder.

He took the prompt for what it was. "As long as I've known her, anyway. It's just something I've got to deal with. Nothing will ever happen, so I need to move on."

"How's that working for you? The whole 'moving on' thing?"

"Yeah. Not so good." He took another swig of water.

"And it pisses you off," she ventured.

"Of course it does." His hand curled around the plastic, crunching it slightly before relaxing. "Why would I want to feel like this? And why am I telling you all this?"

Skye shrugged. "Because I'm not Tim or Dwayne."

"You're Tim's wife," he said, as if reminding himself as much as her.

"Luckily I didn't take a blood oath to tell my husband every single thing I know. Your secret—if it really is a secret—is safe with me. But I'm not really sure why."

"Why it's a secret?" She nodded and he continued. "It's just not going to happen. So why make it more awkward if I try and she rejects me?"

"Is that the only reason?"

"It's a guy thing."

She punched his shoulder. "I'm going to pretend you didn't say that. As a feminist, I'd be honor bound to kick your butt. And I just don't have the energy right now."

That dragged a small smile from him. "You don't mess around with your best friend's girl, or his sister. It's just a code."

Skye mulled that one over. She could see the logic behind it, twisted though it may be. "Okay. But what if the sister makes the first move? What if it's what she wants? Don't you think a caring, loving brother and friend would make an exception to 'the man code' as you so delicately put it?" She used quote fingers, and he smiled more.

He stilled, as if she'd hit on something without even realizing it. But then he shrugged. "It doesn't matter. We're not going to go there. I'm not going to find out."

"But if you—"

"I'm not going to find out," he said more firmly. The equal parts hurt and determination in Jeremy's eyes made her heart ache for him.

"Okay." She slipped down off the counter. "If you want to talk, I'll listen. Until then, if you plan on keeping things as normal as possible, you might want to rein in the possessive boyfriend attitude. Tim's clueless right now, but he's no idiot. He'll figure it out sooner or later that you want Madison."

As she rounded the corner to the dining area, he called, "You're not going to say anything, right?"

"No." She shook her head. "Not my place, no matter which angle I look at it from. I told you what I think, and that's enough."

He stared at the bottle for a long moment. "Okay. Maybe you aren't as crazy as I originally thought."

Skye figured that was as close to a compliment she'd get from Jeremy, so she took it.

Tim listened to Skye hum along with the radio on the way home. It was a short drive, only ten minutes without traffic between Madison's apartment and his. But he felt like he needed to fill the silence.

"Are you keeping your name?"

"Hmm?" Skye turned to him. Her profile was washed in the late afternoon light. She might be dressed as an average, ordinary housewife, but she still gave off some vibe that drew him in, made his chest burn. Made him want her more than he'd wanted almost anything.

"Your name. Are you keeping your last name?"

"Oh. Actually, I hadn't thought about it. I'd like to

keep it. But…" She looked toward him, chewing her bottom lip.

"But?"

"Isn't that kind of frowned upon?"

He sighed, wondering why he'd opened his mouth. "It's not frowned upon. Just not as common." Not even close to common.

"Oh. I don't mind being uncommon," she said brightly.

Understatement of the century. "We can take care of the IDs on Monday. How's that sound?"

"Sounds good." She looked happy, like he'd told her they were going to buy her a new car. Of course, she'd only be this happy if the car was a hybrid with low fuel emissions.

Never in his life would Tim have thought he'd be asking his wife whether she wanted to keep her name. His upbringing was as traditional as apple freaking pie. With any other woman, he wouldn't have even asked. He'd have just driven her to the proper office to fill out forms for a name change. But Skye… Skye was different. In every good and confusing and frustrating sense of the word.

Tim had a feeling that, for as long as their marriage lasted, he would be kept on his toes.

But was that what he wanted? He spent his career on his toes. Half the decisions he made could end up being life or death. For months on end, he didn't sleep well thanks to the worry that shrouded his mind during deployments. Even the most simple choices could, in the long run, end up being a mistake that cost someone their lives.

What did he want at home? Peace. He wanted to

walk through the front door each night and feel comfort. Security. A stress-free zone. A well-maintained place of refuge.

Like what they'd had the night he'd come home with the black eye. Peace. Serenity. A soft place to fall, and a soft woman to fall with. A nice, hot, sweaty round or two of sex wouldn't hurt the deal either. But that would come. In time.

What he wasn't sure of was how peaceful Skye would make his life at home. She was energetic and lively, yes. Both great qualities. But the moment something irked her, she went from lively to live wire. Exploding all over the place. A serious short fuse. She cooled off quickly enough, at least so far. And thank God for that. But would the ups and downs of keeping time with her moods wear over the years? Would they slowly eat away at his reserve until he didn't want to come home anymore?

He'd seen it. He'd seen it more times than he wanted to admit. Marines who would rather stay with their stressful job twenty-four seven than go home to a more stressful home life. Hell, some volunteered for deployment slots to escape the madness of their marriages.

You know it's bad when a Marine would choose war over wife.

Was he just shooting himself in the foot by continuing this impromptu marriage instead of cutting his losses? He could have said no. He wasn't the first idiot to get plastered in Vegas and get married. It didn't have to mean a life sentence.

Once more he glanced over at Skye, watched as her head bobbed along with the music. Laughed to himself when her lips mouthed the words. Felt that all-too-familiar tug of desire low in his gut when she turned to him and smiled.

No, he didn't make a mistake. Even if this ended a year down the road, it wasn't a mistake.

He'd just have to find a way to keep his wife and his peaceful home. He'd figure out a way.

Chapter 11

TIM'S PHONE RANG DURING HIS LUNCH HOUR. UNFORTUNATELY he didn't have time to take a lunch, and wouldn't in the foreseeable future, thanks to a miscommunication on ordering weapons. If he left the battalion before eight, it'd be a miracle. The ID office had taken way longer than he anticipated that morning. How was it possible it took two hours to wait for something that took ten minutes to do? He swallowed the bite of his turkey club he'd had delivered and punched the speakerphone button.

"O'Shay."

"Timmy!"

"Mom?" The sandwich he'd just swallowed struck his stomach like a bomb. "Hey, how's it going? How's Dad?"

She scoffed. "Oh, he's fine, as usual. The man has more energy now than he did during the Gulf War. Retirement, shockingly, still agrees with him. Everything's great. How are you doing, sweetie? I feel like I haven't spoken to you in forever. What's going on in your life?"

Oh, you know, the usual. Went to Vegas, got hammered, got married, forgot I got married, almost deployed, then didn't deploy, then had my wife show up on my doorstep, and now she's living with me. But in separate rooms, so it's completely logical. "Not much."

Damn. The last time he'd spoken to his parents, he was on the way home from Quantico and had no clue what was going on with Skye yet. Since then, he hadn't had the chance to call and let them know what was going on.

Okay, he'd had plenty of chances. But this just wasn't an easy conversation to have with his folks. The one thing he never wanted from them was disappointment. And he had a feeling they'd be giving it in spades when they heard about this mess.

He would tell them. There was absolutely no way to avoid it. He just had to figure out the right angle to come at it from. And he wanted to be a little more secure with Skye first. It was all still too new. Too tentative.

"We have some news for you," his mother chirped into the phone. As usual, Susie O'Shay was cheerful and sunny. That much, she and Skye had in common. Likely the only thing.

Tim shuffled through the papers on his desk, looking for the one his assistant was waiting for him to sign off on. "Hit me with it," he said.

"Your father and I bought an RV."

"Whoa. Going to do the cross-country thing? Didn't you get enough traveling in courtesy of the Corps?"

His mother laughed, a light tinkling sound. "Never. You know I would have followed your father everywhere. And now he's bound and determined to see the country at our own pace."

"Sounds like a plan." His parents, though officially retired, would never slow down. It wasn't in them. Tim only hoped he would be the same at their age. "So where are you starting this glorious road trip? Maine? Florida? Alaska? Abroad?"

"California, silly."

That gave Tim pause. It was a big state, after all. "Where in California?"

"Actually, we surprised your sister this morning. She had to go to work, though. Poor thing will be up half the night. But we're in town! Isn't that fantastic?"

Red alert. Red alert. Man your battle stations. "Wow. That's… quite a surprise. And Madison didn't know?"

"Oh, no. She was shocked."

Oh fuck. Tim dug through the papers on his desk until he reached his cell phone, which he'd turned on vibrate earlier. Sure enough, seven text messages. All from Madison. Without even opening them, he knew exactly what they'd say.

Get your shit together, O'Shay.

"I originally wanted to use Madison's spare key to swing by your home and start a nice pot roast for supper as a surprise. But Madison talked me out of it. She said you'd probably want to go out for dinner."

Thank you, sweet baby Jesus. Madison always had his back. He felt ten again, in cahoots with his own sister, plotting some scheme against their parents. "She's right. You're a guest; you shouldn't be cooking. We'll go out. How's that sound?"

"You know I never mind cooking for my family. That's never been a chore to me."

No, it really hadn't been. Susie O'Shay showed love through serving others. She would have made June Cleaver look like a lazy slob. A job outside the home had never been appealing to her. But God save the person who tried to tell her she didn't work. The woman could rattle off a list of her daily "work" faster than you could say "holy housewife."

Tim realized it was now or never. He'd wanted to hold off explaining the marriage, but life had other plans. Much like a mission gone bad, it was time to re-strategize, re-plan, and react.

"Mom, I've got a ton of work still to do. But how about I call you or Dad on your cell when I'm ready to leave and we can make plans from there. Sound good?"

"I think we can do that," his mom replied. "Look forward to seeing you. I'm so glad you're still here!"

"Me too, Mom." He kept his tone light as he said his good-byes and hung up. But dread anchored him low like nothing he'd ever felt before. This was definitely worse than the time he had to explain why he was caught skipping seventh period in high school.

Wow, was that really the last time he'd had to admit some sort of wrongdoing? And what kind of lame existence was he living? No wonder he'd freaked in Vegas and had an experience of a lifetime.

Moreover, could he really call his marriage a wrong-doing? That didn't seem fair to Skye, or to their fledgling marriage.

Tim gritted his teeth and turned his thoughts back to the unaccounted-for weaponry. He had eight hours of work to cram into less than four, so he could beat it home and have a talk with Skye before Momma and Poppa O'Shay beat him to it.

Skye was sitting on the patio, iced chai tea in her hand, reveling in the great day. First thing, she'd received her ID. So the picture wasn't overly flattering, but that almost made it all the more real. Like a good-looking driver's license photo—they didn't really exist. Then she'd excelled during her first day of training. Mac had been beyond impressed with her knowledge of front house service as well as her patience and understanding of customer relations. They would be cutting her training in half, he'd said, and she would be ready for solo management by next week.

She stood and walked back in to refresh her drink and grab a book so she could read outside. It was hot as blazes, but she'd changed out of her management uniform of pinstripe pants, white button-down shirt, and matching pinstripe vest—almost a complete match to her uniform in Vegas—and put on her favorite pair of ragged cutoff jean shorts that had more than one patch on the butt, a spaghetti strap tank, and her favorite footwear: nothing. Her unruly waves were anchored to the top of her head with a big clip. Perfect outfit to relax in the backyard after a long afternoon on her feet.

She had nowhere to go, and Tim wasn't due home for another few hours. More, if he got caught up in paperwork like he warned. The man left before seven and didn't get home until eight. He worked too hard. But then again, was there such a thing as working too hard in the military? If there was any career where cutting corners should probably be avoided, it was likely the military.

She replaced the pitcher in the fridge when she heard the front door open. Hmm. Tim was home earlier than expected. A quick glance at the clock confirmed he was hours ahead of his schedule of late. Popping up to sit on the counter, legs dangling against the cabinets, she waited until he made his way back to the kitchen to talk about his day.

Instead of Tim, though, a woman in her fifties turned the corner holding a paper grocery sack. She caught sight of Skye and dropped the bag. Something that sounded like eggs made a sick squishing noise. Oranges rolled across the floor and came to a stop under the kitchen table. The woman stood with her mouth open.

Skye froze, unable to move thanks to shock, and tried not to panic. Did Tim have a cleaning lady? No, she'd been there over a week. He'd have mentioned one by now, wouldn't he? Well, whoever this was had a key, because she was positive she'd locked the door behind her coming in. Burglars didn't have keys to the front door. Burglars didn't bring food with them for a heist, did they?

"Who are you?" the woman demanded.

The question snapped her out of the semi-trance she'd been stuck in. "Skye." She hopped down and held out a hand, for lack of any other idea. "You would be?"

"Susie? Where'd you head off to?" a man's voice called from the front of the house. More? There were more of them? Now she was starting to worry.

"I'm in here!" the woman called out, not taking her eyes off Skye.

Skye dropped her hand, losing the friendly tone. "I don't know how you got in here but I think you should leave." The woman didn't budge.

"Susie, there you are." A man who looked to be in his late fifties rounded the corner and stopped next to the woman. "Who's this?"

"I don't know. She hasn't said."

"I did," Skye reminded her. "I said my name was Skye. And also that you should leave." This was the oddest breaking and entering she'd ever heard of. She could see the headlines now: *Older couple breaks into house, stocks fridge*.

"Timothy, why would she be here?"

Timothy? Skye took another look at the man. In a polo shirt and pleated slacks, with a thick gold watch around his wrist, he could have stepped off a country club golf course. He was fit, and his skin had a healthy tan. His hair was silver, cut the same way she'd seen Marines wear theirs, and his eyes were a piercing blue.

And in thirty years, Tim would look exactly like him.

She analyzed the woman. Early to mid fifties, silvery blond hair cut to chin length. Shorter than Skye in bare feet, wearing a light cardigan and a khaki skirt with low heels. Discrete jewelry winked from her ears and hands. Conservative chic.

"Are you… are you Tim's parents?"

"Yes," the man answered gruffly. "And who are you?"

"Oh, boy," she muttered under her breath, then cursed Tim for putting her in this position. They obviously had no clue whatsoever that their son was married. "Let's go have a seat in the living room. I think it'd be easier for everyone if we were all sitting down for that conversation."

———

Tim pulled up, running through every curse he knew—and that was an extensive list—as he saw an RV sitting in front of his townhouse. Apparently his mother had chosen to play the "my son never has a decent meal without me" card after all.

Fuck.

He quickly debated—and rejected—the idea of turning the car around and heading to Mexico. Avoiding his parents' lecture seemed like a good idea at the moment, but he knew from experience the longer he put it off, the worse it would get.

Boots dragging, he walked up the steps and opened the front door.

Three heads swiveled his way. None of them looked overly pleased, but then again, nobody jumped up and took a swing at him either.

Silver lining.

"Hey, Mom. Hi, Dad. Thought we were going to meet up for dinner later," he said casually, setting his cover on the entry table and dropping his gym bag beneath it.

Skye said nothing. She just stared at him, misery plain on her face. And he felt three inches tall.

"Timmy, come over here so I can hug you. And then kill you." His mother's voice was light, but there was steel hidden under the deceptive tone.

"The hug I'll take. You can keep the kill part." He bent and wrapped his arms around her. She was a small woman, but he always thought she was ten feet tall growing up. She squeezed him tightly. She might not like him right now and he couldn't blame her for that—but she still loved him. Love was never a question in their family.

It was harder to turn to his father, to look him in the eye. The man he strove to be like in every aspect of his life. His hero. Sure enough, his father's eyes held disappointment. But he still reached out and pulled Tim into a bone-crushing bear hug. "I'm glad you're safe," he murmured to Tim before letting him go.

There was an awkward silence, then Skye spoke.

"I was just about to tell your parents about my new job. Do you want to go change and come back down so we can talk together?"

She was looking at him calmly, as if nothing out of the ordinary was happening. But he could tell she'd emotionally checked out. There was a wall up. Her eyes, which normally burned with an overall passion for life, were cool and distant. Her voice, always a bubbling brook of excitement, was a placid lake.

It was Skye, but it wasn't.

"Yeah. I'll be right back down." He hustled upstairs to change into a polo and jeans, then jogged back down. If anyone had said a word since he left, he would be shocked. He walked over to the armchair Skye sat in and stood beside it. Did she feel his support? Or did she feel abandoned, ready to be sacrificed at a moment's notice? He placed a hand on her bare shoulder and felt her muscles and tendons stiffen. That answered that question.

"I don't know what Skye told you so far—"

"Enough. She told us enough. How could you get married in Las Vegas, Timothy Francis? Married? Without your family there? Without telling us? This was over a month ago!"

"Mom. Calm down."

"No, I won't calm down," she said fiercely. "My only son gets married and I'm not even there to see it and he wants me to calm down?" Her voice hitched and she bit her lip. Tim wanted to throw up. The only thing worse than watching his mom cry was knowing he caused it.

"What she's trying to say," his father stepped in, "is that this just isn't like you, Tim. This sort of impulsive behavior, especially with something so serious as marriage, is not you."

"I explained to your parents that we met in Vegas while you were there on leave. How we connected so quickly. And that I was the one who pushed for it."

Tim looked down into Skye's eyes. She'd tried to deflect the situation onto herself. Take the hit in front of his parents. He was stunned.

"That's not entirely true. This was my choice. Skye was no more responsible than I was. I asked her to marry me and she said yes. My choice."

He watched as Skye's eyes softened, and her mouth lost its hard edge. The ball of tension playing pinball in his stomach slowed down.

"Timmy, I think we'd like to speak with you alone." Susie turned to Skye, her voice polite but firm. "I hope you understand. This is just a conversation for family right now."

Skye started to stand, but he pressed down on her shoulder. "Skye is my family." In for a penny... "She's my wife. So you can talk in front of her." It was time to take a stand. If he wasn't firm on his marriage, his parents would never respect it, ever. Might not respect him. He couldn't bear either scenario.

His parents exchanged pointed glances that spoke volumes. The benefit of being married several decades—silent communication. Finally his father spoke. "Your mother and I simply wonder if this is the best choice. For everyone involved," he hastened to add. "Whether it wouldn't be just a good idea to accept that a mistake was made and everyone can move on with their lives. Know when to retreat."

This was the delicate part. Standing up for Skye and their marriage without completely pissing off his family. "I appreciate the advice, sir. But here's the thing. Skye and I are married. And we'll continue to be married for the foreseeable future. I understand you're hurt by my choice of weddings, but I'm going to ask you to respect my marriage. And especially my wife." He squeezed Skye's shoulder, and her hand slid up to hold his.

His mother's eyes narrowed in on their connected hands, then she stood up. "Well, I have to say, I'm a little relieved."

"What?" he and Skye asked at the same time.

A small smile curved his mother's lips as she walked over to plant a kiss on his cheek. "If you hadn't stood up to us, then it wouldn't have meant anything. I'm still a little confused," she added cautiously. "This just isn't something you typically do. Madison is the more rash one in the family," she explained to Skye. "That girl was forever getting into trouble. Innocent stuff, but trouble nonetheless."

"Knew I liked that girl," Skye murmured.

"What your mother was attempting to say is that if this is your choice, then I'm glad you're sticking by it. Not what we expected, but that's what happens with kids." His dad winked. "They grow up and continue surprising you."

It wasn't the best place to end the conversation, but it certainly wasn't the worst either. "I don't smell a roast. Didn't get here in time, Mom?"

His mother gave a wry smile. "My groceries met an unfortunate end when I was startled by Skye in the kitchen. I'm afraid they're a wash."

"Looks like we're going out."

———∿∿———

Skye absorbed every moment with Tim's parents. These were the people who had shaped his life. Raised him, given him the moral foundation for his existence. By his own admission, Tim's father was his hero and his mother was Superwoman. How could she ignore their influence?

Tim drove them to a chain restaurant. Fletchers might have been nicer, but she didn't want her first dinner with her in-laws to be witnessed by the people she was supposed to supervise. Awkward. While waiting for a table, Tim's father, Timothy Senior, entertained them with amusing stories of his days in the Corps. Every so often, Tim would finish the story, or remind him of a detail he'd left out. Obviously these were well-known tales in the family told mostly for her benefit. But she soaked up every word. His humor was at times a bit raunchy, a bit on the crude side. And more than once Tim's mother gave him a playful swat on the arm and told him to watch his language in a mild tone.

So much of her husband was mirrored in his father's movements. His speech. The way they both tilted their heads back when they laughed. Timothy was a good-looking man, fit for his age, and she found him charming and utterly endearing. She could see Tim being very similar in appearance and mannerisms in thirty years.

Why she was thinking thirty years down the road when she wasn't even sure about tomorrow was beyond her.

His mother was another story altogether. Where Tim's father was loud, she was soft. While Senior used rough language at times, her vocabulary was more refined. She was graceful and serene. Able to command attention and respect through her understated nature. Some shouted to be heard in a crowd. Susie O'Shay merely had to whisper.

And while her husband seemed almost to forget entirely the manner of their elopement, Susie was definitely on her guard. While Skye was observing Tim's parents, she realized she was being watched in return. Though his mother made no comment as to her observations, Skye felt very much like a bug under a microscope.

Skye had to admit, she likely wasn't even coming close to measuring up to Tim's mother's standards. The woman had been wearing the same outfit all day, and it looked as crisp as when she'd first scared Skye in the kitchen. Meanwhile, Skye had changed into fresh clothing before leaving—a pair of white cotton pants and a bright tunic—and she felt her outfit already drooping and wrinkling. The woman's jewelry was understatement personified, and Skye's made a great big statement. Skye hoped it was that she liked fun, colorful things and bright accessories. Her fear was that Susie read the statement more as *I like cheap stuff*.

Not that she was attempting to impress. No, that wasn't the point. But all the same, she didn't want to alienate Tim's family. Skye couldn't help but look at Tim's mother and realize this was the type of woman Tim likely had been waiting for. A calm soul with a quiet nature. Simple refinement wrapped in a beautiful, sophisticated package and tied with a classy bow.

Skye couldn't find the word "calm" in the dictionary.

Tim's father finished another joke and she saw her opportunity.

"Tell me a story about Tim as a child," she asked.

"What kind? There are millions," his mother said with a smile.

"Something embarrassing," Skye replied, giving Tim a wicked grin. "Something I can pull out later to tease him with when I need to keep him in line."

His mother considered her for a moment, then nodded. "Let's see. An embarrassing story. Oh! Has Madison shared the laundry mix-up?"

"Nope. Sounds promising though. Let's hear it," Skye said, leaning in conspiratorially.

"Mom. Come on." Tim groaned.

"Shush. It's story time," Skye reprimanded.

Tim merely buried his face in his arms and groaned again.

"When Tim was in the seventh grade—"

"Sixth," he corrected in a muffled voice, not looking up. Skye bit back a laugh and rubbed his neck soothingly.

"Fine, sixth," his mother continued, unruffled. "Timothy was deployed and I was ill. I'd been sick for days, running a high fever. But the kids were so active at that point, they weren't around to help out with chores much. So I had to manage the bare essentials myself until I was feeling better. Laundry was the worst. My most hated chore," she explained.

"Mine too!" Skye said on a laugh. "There's nothing more boring than folding clothing."

"Nothing," Susie agreed. "In my feverish delusions, I'd put the laundry in the wrong places. Unfortunately, Tim had this habit of waking up with a minute to spare to get out the door for school. He had it down to a science, how much time he needed to get up, get dressed, grab a handful of breakfast, and go. We're talking nanoseconds."

"Susie quickly learned how to turn most of her breakfast foods into on-the-go meals that Tim could eat on the bus." Timothy laughed.

"Adapt and overcome. If you need a good recipe for a breakfast wrap, let me know," Susie said dryly. "Apparently he was running a few nanoseconds behind one morning, grabbed the first thing out of the drawers to dress in, not caring if it matched, and took off to school. And when he got to gym class and started to change, there was an unfortunate surprise."

Skye smiled, sure she knew what was coming.

"I had mixed some of Madison's favorite workout shorts in with his boxers."

Skye laughed. "Tell me they were hot pink."

Susie's eyes gleamed with amusement. "Better. Powder Puff Girls."

"And boom goes the dynamite," Tim muttered to no one in particular.

Skye couldn't contain the hoot of laughter, picturing the twelve-year-old version of Tim wearing his sister's shorts, face beet red. When she had wiped a tear away, she turned to Tim and said, "But you always wake up early now."

"And now you know why," he replied, sending her on another round of laughter.

Chapter 12

Their food arrived, and Skye dug into her salad, starving after a long day at work.

"Tim, do you want a part of this chicken? I won't eat it all."

"Sure." Tim held his plate out for his mom to slip some meat on. He nudged Skye with his shoulder. "I won't bother asking if you want some of my steak."

"Oh, but sharing's what married people do," his mom said in a teasing voice.

"That's okay, I don't eat meat," Skye said easily and took another bite of salad. But the food stuck in her throat when she looked up and saw the stunned faces of her in-laws.

"None at all?" his father asked, apparently too shocked to comprehend the concept.

"Rarely. I'm not a die-hard vegan, but I don't eat it when there's a non-meat option available." She worked hard to keep her voice even. Why was it hitting her so hard? This confusing *do they like me?* trap she felt stuck in.

"That must be hard," Susie murmured. Her face was passive, no censure.

"It can be. But it's just how I was raised."

Susie smiled then. "I guess I won't be passing on a copy of my recipe box, since nine out of ten have meat in them for these carnivores."

Skye laughed, glad for the mild joke to keep things light.

"I remember you said you're working?" Susie asked, taking a sip of water.

"I am. Today was my first day. I'm a floor manager at Fletchers, downtown."

"Skye worked at the hotel that the guys and I stayed at in Vegas. She snagged a job fast down here thanks to her experience."

The pleased, proud tone in Tim's voice made her flush. She took a sip of water to hide her smile.

"Sounds like you've got a knack for customer service," Timothy said.

"I like working with people. They make it interesting. I'm not sure I could ever be a manager that just runs books and has business meetings all day. I need the interaction with people. I'd die of boredom otherwise."

"Will you want to continue working or stay home eventually?"

"Um…"

"I mean, when you have children. Will you want to stay home when you start a family?"

"Mom." Tim's voice was quiet but solid as steel.

"Is restaurant management something you can move around with?"

"Susie," Timothy muttered under his breath.

"What?" She looked at her husband, then sighed and folded her hands on the table. "I'm sorry, but I simply can't ignore the elephant in the room. They're married now. These are things that Skye needs to consider. They both need to consider."

Tim said something to his mother, but Skye didn't

listen. Children? Portable careers? Staying at home? The possibilities, options, and choices swirled in Skye's head. Susie was right. Once again, these were things married people knew before they took the plunge. And what were Tim's expectations? Did he want kids right away? Did he want to wait? Did he not want them at all?

For the first time in her life, Skye felt a moment of true panic. Her "go with the flow, follow Fate wherever it leads" attitude suddenly seemed less like a good idea and more like a liability.

Liability—oh. Was that how Tim would see her? Dragging her from spot to spot?

You're getting way too far ahead of yourself. Three deep breaths, and let it go. Either things will work, or they won't. But having a panic attack in front of Tim's parents won't help a damn thing.

"So that's the end of it, Mom. No more butting in."

Tim's mother nodded, her mouth drawn into a tight line. Part of Skye wanted to add in a few choice words herself, and the other part whispered she was just a mother protecting her child the best way she could.

The conversation came to an awkward halt thanks to some silent agreement to not bring up their marriage or the future in any capacity. Small talk was attempted but often flatlined after a few minutes. There was only so much praise one could lavish over a Caesar salad before you sounded like a moron.

The drive home was almost worse. His parents mentioned wanting to hit the road early in the morning. Tim said good-bye to his parents outside their door and Skye slipped in to give them some privacy, kicking off her sandals in the entryway. As she wandered around the living room, she took stock of what she'd gleaned from his parents.

They loved Tim more than anything. She could understand, even appreciate, their automatic protective stance against her and their marriage in the beginning. It wasn't what they had expected. And to be fair, it wasn't what Tim had expected either. But his father had jumped on the "go with it" bandwagon early on. At least by appearances, anyway.

His mother was another story. The woman was reserved with Skye. Not cold, but cool. Observant, most likely judging. But didn't everyone judge? Skye only wished she knew what his mother's overall impression was.

Or did she? If Skye ended up in the negative column on Susie O'Shay's list, would knowing that fact help matters?

The evening had served to make her feel closer to Tim, and yet farther away. The niggling fear in the back of her mind that she was less than what Tim expected couldn't be ignored. Not entirely.

Skye wandered into the kitchen and aimlessly opened the fridge. She wasn't hungry; she hadn't even eaten all of her dinner. But who could swallow around the mouthful of inadequacy she'd been chewing on the entire night?

She was the one who had pushed for the marriage. She was the one who had felt—still felt—the importance of what they were trying to work through. Tim was giving it his all; she had no complaints on that point. But would his reluctance in the beginning translate to an easy-out attitude later?

The front door opened, then closed. Skye scanned the shelves and picked up an apple and turned around.

"Thanks for that." Tim turned a kitchen chair around and straddled it, arms folded over the top.

"For what?" She hunted around until she found a knife and cutting board, then began to slice the unnecessary apple. Having something for her hands to do—a prop of sorts—gave her more confidence.

"Dealing with my parents. They're great people. It's just a little hard on them."

Skye didn't turn around, concentrating on her slices. She could read between the lines without facing her husband. "I'm not mad, if that's what you're worried about. I understand why you didn't mention the marriage. I just… I think we both wish we'd had some time to prepare." She wanted to ask about his mother. Ask about his wants from a wife. But the words wouldn't squeak by the lump in her throat. Did she want to know the honest answer?

No. Not yet.

"You were good with them." His voice was closer now, but she didn't turn around.

"They were nice. Made it easy." For the most part, anyway. "Did you expect me to bite?" she teased as she took a step to the left to drop the knife in the sink.

His hand caught her wrist. She barely had time to gasp before he whirled her around, pushing her back against the fridge door.

Tim's mouth was on hers in an instant. Aggression, possession. Everything ruthless, insistent, nothing sweet. His lips pried hers open, tongue thrust in to claim the recesses of her mouth. His feet bracketed hers. The outline of his erection was impossible to miss.

They were supposed to be taking it slow. Chaste, closed-mouth kisses were all they'd allowed themselves. All they'd managed to suffer through. But feeling his need, his desire in such a dark way, put a serious crack in the reserve she'd been holding onto.

But there had been a purpose. A damn good one. Relying on sex wasn't going to get them any closer to a true marriage. Instant gratification always felt fantastic in the moment. But afterward? Never as good as the thing you waited patiently for.

Now, could she just get her body to catch up to where her mind was headed?

"No," she breathed as his mouth worked over to her ear. His teeth nibbled, nipped, worked her lobe until her knees were spaghetti, along with her resistance. "No, we said—"

"We said no sex," he said, breath tickling her ear. "This isn't sex, is it? Not yet, anyway." His tone said there was always hope.

True. No, wait. This wasn't supposed to happen. But oh God, it felt so good.

One large hand crept down her rib cage with steady confidence, fingers bunching and pulling at her tunic until it sat above the waistband of her cotton pants.

She sighed when his fingers finally touched skin. The light caress of his rough fingertips over her belly spread heat and desire across her skin like a flash fire. She ached for him. Was too aware of the emptiness where he should be. Had been once before. Her mind drew a blank on reasons to stop his exploration. But there was one large, insistent reason to keep going, and it rocked against her hip with obvious impatience.

"Let me," he panted against her cheek. "Let me." His hand was untying the drawstring to her pants, tracing the skin above the waistband, making her shiver.

"Yes," she whispered. As if she could say no. Not now. She was too far into it now to dig her way back out. Logic and reason be damned.

His fingers walked their way beneath the waistband, beneath her thong. Pressing into her core, massaging down to the place she wanted him most. He was taking forever and she squirmed to silently hurry him along. Instead he stopped completely.

"Wh—what are you doing?" Did her voice just break? Was she that far gone? Embarrassing. *Pull your-self together, McDermott!*

"Slowing down. My pace," he said, his tone hard. The other hand pushed her hips back against the fridge, removing her wiggle room. Taking complete control, demanding submission. "I lead."

Every feminist, dominant cell in her body revolted. But when she gave him a hard stare, he only gave it back tenfold. The heat of his fingers only inches from her core was a burning reminder of what she had to lose if he changed his mind.

The man wasn't joking. She had a very good feeling he'd rather walk away and suffer the blue consequence than relinquish control.

The message was clear. He might be indulgent with some things, letting her have her way. But when it came to this very base, carnal area of marriage, he was alpha dog. And that thought made her want to scream with frustration, all while she felt the faint, annoying flutter of excitement.

"Fine," she said through clenched teeth. She would play his way. For now.

Later, all bets were off.

"Good choice," he said, voice husky, and took her mouth with his once more.

Inch by inch, his fingers brushed down until they traced the slick outer edges of her folds. She shuddered but forced herself to stay still. Torture. Absolute torture. One long finger dipped in, then pulled out. Her hips lifted to keep the contact, but he pushed her back.

"Cheating," he murmured and started to pull his hand out.

"Okay!" She growled and fought back the urge to kick him in the shin. Had she really thought this domineering bit was sexy just a minute ago?

He rewarded her with another long, lingering stroke of his finger, grazing the bundle of nerves and making her whimper. But with supreme effort, she stayed in place when he retreated.

"Good."

The single word of praise made her flush with pleasure.

Okay. Maybe the domineering thing was a *little* sexy.

His breath fanned over her collarbone as he worked his way down. The tunic's wide neck gave him plenty of skin to caress, kiss, light on fire with his touch. One finger entered slowly. Her breath caught. The smooth glide in made a dent in her emptiness, but it wasn't enough. Not nearly enough. As if hearing her thoughts, he added another finger, filling her more. Stretching her.

Skye's head thumped against the freezer door. Every ounce of control in her body was focused on not thrusting up to meet his questing hand, to force the rhythm. She was pleased with her restraint... until he added his thumb.

The pad slowly pressed on her clitoris like a button, then released. Her body shook with the effort to remain motionless, to abide by his stupid rule. His fingers worked her faster, and his thumb pressed against her once more, then moved away.

It was maddening. No rhyme, no rhythm to his attentions. She had no way of anticipating his next move. Just his labored breathing against her shoulder, and the knowledge that at some point, when he felt like it, he would—ah, there!—touch her where she wanted it most.

The pressure inside built up like a teakettle, low in her belly. Her muscles were contracting; she could barely stand. He had to feel her straining with the effort to stay immobile, had to recognize how close she was to dropping like a sack of potatoes. He must have realized how unsteady she was, because he used his free hand to wind her arms around his neck for support.

"Tim. Tim, I need—" She couldn't catch her breath. She was going to black out from lack of oxygen. And it would be all this infuriating man's fault. All his fau—

His thumb brushed against her, circled this time, continued the pattern with more force and didn't let go.

And the top blew off the teakettle.

Everything inside her shifted, shook, and exploded. Like the champagne bottles they served in Vegas, her insides roiled, rattled, bubbled until they had nowhere to go and she shattered. Her knees gave and Tim helped her sink to the floor, sliding his hand away as she landed with an ungainly plop.

After a moment of deep breathing, he pulled her onto his lap and rubbed her back in soothing circles. He pressed a kiss to her temple and murmured soft words while she came back to her own body. Her limbs felt like dead weight; her joints were loose and useless. But even as she shifted, she felt his cock still hard, still insistent, and she felt guilt.

Her own rule, and she broke it. Quickly. The man somehow managed to kill every single thread of resistance in her, even on something so serious as this. If he'd pushed, she had no idea if her body would have caved into the temptation to go at it like teenagers on the kitchen floor, damn the consequences.

Guilt, yeah. She had it. And a little bit of shame.

"Stop thinking so loud."

She leaned back and looked into her husband's eyes. "If you can hear, what am I thinking of?"

He lifted a brow, as if to say, *Like this is even a challenge*. "You're beating yourself up over what just happened because of your rule. But you shouldn't be. Know why?"

She shook her head, curious to hear his interpretation.

"I think in your mind, sex is a wall. But what if it's not? What if it's really a bridge, leading us to the better parts?" He shrugged a shoulder, her head bobbing with the movement. "We're hot for each other. That's good. You need that in a marriage, and it's natural. I'm not going to push it though. So we took the edge off. And from here, we can just go on. Right?"

Mutely she nodded. How could she argue with that? He'd explained her thought process to a T. And released just a little bit of the shame that she'd felt creeping in.

It didn't, though, make her feel any different about her choice to forego sex for the time being to strengthen their bond. Well, from here on out.

Tim nudged and pulled until she was on her feet.

"I'm going to go take a shower, and you're going to... do something. That doesn't involve me or the shower. Understood?"

More commands. More orders. She wanted to bark at him that she wasn't one of his Marine minions. Instead she nodded. Because in the end, this was the whole point. And he was holding up his end of the agreement.

He blew out a breath, as if he'd just been given a reprieve from the governor not a moment too soon. Then he kissed her forehead and left, walking with a slight hitch.

She bit back a giggle until she could hear his uneven footsteps tromping up the stairs. Then she chuckled and turned back to her abandoned apple slices, then bit into one for the satisfying crunch.

Doing the honorable thing was killing him, but he was doing it. She'd accidentally chosen her husband well.

For the first time in a few days, confidence seeped back into her bones, warming her. This was going to work.

―――

Hiding in his guest bedroom like a fucking coward was not how Tim planned on spending his Saturday morning. But after leaving Skye in the kitchen the night before, after instigating the break of her no-sex rule, that's exactly what he was doing.

The way Tim saw it, he had two options. He could climb out the window, shimmy down the drainpipe, and head toward the nearest golden arches for breakfast. Or he could stay in the guest room until he died of hunger.

Or you could choose door number three: Grow a pair and go downstairs, O'Shay. She might not even be upset.

Right. And a wet cat might not be spitting pissed.

As his stomach rumbled, he realized he had no choice but to find out the depths of her anger. He walked down the stairs, prepped and ready for a fight, to give in-depth explanations, to apologize.

Instead he found breakfast cooking. Smelled like—he stopped to take a sniff at the bottom of the stairs—smelled like bacon and eggs. The good stuff, no tofu required. He shuffled into the kitchen to find Skye in another of her trippy outfits, this one a black ruffled skirt that came down to her knees, tan and pink striped leggings, and some sort of baggy purple top. Her hair was, as usual, pulled into a messy knot at the top of her head, which bobbed with every movement she made.

The radio was on; some top forty song blasted. Just not loud enough to drown out her unfortunate singing. Tim smiled at the picture she made. It was definitely not his mother's famous Saturday morning pancake buffet. But it was something he could get used to. Especially if she was making *real* food, not something that rabbits would eat.

Hedging his bets, he walked up behind her and snuck a kiss on her cheek. She gasped, whirled around, and smacked him in the chest with the spatula, splattering what he hoped—and feared—was egg residue on his shirt.

"Good thing I didn't wear my favorite shirt," he joked as her eyes widened. "It's okay." He carefully unclenched her fingers from the utensil and set it aside, then reached behind her and turned down the burner.

She started to protest, but he kissed her soundly, and she melted like butter in the frying pan. Just a quick one, then he stepped back.

"Needed a good morning kiss." Was she going to smack him? Make some comment about last night? Fling the half-done eggs in his face?

She only smiled and turned back to the stove. "That was nice."

Hmm. It was, but that wasn't quite what he expected. In fact, he found himself waiting for the other shoe and almost enjoying the anticipation. But she merely hummed along with the next song and flipped eggs.

He grabbed a glass of juice and sat at the table, waiting for some sign that she wanted to talk. But all he got was the opportunity to watch her flit around the kitchen with no real pattern until she had two plates full of bacon and eggs. She placed one in front of him, sat the other in front of the seat next to him, and plopped down with an exaggerated sigh.

"Whew!" She grinned. "I'm more of a cereal person. But I felt like doing something extra today."

"I'm not going to argue," he said and took a bite of bacon. "Hmm. Did you season this with something? Tastes different. Good though," he added and took another bite.

"You like it?" she asked uncertainly.

He killed off the last bite and grabbed another slice. "Yeah."

She sat back a little and blew out a breath. "Good. I was afraid you wouldn't like the fakon."

Tim paused with the next slice halfway to his mouth and eyed it warily. "The... what?"

"Fakon. Fake bacon." She picked up a slice and bent, smiling when she heard the crisp snap. "It's a vegan bacon substitute. Like I said, I'm not a big meat eater, but I know you are, so I was looking for ways to combine meals." She smiled brightly. "I guess this is a score." And with that she picked up her fork and dug into her eggs.

Or were they eggs? He glanced at the simple, fluffy yellow concoction on his plate with new curiosity. If he poked it, would it poke back?

Skye glanced his way, her smile slipping a little as she noticed his frozen state. Quickly he shoved the entire fake food product in his mouth and chewed with renewed vigor. Then he grabbed his fork and shoveled a load of I-hope-it's-egg into his mouth and swallowed before he could taste it. With a large grin, he said, "It's great!"

She smiled again and went back to her meal. "They're real eggs, you know," she said, and he could hear the smile in her voice. "I'm a vegetarian, not a vegan. I actually like eggs."

He sighed with relief and glanced over. She was looking down at her plate, but the corner of her mouth tilted up.

A few minutes and two more slices of fakon later, he asked, "Do you have plans for the day?"

"Nope. I have today off, then work six days straight."

Tim opened his mouth but shut it again as he watched Skye drag her tongue over the tines of her fork. Her taste buds rasped over the cool metal, slipping between to grab every last bit of egg. His body hardened instantly. Was that her plan? He glanced at her eyes, but she was staring innocently at the vase of flowers she'd set out the other day.

He cleared his throat and tried again. "There's a mixer today at the battalion if you're interested. Guys bringing their wives and kids. Barbeque gets going. That sort of thing."

"Oh." She glanced at the clock. "Is this a last-minute thing they put together?"

Of course not. The MWR put these things together weeks in advance. But between putting off announcing his marriage and just not being used to RSVPing for an additional person, he realized this was the first he'd mentioned it to her. Shit. "These things are pretty casual," he hedged. "I'll probably just wear this." A polo and khaki cargo shorts were basically an out-of-uniform uniform for most Marines. "Well, minus the egg."

"Ah." She glanced at the clock again and nodded. "Sounds good. I'll be ready to go in two hours?" When he nodded, she stood up and took her plate to the sink. After rinsing and putting it in the dishwasher, she came back and gave him a dazzling smile that made his lungs burn and his cock stiffen almost painfully.

"Thanks for asking me," she said and bent down to give him a kiss.

Tim clenched his hands around the seat of the chair to keep from pulling her into his lap and spending the day remembering every spot on her body that made her moan. But no, he'd invited her to a battalion barbeque and he'd live up to the promise. Because for some unknown reason, it made her ridiculously happy and grateful.

As she disappeared up the stairs to do who knows what girly things that were required before leaving the house, he wondered about that. Mandatory fun, as they often liked to call "recommended" off-duty events, were usually attended grudgingly, at best. People didn't like giving up an afternoon out of their free time. But Skye had acted like he'd presented her with the chance to go deep sea diving or take private flying lessons. It was just a barbeque.

Right?

So why did he feel the intense need to man the battle stations?

Chapter 13

SKYE'S BOTTOM LIP FELT RAW BY THE TIME THEY PULLED UP to the battalion. It was never a good sign when she chewed on her lip that much. She'd agonized over everything from her outfit to her makeup to her hair.

And how annoying was that? She wasn't a self-conscious person. For the most part, people could take her or leave her, and she was fine with their decision either way. It's how her parents raised her. And thanks to her admittedly unique views on life, she had run into judgmental people all her life. But this was different.

These were Tim's people.

And much like with his parents, she didn't want to embarrass him or have anyone judge him based on her actions. Nobody wanted to be *that girl* in groups. The only problem was, in this situation she had no clue who or what *that girl* was. Or how to avoid becoming her.

Out of her element did not begin to describe the sensation she was feeling.

They crossed the grassy field toward the tents set up behind the building that she and Madison had visited Tim in. She could already smell the smoke, the cooking meat, hear the music blaring, and see the children sprinting in circles around each other. A group of shirtless guys played volleyball in a sandy court a few yards beyond the picnic area. It should have been welcoming, comforting.

Instead she just felt nauseous.

No. She wouldn't let this defeat her, Skye scolded silently. It was important for Tim, and she wouldn't act like an idiot and run back to the car to hide. She would just be herself. *Herself* was a cool, interesting, down-to-earth person. There was no reason someone shouldn't like her. It would be fine.

The pep talk worked, and as Tim steered her toward massive coolers where people were bending over to grab drinks, her nerves started to settle.

Tim said hello to a few people in passing. He grabbed her a bottle of water and a beer for himself, then headed toward a group of both men and women standing to the side.

"Hey, guys."

They greeted him back, then Tim slipped an arm around her waist and pulled her close. "Someone I want you to meet. This is—"

"Hey, O'Shay bagged himself a nice weekend piece," one obnoxious man slurred. For the love of the ozone, it wasn't much past noon and he was already drunk? In Vegas, this would have been typical. But here, it seemed a little unnecessary.

"Shut up, McNelson," Tim said quietly. Though he'd made no threat, a person would have to be stone drunk not to hear the venom in his voice.

Like McNelson. "What? I won't poach. I'll just wait until next weekend. You'll be free, right, sweetie?"

Before Tim could say another word, Jeremy stepped over and slung an arm around his shoulder. "Hey, McNellie, since you were gone all last week, I wanted to ask you a question." Jeremy's voice faded as he led the intolerable drunk away from the group. Everyone else stood in uncomfortable silence.

All that was missing were some cartoon cricket noises to make the entire thing more bearable.

"Tim, weren't you going to introduce us?" one blessed woman spoke up, giving Skye an encouraging smile.

"Right. Thanks, Beth. This is Skye. My wife."

And they were back to awkward silence. A few people looked at each other from the corner of their eye, but nobody said a word.

"Holy shit, so the rumors are true," one short, bulky man finally breathed. An even shorter woman to his left elbowed him in the ribs.

Had he not told any of his coworkers about her? What was she, some dirty little secret?

No, that's not right, she chided herself. He wouldn't have brought her with him to the barbeque if he didn't want people to meet her.

Tim went around the circle, introducing the group. Names were never her specialty, but she tried her hardest to concentrate. After she'd shaken hands and said hello, Dwayne leaned over and gave her a kiss on the cheek.

"Good to see you again."

Ah. She loved Dwayne. He was a teddy bear. "Thanks. Wait, I thought you were deploying again."

Dwayne rolled his eyes. "Any day now, they tell me. Any day now." He scoffed. "Which could mean in an hour, or in three weeks. Meanwhile, my guys get to suffer through never knowing if this is the day they leave. Hovers over their heads like an anchor. Sucks."

There were murmurs of sympathy from everyone, all of whom seemed to relate to the unfortunate situation.

After a moment the men slipped into what Skye could only consider "shop talk." Weapons and training exercises and travel arrangements sounded like gibberish to her, but she did her best to at least appear like she was following the conversation.

A tug on the crook of her elbow had Skye looking behind her.

The woman Tim had introduced as Beth was standing, one hand on Skye's arm. She gave her a warm smile.

"Time to escape the man cave," she said with a wink and a grin. She tilted her head to indicate a group of women twenty feet away. "It's safer over there, in the estrogen zone."

"You had me at 'escape,'" Skye joked and followed Beth, who linked arms with her. Already, Skye felt the buzzing nerves start to settle down. Here was someone that had reached out. Maybe Beth would become her new Tasha. She could use a best friend about now.

"I know my ears start to ring and my brain starts to ooze after ten seconds of listening to that macho stuff," Beth explained as she led Skye to the gaggle of women. She carried a Southern accent dripping with genuine warmth. She could have been Dwayne's sister with that accent, if they'd looked anything alike. "I just had to save you."

"You are my new best friend," Skye said earnestly, and Beth laughed.

"Ladies," Beth announced as they approached the circle. "This is Skye. She just married Tim O'Shay and she's new to the area."

Heads swiveled, and once again Skye felt herself being evaluated. For a moment she longed for Vegas, where nobody looked twice at you whether you were wearing a ball gown or an Elvis costume. Everyone stood out, which meant nobody stood out. It was safe, comfortable.

Beth performed introductions. More names she'd forget. Skye slyly checked each woman's outfit—as all females do—with each introduction.

Many were wearing simple jeans or capris and shirts. A few wore khakis. Some were in skirts and cardigans, much like Susie O'Shay. But they all seemed to wear more muted colors; their outfits were subtle.

"Where did you get your skirt?" one asked with a smile. "I love the color."

Name. What was her name? Amanda. Yes. "Thank you. I actually got it in Vegas, at this cute little boutique that's way off the strip. Some of the best shopping is so far off the strip you wouldn't find it if you didn't live there."

She'd worn her favorite skirt and shirt, sort of a confidence boost. The vibrant purple of the skirt had cheered her up in the privacy of her own room. But now she felt loud. Garish compared to the other spouses in their muted pallets and simple outfits.

"I actually really like this shirt." The woman to her left reached out and fingered the puffed sleeve on her shirt. "It'd look awful on me, but it's great with the skirt."

"It wouldn't look awful on you," Skye protested, starting to feel a little better.

When in doubt, a woman's group turns to fashion. They started to comment on her jewelry, her sandals. What shopping was like in Vegas. And Skye relaxed with each question. They might not dress like her, but they didn't seem to think she was a freak either.

"It's like, boho chic, right?" one asked, tilting her head and studying Skye from head to toe and back again. "Very Mary-Kate Olsen. Though sometimes she just looks homeless." Her eyes widened, as if she just realized what she'd said. "And you look cute," she added quickly, and the group laughed.

"Okay, who wants to go grab some pig? I'm starving," Beth announced, and others agreed. Skye followed the women to the food line, grateful for something else to talk about besides her own fashion choices. They had been kind, even complimentary. But it just served as another reminder that she was very different from the other women.

Variety is the spice of life.

Except, looking around, Skye realized she seemed to be the only spice at the party. At least from her eye line.

She contemplated heading to Tim's table, but all the women sat together and she was having a good time with them. Plus, there was only so much gun-talk a pacifist could listen to before wanting to cry.

As she dug into her salad, one asked if she worked. Skye talked about her job at Fletchers, and a few others mentioned their jobs. One nurse who worked at the naval hospital like Madison. Another hospital worker, this time clerical. One teacher. And the rest stayed at home, either with children or without.

Beth told a joke, and Skye couldn't help but laugh, full out. It felt good, too good. She hadn't laughed that hard in a while. Then she realized that others had laughed as well, but more lightly. A polite chuckle, really. And here she was, braying like a donkey.

Well, it'd been funny.

The other women seemed to be more reserved, but not in a snotty way. No, they were just more quiet in spirit. Their very nature seemed a little more relaxed, calm.

Skye's spirit, as her mother used to say, was louder than a ticker-tape parade.

So you'll just be the big mouth. Every group's got one.

An hour later, they all gathered around an open space while a few of the Marines were coerced into playing a relay game designed to make them look silly. Tim walked up behind her and wrapped his arms around her torso; she felt relaxed enough to lean into his supportive embrace.

"How's it going?" he asked in her ear.

"It's going well," she said and meant it. Mostly.

Tim watched from a distance as Skye laughed with another wife. And he breathed.

Skye—the beautiful, funny woman he'd married—had been winning people over left and right. Nobody had made a huge deal about their marriage to him, or to Skye as much as he could tell. Minus the debacle with McNelson and his drunk ramblings, the barbecue had gone well. And as far as he could tell, she wasn't holding a grudge against him for not mentioning the gathering sooner.

"She's not what I would have expected," a voice said behind him.

Tim felt the temperature around him drop twenty degrees, and he internally groaned as he turned and held out a hand to his CO. "Sir. Afternoon."

Colonel Blackwater shook and clasped his other hand over Tim's shoulder. Though the man had an enviable military career and was a respectable CO to serve under, Tim could never entirely shake the uneasy feeling around him. He seemed to set himself in the father figure role for most officers, playing both professional and personal confidant.

Tim didn't need a father figure. He already had one. A great one.

"She's unexpected," Col. Blackwater repeated.

Tim felt backed into a corner. He didn't want to say anything about his personal life, period. It was nobody's damn business unless he chose to share. But it never paid to tell the boss to back the fuck off, either. "She's great," he said neutrally.

"From what I've seen of you, your wife is the complete opposite of you in almost every way."

"Opposites attract." How soon could he escape?

"So goes the saying," the Colonel said wryly. "Ah. Here's my own other half."

A woman with shoulder-length dark hair and tight lips came to stand beside him.

"Tim, I believe you've met my wife before, Patricia. Patricia, Captain Timothy O'Shay."

"Ma'am," Tim said, shaking her offered hand.

"Captain O'Shay," she responded. Her lips barely ever moved; her expression never changed. It was like talking to a wax figure in Madame Tussauds museum. In the past he'd asked her to call him Tim, but she'd ignored his request. So he stopped bothering. The Colonel wasn't kidding when he said Patricia was his other half. Mrs. Blackwater was his match in every way, including the old-school family values she tried to push on every wife she met. The woman always had a pinched, almost pained expression on her face. Likely still recovering from the pole she had shoved up her—

"Tim, hey." Skye appeared at his side, nearly out of breath. Her hair was falling around her face in a curtain of unruly curls, her face was flushed, and she was smiling.

He wanted to kiss her sun-warmed cheeks. Let his fingers thread through her heavy hair. Feel her sweet, curved body pressed up against his side.

No, he really wanted to find the nearest horizontal spot, flip her skirt up, and consummate their damn marriage. Again.

But he refused to give the CO even a small hint into his personal life if he could help it. Maybe that was childish, but oh well. Keeping a small distance between himself and Skye—which hurt more than he wanted—he said, "Skye, you remember my CO, Colonel Blackwater."

"Right, hi." She held out a hand and shook firmly, a friendly smile pasted on her face. But he could see the nerves taking over as she smoothed hair back from her face and her fingers shook. And she was chewing on her lip again, just like in the car on the way over.

"This is my wife, Patricia."

Patricia held out a limp hand, giving Skye an obvious once-over. "Interesting outfit for a barbeque," she said, her lips pinching together.

"Oh. Um. Thank you. I like bright colors," Skye said, her voice trailing off quietly.

Damn. This wasn't how he wanted her to feel. "I think we were about to make the rounds and say good-bye to everyone. If you'll excuse—"

"How about dinner next weekend?" Colonel Blackwater said, cutting Tim off without hesitation. "I was thinking of inviting a few other officers and their wives over for a little get-together. Saturday night, our house."

"I don't know. Skye might have to work," he put in quickly before she could say a word. When she shifted to look at him, he put his arm around her waist and squeezed meaningfully. She kept silent. God bless his intelligent wife for being quick on the uptake.

"Work? Surely you can ask off for important things. Your husband's boss invites you to dinner, that seems like something you would want to attend," Patricia commented sourly. Her voice said she was shocked it even had to be debated.

There was no way to back out of that. "Great. Sounds great." He excused them and headed for the parking lot, all but dragging Skye behind him.

"Got everything?"

"Yeah, I do... but, Tim," she panted behind him. "Why are we leaving so fast?"

"I'm just ready to go." It was an asshole answer, but he didn't want to get into why he was pissed while they were there. Frankly, he didn't want Skye to know his misgivings about the CO at all. She seemed nervous enough as it was. No point in giving her something else to worry about on top of her nerves.

He didn't relish the thought of having dinner and mixing more of their personal life with work. But there was no way to get out of it now. They'd push through and move on.

"Tim, do you really want me to ask off for next week?"

He caught movement from the corner of his eye and glanced over. Skye was in the passenger seat, her fingers scrunching and releasing the hem of her purple skirt. "Do you work on Saturday?"

"I don't know yet. Won't know until Monday, when Mac has the new schedule out. But it's easier to ask off before he makes the schedule than it is to trade a shift. So if you want me to…"

Tim swallowed. "I'll be going either way. But I don't want it to mess up anything with your work schedule. I know work is important for you." Despite what Patricia Blackwater thinks. The old bat.

Skye was quiet for a moment, then said, "Thank you."

"For?"

"For acknowledging that you understand working is important for me." She took a deep gulp of air. "I don't know if you expected your wife to work or not, since we never really talked about that. We didn't have the chance. But to me, it's not just about adding to the income. It's something that I enjoy, and it makes me feel independent and my own person aside from the relationship. So it's a big deal for me."

Matter-of-fact, when Tim thought back to his vague "someday" version of marriage he'd always carried in the back of his mind, his faceless, nameless wife hadn't worked. Maybe that was because his mother didn't work outside the home, maybe he just knew he would always be able to support a wife so she wouldn't have to work, or maybe that's because he just had no imagination.

For which Skye would make up for quickly.

But despite the fact that he never expected her to hold a job or contribute financially, he really didn't mind it.

"It's not a big deal for me. If you like your job, then that's what matters. If you don't, then quit. Stay home and make crepe paper flowers all day. Do what makes you happy."

Skye's face split into a huge grin, and she leaned over to give him a kiss on the cheek. "That's really sweet of you to say. Do what makes you happy. I think there might be a little hippie in you after all, Timothy O'Shay."

Tim scowled at that. "Don't get too ahead of yourself. I'm not running out to hug trees or save otters or whatever."

Skye settled back in her seat, a smug smile curving her lips. "Mhmm. Just keep telling yourself that."

He wanted to laugh, but he didn't. Skye might think she had the upper hand in some things, but Tim's personality was too dominant to let control pass him by for too long. It wasn't a matter of need. It was pure habit. He was in control all day long, making decisions that affected hundreds of people. But he could relax that from time to time. At least, he hoped so. Marriage was about give and take, he reminded himself. He had to give up control as much as he used it.

"So I'll just ask Mac if I can make sure to have Saturday evening off."

"Are you sure?"

"Yup. Give and take, right? That's marriage."

Skye went back to humming with the radio, but Tim had a moment to wonder if he'd been thinking out loud. No, she was just repeating a well-known phrase. That's all. "Did you have fun?"

"I loved meeting the other women. And Beth was a

hoot. That sweet Southern belle routine is all a front. She's a feisty gal for sure." Skye gave a dreamy smile. "I'm glad I found some friends. I love hanging out with Madison, but I need some variety. They were all really nice. Except, well…"

When she didn't finish, Tim prodded, "Well?"

"I don't think Patricia Blackwater really thought very highly of me," she said carefully, and went back to fingering the hem of her skirt. He watched as she caught the bottom of her lip between her teeth.

Reaching a red light, he leaned over and put his thumb against her lips to stop her from biting harder. "Well, I think it looks nice on you." And it did. The vibrant color made her skin glow, and the material flowed around her like a cloud, following her curves lovingly without being overly sexual. Just a sweet hint of the body beneath.

Instead of biting her lip, she took the pad of his thumb in her mouth and gently closed her teeth around it.

Tim hissed in a breath. "Maybe the best place to tease me isn't in the car, sweetheart."

With obvious reluctance, she pulled away, teeth grazing his thumb until he was free.

"Thanks for saying I look nice."

Tim struggled to downshift from the mental image of pulling into the nearest parking lot and tossing her in the backseat for a reenactment of his teenage years. "It's just the truth."

"Hmm," was all she said. But the fantastic mood she'd shown while talking about Beth had somehow dimmed.

Tim hated that—when she turned inward and somehow the thing that made her Skye became shuttered. So he did the only thing he could think of.

"I'd love for you to come to the dinner. It would be nice having you there with me."

She smiled again, more genuine this time. "Okay."

Chapter 14

SKYE LET OUT A FRUSTRATED GROAN AS A CAR CUT HER OFF. Her hand hovered over the horn, then she counted to ten and went back to clenching the steering wheel. Time for self-inflection. The traffic wasn't the true source of her frustration. Her lack of loving was.

She was the one who made up the stupid "no sex" rule to begin with. Shouldn't she be the one who gets to take it back? What the hell kind of game was Tim playing? She'd been putty in his hands the other night in the kitchen. And he just... walked away. Who did that? What was his end goal? Or was it the same as hers, and she was just paranoid?

She caught herself hitting the gas a little too hard and eased off. Getting a speeding ticket would have just been the cherry to her craptastic sundae.

Skye rarely saw her husband at all during that week. The universe was conspiring against her. Thanks to being the new kid on the management block, she still worked long hours. It was always an adjustment working at a new restaurant. And she refused to look like a slacker. So she came in early to make sure she was prepared, and stayed way beyond "late" to read up on procedures and ordering and to organize her own work space. Not her favorite way to spend evenings, but she was dedicated to being a good employee. It mattered.

Skye flipped her turn signal on and merged onto the

exit ramp like a civilized human. It was more than plenty of the drivers on the road today were able to say. Three more calm breaths as she headed her car towards the mall.

Tim seemed to spend more and more time at the unit than ever. He always had good reasons. Paperwork that couldn't leave the office due to security. A problem with a training manual. Helping Dwayne work out kinks before their company deployment.

He assured her after Dwayne's company left that things would be easier. And once she had complete confidence in her spot at Fletchers, she would be able to leave as soon as her shift was over. But until then, she and Tim were like passing ships in the night. If she got a goodnight kiss from him, she felt lucky.

'Cause she sure as hell wasn't getting anything more than kisses. Not at this point. He'd barely put his hands on her since the night he'd given her pleasure against the fridge. And it was eating her alive. Every moment of her day seemed to remind her of their lack of intimacy. Jealousy flared when she saw couples on dates, holding hands at the restaurant. Sharing kisses between courses or sneaking peeks over menus. The radio always knew she was listening. Every station managed to play some soft, slow ballad about love and lust and finding that special someone. The languid beats were just the right rhythm to make love to.

Which, from a more logical standpoint, she knew was wrong. Because she was the one who started the whole "no sex" rule in the first place. And it had its merits. They needed it. A little breathing room, a chance to get to know each other without letting physical intimacy get in the way.

She just really, seriously hoped they'd be in a good place and ready for sex soon. Very. Very. Soon.

Even her dreams were plotting against her, taking her to the brink of sanity. Images of Tim, naked and sweating in bed, infused her nights. Her straddling his legs, his hands bruising her hips with his grip. His rough play when he flipped her around to take her how he wanted…

And yet, the only times she saw him were buttoned up and laced into his stuffy uniform. Or when he was already heading to bed, and she was still in her own starched manager's outfit, just home from work.

God, she had ideas. Hundreds of ideas. Thousands of ideas how to get rid of that damn camouflage. Rip it from his body. Tear seams. Pop buttons. Take a knife to it and cut the material away. Burn the damn thing.

Of course, Tim would probably call that blasphemous or something ridiculous. She'd make it up to him though. Inch by sweaty inch.

But first she had to get through this dinner at the Blackwaters' house. The dinner that, despite his best effort, she could tell bothered Tim. He wouldn't say why. Whether he disliked his boss, or he was worried about introducing her, or maybe he didn't care for the other people who would be there… her mind ran wild with possibilities. As usual. Nothing could be simple or straightforward in her mind. Whatever the reason, Tim was definitely anxious about the evening coming up, and Skye refused to make him regret asking her to come along.

The dinner felt almost like a test, some real, tangible hurdle for their relationship to leap over before they could really make a go at being married in truth.

And she would pass. For the love of Mother Earth, she would pass. She slammed her car door a little harder than necessary and closed her eyes. One more breathing cycle and she felt calm enough to walk into the department store and meet up with Beth.

"Now tell me again, why do you need my help picking out an outfit?" her new friend asked, holding up a dress. She presented it out to Skye, then shook her head and put it back without Skye's opinion.

"Because I seem physically incapable of picking anything remotely conservative. Even when I try to be more proper I end up looking out of place around here. The only thing I own that looks remotely proper in a moderate sort of way is my uniform for work. And I can't wear that, obviously."

"But I like the way you dress," Beth pointed out. She flipped through the racks of clothing with expert speed. This was not her first last-minute shopping expedition. That much was clear. Once again, Skye blessed the stars she had thought to invite Beth out for help with an outfit.

"I do too," Skye said, doing her best to keep the whine out of her voice. "But obviously what I wear isn't appropriate for certain functions. And since everything I have with me I wore in Vegas, where anything goes, I need to get an outfit for this dinner on Saturday."

She didn't want to embarrass Tim in front of his boss. It hadn't escaped her notice how quickly Tim tried to drag her away from the Blackwaters at the barbeque. It was almost as obvious as Mrs. Blackwater's distain for her colorful outfit. An average person's scorn for her fashion sense would normally make Skye roll her eyes and move on with her day. But the boss's wife was different. Just like Tim's mother was different. She wouldn't flaunt her problems blending in front of the boss. Not when she could fix it with a shopping excursion or two.

"True. I'm probably the most boring dresser ever and even I have to think twice before heading over to their house," Beth conceded. She pulled out a shirt the color of drywall and tossed it over her arm.

"You're not a boring dresser," Skye protested.

Beth stopped in the middle of the aisle, held her arms out, looked down at herself, then back up at Skye. One eyebrow arched in a silent *who do you think you're kidding?* question.

Her friend's shell tank in light pink, khakis, and black flats would be five kinds of torture for Skye to wear. But she smiled and said, "I think it works for you. Bolder colors would overpower your smaller frame. Do you go over to the Blackwaters' often for dinner?"

"Nice topic change," Beth said with a smile and tossed Skye another skirt. "No. I've only been over twice. To my knowledge this isn't something they do often. At least, that's what Toby says."

"Does Toby care what you wear to this kind of event?"

Beth snorted. "No way. He wouldn't know female fashion if it slapped him in the ass and called him Harry."

Skye laughed and slung an arm around her friend. "I knew I was going to like you. Now come on. We've got some beige to try on."

―⁓―

Skye draped herself over the bed and let her shoes fall to the floor with a thud apiece. Bags littered the floor around the bed, but she was too tired to put them away yet. Exhausted from shopping for clothes she didn't really like, combined with the insane schedule she was working this week and no afternoon nap, had her feeling depleted. And not just physically. She was missing Vegas in a big way, for more than one reason. Her Skye-tank was running on E. Time to fix it the best way she knew how. Without another thought, she grabbed her cell from the nightstand and dialed. And her heart jumped with joy after the first word.

"Hello?"

Skye swallowed around the lump forming a block in her throat. "Hey. What are you doing?"

"I'm sorry. I must need to get my ears checked. This sounds like a friend I once knew. Skye was her name…"

"Ha. Ha." Skye rolled on her back and smiled to the ceiling. "How's life, Tasha?"

"Oh, little of this, little of that. Had a date the other week with a guy I will now refer to as Grabby Hands McGee. Almost had to beat his fingers off my ass with my purse. So of course I'm seeing him again next Thursday."

"Of course," Skye agreed, because it was so like her friend.

"They found your replacement at work. He sucks."

Skye chuckled, then gave a half-hearted apology. "I'm sure he's not that bad."

"Uh huh. Liar. You're not sorry at all. You're holed up in domestic bliss somewhere in California, leaving behind us poor single people without big strong Marines to keep us warm at night. Traitor."

"Domestic, yes. Bliss? Still up in the air."

Tasha was silent for a minute. "Well, he did take off the morning after your wedding. I warned you that wasn't the greatest of signs."

"He didn't know we were married," Skye reminded her.

"Always what you want to hear about your friend's husband. That's not exactly a point in his favor, you know that, right?"

"Hmm." Skye only made a non-committal response, knowing that's all her friend really required to keep going. Sure enough...

"But I thought things were getting better. Or at least there was effort on his part. Is it not? Getting better, I mean?"

"Getting better..." Skye sighed and covered her face with a corner of the bedspread. "Yes and no."

"Which is it?"

Skye said nothing.

"That bad, huh? Are you coming back? 'Cause I guarantee you, the GM would drop this new guy like a bad habit and grab you back. And never let go. At this point, I think he'd tie you to the bar with a bungee cord if he could get away with it."

"No," Skye said firmly. "No, I'm not coming back. This will work. It has to work."

Tasha blew out an impatient breath. "Has to? Skye, I know you believe in Fate and that everything has a reason and all that, but have you ever thought that some- times things just happen because they happened? And that we just have to find the quickest and most painless way out of them? Like ripping a Band-Aid?"

"No," she said again. "This marriage means some- thing. We both walked into it with eyes wide open—"

"One of you was wearing beer goggles," Tasha interrupted.

"Eyes wide open," Skye repeated more forcefully. "And we're both determined to make the best of it. Think about it, why would a stable guy like Tim who has absolutely no belief in destiny or Fate agree to stay married? I mean, that's got to mean something!"

"It might mean he likes having a convenient booty call."

Skye mumbled something into the bedspread.

"Say again?"

"I said we're not having sex," she said through clenched teeth.

Tasha whooped with laughter. "So you're telling me," she gasped through the gut-wrenching laughter, "that you've got all the duties and responsibilities of a marriage, all the shit that comes with tying yourself to someone for the rest of your foreseeable future, without any of the actual perks? And he agreed to that?"

"Yes, he did. Which only proves my point that this marriage is meant to happen. Besides, there has to be room for adjustment. You've seen enough newlyweds in Vegas to know things aren't magically perfect. Fate takes her sweet time."

Tasha's laughter died down. "Then why don't you sound more happy?"

Skye examined her fingers for a moment. Short, clean, but definitely made for work. Not the hands of a cute housewife. "I don't really fit in here."

"Why the hell do you care?"

"Because it matters to Tim."

"He said that?" Her friend's outrage was clear through the phone.

"He wouldn't. But... it's just obvious. I stand out, big-time. And as much as I think everyone wants to pretend otherwise, it matters to his boss."

"So his boss can take a flying leap."

"I'd love to agree," Skye said dryly. "But his boss is the one that can make or break Tim's career. I mean, I'm not running around the office distracting Tim or anything. But there seems to be an emphasis with this colonel guy on family values. And apparently my values aren't stacking up." Maybe that was just her own negativity talking.

"What the fuck does he know? My best friend has unquestionable values and morals. You're one of the most selfless, amazing people I know, Skye. And if you let some dickweed with shiny medals tell you otherwise, I'll personally come down there and beat you for it."

"Thanks." It helped to hear it. Tasha, for all her jokes and sarcasm, was a mama bear when it came to defending her friends.

"Please tell me Tim hasn't said anything about your values or morals. He doesn't agree with this guy, right? 'Cause I can just add him to my list of 'People Tasha's Beating Today.'"

"No. I don't think he ever would. But he could still resent me. If I was hurting his chances for promotion, or making things harder for him at work, why would he want to stay married to me? It's not because he loves me." Why did that truth hurt so much? She could honestly say she didn't love him. Not yet. But she also feared that her love might come much faster than Tim's ever would, if at all.

"So get out. It's not worth it if you're unhappy."

"Just for a little while. I'm learning."

"Learning what?"

"How to fit in."

"How to be one of a million? Skye, come on. That's not your thing. You're you, and you are pretty freaking awesome. If Tim doesn't want that amazing package—"

"We don't know that," she interjected, standing up for her husband.

"If. If he doesn't want what you have to offer, then you're better off."

"Why is it that everyone always tells the dumpee they're better off? Is that standard breakup procedure?"

"Yes," Tasha said without hesitation. "But in this case it's true." She paused, then added, "You're always welcome here, you know. I've got a sofa bed that might paralyze you, but you're welcome to it for as long as you need."

The offer warmed her heart. She truly had some of the best friends in the world. "Thanks, sweetie. But I'm sticking. I just have to figure out a way to tone down my Skye-ness in certain situations and make sure that I'm not getting in Tim's way. At least for now. Maybe later it will be different."

"Maybe." Tasha didn't sound hopeful. "Remember the sofa bed."

After Skye hung up the phone, she played with the corner of the bedspread, letting it flow between her fingers. The material was soft, a little faded, but still in good condition. The patchwork was beautiful, and she wondered if it was homemade. Probably from his mother, or maybe his grandmother.

Could she do this? Could she really dim her own

light, even for a little while, to make sure that Tim's career wasn't compromised? Was that fair to her?

It was fair to her marriage to give it a try, she scolded. It might not always be fun, but sometimes in life we had to do things that weren't fun to make up for the good parts.

She could always look at it as acting. A sort of ongoing performance. At home she could be herself, because who was there to notice or care besides her husband? And he'd already seen her. But in public, she could work on it. A little more quiet in spirit, a little less bright clothing. That's all. Nothing drastic.

Yes, she thought as she sat up in bed, feeling more energized. It really wouldn't be that bad. Just for a while she could play the part in public. If that's what Tim needed for his career, she could do it. And then things could slowly drift back to normal.

Skye started rummaging through the sacks of clothing, deciding what to put where, and feeling much better about things.

Tim sat on the couch, feet twitching in some obnoxious rhythm he couldn't seem to stop. His slacks were creased, his shirt was ironed, face freshly shaved, and he'd had a haircut that morning. Despite his own hesitations on interacting with Colonel Blackwater outside the battalion, he knew he had nothing to worry about. At least with himself.

There was a muffled thump above him, and a not-so-ladylike curse.

He winced. Skye was another story.

She was already hopped up on adrenaline, having switched shifts today so she could make it to the dinner. Then her lunch shift ran over with an unexpected wave of customers. She'd rushed in the door without so much as a "hey how are ya" and sprinted up the stairs to jump in the shower. And upstairs she'd stayed ever since, getting ready. How she was doing, what she was planning to wear, how nervous she felt... he had no clue. He did know she bought a new outfit for the night, but past that, he was clueless. Knowing Skye, though, she would stand out.

He knew she could shine. Skye had already won his father over. His mother, a tougher sell, had softened. The other wives seemed to enjoy her company.

But he knew the other Marines and their spouses weren't who concerned her.

"Okay. I'm ready," she called out from the stairs. "And if this outfit isn't Captain O'Shay approved, I'm not going at all."

Tim rubbed his sweaty palms on the sofa and stood. Then sat back down.

He wasn't prepared for what walked in the living room.

Skye entered without her usual swish of fabric, her pop of color. Even her gait was subdued. Her hair was straight for the first time since he'd met her, and much longer than it was when it curled, reaching halfway down her back. With the brunette strands pulled up on either side, he could see simple gold studs in her ears. A pale blue button-down shirt with no frills was tucked into a straight black skirt ending at her knees. On her feet, black shoes with a small heel. One of those feet was tapping an annoyed beat, and he looked up to see her hands on her hips, head cocked to one side.

"Well? Will it do?"

She was beautiful. She was adorable.

She wasn't his Skye.

But that wasn't what his wife wanted to hear. He mustered up an encouraging smile and said, "You look great. Where'd the clothing come from?"

Skye reached up to smooth down her hair, then dropped her hand as if she'd thought better of it. "I went shopping with Beth."

Toby's wife. Sweet woman. Dressed a lot like what Skye was wearing at that moment. "It's... it's different. But nice."

She pulled the shirt a little, then turned her head as if she were trying to see her backside. "It's appropriate for something like this. Right?"

For a dinner with the Blackwaters, absolutely. Mrs. Blackwater's mouth might drop open at the change in her.

She was trying. That's what this was all about. She was trying her hardest to help him, to show her support. She cared. His heart beat just a little faster at the thought.

He stepped to her, cupped her face in his hands, and kissed her slowly. His wife didn't even put up a token protest, just melted against him and wound her arms around his neck.

If they had time, he would have stripped the outfit from her button by button until she was bared to him. He would have carried her upstairs to her—no their, it would be their—bedroom, set her down on the soft, warm comforter, and made love to her with every ounce of strength he had. Fast the first time. Fast and hard and more than a little rough. It'd been too long. He'd wanted for too long.

But slow the next. So slow she'd think they were moving underwater. Drag out every possible ounce of pleasure until they'd wrung their bodies dry.

If he had time.

With regret, he broke the kiss and stepped away. Fierce pride filled his chest when he saw his woman's face. Lips swollen, cheeks flushed, hair falling out of its pins on one side.

"Yeah. It's appropriate."

Skye blinked, a little like an owl, and walked to the fireplace to glance in the mirror above. Her hands weren't entirely steady as she fixed her hair, he noticed. Good. She was as affected as he was.

"That was quite the pre-party," she joked.

"You just looked too irresistible," he answered, because it was easier than explaining how much her effort meant.

She smiled at him from the reflection. A glimpse of the real Skye. She was still in there. Surprisingly, that caused him a moment of relief.

"I'm ready to go if you are, Captain O'Shay," she said teasingly and held out a hand.

Slipping his hand into hers was the most natural thing he'd ever done.

Chapter 15

SKYE WONDERED WHY SHE'D PULLED SO MANY STRINGS AT work to make sure she could come to this dinner only to wind up dead.

Dead of boredom.

"I don't know that you've ever cooked such a delicious meal, sweetheart." Colonel Blackwater patted his wife on the hand and gave her an indulgent smile.

Skye poked once more at the rubbery chicken on her plate, which sat beside her untouched mashed potatoes devoid of any spice or salt. Not to mention the limp green beans. Even Tim, who liked meat, had barely eaten anything. Though he'd done a much better job at moving food around his plate to seem like he devoured it all. Smart man, her husband. The entire meal was devoid of all spice or originality, which only matched the yawn-worthy décor in the Blackwater home. Everything was white or cream or beige. Including Mrs. Blackwater's outfit. Had these people ever heard of color?

"Oh, it was just delicious." MaryAnn, that was her name, all but fell to her knees in gratitude and worship once again. Pretty soon she'd have rug burns from all the adoration. "You'll have to let me copy down every recipe."

Laying it on a little thick there, aren't we? Soon they'd have to call for the jaws of life to pry the woman's lips from the Blackwaters' asses.

Mrs. Blackwater gave a small smile that said such praise was only her due. "I'm sure I can write it down for you, dear. I always love to hear when a wife wants to provide a healthy meal for her husband at the end of the day."

"I absolutely agree." Apparently not to be left behind, Julia joined in the blatant ass-kissing. It was an ass-kissing free-for-all. Her serious face only made it more amusing. "Making sure our men are taken care of is truly the most important job we'll ever have."

It was official. Skye stepped out of the car and into a time machine. They were currently in 1953, and any second now Wally and the Beaver would burst in through the back door.

But then she watched as Julie's hand clenched a little harder around her fork, how her mouth pulled, almost as if she was fighting against another, more realistic response. And Skye wondered if Julia might not be more like her and Beth than she originally thought. That she assumed she had to play good wife and make nice with the boss's wife.

To a degree, Skye could relate.

Besides Skye and Tim, and the Blackwaters of course, there were three other couples sharing the *oh so special* evening with them. One included Beth and her husband Toby, who was almost as quiet and reserved as Beth. Thank goodness for those two, or Skye was sure she'd have never survived. The other couples were ones she vaguely remembered from the barbeque, but they hadn't clicked.

Probably because they seemed to click with the Blackwaters. Or pretended to click, in Julia's case. Skye didn't think she and Mrs. Blackwater would click if they knocked their heads together.

The thought of literally butting heads had her trying to swallow an inappropriate chuckle.

The only problem with holding back a laugh is that it seems to multiply as you hold back. She gripped the edge of her chair and prayed nobody would notice her eyes watering and chest heaving with the effort. But then Tim, damn him, nudged her and she let out a bark of laughter.

Conversation stopped, and all eyes turned to her.

Skye quickly grabbed her napkin and coughed delicately, patting her chest with the other hand. She shot an apologetic smile to the rest of the table. "I'm sorry. Water went down wrong."

The answer seemed to pacify the group, though Mrs. Blackwater eyed her sharply for another moment before turning her attention back to her husband.

"What the hell was that?" Tim murmured.

"Not important," she whispered back. She caught Beth's inquiring look, but she only shook her head and did her best to be invisible for the rest of the meal.

After dinner was over, the Colonel led the men out to the back porch for a cigar, and the women moved into the living room for coffee.

What is this, 1812? The little ladies shift to the parlor so the men can enjoy their brandy and cigars in peace?

But she saw her moment for escape and asked for the powder room. Beth discretely followed until they were alone in the hallway upstairs.

"Hey there, Giggles." Beth laughed quietly. "What the heck was that all about?"

"I'll tell you later." Skye leaned against the wall and breathed deeply—the first relaxed breath she'd had all night since walking down their stairs to see Tim. Keeping her voice low, she asked, "Are functions always like this?"

Beth shook her head. "No way. The CO at our last battalion was all about a party. He used to have pig roasts in his backyard, complete with kegs of beer. Every CO is different on how they like to run things." She sighed and leaned against the wall opposite Skye. "I'll admit, this one seems more than a little stuck up."

Skye snorted. "A little?"

Beth laughed. "Okay, okay. A lot. MaryAnn, I've never really connected with. Julia's a good sort. But her husband really pushes her to try and get on the CO's wife's good side. She's a sweetie, just wants to help her husband and thinks this might be a way."

"Hmm," was Skye's reply. She'd never considered sucking up. It was enough to make sure she didn't screw up.

"You look nice, by the way."

Skye looked down at her conservative costume, as she liked to think of it. "Tim certainly thought so. He showed his appreciation before we left," she confided.

Beth giggled, then covered her mouth and looked toward the stairs with wide eyes. When no sign of eaves-droppers developed, she giggled again. "We should probably head back down."

"I'll go first. Man, who thought dinner with the boss would turn into such a covert operation?" Skye walked down the stairs, Beth's faint giggles following her.

It was like the temperature dropped ten degrees as she walked into the living room after leaving the warmth of friendship upstairs. The obviously fake smiles the three women sent her as she sat down left her wanting to check for frostbite. But she took a second glance at Julia and found Beth might have been right. There was something there besides cold formality. An extra tilt to her lips after the other two women had turned away. A little crinkle to her eyes.

"I like your outfit, dear," Mrs. Blackwater said, her voice cool.

"Thank you." Desired effect achieved. She smoothed down the skirt a little and wondered how well the fabric would burn.

"I assume the outfit you wore at the barbecue was more of a joke. A prank of sorts." Mrs. Blackwater tisked her tongue. "Not the most proper thing for a new wife to do. But still harmless. It's nice to see you have some taste after all."

Skye bit her tongue so hard she would have teeth marks for a week. A quick glance at MaryAnn showed no aid from that direction. Julia squirmed just a little but said nothing either. Each were looking around the room randomly, their eyes landing anywhere but on her or Mrs. Blackwater.

Well, she couldn't really blame them. Who would want to tackle the Dragon Lady, as she was starting to think of Mrs. Blackwater.

"I don't mind experimenting with clothing every so often." There, that was neutral, wasn't it?

"I'm sure. But it's nice to know that our Marines have a solid, comforting home to return to after such a long day. Or even a long deployment. Loud, lewd clothing indicates a more… unsettled home life, I would think.

Your outward appearance is simply a physical manifestation of your inner self, I always say."

Sounds like something you dragged out of a Psych 101 textbook from the fifties. Like everything else you say.

"But my husband always has an eye out for what is in his Marines' best interest. There was one young man—you ladies are too new to the battalion to remember him—who met and married a woman within a week of meeting her. Oh, it was unbelievable. Horrible example for his subordinates."

Skye almost choked on her coffee.

"As it turns out, the woman was a..." the woman glanced around, leaned forward, and lowered her voice to stage whisper, "a stripper."

MaryAnn gave a delicate gasp of horror, as if Mrs. Blackwater had just revealed the wife was a member of al-Qaeda.

Beth walked in silently and took the seat to Skye's right. "What's going on?" she murmured.

"We're learning about the domestic terrorist also known as exotic dancers," Skye murmured back, and Beth snorted.

"I don't have to tell you the amount of grief that Marine was given. My husband had to pull him aside to counsel him on the situation. It ended up affecting his entire career, the poor man." Mrs. Blackwater shook her head and lifted the coffee cup to her lips, though Skye would bet she didn't take a sip. "Some things you just cannot come back from."

"The soaps in the bathroom were lovely, Mrs. Blackwater," Beth interjected smoothly. "Where did you get them?"

Pleased with the compliment, their hostess launched into a lecture on the importance of coordinating bathroom themes, which turned the conversation to the safer topic of home décor. Skye was half-tempted to say something about incenses, black light posters, and Bob Marley music. Why not play up the "dirty hippie" label to its fullest potential?

Because Tim was counting on her, that's why. So she managed to make it through the evening using short sentences and elusive comments. Shortly after the men returned, the "party" died and everyone headed for their cars.

The ride home was silent. Skye opened her mouth once to ask how the manly meeting outside went, but she didn't. Tim seemed to be brooding almost as much as she was. Had his meeting outside not gone well? Did someone say something about her? Was she the new terrorist stripper?

Skye mentally shut down the worry center of her brain. There was nothing she could do about it now. Her outfit was conservative, she had held her tongue more than once during the evening, and there was nothing she would have changed.

"Thank you for coming."

Tim's deep, softly spoken words shook Skye out of her own momentary depression. "No problem. I had fun."

He snorted.

Skye glanced over and caught the slight lift to the corner of his lips in the bluish streetlight.

"I won't pretend that I had fun, so you don't have to either. Some things are just obligations in this field of work, and having dinner with people you don't particularly care for is one of them, unfortunately. Just like any other job. Boss invites you over, you go."

"I can understand that." How many times did she have to do something she didn't want to at her last job?

"But thank you for the effort."

"Effort?"

His hands tightened on the steering wheel. "For, you know." He glanced quickly at her outfit then back to the road. "Did I say you looked nice?"

"Yeah. You did." She waited for him to elaborate, but he didn't.

Ah. He didn't want to say it. But her husband wanted her in more conservative clothing. Liked her in these clothes.

Did that mean he hated her normal wardrobe and just didn't know how to say it? Skye fingered the hem of her skirt. Maybe it wouldn't be tossed in the first fire she came across after all.

Skye bounded up the stairs the moment they walked in the front door. "I'm going to change, then I'll be back down," she called. "Do you want to watch a movie?"

"That's fine," he yelled after her just before the master bedroom door slammed. He smiled to himself. Even dressed like an attorney, she couldn't completely contain her impulsive, grab-life-by-the-horns personality. Thankfully.

At a more sedate pace, he headed into the guest room to hang his clothing up. Skye's clothing, he assumed, would end up on a heap on the floor. Just like most else she owned. Of course, half of her outfits were designed to look wrinkled even when freshly laundered, so he'd never know whether it came from the floor or the closet.

But one thing was for sure… the woman was not keen on hanging her things up.

But that was part of the fun with Skye. You never knew, period, what you were going to get.

Tim paused, dresser drawer half open. Wait, part of the fun was never knowing? When had he adopted that line of thinking? Consistency. Consistency was his favorite. He liked rules, schedules, stability. He lived his life by it. He breathed reliability.

He shook out a pair of basketball shorts and an old Academy T-shirt and slipped on the comfortable outfit. A night snuggling on the couch with Skye seemed like a great way to end a shitty day.

Maybe he'd even cop a feel, straight out of a middle school handbook.

But when he jogged back down the stairs, hitting second base was the last thing on his mind.

Skye stood with her back to him, debating the DVDs in the entertainment center. As usual, she swayed from side to side as if she couldn't stand still, as if some song in her head compelled her to move and dance.

She'd twisted her hair into a knot, though a few tendrils had already escaped and were flowing down around her neck. What he could see of her legs were encased in black leggings, though her feet were bare. But he'd recognize that top anywhere.

That was his favorite sweatshirt from college. The soft gray material was always a comfort on chilly days. The N with a star on the front was starting to crack and peel off. A size too big on him, it swallowed Skye's torso whole, falling almost to her knees. He'd lost it weeks ago. Or so he thought.

She must have had it for a while now. How long had she been wearing it?

And why did the thought of her in his clothing turn him on so much?

"Where did you get that?"

She whipped around, her knot of hair bobbing. Following his gaze, she glanced down at the sleeves that dangled over her hands, too long for her arms by half. "Oh. Um." Her teeth caught her bottom lip like they always did when she was worried.

"I'm not mad. Just, where did you find it? I thought it was lost."

"It was in the laundry basket one day." Skye crossed her arms over her chest, hugging herself. "I was cold with the AC on so high, but I didn't want to turn it down, since you're always so warm when you get home. And it smelled like you…" Her voice trailed off as if she just realized what she'd said. Then she shrugged. "I wear it to bed a lot. I get cold at night."

The sweatshirt was like a brand. His mark. His woman. Whatever tentative hold he'd had on his urges, his cravings collapsed faster than an untrained platoon of privates. He took the three steps across the room and grabbed her by the shoulders, hauling her into his body. She grunted but didn't resist.

And when he lowered his lips to hers, she rose up to meet him.

—⁘—

Finally.

Tim made the move. And Skye wasn't going to let him back out now. She reached up to meet his dipping head, their mouths coming together in a clash of passion and need. His lips were warm on hers, moving with hunger more than skill.

As if he couldn't get enough soon enough. As if she were a lifeline.

"Tim. Tim."

"Don't say no." He spoke against her ear, his breath hot on her skin while he kissed a path down her cheek, her jaw, her neck. "Not now. Don't tell us no."

Us. Not him. Us. If she'd had any intention of saying no before then—and she hadn't—all resistance would have melted away with that one word.

"Tim, I—oh!"

Any sweet speech she had was cut short by her husband stepping back, shoving his shoulder in her stomach and standing. One arm locked over her knees to keep her in place, he walked toward the stairs.

"What... are you... doing?" She could barely catch her breath from the shock, let alone speak in full sentences.

"Not giving you a chance to say no," he replied as he started up the steps. Like it was the most normal thing in the world to just hijack your wife and carry her upstairs fireman style to be ravished.

Oh, ravished. That was a brand of "normal" she could get used to.

"I wa—hmm." She almost told him she had no intention of saying no, but why spoil the fun for them both? Letting Tim have the chance to "change her mind" might be even more pleasurable than the main attraction.

Maybe some token resistance to show he's not her boss.

"Tim, this boorish behavior is really—"

Swat!

"Hey!" She reached back to rub her butt.

"That's what wives who talk back when their husbands are hauling them to the bedroom get." Tim's voice was completely natural. He wasn't even breathing hard.

He nudged open the door with his foot and swung her down to bounce on the bed. Skye leveled herself up on her elbows and watched as he opened the shades. Silvery light illuminated the bedroom, outlining shadows and highlighting Tim's tall frame, his wide shoulders, narrow waist—

Skye stopped short of licking her lips. But it was a near thing.

"I wanted to see you," he explained, crawling on the bed over her body. "I haven't been able to see you nearly as much as I wanted to." He slid his hands under the bottom of the sweatshirt, pushing up. His calluses rasped against the skin of her stomach. With each inch he uncovered, he pressed a kiss to her skin.

"I plan to rectify that problem right now." His breath warmed her, chased away the chill in the air. "Every last patch of skin, I want to know."

"You've already seen me."

"Again. I want to know again."

Skye shifted so he could push the sweatshirt over her head. Her lace bra was no match for the air conditioning. Beneath the see-through material, her nipples hardened, tightened to peaks.

Tim slid one hand under her back and used his fingers to sightlessly flick her clasp open.

"Nice moves," she said as he drew the bra off her shoulders.

"Thanks," he said and latched onto her breast.

Skye cried out in surprise, in pleasure, in relief. His mouth was insistent, pulling and testing her flesh, not giving in when she mewled or moaned.

He wasn't a gentle lover. Hasty. Needy. But always in control. He switched breasts, the cool air coursing over the abandoned nipple still wet from his tongue. She shivered against the cold.

Then he worked his way down her stomach, circled his tongue in her navel. He sat up long enough to pull down her leggings, stripping her panties with them. But if she would have felt embarrassment at being so rapidly stripped, she didn't have time to realize it. No, he was too fast, too insistent for her to gather any coherent thoughts. Shouldering her legs apart, his mouth found her warm, wet center.

Skye arched into his questing tongue, wanting the quick pulse, the flash release. But he avoided the one aching, essential spot. Teased around it with quick flicks and long strokes of his tongue.

"Bastard," she muttered and let her nails bury into his shoulders. Louder, she moaned. "Tim."

Hearing the unspoken plea, he trapped her nub between his teeth and sucked.

The climax threw her back. Skye dug her heels into the mattress, pulsed in unconscious rhythm as he dragged her through the storm, never relenting.

"Stop," she gasped when the sensation was too much. "Stop, Tim."

He launched himself over her body, and she clawed at his shirt until he helped her remove it entirely. His chest was like marble, smooth and hard. Unyielding. But where stone was cool to the touch, his skin burned as she ran her palms down the muscles to find the waistband of his shorts.

"Off. Off." She panted, fumbling with the elastic. Her arms were too short. She couldn't reach down far enough to push them down.

Suddenly her arms were pinned by her head, one large hand holding her wrists captive.

"There's only one boss here," he reminded her with a punishing nip to her bottom lip.

Skye opened her mouth to argue, but he took the opportunity to kiss her. Arguing suddenly was the last thing on her mind as his lips moved over hers, as he whispered words that would make her blush in the morning.

One knee wedged between her thighs pried them apart. Then the blunt head of his penis pushed between her slick folds. When had he had the chance to remove his shorts? Ah, when he was kissing her stupid, that's when. He pushed, inched in with aggravating control.

"Arg!" She was going to lose her mind before he was halfway in. Bucking up did nothing, as he countered every maneuver.

"I'm not moving until you hand over the reins," he said, his voice fierce. "Skye. Trust me."

Fighting was fun. A battle to grab for the edge. But those two words—trust me—hung in the air between them.

Just this once, she promised herself and surrendered.

"There we go," he breathed, and he pushed until he was fully seated inside. Her body sighed with pleasure, pulsed around his cock. The low glow of a fire started in her belly.

Then he rocked out and back in; the long glide had her gasping and reaching for more. More friction, more depth, more Tim.

"You'll get more, sweetheart," he murmured into the hollow below her ear.

Oh for the love... Had she said that out loud?

Tim thrust faster, harder, deeper, and she couldn't hold back any longer. Flames flicked along her nerves, blazing through her veins.

"Tim. Oh, God. Tim, I'm... I'm..."

"I know, baby. I'm with you. Let go."

The burn, the fire was too intense to shut down. There was nothing she could do to hold back the inferno.

So she jumped into the flames.

Her body tightened, fluttered, flexed around Tim as she cried out with the ultimate release. The satisfying sizzle and burn engulfed her, and for a moment she was deaf and blind, drifting in a dark pool of satisfaction and lush fulfillment.

Tim's own groan brought her back to the present. He nuzzled into her neck; his plunging rhythm became erratic. Then his body stiffened, thrust to the hilt, and he collapsed over her, surrendering to the same pleasure-tinged blaze as she had.

And to think I purposefully said no to sex... I'm an idiot.

It was the last thought before she drifted to sleep.

Chapter 16

SKYE WOKE TO NEEDLE-SHARP PAIN IN HER ARMS, A HEAVY weight over her legs, and a blinding light in her eyes.

The last was the easiest to identify. The blinds were open, letting unadulterated morning light pour in much earlier than she would ever dare wake up on her own. The weight, she quickly discovered, was her husband's thigh thrown over her own legs. His head was pillowed by her breast, an arm draped possessively over her stomach.

And the source of her pain was his hand, still pinning her own arms above her head in an awkward, unnatural position, resulting in her limbs falling asleep.

She shifted enough to pull both wrists out of his lax grasp and lower them, only to double over in pain as the blood rushed back. A low groan escaped from deep in her chest. Tim was up in an instant, crouched low on the bed. Naked as a jaybird. Battle ready and fierce, prepared to fight whatever enemy dared to sneak into his sanctuary.

Too bad the enemy was a burning, tingly feeling from hell and completely resistant to combat. The entire thing would have been hilarious if the pain wasn't overriding her brainpower.

She rolled to one side and curled up in a ball. How could something so simple hurt so badly?

"Hey, Skye. Baby, what's wrong?" Large, gentle

hands rolled her to her back. His concerned face appeared around her shoulder, desperate to solve her problems. He was so handsome, even with the crease over one cheek from the pillow. If she hadn't been in pain, she could have appreciated the sight of her rumpled husband more.

"My arms hurt. Fell asleep. Blood rushing. Hurts."

"Okay, all right. Shh," he murmured. Softly, he massaged one arm while she stayed curled on her side, starting at the shoulder and working his way down to her wrist, then back up again. The burning started to subside, and her body relaxed marginally. He rolled her onto her stomach and repeated the gesture with her other arm. The massage continued down her back and she melted into the bed as tension seeped out of her body.

"Feel better?"

"Mmm hmm," she sighed into the pillow. She didn't want to talk. Just focus on the magic those big strong hands were working over the knots from her weeks at the restaurant bending over tables, the stress, the worry...

He chuckled but didn't stop the massage. Lower his hands searched for tense muscles to knead, reaching her ass. The shock had her tensing again, but his effortless ministrations made it easy to unwind once more as he continued to work down her legs.

He pressed on the arches of her feet with his thumbs and the heavens opened up. She could see the light of the pearly gates. This had to be what heaven felt like. Some out-of-body, weightless experience, floating on puffy clouds of happiness and contentment.

Maybe marriage didn't have to be so hard after all.

"Are you okay? From last night, I mean?"

His hesitant question brought her back to earth. How could he even be worried? Did he miss the multiple orgasms? She turned her head to one side so he could hear the answer clearly instead of mumbling into the pillow. "I'm fine. Better than fine, really. Great. Last night was…" She didn't think she could sum it up in one word.

"Yeah." He paused. "Uh, I forgot to use something last night. But I checked out clean during my pre-deployment physical, and I haven't been with anyone but you since."

"I'm fine too." She thought about it for a moment, then added, "I'm on the pill. We're good."

She heard his sigh of relief. Always the responsible one, she mused. Thinking of everything, even if it was just a tad too late. But she had to smile into the soft cotton of the pillow. Just another thing to write down on the Things Married People Should Already Know list. The damn thing was growing rapidly.

Tim's hands worked their way back up slowly, making sure no muscle or tendon went untended. As he rubbed her down, Skye thought back to last night. What had sparked the out-of-the-blue passionate response from her husband? He had been so adamant about holding off, on keeping clear of physical anything. What was the difference last night?

Her outfit at the dinner.

Nothing else out of the ordinary had happened.

When she'd come down the stairs in her outfit, he'd given her a toe-curling kiss. And he'd thanked her for wearing what she did, for playing the part. Was that what made the difference? Playing the expected role in their marriage, the type of wife he'd wanted?

Or was she selling herself short?

Maybe. She'd have to think about it some more.

"Do you work afternoon or evening today?"

"Afternoon," she answered. "But not until eleven."

He crawled down next to her, then wrapped one strong arm around her and pulled until her back was against his chest. "So you have the morning free."

"I do." She wiggled her behind a little and felt the obvious morning wood he was sporting. "What did you have in mind to pass the time?" she asked slyly.

"Checkers." He stroked his fingertips down one arm, leaving goose bumps behind. His palm came to rest on her breast, kneading gently. "I always love a rousing game of checkers in the morning."

"Rousing?" She turned in his arms to face him and reached down with one hand. Circling the thick flesh, she stroked. The satiny skin was blazing hot beneath her palm and hard as iron. "Hmm. Seems pretty roused already. I better go have a closer look."

She waited for the commanding tone, the orders, the push-pull of fighting for who had control. Instead, he gave her a devilish smile and fell to his back with passive ease. "I think that's a great plan."

"Just when you think you've got them figured out," she muttered. He chuckled and she bit his rib.

"Ow!" Tim tugged her hair until she looked up into his stern face. "Play nice."

There was that familiar old bossy nature. And for some reason, she'd wanted it. That either made her the most pathetic feminist on the planet, or she was just becoming used to her husband's domineering ways and seeing them for what they were.

His way of showing he cared.

The idea floored her, and she took the gentle approach. Feathering kisses over his abdomen, she took silent pleasure in the way his muscles quivered with each light brush. To be more of a tease, she quickly yanked her hair-tie out and let her wavy tresses fall in a curtain around her. The locks brushed his stomach and thighs when she moved, tickling and provoking a harsh breath from him.

Not so stoic after all. She smiled against his hip and planted a sweet kiss before turning her attention to his cock lying against his lower stomach, twitching with anticipation.

Working her way carefully around the aroused flesh, she tormented him with licks and nips, coming close but never touching his erection. At one point his fingers curled around her skull, putting slight pressure to guide her to him. But she pulled back and he let go.

Smart man.

She rewarded his decision with a long lap up the underside of his shaft, ending with the tip flicking to taste the drop of pearly liquid at the head. Skye looked up to see Tim's jaw clenched. His fists covered his eyes as if he was using every ounce of restraint to not look or touch.

There was such power in being a woman sometimes.

She wrapped one hand around his erection. Her other she used for balance. And breathing deeply, she took him in a centimeter at a time.

The salty taste caught on her tongue, and she swirled around until Tim moaned. The sound was a deep rumble in his chest, vibrating through his body.

Gliding down and back up again, Skye chose a rhythm she wanted. One that kept him twitching. One that would draw out the pleasure until it bordered on pain.

"You're killing me," he complained.

She pulled away, breaking the suction with a pop. "I can always just go downstairs and start some breakfast," she said and started to shift.

One heavy leg clamped around her calves, making it impossible to move. "Don't you dare," he said, giving her the evil eye.

"Poor Tim. So sad." She scratched her nails up and down his stomach, watching him relax until his head dropped back onto the pillow. "How do I make it better?"

When she took him in her mouth again, she picked up the speed, using her fist for additional friction. His hips pumped, as if he couldn't hold back if his country depended on it. And she didn't want him to. Holding back was the last thing she wanted from her husband. In bed or out. But for now, she'd start with this.

"Skye, I'm close. Come here." His hands gripped under her elbows, but she ignored them. Not this time. This time she wanted to finish.

"Skye. Christ. Skye!" Tim's arms dropped, his back arched, and he grunted as the climax took him over. When he fell back, silent and still, she gave one last lick—just because she could—before releasing him. She crawled toward the headboard.

Tim was still as stone, one forearm draped over his eyes. All signs of life gone but for the rise and fall of his chest. He looked vulnerable, the position leaving him open and defenseless. It was an oddly endearing thought. But then, she thought, he was always so strong.

So in control. Showing his emotional soft underbelly for even a moment was a triumph for both of them.

Of course nobody would mistake the vulnerability for weakness. No, not with arms so thick she couldn't wrap two hands around. Or the cut muscles of his chest, the ladder of abs working down to his rock hard thighs.

No wimps for the Marines, she thought and laughed.

"What's so funny?"

She looked back, seeing he hadn't moved. "Just wondered something."

A moment of silence, and then, "Are you going to share?"

"Hmm. Sure." Of course she wasn't. She could only picture the look of horror on Tim's face as she explained the beauty of his vulnerability. The image made her laugh again. So she improvised. "I was curious if you were ticklish." And with that, she poked him in the ribs repeatedly until he grunted and rolled around to pin her beneath him. His strength vibrated from every muscle.

Yes, vulnerability was a beautiful thing. But her husband sure as hell was no pushover.

Tim took the offered beer and sat back in the recliner, making sure his feet were propped up at just the right angle to aid in optimum beer and snack consumption and game-watching.

Dwayne plopped into the opposite recliner, going through the same motions until he was settled, then turned his eyes to the television.

"How goes married life?" Dwayne asked.

"Great." When Dwayne raised an eyebrow, he

shrugged. "It is. Look at this. I'm at a friend's house on a Sunday afternoon watching football and she's not even ragging on me for it."

"I thought you said she was at work," Dwayne chimed in.

"I thought you would be deployed by now."

"Any day now. Or so they tell me. Any fucking day." Dwayne saluted him with his beer. "Lame distraction, by the way."

"Fine. Yes, she's at work. But she's still not ragging, is she?" Tim pointed out.

They watched in silence until a commercial.

"How was the thing at Colonel Blackwater's house?"

Tim sighed. "Uneventful, luckily."

"Was there a concern?" Dwayne asked. "And with who—you or Skye?"

"Skye, mostly. The way the Colonel's wife tore into her outfit at the barbeque, I was sure she'd wear something even more... hippieish. Just to spite." Part of him—the insane part, clearly—had even been looking forward to it. "But instead she hauled ass the other direction and wore something that looked completely..." Tim shrugged his shoulders. "Not her. It wasn't her at all. It was conservative and boring. Some black skirt and a blue shirt. No funky jewelry, no patterns. Nothing. The model of conservative."

"Sounds familiar," Dwayne drawled.

"What are you talking about?"

Dwayne sat up and pushed the leg rest in. Then he leaned forward, rolling the beer bottle between his palms. "Oh, I'm just thinking back to all the women you've dated. How they were all nice, simple, dressed like that. Conservative all around. Safe. Basically, the female version of you."

"What? No." Tim shuffled through his mental file cabinet of old girlfriends. How did they dress to go on a date? How did they look at home? How did they act?

Damn. Dwayne was right. "Well, okay. You have a point. But that's what normal women dress like. Act like. It's a responsible mode of clothing. Those women were usually coming from work or something," he justified. "Banks or attorney offices. Of course they'd dress and act conservatively."

"And yet, instead of being pleased with how Skye looked—and I can imagine she looked pretty damn fine in the outfit because she's a beautiful woman—you're bitching about how it didn't look right on her," Dwayne pointed out smugly. The bastard.

"It did look nice. She looked great. It just wasn't what I'm used to from her." Tim took a sip of beer to wash the dusty feeling from his throat. "Besides, I doubt she'll dress like that much anyway. I could tell she was uncomfortable, and she switched outfits as soon as we got home."

An outfit that turned him from an average, semi-sex-starved husband into a full-blown lusting animal with almost no finesse. God, he'd practically attacked her and dragged her back to the bedroom, Neanderthal style. All that was missing was pulling her by the hair to his cave.

She didn't seem to mind.

Didn't matter. Next time he'd show at least a tiny bit of skill. Show her he was at least one step up from a hormonal teen fumbling in the backseat of his father's Jeep.

"Basically what it sounds like is she was being

practical. Assessing the situation and making adjustments to her normal routine as necessary." Dwayne killed the bottle and sat the empty one down on the coffee table between them. "It's logical. Can't complain there."

No, he couldn't. The fact that Skye understood how important staying on the CO's good side was to his career pleased him. She was putting in the effort. That more than the outfit itself was what hit him the hardest. When she said she wanted to give the marriage everything she had, she hadn't been kidding.

Maybe this wasn't such a crazy idea after all.

Tim opened the front door, cursing when it slammed back at him.

"What the hell?" He pushed harder and finally managed to squeeze in. When he shut the door behind him, he saw the culprit.

A shoe had bested him. A tennis shoe must have fallen from the mountainous pile of Skye's footwear and wedged itself under the door when he pushed open. He kicked the offending shoe back into the pile, only to watch five more tumble down and litter the entryway. He turned to leave, then couldn't. Lining all the shoes up along the wall made him feel slightly better about them being where they didn't belong. Slightly.

On his way to the kitchen, he smelled something different. Definitely not the air freshener Madison had left behind when she moved out. It was too earthy. He sniffed again, following his nose Toucan Sam-style until he halted in front of the fireplace. Incense. A lot of them. Lined up on the mantel between pictures of his family and little statues of… someone. He picked one up, amazed by how heavy it was. Definitely not the fat Buddha guy. But it looked like some pagan god of some sort. He placed it back warily and took a step back, almost tripping over a stack of magazines.

His house was booby-trapped. Against him.

Finally he made it to the fridge for some water when he saw the check hanging by a magnet.

"Skye?" he called out, waiting for a response, the check between two fingers like he was holding a vial of deadly swine flu and wanted nothing to do with it. "Skye, where are you?"

"Back porch!"

Tim walked out the back door of the kitchen to find his wife lounging on one of the patio chairs in the sun. Sunglasses shaded her eyes, her arms were tossed over her head as if she were napping. One knee was bent, the other straight out in an unconsciously provocative pin-up girl pose. If she had been wearing an old-fashioned 1940s bikini, his heart might have stopped. As it was, the thin tank top and ripped denim shorts had his heart skipping a few beats.

"Skye, what's this?"

"Dunno." She didn't even turn toward him to see what he was referring to.

He sighed and walked in front of her. When she didn't move, didn't even tilt her head, he gently reached over and pushed her glasses to the top of her head. They left a cute red mark on the bridge of her nose. The sun had bronzed her skin, highlighting a few freckles over her cheeks. What would she do if he—

"Looks like a piece of paper to me. Too far away to see more."

Her answer snapped him back. "It's a check. Written to me."

Her nose scrunched at that. "If you know what it is, why are you asking me? I was taking in a nice afternoon nap." Her eyelids dropped and her voice became husky. "I didn't get much sleep last night, as you well know."

He did remember last night. And the night before. The past several nights, actually, and it was taking all his willpower not to roll on top of her on the lounge chair and repeat the performance.

Jesus, Tim. Sex outside? Seriously? This isn't you.

He dropped into the other patio chair... very much out of arm's reach. Take that, temptation. This situation was going to be annoying enough without battling a raging erection. "It's a check from you. What's it for? Why are you writing me checks?"

"Oh." At the clarification, she sat up and brightened. "It's for this month's mortgage payment. I took a peek at the statement when I saw it sitting on your desk. No, don't get mad."

"I'm not mad."

"Yes you are. Your jaw looks so tight it might snap. I live here too. I should know what it takes to keep this place running."

Tim rubbed the ache that started to form between his brows. "Okay. Besides the fact that you snooped through my mail—"

"Not snooping. It was just sitting there on the desk and I noticed it. And it saved me the effort of asking you about—"

"Aside from that," he repeated, "why are you writing me a check for half the payment?"

She looked at him, her head tilting like a dog being given a command it didn't understand. "Because I live here too."

"I never asked you for any money."

Her expression cleared, as if realizing the problem. Then she patted his knee and pushed her glasses back down on her nose. "I know. But I fixed it. So now I know what I need to contribute every month. We're all set."

He stared at her, no clue where to go from there. "Um, no. We're not all set. You're not some roommate, Skye. You're my wife."

No response.

"So as my wife, you're not obligated to pay rent."

"It's not rent. It's a contribution. If you just let me know when you get the electric, I'll do my best to get you a check fast. Although I really should call my old bank and have them issue new checks with the new address on them. Do you think I should switch to a local bank here? Or maybe open an account at whatever bank you use…"

"Skye."

"I mean I don't think a joint account is the right thing to do right now, but maybe if we—"

"Skye."

"No, you're right. I'll just find a bank that I like myself. No need to—"

"Skye!" Jesus, she could go on for hours.

Her head snapped back. "What?"

He ripped the check in two and let them fall to her stomach. And had the satisfaction of watching his wife's mouth drop open without a word to say. Speechless. For once. Maybe he should grab a calendar and write it down.

That lasted a whole ten seconds.

"What was that for?" She stood up and thrust the patio chair back. "I only have a few checks left that have to last me until the new ones come in. What the hell, Tim?"

"My wife doesn't pay rent. I provide."

Once again, her mouth hung open like a flytrap. Then it snapped shut with such force he was shocked she didn't wince with pain. "You forgot to scratch yourself and mutter in Prehistoric Caveman while you said that. Oh my God, did you spear us a mastodon for dinner too, dear?"

"Look, don't get all feminist about this. It's just the way O'Shays work. Husband provides. I am more than capable of providing the roof over my wife's head."

With the sunglasses shading her eyes, it was impossible to tell what she was thinking. But from the way she was trembling, he could easily guess she wasn't thinking about sunshine and rainbows. Then she raised her shaking fists, tilted her face heavenward, and let out a strangled, blood-curdling scream. Tim barely resisted the urge to cover his ears.

"Christ, Skye. The neighbors are going to think I'm out here murdering you!"

Without notice, she walked barefoot down to the small patch of grass they called a backyard and started to pace. And pace. And pace. Tim could have sworn steam actually poured out her ears. The entire time, her mouth was moving, and he could faintly hear her voice. But the words were undetermined. He didn't have to hear them to know that they wouldn't be flattering to his ego.

He wanted to tell her that people would be staring out their windows and thinking she was crazy, but he couldn't. He couldn't take his eyes off her. Chestnut hair flowing behind her with every turn, body vibrating with energy—even angry energy—legs eating up the ground with purposeful strides… she was magnificent. Even if she was causing a scene for anyone in the townhouse complex to see. His body tightened in response, even as his brain was shouting to stay alert because with Skye, who knew what she would throw at him next?

Finally she stopped, turned on a dime, and stared at him. With precision and care, she lifted her glasses with one finger and stared at him. Her voice was calm—too calm—when she spoke.

"I am a capable, intelligent, independent woman."

She paused, as if giving him time to either agree or fight. Tim kept his mouth shut. This would be what his father called a no-win situation for males.

"I am completely able to contribute to the house that I am staying in. It just so happens that this house is my husband's home. My helpmate. Isn't that what a spouse is? There to help? Well, I want to help."

Tim wanted to say she helped in other ways, by cooking and cleaning and seeing to the domestic chores. But that'd be a lie. She didn't cook any more than he did, and her idea of cleaning was to shove everything under the nearest piece of furniture to hide it from view. It should bother him. It didn't.

"I refuse to be a dead weight around here."

"That's what you think? That you're dead weight?"

Tim thudded down the wooden patio stairs to stand in front of her. Though it was a risk, touching someone who still looked like a live wire of energy, he put his hands on her shoulders. "That's not the truth at all. This is just how I was raised. That the man—"

"Provides. Takes care of the women. Yeah, I know." Skye rubbed her temples and gave a shy grin. "I'm sorry. I get a little upset at the whole male macho 1950s routine."

"This is you a *little* upset?" The screaming, the pacing, the calm-before-the-storm attitude?

God help him if she ever got well and truly pissed at him. And why did that thought make him want to smile?

She shrugged then walked up the stairs to the patio chair she'd vacated ten minutes earlier as if nothing happened. "So will you let me help with the bills?"

He rubbed a hand over his hair, feeling completely trapped. To say yes meant going against his entire upbringing, an upbringing he happened to believe in. But saying no obviously didn't yield desirable results with his wife.

As if sensing his problem, Skye waved him to sit down in the other chair again. When he did, she held out a hand until he placed his in it. Her skin was soft, warm from the sun. He wanted to see if she was warm all over.

"Please." It was all she said, and he felt helpless to deny her at that point.

He raised their hands and kissed the back of her fingers. "Okay."

Though it gave him a little twist in the gut, her smile unraveled it and soothed the churning. He still felt like he barely knew her. But to see her smile like that, Tim knew he would do almost anything.

He waited until she relaxed before he scooped her up in his arms. And he walked the shrieking, laughing woman back up to their bedroom to spend the rest of the afternoon finding other ways to make her smile.

Chapter 17

SKYE PLODDED INTO THE KITCHEN, EYES BLURRY AND DROOPY with sleep. Reaching in the cabinet, she pulled out the makings for tea. Right now, coffee would be nice. Except she didn't drink it. But the kick it could give her was enviable. Instead she picked the strongest tea she had and started the water.

Her day off, and she'd slept half of it away. Then again, understandable since she'd had a late night. A private party kept her at work two hours past expected close time. And Tim had kept her awake well into the early morning hours.

Skye's skin tingled as she remembered the rapt attention he'd paid to her body in the dark. The tireless energy he'd used over and over, pushing her past every physical, sexual limit she thought she had. The man definitely knew which buttons to push. That part she couldn't complain about. The lack of sleep though... that was going to be something to get used to. Every night since the dinner party at the CO's house, she'd averaged less than half her usual shut-eye.

You'll take catnaps. If the payoff in bed is that *good, you adjust. So, adjust already.*

The phone rang as she took her first sip of fortifying tea, and Skye reached blindly for the receiver.

"Hello?"

"Skye, it's Beth. How are you?"

Skye smiled and stretched her sore muscles. "Good. Really good. How are you?"

"Panicking. I'm desperate."

That shook her out of her private sexual gloating. "What? Are you okay? Are you hurt?"

"Huh? No. No, nothing like that."

Skye breathed a quick sigh of relief. "Okay, start from the top."

Beth took an audible breath and blew out. "My in-laws are coming to town for a *surprise* visit." Her friend's tone told Skye exactly how welcome the surprise was.

After the shocking visit she'd had with Tim's family, she could relate.

"All right. Not everyone's favorite situation in the world, but survivable. What do you need?"

"I need you to host the spouse coffee."

"Host the what?"

"The monthly spouse coffee. It's my turn to host this Saturday, but with Toby's family in town, I can't. I just can't. I love them, but they're embarrassing and pushy and it would make everyone miserable. Me more than anyone." Beth sounded close to cracking. "Please host the coffee. I will help you with anything you need. Just provide the place and play the hostess. I beg of you. If I have to host this thing with Toby's parents around, men in white coats will be dragging me out the door."

Skye stared into her mug of tea. "But I don't even drink coffee." Regrettably, on mornings like this.

At that, Beth laughed. "No. I mean yeah, there's usually coffee. It's just called a coffee. But it's basically a get-together of the spouses. A little meet and greet.

Ten to twenty women, usually. I'd bet more this time, just because people will want to meet you. We chat, we catch up, we find out the good gossip from around the battalion like deployment changes and training dates and stuff. And then we go home."

"I don't know. I mean—"

"I would ask someone else, someone who has experience with these. But everyone I know has already hosted one recently and I feel bad imposing on them."

"Just not bad about imposing on the new girl."

"Well, you're new. You need friends, so you can't hold a grudge against me."

She laughed at that. "Point taken."

There was silence. Then softly, Beth said, "Please."

Skye sighed and stirred her tea. Time to talk Beth down from the ledge. "And you'll help me plan everything? It'll be a hands-free thing?"

"Yes! I will give you my outline down to the last detail. It's really simple, I promise. Don't panic."

"That's your job, right?" Skye asked.

"Exactly." Beth's voice was relieved, even upbeat now. "I'll email you the plans I created. It has the food list, though you could make substitutions if you have a good cookie recipe or anything you might want to put out."

Skye thought of her favorite stone ground crackers and soy veggie dip. Probably not a crowd favorite.

She hung up the phone a few minutes later, promising to call Beth later to confirm the plans. Beth, for her part, would take care of changing the invitation and informing everyone.

Letting her head drop to thunk against the fridge

door, she beat it gently a few times. The stainless steel was cool against her skin, helping to douse the flush of nerves.

What the hell had she just agreed to? Showing up to an event was one thing. But inviting people into her home… it was like an invitation to judge everything she'd done wrong… in their eyes, anyway. *Here, please have this intimate peek into my life, and go ahead. Tell me where I'm lacking, Mrs. Blackwater.*

Wandering around the house, mug of tea in hand, Skye took stock of the home that would be infiltrated with women in a few days. What would they think?

Tim's home was clean, though not pristine. With a quick glance around the room, she realized the last part was basically her own fault. A small pile of magazines sat stacked on the coffee table. A pair of shoes sat to the side of the couch. A pile of clothes she'd started to fold but never finished lay in a heap on the armchair. Her incense and goddess statues cluttered the fireplace mantel.

And yet, Tim never said a word. Her fastidious husband never complained about the wreck she'd created. How unfair was that to him? The more she looked around the room with an objective eye, the more it looked like a Skye-bomb exploded.

Skye set the mug down on the coffee table, then had a second thought, grabbing a coaster from the end table before putting it down again. She rubbed her hands and went to work.

An hour later, Skye flopped down on the couch and surveyed her work. The place sparkled. Or at least, the mirrors and windows did. Everything was neatly tucked away, polished, or vacuumed. Even her incense had found a new home, upstairs in the guest bedroom.

A small sense of pride pushed her to take one step further. Before she could change her mind and give in to the physical desire for a nap, she grabbed her phone.

"Madison? Hey, when do you work today? Okay, if you get off in an hour, can you meet me at the mall? I have some shopping to do."

Skye shut her phone with a snap. No lounging in bed today. She had some serious work still ahead of her, and a deadline looming.

Skye fingered the collar of a simple white button-down shirt. No ruffles, no color, no design. Absolutely nothing that set it apart from anything else in the store.

She grabbed two.

"I'm still not sure why you need to go this far out," Madison called.

She turned around to find her sister-in-law-turned-pack-mule behind a pile of clothing. "Because it seems like these functions pop up all the time. These spouseish things. And what I'm learning is in situations like this, it's easier to swim with the flow than fight upstream." She turned and started to rifle through another rack of clothing. "Especially when the answer is as simple as an outfit."

"But I like your clothing," Madison complained. "It's you. It's who you are. It's not scrubs!"

Skye laughed. "Scrubs are adorable on you. You're a nurse, after all. What else would you wear? Thanks for meeting me here after your shift, by the way. I'm sure you're exhausted."

"You're right." Madison plopped down on a riser holding a few mannequins dressed in what Skye could only call Country Club Chic. "ER is definitely not my favorite rotation. But when someone says shopping, I heed the call."

"That's why I love you," Skye called out an aisle away.

"Can I start a fitting room for you?" a sales associate asked Madison.

"Oh, thank you, God." She dumped the pile of clothing in the capable woman's arms and dusted her hands. "Skye, I'm no expert with shopping, obviously," she started, fingering her light blue scrub shirt and smiling, "but aren't you buying a few too many clothes for the purpose? To have something on hand for those rare spouse occasions? One or two things should do it. But the way you're picking out clothes makes it look like you're on *What Not to Wear*. Are Stacy and Clinton going to pop out from behind some rack of clothing and scare the shit out of me?"

"I don't want to leave anything to chance. I just need to have a few different options." Skye battled back the feeling of defensiveness. Madison was being kind, because that was who she was. There was no way she'd put Tim in the position of having to defend her or be embarrassed by her. She wanted to be prepared for any occasion.

"I still think you're overreacting. I bet a lot of people think you dress cool. And if they don't, then screw them." She held out a vibrant green and purple tank and thin sweater set. Skye shook her head.

It was so simple for Madison. Skye envied her that. "Easy for you to say. How hard do you have to think about what you put on before you go to work?" Skye grabbed an oatmeal-colored sweater and held back the shudder.

"Point taken," she conceded. "But still. My brother likes you for you. Clearly. He married you."

Skye turned and stared at Madison, one eyebrow raised. There wasn't any need to point out the obvious out loud. *He married me drunk off his ass. He didn't know if he liked me.*

"Okay, well, I mean he's *still* married to you. He would have left by now if he didn't like you. Tim's not one to surrender quickly, but he also knows when to cut his losses. They kind of drill that into their heads from the minute the ink's dry on the commission paperwork."

"I appreciate the sentiment. And it does make me feel better. But this is something I need to do." For my marriage, she silently added and hauled a pile of shirts to the dressing room. She undressed and stared at the pile of colorless clothing on the bench. Screwing her eyes shut, she grabbed the first thing and pulled it on. *Okay. Time to open your eyes and look. Open. Open your eyes, Skye.*

She cracked one lid and glanced in the mirror. The lumpy brown summer cardigan had no shape, no definition. The light, loose knit was woven into something resembling a swirling pattern over the front. It hung well past her hips. Okay. This could not be right.

"Come on, Skye. Do you have something on?"

"Um." It was… something all right. Something horrid.

"Just come out so I can tell you it's awful and we can move on."

She stepped out of the dressing room to find Madison

sprawled over a bench, shopping bags tucked under her feet. Her sister-in-law's eyes widened almost comically, then she snickered.

"I'm sorry. Exactly what were you going for again? Crazy Cat Lady Chic?"

"Bite me." Skye turned back into the dressing room and shut the door. Okay. Number one was a failure. But now that she looked at the sweater again, that's because she just grabbed something at the end out of frustration. Time to try on something more normal. She slipped into a pair of black capris and one of the white button-down shirts. It wasn't ugly. Turning around, she gave her butt a good once-over. At least it fit her. Braced for criticism, she stepped out.

Madison gave her a long look and shrugged. "It's fine."

"Fine?" After the stress of picking something out and trying to not look like someone's shut-in aunt with too many felines, fine was no longer good enough. "Fine."

"Yeah. It's fine." Unaware of Skye's inner turmoil, Madison stretched and rolled her shoulders. "Don't you wear something like that to work at Fletchers?"

She looked down, then in the three-way mirror at the end if the dressing room. "Oh my God. You're right."

Madison laughed again. "Trying too hard. Just pick out something you actually like." She sobered a little. "You don't really think my brother cares what you wear, do you?"

Skye glanced back at the pile of clothing and didn't answer the question. "This might take a little longer than I thought. Do you mind?"

Madison sighed and sprawled across the bench,

waving her hand toward the stall. "Shoo. Go find something. But you owe me ice cream after this."

"Deal."

—*✦*—

Tim came home to a pristine living room. The floor was
vacuumed, the tables were dusted, he couldn't see a hint
of clutter. It smelled cotton fresh, like laundry just out of
the dryer. Even the couch throw pillows looked fluffed.

There was only one explanation.

Little elves had broken into the townhouse and cast
some magical cleaning spell.

No, that wasn't fair. She was more than capable of
cleaning up the house. It just didn't occur to her. Messes,
a little clutter, disorganization never seemed to affect
her like it did Tim. But then, Skye's own mind seemed
a tad cluttered at times, in the scatterbrained sort of way.
It wasn't laziness, just, well, Skyeness.

But at the same time, the sight of no cups or magazines or opened junk mail scattered around his home
made him smile. Tim dropped onto the sofa and took
stock of the clean room. She'd even polished the mirrors
and glass on the entertainment center. It was amazing.
Relaxing. Normal.

No. Not quite. Something was off. Tim couldn't
ignore the little voice in the back of his mind saying that something wasn't right. He scanned the area,
looking for things out of place. Something broken.
Something missing.

Something missing. Skye.

Not the woman. The presence. Skye's things were
gone. It was always Skye's junk mail and magazines

cluttering the coffee table. Her mug of half-finished tea leaving a ring on the wood. Her clothes draped over various pieces of furniture. Her little stick things burning on the mantel.

It was all gone. As if all signs of her existence in his home, and his life, had evaporated. Someone walking in at this very minute wouldn't have a clue he didn't live alone. Where was she? Skye the woman, that was. It was her day off. He assumed she'd be lounging on the couch watching a movie when he came in, ready to snuggle until dinner.

"Skye?" he called, standing up and heading to the silent kitchen. No surprise, no Skye. He headed toward the stairs, listening for the run of water or a door closing. Something.

Silence.

He jogged up the stairs calling her name. Then he had a thought and peeked through the window at the top landing to the street. Her car was gone. How had he missed that when he first pulled up? Must have been on autopilot, too intent on getting inside to notice.

But even as he started back down the stairs, he heard a car pull up. He opened the front door just in time to see Skye struggling with a handful of massive shopping bags.

"Good timing." She thrust one handful at him and waddled around until she could drop the lot in a pile next to the couch, then sank down to the cushions herself.

"Busy day?"

"Whew. Shopping has never been so difficult," she said with exaggerated exhaustion.

Tim surveyed the haul. "Did you leave anything for the rest of the city?"

"A few things. The very ugly things. Including a

lovely brown sweater that will go well with a cat," she said with a laugh. "Madison says hi, by the way."

"Oh." That was new. He'd never had any of his previous girlfriends spend quality time with his sister before. "So she was your partner in crime for the shopping spree. She didn't encourage you to wipe us out, did she?"

"Nope. It only cost me a giant ice cream cone as payment. She wasn't too excited to be dragged out after her shift, but I wanted to beat you home." She blew out a breath, shifting a curl that draped over her cheek. "Not that it worked out. Come help me drag these upstairs?" She pushed herself up with a delicate grunt and headed for the stairs.

"Yeah. Sure." As he followed Skye up, he made the split-second decision to ask, "Do you want to go out tonight for dinner?"

Skye paused at the top and shot him a grateful smile. "Bless you, child. Yes. The thought of having someone else cook for my tired butt is vastly appealing. I can try on a new outfit too," she mused as she headed for the bedroom.

Tim wondered if any of the sacks contained something sexy for her to wear later that night. Maybe lace, sheer, even completely transparent... The thought had him hard in an instant, and he shook it away the best he could. Now wasn't the time.

Or was it?

Skye dropped the sacks on the bed—the made up bed, surprisingly—and stripped her tank off in one smooth motion. The creamy skin of her belly had his muscles tightening, coiled, and ready to pounce. He started to reach out for her. But she barely even registered his presence as she dug into one sack, then another, looking for something. She glanced up and asked, "You're not wearing that, obviously. Change."

He looked down at his cammies and boots and laughed at himself. He hadn't even taken the time to change after he got home. Too blown away by the state of cleanliness.

Rifling through one of the drawers he wondered what plethora of colorful concoctions Skye had come home with this time. What sunburst of design would she grace the world with that evening?

"Where did all your stuff go that was on the fireplace mantel?" he asked as he folded his uniform. "The incense and the statues."

"Oh, I put them in the guest room for now. I promised Beth I'd host the spouse coffee on Saturday for her. I should have asked you first, but she absolutely panicked so I just said yes. And I figured I would put that stuff away for now. After Saturday I can put it back out."

The plan made sense. Though he wasn't pleased with her feeling like she had to hide the stuff. But maybe it was just easier to host with less things around. He turned to ask her but stopped with his mouth open.

Skye stood with her back to him, fiddling with something in another bag. She wore a lightweight sweater in pale green, the sleeves hitting just below her elbows. A pair of crisp khakis elongated the line of her legs. And on her feet were a pair of simple flat shoes in the same color as her pants.

She glanced up at him as she fixed an earring. A tiny

earring that he could barely see across the room. A very un-Skye-like earring.

The dazzling smile she sent him took his breath away. "Do you like?" She spun around with her arms out, showing off the conservative outfit.

The slacks showed off how long her legs were, the sweater skimmed the top of her breasts, the color was nice against her mahogany hair.

But, much like the ever-dreaded question of *does this make me look fat?* there was no right answer here.

"It's nice." And it was. It just wasn't Skye. It wasn't the woman he had grown accustomed to. The wife he'd come to desire. It was like a peacock covering its plumage. "Is there more in the bags?"

"Oh, yeah. Took me forever to decide. But I figured I could splurge a little bit."

Skye's idea of a splurge was to tone down her look? Huh. Women truly were an odd species. "Ready for dinner?"

She smiled so brightly he knew he would rather cut off his arm than admit he wished she changed back. So he held out his hand and took his wife to dinner.

"Hello?"

"Tim. Man. Why the hell do you sound so tired?"

He checked his bedside clock. O-fucking-two-hundred on a Thursday night. No, Friday morning. Either way, he had work the next day. "Because it's the middle of the night, dipshit. I'm sleeping. This better be important. Like, *near-death or profusely bleeding* important."

Dwayne chuckled. "Never used to need so much sleep, old man."

Beside him, Skye shifted. Her soft breasts pressed into his back as her arm slid around his waist. "Never really had much of a reason to head to bed early before, did I?"

Skye's arm tightened in silent response.

"Point taken. Sorry, totally forgot you weren't alone, or I would have waited. Just wanted to tell you that I finally got the call."

Tim sat up, sorry for disturbing Skye... but still. He needed to be upright. "When?"

Dwayne understood the question wasn't when he got the call, but when he'd leave. "Seventy-two hours. Well, that was a few hours ago. So about sixty-six now."

Leave it to D to joke about a deployment. "You, me, and Jer. Tomorrow night. I have to be out of the house anyway."

"Right. Last guys' night." Dwayne blew out a breath. "Sounds good. I'll see you tomorrow, then."

Tim hung up the phone, then stared into the darkness for another minute.

That was his deployment. His missed opportunity. Though not always fun, deployments and extended training missions were how he honed his skills. It's what the practice was for. He'd been resentful before about being left behind. Jealous about the things, the experiences, he would lose out on. Work was his number one. His driving force. Anything necessary to climb the next step.

"You okay?" Skye's voice was soft in the night, as if she didn't want to bother him. With a gentle touch, she rubbed slow circles on his back.

Hearing her, feeling the warmth of her body next to his, knowing it would be there again tomorrow night, and the night after… he couldn't quite force himself to feel bad about staying back. Not now. Now when he had things to accomplish at home.

There was a new number one goal. Family.

"Yeah. I'm great."

Chapter 18

SKYE SANK DOWN ON THE COUCH AND RAN A HAND OVER HER completely frizzed hair. Defeated. She was completely defeated... by an appliance. How pathetic. The thick, choking smoke from the last batch of ruined cookies still filled the air, despite having opened all the downstairs windows and fanning the air with a clean cookie sheet. The only clean sheet left.

On the upside, she now knew how to turn off the smoke detector.

This should not be so hard. Women made cookies from scratch every day. Hell, *children* made cookies. How could someone with a college education who had worked in restaurants since she was eighteen not be able to make a freaking cookie? This wasn't rocket science.

She sat back and brushed hair out of her face, then picked up the discarded hair clip and pinned her frizzed out curls up, fighting back tears.

The outfit she'd put on was already wet with perspiration, thanks to standing in the hot-as-Hades kitchen all day. The house wasn't even remotely clean yet. She'd burned or ruined every batch of treats so far. And her own stubborn self hadn't bothered to buy pre-made food since she was determined to get it right from scratch. Because, hey, anybody can read directions and follow them, right? But Betty Crocker, she was not. More like Betty Full of Crock. If there was time to run to the store and still get everything finished that she needed to, she would have.

This coffee was turning into an utter disaster, and it was still two hours before showtime. At this point, all she had to offer the ladies was, literally, coffee.

Skye eyed her cell with renewed hope, wondering if she could beg Tim to buy some cookies and bring them back so she could finish cleaning before the women arrived. Somehow, that felt like cheating.

Visions of a dozen women standing in her living room nibbling on black cookies and grimacing filled her mind.

Oh, to hell with cheating. She picked up the phone and called his cell, only to reach voice mail.

Skye was debating whether it was better to have food, but a disgusting kitchen, or a squeaky-clean kitchen and no food when the front door opened.

"What the hell is—is that smoke? Skye! Where are you? Are you okay?"

"I'm on the couch." Why was her husband home? She'd banished him hours ago to Dwayne's apartment— who was set to leave the next day—to have a guys' night.

"Did something burn? Was there a fire?" He rounded the corner at a jog and spotted her on the couch, stopping in his tracks when there were no flames to battle or damsels to save.

"Oh. Something burned. Repeatedly." Admitting failure was not one of her best qualities, but she sucked it up in the name of the coffee. "Tim, could you run out and grab a few dozen cookies? I seem to have ruined every batch I made… along with a few cookie sheets."

"Hmm. I wondered how this would go when you said

you don't bake very much but insisted to do it all from scratch. I'll be right back." He turned around and left.

Yeah. She didn't bake. It was the twenty-first century, for the love of feminism. Prepackaged food and supermarkets existed for a reason. Betty Crocker was a masochist.

It occurred to her she hadn't told him what kind of cookies to get, but at this point it didn't matter. Having something—anything—edible was better than an empty table and smoky air to breathe.

Tim came back two minutes later holding two bags. He let one bag drop gently into her lap, the sound of crunching plastic piquing her curiosity. She looked in and found what appeared to be several containers of fresh-baked cookies from a local bakery.

She snuck a look at him out the corner of her eye. "You don't by any chance have little elves that live in your car and make baked goodies all day, do you? 'Cause I thought they lived in trees in the woods and only came out to make commercials."

Tim shrugged. "I figured they'd be good for the guys and me to gorge on tonight. And in the event that you needed some backup," he added with a kiss on the top of her head, "as even the best of chefs do, they would come in handy. Just arrange them on a plate and say they're a family specialty. My mom pulled this trick once or twice when she ran out of time and had unexpected guests. That's where I got the idea."

"This is great. Thank you." She fought back grateful tears and gave him a rueful smile. "But what do I do with the smell? The worst of the smoke will die down soon, of course, but it might linger."

"Ah. Now this one, I'm taking credit for." He handed her the other bag, much heavier than the first. She reached in and pulled out two candles.

"Cookie-scented candles?" she asked with a laugh.

"Yup. I'll bring the fans down here, get some of the smoke moving out, and then light those suckers about an hour before people get here." He looked pleased with himself, as well he should be.

Skye set everything on the table and stood up, launching herself into his arms. He caught her, like she knew he would, and squeezed tight.

"Thank you," she murmured into his neck. "Thank you, thank you, thank you."

"Anytime," he replied, and she burst into tears.

"Hey, hey. What's this?" Scooting to the couch, he pulled her down into his lap. One hand smoothed her hair while the other rubbed up and down her arm.

"I just… I can't… and I couldn't… and I hate it… stupid cookies!" she wailed.

Tim chuckled, the sound a rumble in his chest. "I'm going to pretend I understood that. It's okay. We all need some help every so often." He rocked her a little, the gentle nonsense murmurs he whispered going a long way to calming her down.

Skye gave a watery laugh. "I can't believe how worked up I got over cookies."

"It happens." Tim pressed a kiss to her temple. "You just got too fixated on one thing and let it consume you. Step back and do the big picture thing for a while. It'll be fine."

"I'm not a perfect hostess."

"No. But you're a perfect Skye. And people like you,

they enjoy being around you. So just let it go. Put out the cookies, light the candles, and try to have fun. Everyone else will follow your lead. And if they don't, then they don't know what they're missing."

"You're good for my ego, Timothy O'Shay." She tilted her face up for a sweet kiss.

"You're good for me, Skye McDermott."

The words warmed her from the inside and lodged a not-so-small lump in her throat. Standing, she made a good show of straightening the outfit she would have to change out of anyway and cleared her throat. "You should go. Jeremy and Dwayne must be waiting for you."

He gave her an assessing glance but said nothing as he stood and walked to the door. "Call me if you need anything else. I'll be here for you."

"Yes, you would," Skye whispered as Tim shut the door. "That's what you do."

—⁂—

"So how goes the marital bliss?" Jeremy asked as Tim sat down in the recliner.

"Great. Fantastic. Couldn't be happier." Tim shot him a *shut the hell up* look and took the beer Dwayne passed him. "You might try it sometime."

Jeremy scoffed. "Being married?"

"Being happy," Tim shot back. "You've been moping like a girl dumped the day before prom for weeks now. What the hell is your problem these days?"

"How about you mind your own problems?" Jeremy growled.

"Ladies, ladies. How about you both shut the fuck

up?" Dwayne paused the movie. "Not to be all *look at me* here, but damn. We're supposed to be having a last guys' night before I take off. Can you just stop bitching at each other? Save it for when I'm gone." His speech concluded, he hit play.

There was silence for a moment while they watched Optimus Prime and Megatron battle.

"Where's the food?" Jeremy asked finally.

"I had a small delay at home," Tim said. "So I asked Madison to bring it over in exchange for some handyman work around her place and a few slices of pizza."

"Good idea. Let her stay for a bit," Dwayne said. "I'll miss the rugrat, and with her work schedule I don't know if I'll get to say good-bye again."

"It's guys' night." Jeremy shifted in his seat and scowled.

"Dude. It's just Madison. I'm not inviting a harem up here." Dwayne gave him a quizzical look.

Jeremy grumbled about the sacred theory of male bonding and how women were the ruin of all things good. But the moment the doorbell rang, he jumped up. "I'll go get it."

Tim settled further back in his armchair. "What crawled up his ass and died?"

Dwayne shook his head. "It's Jeremy. You know he broods sometimes. He gets all… introverted and shit. Dude spends too much time in his own head." D used air quotes around the word *introverted* and grinned.

"I know he broods, but damn." He waited to hear Madison's voice coming down the hall but heard nothing. "Must not have been the squirt. Our ears would be bleeding by now with all her chatter."

"Might be the hot piece across the hall. I caught a glimpse of her earlier," Dwayne said with a smile.

"You leave in a day," Tim reminded him.

"Always good to remember there are things worth fighting for."

———⟋⟍⟍⟍⟍⟍⟋———

"Delivery, fresh from the ov—oh. Jeremy." Madison lowered the pizza boxes, the smile sliding off her face. With his body rigid and his face an impassive mask, Jeremy was giving off the most intense *Leave. Now.* vibe she'd ever felt. Definitely not happy to see her. And here she thought that the promise of food might at least make him crack a smile.

"Tim says thanks and he owes you one." Jeremy held his hands out, his body blocking the door.

She glanced around, but there was no way to get through the door without him moving. And he definitely wouldn't budge. The message was clear… she wasn't welcome inside. But why? "Is that all Tim wanted to tell me?"

"Yup. Hand 'em over. Do we owe you cash?"

Madison narrowed her eyes. "So if I yell for Tim to come out here, he'll tell me thanks for the pizzas, now beat it?"

"All said with brotherly love, I'm sure."

Madison bent over to set the pizzas down and took a deep breath. But she didn't even get the first part of a squeak out before Jeremy's hand clamped over her mouth. He whirled her around until her back hit the outside wall of the apartment by the door.

"Well, this is a new spin on an old dance," she mumbled into his hand.

"Madison. I'm asking you to go." His eyes were fierce, his body tight and ready for a fight.

She reached up with both hands and gently tugged his hand away. It fell without resisting. "Why, Jeremy?" When he said nothing, she added, "Tell me why, and I'll go."

"Because I can't be around you. Not right now."

Madison watched his lips thin into a straight line, his jaw clench in stubborn determination. God, why did he always shut her out? Why?

"It was a kiss. We're adults; we can forget it happened," she said softly.

"Can we?"

No. She couldn't. Madison had been waiting almost ten years to know what kissing Jeremy would feel like. And the moment she got a taste, he ripped it away from her. But if it took playing it cool to be near him, even a little bit, she could act the part. "Yeah. Sure. No biggie. People kiss, they move on."

She patted his cheek in a smartass gesture, but his hand snatched hers before she could take it away. He pressed her palm to his skin. His eyes closed, as if he was creating a memory file of the moment to store away and take out later when he had more time to linger.

"Jeremy," she whispered.

He leaned in, body brushing hers, lips a breath apart when he snapped back. Snapped out of reach. Physically and emotionally.

The wall was back up. His eyes were blank, as if desire hadn't just been there. As if he wasn't fighting the same demons she was.

"Thanks for the pizza. I'll tell Tim you had things to do." He picked up the boxes and stood by the door.

She'd been dismissed. Wrapping as much dignity as she could around her like a suit of armor, she walked down the building stairs without saying good-bye.

He didn't deserve anything from her.

———∿∿———

Skye opened the door, smile plastered on her face, ready to greet the next woman who would walk through and join the coffee. The smile froze when she saw the CO's wife, Patricia Blackwater, standing on her porch holding a platter of what looked like brownies.

"Mrs. O'Shay." She nodded once.

"Mrs. Blackwater, hi. I didn't realize you would be coming." Skye stepped aside and let her through the doorway, grabbing the platter as the older woman thrust it toward her. "I'm so glad you could make it."

Did that sound sincere? Well, it was her best effort, so here's hoping.

Mrs. Blackwater stood in the entryway, not-so-subtly observing—and judging—the home. "It's nice, for a townhouse, Mrs. O'Shay."

"Please, call me Skye. Tha—"

"I prefer more space, naturally. Townhouses always just feel so… incomplete. Does that make sense?" And with that, the woman brushed past Skye and farther into the home.

"Gee, thanks for the treats. Please, join us in the living room," Skye muttered after the woman was out of earshot. Then she steeled herself against any negativity. It could only hurt the cause to get bitchy at this point. She had followed Beth's instructions to a tee, so there should be nothing to worry about.

At least now, thanks to Tim and his lifesaving cookies.

Skye followed Mrs. Blackwater into the living room to see that the social temperature had dropped about fifteen degrees. Where women had been laughing and chatting before, completely comfortable and making Skye relax with a feeling of accomplishment, the older woman's presence suddenly changed the tempo. People's conversations were quieter, or nonexistent. A few shifted uncomfortably in their seats, like they were mentally looking for an excuse to leave the room.

Skye was pretty sure that the discomfort had nothing to do with Mrs. Blackwater being the CO's wife and everything to do with Mrs. Blackwater just being herself, period.

"Ladies, gather around," Patricia called, clapping her hands together briskly like she was getting the attention of a group of ADHD kindergarteners. She took the large armchair for herself, like a queen sitting on her rightful throne. She sat down on the edge, with as little of her body actually touching the seat as possible. Then she pulled out a thick binder and a pen and waited, an annoyed, expectant look on her face. Women slowly sat down on the couch and in the folding chairs and kitchen chairs placed around the room. A few even sat on the floor.

Suzanna—another of Skye's favorite wives, and her guardian angel for the evening—paused at the refreshment table. "The queen has spoken," she murmured in Skye's ear and gave her a wink before heading into the living room.

Thank God it wasn't just her. Someone else had validated her opinion of the Head Bitch in Charge.

Skye managed to fit the platter of brownies onto the kitchen table, grabbed a cup of tea for herself, and headed in. Exactly what was going on, she had no clue. Please, God, let this not be something like baby showers where people played embarrassing games.

Mrs. Blackwater tapped the tip of her pen rhythmically against the binder's hard plastic cover until all the women were seated in a circle, waiting for the queen to speak.

"Well. First off, let us thank Skye O'Shay for her quick work to step in and host this coffee for us. She went above and beyond for a new wife."

The words were right, but the woman's tone couldn't be any farther from sincere if she tried. Skye bit her tongue on correcting the woman on her last name while there were polite, soft claps. Suzanna nudged her with a shoulder as a silent congratulations.

"Now let's get down to business. As we all know, Charlie Company will be deploying tomorrow. That means a few of you will now be husbandless for the next several months. Charlie wives, please raise your hand. Not all are here, naturally. But a few. Everyone look around and see your fellow wives who will need your support."

Skye glanced around and saw a few women with their hands up. Nobody was teary-eyed. Nobody sniffled or sobbed. There was simply a grim acceptance in their body language, steel in their spine, and determination written on their faces. These women weren't ones to need their hand held often. Her respect for the women in the room grew exponentially.

"Thank you, ladies. We will try to wrap up as

soon as possible to get you home to spend time with your families."

As Mrs. Blackwater continued on about the changes from the entire battalion deploying to now only having one company gone and what that could signal for a spouse, Skye's mind drifted. What would it be like if Tim were the one leaving instead? He almost had been the one taking off. How would she feel, losing him for months at a time? Would she be stoic in the face of a deployment like these women? Or would her emotional side get the better of her? Likely a bit of both.

But she hated the thought of him leaving at all. They were just getting started on this life journey of marriage. To lose him again for so long would be cruel. Thank goodness he was sticking around, at least for now.

"And that concludes the official business, unless anyone else has anything to add. No? Well, then. Now for the good stuff." A wicked gleam came over Mrs. Blackwater's eyes as she leaned forward. "Did anyone see the base CO's wife at the fund-raiser last week? If not, you missed something good. The woman was dressed in this ridiculous outfit. She—"

Skye popped up, completely unwilling to sit through a woman-hating session, even if it was a one-woman show. "I'm sorry to interrupt, Mrs. Blackwater. Does anyone need a refill or want another plate?"

A few women glanced her way, and she thought she saw gratitude in their eyes. Several held up their hands, asking for more tea or coffee.

"A plate of treats wouldn't be unwelcome, sweetie," Mrs. Blackwater called without making eye contact.

"Sure thing," Skye said, using her best *you're the*

customer so you have to be right, but mentally I'm kick-ing your ass to Kentucky voice. She turned toward the kitchen, orders mentally filed.

"I'll give you a hand with those." Suzanna popped up and shuffled around the chairs and women to get to the kitchen.

Once in the privacy of the kitchen, Suzanna started giggling. In a low voice she said, "Nice work. Almost none of us likes to listen to that woman go on about who she saw wearing what or doing whatever in the com-missary. But she does anyway. And nobody can figure out how to shut her up without enduring her wrath or worrying if she'll take it out on *our* husbands through *her* husband."

Skye nodded, understanding completely. But still, she tried for diplomacy. "It must be hard, being the CO's wife. I mean, her husband is in charge of our husbands, so maybe it's difficult for her to figure out how to fit in."

Suzanna snorted and started making up paper plates of veggies and dip. "The last CO's wife was seriously kick-ass cool. She never gossiped, she never spoke about anyone behind their backs, and she was always the first one in line to help out the new spouse. She even showed up to help me paint my living room when I mentioned offhand that I was going to start the next day. Trust me, it's the individual, not the job description. And that individual is… something else." She pointed toward the living room with a celery stick.

Once again, no shocker to Skye. Though the military community was new to her, the general rule of thumb about treating others as you wanted to be treated seemed to apply. She gathered the tray of refilled drinks and hefted it up. "Ready to go back into battle?"

Suzanna grinned and followed her in just in time to catch the tail end of some story Mrs. Blackwater was gracing everyone with.

"And I just thought to myself, 'Flip-flops? Who wears flip-flops in public? And to the exchange no less? They're so tacky!'" Mrs. Blackwater tossed her head back and laughed.

Skye watched as the wife sitting directly to Mrs. Blackwater's right flushed and tucked her feet—which had adorable jeweled flip-flops on—as far under her seat as possible. Poor thing.

"Cookies and tea, get 'em while they're hot!" Skye announced cheerfully, setting the tray down on the coffee table so everyone could reach for their cup or a plate.

Mrs. Blackwater sat back, a bakery cookie in one clawed hand. She took a bite and made a shocked face.

"These are delicious, Skye. I have to say I didn't take you to be the baking sort. Too... domestic for your type, if you know what I mean."

Skye knew exactly what she meant. But she resisted flipping her the bird as thanks.

"You'll need to give me your recipe."

It was all she could do to hold back the snort of laughter. "Sorry. Family secret. I was sworn to secrecy." Before the woman could launch into another tirade on an unsuspecting victim, Skye asked, "Has anyone seen the new movie that just came out? The one with that singer-turned-actress... oh what's her name?"

"I did!" the woman wearing flip-flops all but shouted and jumped out of her chair with gratitude.

"You did? Did you like it? Oh man. I can't decide if it's a good date night movie for us or not."

She could almost hear the audible group sigh of relief as women settled back into their chairs, getting comfortable. If nothing else, she would consider this moment of group happiness a triumph in her first coffee.

"You did great. I'm really impressed." Suzanna tied off a garbage bag and hauled it to the corner of the kitchen.

"Thanks. But you didn't have to stay and help," Skye protested for the fifth time.

"I know how quickly the mess piles up," she said, opening another garbage bag with a flick of her wrists and a pop of plastic. "And we're all grateful that you could have us last-minute. These coffees can be really great for wives to meet each other and bond. A good way to make friends for those who are new to the area. So when you stepped in to pick up the responsibility, we were relieved."

"I was just doing a favor for a friend. It was no big deal," Skye said and thought about the devoured plate of cookies. She bit back a smile as she set dishes in the sink to wash later. "I've never been to one of these before, but it was nice."

"They can be," Suzanna agreed, sitting down in a kitchen chair. "All depends on the group of women, just like most things. Too many pissy cats and the group starts to fall apart. But often they can be a great night with girls. This is a pretty good group."

Skye said nothing.

"The good thing is that the Blackwaters will be taking

off soon enough. Commands come and go. We'll get another CO, and here's hoping they're a little more relaxed this time."

"Hmm," Skye said noncommittally as she put the leftover iced tea back in the fridge.

Suzanna had shown up fifteen minutes early and declared herself Skye's ambassador for the evening. In other words, a guardian angel sent by Beth to smooth the way. Skye couldn't have been more grateful if she'd fallen on the woman's feet and kissed them.

Suzanna sighed and slid into a chair. "I have work in the morning, but I'm so not ready to go home and face the brood quite yet."

"Where do you work?"

"Manager at a bank." She named the chain. "It's nice, there's one almost everywhere we go. So far, I haven't had any trouble moving into a new job when we PCSed."

With quick side glances, Skye studied the graceful woman at the kitchen table. In a halter-style dress with soft pastel washes of color, she was the epitome of everything Skye was hoping to emulate and had no chance of coming close. But she was sure as hell going to give it her best shot.

Suzanna lifted the hair off the back of her neck, and Skye caught sight of a small tattoo just below the hairline. Completely covered when she wore her hair down, the tattoo was tiny and likely very personal. She didn't ask. But it did make her smile.

Chapter 19

Suzanna left a few minutes later with the promise of calling. As Skye walked her to the door, she noticed another car sitting in front of the house. A closer inspection told her it was Madison's.

While Suzanna drove away, Skye stood on the front porch waiting patiently. Finally Madison opened the door and trudged up the driveway. A prisoner walking the last mile couldn't have looked more depressed.

"Hey." She threw her arm around Madison's shoulders. "What's with the mope? Did your dog die?"

"No, not my dog. My dream," Madison muttered.

Skye could easily guess what that was referring to, and her heart hurt for her new sister. "Okay, that's it. You're coming in and we're having a bitchfest." When Madison paused in the doorway, Skye added, "I have leftover brownies... and booze." That seemed to convince her. Skye shut the door behind them and walked her to the living room.

"How did you know I needed to bitch about something?" Madison asked as she flopped down on the couch.

"You just have the look. You want something to drink?" Skye floated to the kitchen.

"If you're referring to water, the answer is no. If you mean something with a kick, bring it on."

Skye smiled as she mixed two rum and Cokes, heavy on the Coke. Bringing out the glasses, along with a plate of Blackwater brownies, she sat down next to Madison and propped her feet on the couch. She waited, taking slow sips until Madison was ready.

It didn't take long.

"Why? Why are men so stupid?"

Having just been on the receiving end of an extremely thoughtful act by a male, Skye wisely kept her mouth shut.

"They say no, they mean yes. They show yes, then they act all no." Madison waved her arm around, liquid sloshing close to the rim. Skye reached for the glass.

"I'll take this so you don't spill."

"Mine," Madison all but growled and downed the drink in three quick gulps. Skye mentally cringed. Madison held out the empty cup. "Any more in the kitchen?" Before Skye could answer, she stood. "Never mind. I'll pour my own." She shuffled into the kitchen then right back out again, holding the bottle of rum and liter of Coke. Sitting back down, she poured another glass of rum and Coke. Heavy on the rum this time.

"Okay, time to talk before you start slurring," Skye decided. "I need more information than just how much men suck."

Madison took a fortifying gulp and sat back, resting the glass on her abdomen. "This might come as a shock, but I've got this... thing for Jeremy."

Skye snorted before she could stop herself. When Madison gave her a dry look, she said, "Sorry." Then taking another tiny sip of her own drink, she waved with her hand for Madison to continue.

"As I was saying, I've had a crush on him for God

knows how long. I think since I met him, even though I was only like sixteen, maybe seventeen at the time. Not surprisingly, he didn't notice me at all. I mean, he was graduating TBS. Different places in life. But now, in the same place at the same time, with both of us being unattached adults, I thought maybe…"

A lifetime of hope hung in that one word.

Madison blew out a breath and drained her glass, leaning forward to fill it up once more. Skye debated telling her to slow down, but then thought, *What's the point?* Madison was a big girl. She'd just take her keys and make sure she crashed in the guest room.

"One minute he hates me. Wants nothing to do with me. Pushes me away. Then the next he's practically pawing me, slamming me into walls so he can—" she gestured with her glass again, now thankfully half-empty, "you know. The good stuff." She slammed the rest of the drink back.

"Um, do you want something to eat?" *Please say yes.*

"Not hungry." As Tim's sister leaned forward to grab the Coke, her first swipe turned up air. "Damn bottle moved," she muttered and nabbed it on the second try.

"Madison, you're already on your way to Drunkville. Should you maybe slow down a bit?" Skye pried the glass out of her lax fingers and set it down.

"Not Drunkville. Tipsy Town, maybe," Madison corrected with careful diction. "Tipsy Town. What a stupid thing to say…"

"How can you be drunk off of three glasses?"

"Oh, hell. I'm a buck-ten and I didn't eat dinner," she responded with clarity that should have eluded her, pouring drink number four. "Bastard stole my dinner on top of everything. I'm not a lush, you know. I just want to forget. For the moment, that's all."

Since Skye knew she wouldn't be driving, and was pretty sure Madison wouldn't become a destructive or violent drunk, she saw no reason for the poor girl not to indulge the whim for the night. She'd likely pay for it in the morning, anyway. "Tell me more about the problem with Jeremy," she prompted, relaxing back and taking another sip.

"Telling is not forgetting. But what the hell." Madison stood up then, pacing in front of the coffee table. After a moment, she stopped and turned her too-bright eyes to Skye. "You know, I see why you pace when you're angry. It really helps the thoughts flow, doesn't it?" Before Skye could respond, she went back to pacing and talking. "Jeremy wants to pretend that there's no attraction between us. I don't know why; it's no small thing. There are times I want to just shove him in the first available room with a door and rip his clothes off. And then the rest of the time I want to beat his head with a skillet."

Skye couldn't hold back the laughter then. "Sounds completely natural."

"There are times that I hate him so much because of how he treats me. And those times I wish I wasn't hating him. Because hatred is too much for him, too much energy. He drains me when I'm around him. But then there are the other times when I almost wonder if I love him. If my childish crush wasn't just a warm-up for the real deal.

"And it's impossible to figure out what he's thinking, or why he's acting the way he is," Madison went on.

"He's always so quiet and reserved. Which normally I find immensely sexy—though God knows why. He's a brooder. And I hate brooding. But on him, the quietness is somehow, I don't know. It's magnetic. Like it's just inviting me to try to learn his secrets. Like he won't share them with anyone but..."

"Someone he loves?" Skye supplied.

Madison's eyes wandered the living room, and if she'd heard Skye's question, she didn't show it. "Why haven't I kicked any dirty laundry?" She turned a tight circle, like a dog chasing its tail. "Where's all your magazines? Where are the candles?"

"I cleaned up before the coffee," Skye said gently. "Along with buying the new wardrobe."

"Ah." Madison gave Skye a blurry-eyed once-over. "This looks more like Tim. More like how I pictured it being with him. This whole... thing." She waved her arms around the room wildly.

Something cold slithered down Skye's spine. "What do you mean?"

Madison filled a fifth glass—mostly with Coke, to Skye's relief—and continued pacing. But slower this time, taking in the surroundings. She ran a finger along the mantel, pausing to trace a picture frame. Her movements were languid, as if she moved underwater.

"How I pictured marriage. For Tim, anyway. Easy, neat. A place for everything, and everything in its place, including his wife. You look like you belong here, in this room, in that outfit."

Skye wondered if Madison even realized she was talking out loud. She sat perfectly still, not wanting to break her sister-in-law's train of thought.

"I just always thought he would find a wife very much like him. One that would slip into his life almost unnoticed. Stealth. Just make herself at home, as if she'd always been there. No waves. No worries. That's who he's always dated in the past. Female versions of Tim. Straight-laced, understanding of the Corps and its hold on his life, steadfast."

Something clawed the inside of Skye's gut, and she set the glass down quietly.

"He found you instead." Madison turned now, a glazed look in her eyes, loopy smile pasted to her face. "You like incense. And clutter. Clutter is fun, right?"

The way Madison's head tilted, Skye assumed the question wasn't rhetorical. "Uh huh. Fun." She stood and took the glass from Madison's fingers. "You know what else is fun? Sleeping."

"Mmm. Yeah." Madison didn't resist as Skye took her hand and led her up the stairs, supervised as she readied for the night, and tucked her into the guest bed.

"Female Tim never would have let me drink," Madison murmured as she started to drift off.

"I doubt it," Skye whispered back. Female Tim seemed infinitely smarter than her. She set a trash can by the bed in case, though she doubted Madison would need it. With one last check to make sure she was breathing fine, Skye left her to sleep off the rum and pain.

Skye headed back downstairs to clean up the small mess. Normally, she wouldn't mind leaving the entire thing until the next day. Especially not when she was so tired. But something about having Tim come home to a ripped up kitchen and living room made her finish the task. Just another thing she needed to start doing regularly.

She debated calling Tim to see how long he would be out with Jeremy and Dwayne but decided against it. Instead, she put on a pair of his old boxer shorts, an older T-shirt, and crawled into bed. With the thoughts swimming through her mind, Skye was positive she'd be awake for hours. But within minutes she was drifting.

Hours later, Skye woke to cold hands on her abdomen and a warm body pressing against her back. She looked over her shoulder, eyes adjusting to the silvery moonlight creeping in through the slats in the blinds.

"Hey," Tim whispered. His lips moved over her jawline, neck, lower. "I wondered if you'd need help cleaning up, but you're already done."

Skye checked the clock and saw it was barely midnight. When had she started going to bed so early? "I didn't want to leave the mess for later."

Between kisses, Tim murmured, "Madison's car is outside."

She gave up on going back to sleep and rolled over onto her back. "She had too much to drink so she's in the guest bedroom."

Tim's head lifted at that, a slight scowl on his face. "Why was she drinking so much?"

The truth wasn't hers to give, so Skye evaded. "She just got a little carried away. No big deal."

Tim's scowl deepened. "That's not amusing. She should have been more careful."

Skye sighed inwardly. "She was with someone she trusted and she wasn't driving. I made her drink an entire glass of water before she went to sleep and put her to bed on her side. I don't know how much more careful you can get."

"Drinking to excess really is never smart," the walking safety pamphlet responded. "People act like idiots when they drink like that."

Never smart. Act like idiots. The entire reason they were married was because Tim had been too drunk to realize the big step he was making that night in Vegas. And now he wanted to say that it was never a good idea? She shifted once again onto her side, her back toward Tim. Hopefully he would get the hint and drop it before she snarled at him.

"Dwayne wants you to come to the send-off tomorrow," he whispered in her ear, taking a nip out of the skin beneath her lobe. "If you're not working, that is. So do I."

Okay, she couldn't be silent when he said stuff like that. "Did he have fun tonight?"

"Yup. Simple guys' night in. He's ready to get out there. He thrives on deployment."

Skye could hardly imagine someone who could thrive in a war, but she didn't say so. Tim continued his slow meander over her neck, her ear, her jaw. When she didn't respond—with words or action—he spoke again.

"Is something wrong?"

Not according to you, apparently. She sighed and shifted onto her back again, looking in his eyes. His look was sweet, concerned. But all the same, confused. Just like a man. Time to give the guy a break.

Only that I've been busy falling for my husband, and I'm pretty sure he's not falling with me. "Nope. Nothing." She smiled, determined not to bother him with her own rising insecurities. Neuroticism was never attractive.

Tim looked at her another long moment, then shifted behind to pull her back against his chest. His hand moved idly over her stomach, rubbing slow circles over her top until he came to rest under her breast. Her nipples hardened, despite her annoyance. Damn man and his ability to get her going no matter what.

"I missed you tonight." His voice was low, husky.

"You had a good reason to go out." She gave up resisting and nuzzled back against him. His hand pulled her shirt up over her breasts until he thumbed her nipples. They tightened painfully and her breathing quickened.

"Doesn't mean I didn't miss you. And this." Suddenly she was missing one pair of shorts. The man was slick. He pulled her top leg until it lifted up and back, over his own hip. Spreading her wide for his touch. His finger grazed over her warm center and she shivered.

His fingers played her until she was panting. Grazing her clit, never staying long on the spot she wanted him most.

"Relax, baby." His voice was a whisper over her ear.

She couldn't relax. Because when she relaxed, she fell harder. And it hurt.

The blunt head of his cock pushed against her wet folds, insistent and demanding until he was completely seated inside her. His grip was hard, almost harsh, moving her hips until she was exactly where he wanted her.

She arched her back to make the most of the tight angle, not giving a rip that he chuckled at her sudden turnabout.

"More." The embarrassing plea escaped before she could stop it. But he answered with a shallow thrust that made up for any mortification and more. The controlled, narrow space made deep thrusts impossible, but the friction was intense. Soon, too soon, Skye felt that tightening in her belly and reached down for his hand.

Touch me. The request was silent as she guided him to her, but he understood perfectly. And then her body sang as her nerves fizzled and her muscles clenched around him, milking her husband's own climax until he went completely limp behind her.

"Good," was all he could mumble into her neck. She chuckled and nodded.

His hand came up to rub between her breasts. The touch was soothing rather than sexual, and soon enough Skye heard his breathing change to the low, deep rhythm that said he was asleep.

Though she had been dead asleep not long ago, Skye spent the next few hours battling back the thoughts that worked their way through her mind.

"Are you positive Dwayne wanted us here to say goodbye?" Skye couldn't shake the feeling that somehow she was in the way. Didn't belong there.

"Yes. Wait here for a few minutes while I go help them load bags up." He gave her waist a quick squeeze then jogged over to the two charter buses. Somehow, even compared to the multitude of Marines in their cammies, he looked intimidating. Important. Alpha in his simple polo shirt and khakis.

With nothing to do—and not wanting to wander around and get in the way—Skye took in her surroundings instead. There were crying women everywhere.

Little children clung to cameo-clad legs. Hugs.
Whispers. Promises. Kisses.

She felt almost like an intruder on dozens of intimate
marital moments while she watched the Marines of D's
company say their good-byes. But she had nowhere else
to look. Though nobody seemed to mind her presence anyway, as wrapped up in their own embraces as they were.

She looked for Tim and still found him busy loading
bags into the cargo hold of the buses on some makeshift
assembly line. Nothing to do but continue being a fly
on the wall.

The vast difference in emotions was the most interesting. A few wives looked almost bored, as if saying
good-bye was just routine. No big deal. Maybe to them
it was. Depressing thought. Others wept, uncaring who
witnessed their sorrow. The ones who cracked Skye's
heart were the women who refused to show weakness,
no matter how it hurt. They stiffened their spines, rolled
back their shoulders, and said their good-byes with dry
eyes. But as those women turned away from the buses,
she could see their lips tremble, their hands shake, their
eyes blink away tears.

To Skye's surprise, one man said his farewell to
his wife before she boarded. Just a small reminder
that the military wasn't as cookie-cutter as she'd
previously thought.

"I'm pleased to see you supporting our deploying
Marines."

Skye gasped and turned, startled by the voice. "Mrs.
Blackwater. You scared me." *In more ways than one.*
She rubbed a hand over her galloping heart.

"I'm sorry, sweetheart." Mrs. Blackwater gave her a

small, almost sad smile as she turned back to watch the boarding. "Heartbreaking to watch, isn't it? No matter how many times you go through it yourself, or see others go through it… never gets easier." She heaved a small sigh, as if remembering a distant memory. Probably the last time she'd had to watch her own husband leave.

Skye nodded. Interesting. She didn't expect such compassion from the older woman. Perhaps that was her fault. Maybe she'd misjudged—

"Oh for the love… Would you just look at that?" The woman thrust a finger toward a young, very pregnant woman clinging desperately to her Marine. Mascara leaked down her cheeks as she let out a stifled wail. He pulled gently on his arm, but she only dug her heels in, gripping harder. They might have to get a crowbar for that one.

Skye couldn't blame her for being upset. Clearly, her husband would miss the birth of their child. How hard. She couldn't even imagine—

"Someone needs to slap some sense into her. She's causing a scene. This is completely unacceptable." Mrs. Blackwater shook her head and walked toward her husband standing to the side. Most likely to file an Overly Emotional in Public report.

The witch.

Okay. Apparently her initial judgment wasn't so far off to begin with.

"Sucks, huh?" Madison walked up and laid her head on Skye's shoulder. "I'm not gonna cry this time. I swore to myself this time I wouldn't—"

"You always cry. It's how I know you'll miss me," Dwayne said as he ambled up.

With an almost-silent sob, Madison launched herself at D, wrapping her arms around him. "You big dumbass," she choked out into his shoulder. "Of course I won't miss you."

"Of course not," D crooned, his honey-sweet voice soothing even as it gently teased. "I won't miss you either."

Madison sniffed. "'Kay." As she stepped back, Skye took her place in the giant's embrace.

"Stay safe."

"No problem. We'll rarely even step outside the wire. They never let us have any fun." With one last squeeze, she let him go.

Tim slapped him on the back, a manly sign of affection appropriate for public. "Don't do anything I wouldn't do."

"Shit. Now I *really* won't have any fun." D grappled Tim into a bear hug, then pulled Jeremy in for the ultimate bonding moment. "Try not to be bored without me."

"Jesus. I think you cracked my spine." Jeremy rolled his shoulders but smiled. "I doubt boredom will be a problem. Besides, maybe Tim and I will be right behind you."

"Just what Afghanistan needs." With a grin and a handshake for the guys, he jogged to the buses, thick boots thudding on the parking lot pavement.

Maybe Tim and I will be right behind you. The words echoed in her mind as the bus engines roared to life. Tim stood behind her, and she leaned back just a little until she could feel him. Reassure herself he was still with her. For now.

But eventually his time would come. Sooner or later,

he would deploy. She couldn't delude herself into ignoring that fact. And she would be one of the women left behind, saying tearful good-byes. The knowledge that the day would come had been there, somewhere in the deep recesses of her mind.

But now, watching it live, the veil had truly been lifted. This was her life. Could she handle it?

She'd have to.

Chapter 20

TIM STUCK HIS HEAD THROUGH THE CRACKED DOOR OF THE office. "Sir? You asked to see me?"

Colonel Blackwater waved him in without looking up. "O'Shay, good. Come on in; just give me a minute to finish this up."

Tim edged in, taking a seat in front of the massive oak desk in the CO's office. While the Colonel finished flipping through the paperwork, Tim glanced around from the corner of his eye.

Rows of plaques and frames holding awards were lined on the walls, covering almost every inch of space. Several shadow boxes containing ribbons and medals sat on bookshelves or on top of file cabinets. A healthy, vibrant spider plant sat in the corner next to the big window. Probably watered by the administrative assistant, Tim thought. Blackwater didn't seem like much for what anyone would call a *domestic task*. Too feminine.

"So." Colonel Blackwater's voice cracked through the silence, jolting Tim back. "How's life?"

That's what he was called away for? He left the rifle range early because the Colonel wanted to chew the fat? No, there was more to this. Tim approached the question with caution. And he hated that, at any point, he had to question his boss' motivation.

"Training went well, sir. Only two failed to qualify today at the range, though it was a near miss both times. I'm sure tomorrow's reshoot will see one hundred percent."

Blackwater sat back and crossed one ankle over his knee, hands laced on his stomach. A casual pose, if someone was only paying half attention. Tim wasn't fooled. The man was a study in underhandedness.

"Not what I meant, Captain, though I think you know that. How is life? How's marriage treating you?"

Shit. And once again, the Colonel trapped him into personal talk. Tim hated bringing home with him to the office. Often refused to do so. It was nobody's business, period, what went on in a Marine's home. As long as what happened at home didn't affect the Marine's job performance, he never saw a need to discuss it. But try saying that to a superior officer.

"Things are going well, sir. Marriage is... better than I expected."

Blackwater stared at him, waiting for more. When Tim didn't continue, he sighed heavily. "O'Shay, you're going to make me drag it out of you, aren't you?"

Yes. Tooth and nail. "No. I'm just not sure what you're looking for, sir."

"Does your wife support your career?"

Jesus. How was it any of the man's business? "She supports me." He realized, as he said it, it wasn't just some bullshit evasive answer. It was the truth. Regardless of her feelings about the military, she supported him. And that was enough for Tim.

The Colonel leaned forward and flipped a picture frame around to face Tim. Tim glanced at it. It was the Blackwaters, much younger, standing in front of an American flag.

"This was taken the day I pinned on my Captain bars. My wife was behind me every step of the way, without fail. Setting up house, breaking it down before a move. Hosting spouse events, mixing and mingling with other wives. Foregoing a career so she could concentrate on supporting mine. Keeping the home fires burning, so to speak."

So far, it sounded much like his own mother's life. And almost word-for-word what Tim had always expected in a wife.

"The saying is true, that behind every good man is a good woman." Blackwater chuckled.

"Why not next to every man?" Tim murmured before he could think twice.

"Come again?"

"Nothing," Tim said quickly.

The Colonel was quiet a moment. "My wife said she was pleasantly surprised by Mrs. O'Shay's hosting abilities. She's had… concerns. But your wife stepped up to the plate and delivered, as it seems. And also showed some good support during the send-off the other day. She's coming around nicely. So congratulations to you."

"You mean congratulations to my wife. For hosting a successful event."

Blackwater chuckled. "No, you. I had my doubts, I'll admit. When I met your wife at the barbeque, I thought, 'No, this won't work.' I thought you'd shot your foot off with your choice. Knowing you're a career man, I just didn't see what the benefit was having a wife like that."

A wife like that. A slow rage simmered in Tim's gut. How many years would he get in the brig for choking a lieutenant colonel? Too many. He kept his face carefully blank and let the CO have his say. His stupid, judgmental say.

"Turns out I was wrong. Yup, I can admit it when I am. I was wrong. You brought her to heel after all, and in quick time, too."

Brought her to heel. Like a fucking dog. Tim bit his tongue. Every man was entitled his opinion, ignorant as it was. Tim didn't have to agree with them. God, sometimes it sucked to be forced to follow orders.

The older man leaned forward, elbows on his desk, and dropped his voice a notch. "I know some people would say I'm old-fashioned for thinking this, but that's not my problem. The fact is, I think a spouse has everything to do with how far a Marine will go in his career. Wrong wife can be a death sentence to your military dreams."

The statement wasn't even close to surprising for Tim. Many still believed that a wife's "performance" was actually recorded on the military member's service record. Completely false in this day and age, but the myth still persisted. And some felt it did matter. Hell, he used to. He used to think the type of woman he married mattered a great deal. Skye shot that one to shit. And thank God for it.

Colonel Blackwater was well known for his emphasis on "good, core family values." Family values were great. But what Blackwater really meant was every man was to bring home the bacon and every woman was to stay home, barefoot and pregnant, baking pies. Tim almost laughed at the thought of Skye chained to the oven, baking anything other than a disaster in the kitchen. Then the thought of her pregnant flitted through his mind, and he felt a deep tug in his gut. Wasn't hard to identify that one. Longing. God, she would make a fantastic mother.

The CO went on, oblivious to Tim's inner thoughts. "And my wife has mentioned that if Mrs. O'Shay needs any pointers or tips, she'd be more than willing to help out. Lessons on hosting, appropriate dress, that sort of thing."

"I actually enjoy my wife's originality," Tim commented casually. "She's exactly what I needed." And he meant that.

Tim was walking a tight rope. He disagreed wholeheartedly with the Colonel's point of view. But saying so would get him nowhere. Not only would he not change the mind of a man so set in his ways, but a negative review could seriously hamper—or ruin—his hopes of staying on through twenty years.

Blackwater raised a brow but didn't comment on Tim's remark. "So I wanted to just let you know that I was pleased with your situation. You know you are setting an example for the younger Marines. And I look forward to seeing your wife again at the Dining Out next week."

Shit. He'd completely forgot to mention the event to Skye. "Right. Of course."

"You can go now."

Tim left, barely making it to his office and quietly shutting the door before letting his hands fist with anger.

The man was a certifiable jackass. But Tim had to keep reminding himself that one man wasn't the Marines. For every dipshit CO, there were five great leaders. And Blackwater would be leaving soon for a new duty station, hopefully to be replaced by a Marine who understood and appreciated the boundaries between home life and work. Who wouldn't judge Tim's performance on his wife's outfit of the day.

Tim grabbed his cover and left his office, hoping he could catch the two Marines who needed to reshoot the next day. He wanted to wrap up business and head home to his unique and perfect-for-him wife.

Skye plopped down on the couch after another exhausting—but fulfilling—work shift. Oh man, was she ever ready for a nap. Who brought their three-year-old and twelve of his friends into a fine dining restaurant for a birthday party? A parent who didn't mind that she and the staff would be scraping noodles off the ceiling for a week, clearly. Her hair still smelled like marinara sauce and garlic. She wouldn't be able to eat spaghetti for months.

She toed her shoes off and then propped her ankles on the coffee table. Then, with a sigh, she picked up the shoes and walked them to the shoe rack by the front door before resuming her seat on the couch.

When had she started caring about her shoes and where they went? Who cared if they went on the shoe rack? She was just going to put them on again in the morning. So what made her get up to put them away?

Because she now lived with a neat freak, and sometimes people needed to make adjustments and compromises to make a marriage work, she reminded herself. It was a small thing to do, and she was only being snippy because she was tired.

She hoped. Otherwise, her attitude was starting to

become a habit. And *snippy* was definitely not a personality trait she wanted to adopt.

Skye glanced up at the mantel, noticing how stark it was. Her incense and other decorations were still upstairs in a box in the guest room. Hiding. The original plan had been to replace them right away. But now that she stared at the area, she realized how uncluttered it looked. How fitting that was for Tim's home.

Compromise. The word of the day. More like the word of the year. She just had to remember it wasn't that big of a deal. Tim's house worked the way it was. She was newer, her things needed to earn their spot. Perhaps it was rude to just sort of Skye-bomb the place with all her things from the start.

Maybe eventually she could work a few of her own items into the mix. But for now, it seemed like the best thing to do to make Tim—the biggest obstacle in their own marriage—comfortable. The more comfortable he was, the easier, more relaxed he seemed with her, with their marriage. It hadn't escaped her notice at all that since the night of the Blackwater dinner, he'd been much more stress-free. His shoulders weren't tense; his face wasn't screwed up in a scowl. He could just be. And she couldn't help but think the main reason for that was her success in not embarrassing him at his boss' house, at a coffee, and just in general.

This was his life. His livelihood. His childhood dream. To be a Marine and serve his country until he retired. If it took a few years of wearing subdued clothing and keeping her goddess statues in a private room for the time being, she would survive.

Later on she could bring in the sneak-attack.

But until then, it seemed like keeping the place spotless and wearing boring outfits would have to do. She wanted this marriage to work more and more each day. She wasn't going to give up without a fight.

―⁓―

Tim walked in, expecting to find the house back to its original clutter and chaos that he'd come to accept living with Skye. Clothes on the floor, shoes in a heap in the middle of the hallway just waiting for someone to trip over them, some candle burning that he couldn't identify, music he'd never heard of before blaring. Instead, he found the place exactly as he'd left it the night before.

Pristine. Quiet. Sterile.

Had he really lived like that before? Tim glanced around the living room and dining area, marveling at how big the table looked when it wasn't covered in discarded mail, draped with a drying bra or seven magazines with various pages ripped out. The kitchen was sparkling, no hint of a mess or a burned batch of some unidentifiable who-knows-what in the oven.

It was completely devoid of all the little hints of Skye.

A ball of ice formed low in his gut, and he darted to the back door to check the patio. No Skye. He bound up the stairs before remembering her car had been outside. She was obviously still in the townhouse. He forced himself to take the second half of the stairs extra slowly to make up for his unreasonable―and completely confusing―panic. Why was he so worried she would leave?

He saw the light on in the master bedroom and breathed a silent sigh of relief. She was probably practicing some bizarre yoga pose or had placed herself in some restorative trance and hadn't heard him come home.

Instead, he found her asleep. Curled up in the middle of the bed, on top of the covers, she looked so small. And she still had her clothes from work on. Stark black pants molded to her legs, which were folded up, knees almost reaching her breasts. The white shirt was wrinkled and had some mysterious brownish-yellow stain all down one arm. But the color only served to show how pale her skin was. Not two months ago, she'd had a healthy tan, glowing from her time outside.

Was it just from the exhaustion of her day? Could one shift make someone so pale? Maybe she was coming down with something. Twenty-four-hour bug. Or had he been missing cues that she was stretching herself too thin until now?

Tim sat on the bed gently, doing his best not to wake her. One hand was contracted into a fist by her mouth, and he traced over the knuckles one at a time. Empty. Her fingers were empty. She always wore such big, chunky jewelry before. Rings so big he wondered how she could bend her fingers. Bracelets that clinked and jangled all the time and swallowed her tiny wrists.

When had she stopped wearing them? The emptiness of her hands only served as a reminder that he'd never given her a wedding band.

Nice move, dickhead.

Tim vowed to take care of it the first moment he had time.

Skye stirred, and a breathless little mewl escaped her parted lips. Tim was hard in an instant, but he was determined to let her rest. As she shifted, her face turned toward the waning afternoon light, he saw the faint darkness under her eyes.

He was going to take better care of his wife. Starting now.

Her eyes fluttered open and she stared at him, smiling a little. "Hey, you. Good day at work?"

Yeah, if you count a run-in with a jackass of a boss. "It was fine. How about you? Tiring?" He traced a finger down her cheek, heart clenching a little when her lips curved and she closed her eyes as if savoring the touch.

"You have no idea. What kind of parent brings their child to a four-star restaurant for a birthday party and expects the servers to entertain them? That's why man invented Chuck E. Cheese."

Tim chuckled and leaned over for a kiss, rearing back at the smell. "Um, did you take a bath in the restaurant Dumpster?"

She rolled her eyes and sat up. "That would be the combined effort of a dozen toddlers with little parental supervision. I eventually had to ask them to leave, then comp a dozen desserts for the poor people around them to make up for the mess and the noise."

"So, what's for dinner… spaghetti?" When she gave him the evil eye, he laughed. "I'm sorry. Couldn't resist. We can order Chinese or something."

Skye flopped back down on the pillow. He managed to hold back the wince at what her hair and clothing must be doing to the comforter. Barely. "Thank the goddess for that." She leaned over and sniffed her shoulder, grimacing. "Ug, I really should shower first."

He wasn't going to argue with that plan. But first… "Um, I might have forgotten to mention it, but there's this thing next weekend. A Dining Out. It's required for me to go, but you don't have to go. Unless you want to," he added quickly. "They can get boring and long sometimes. But one of the second lieutenants is the vice and he's actually hilarious, so it might not be so bad…" He trailed off, watching as what little color had come back to her cheeks drain out. "Honestly, you don't have to go."

"No. I'll go." She gave a smile, though it looked almost painful. "What do I need to wear?"

"I'll be in my dress uniform, so something that matches that." When she raised a brow, he shrugged. "I don't know. A dress. With sparkles?" he added as she sighed.

"How helpful. I'll call Beth and find out."

He debated how to ask the question, then just decided the hell with it. "What do you think you'll wear?"

Her eyes were averted, but he would have sworn she rolled them. "Don't worry, I won't embarrass you. I'll figure something out."

"No, that's not what I meant at all." The taste of shoe leather was not the most appealing thing. How did he possibly explain? *You don't, that's how.* Let her wear what she wanted. Regardless of what she picked, she'd look beautiful. And if it happened to be something unique and a little off the beaten path, then he would just have fun watching the Colonel's face turn tomato red and silently snicker about it.

"I'll let you shower, then we can order dinner. Sound okay?"

She mumbled something that he assumed was an agreement, plus or minus a few colorful curses. Tim turned to leave but on impulse leaned down and brushed a light kiss against her lips. Skye's eyes opened slowly, curiously.

Had he been so stingy on simple affection? Passion, sure. Burning up the sheets wasn't a problem anymore. But the easy, sweet stuff—did she miss it? He would fix that. Now.

"Or maybe we can both shower, then get some food," he murmured against her jaw.

He felt her smile. "I like that plan much better."

Tim stood at the bottom of the stairs, still not sure why he followed Skye's directions of not peeking at her outfit until it was too late. Not like she would have known if he glanced at it or anything. But it was likely the right choice. Too late now to debate how to handle whatever she chose, so regardless, he would go with the flow.

Funny how that thought didn't inspire the panic and sheer terror it did a few months ago. Going with the flow was about as natural to Tim as walking on the ceiling. But something about Skye's very nature inspired him to just let go more often. To not worry. To trust.

"Are you ready?" Skye called from upstairs.

"Sure am." Tim used the last few seconds to check in the mirror above the mantel that his ribbons were on straight. Nothing like having to use a ruler to get dressed. And for some reason, one wasn't laying flat. He frowned as he tried to even it out just a little bit more. Why tonight of all nights was it—

He stopped, breath sucked from his lungs, as he caught movement in the reflection. He turned to see

Skye standing next to the couch, hands clasped in front
of her in a very un-Skye-like pose.

Her dress was gorgeous. Strapless, it cupped her
breasts like a lover's hand, gently supporting their weight.
The neckline dipped in only slightly, giving a mere hint
of the shadow between. The midnight material molded
down her rib cage to her hips where it flared out gently to
give the hourglass illusion. The black was relieved only
by a hint of shimmer when the light hit the fabric right. A
dainty silver necklace and teardrop-shaped earrings were
her only accessories. Nothing showy, nothing flashy,
nothing that spoke of life or the vibrancy that was Skye.

But her hair—he breathed a sigh of relief—was one
hundred percent his wife. The front made it appear as
though she had tried to tame the heavy mass into submission with two clips pulling it away from her face. But
her hair knew better. Curls rioted everywhere, moving
and twisting with every slight movement of her head,
as if they had a life of their own. As if they couldn't
stay still. Tim's hands balled into loose fists, fighting
the urge to pull the pins out and let it completely free.
Let his fingers sink into the weight and hold her steady
while he reminded her exactly how submissive she really wasn't. He wanted to ask why black. Why choose
midnight, when Skye was as bright as the sun.

But instead all he said was, "You look beautiful."

The uncertain smile that tilted her lips bloomed into
a relieved grin. She gave an exaggerated "Whew!" and
swiped a hand across her forehead. "Had me worried
there for a minute."

He shook his head. "No worries. Did Beth help you
pick it out?"

Skye nodded and picked up the handbag she'd placed on the side table earlier. "Yes, thank goodness. She showed me the dress she picked out and I went from there." She chewed her lip for a moment. "I just don't want to embarrass you."

How the hell did he show her that she wasn't an embarrassment at all? Where the fuck was his wife? The one who would have worn neon orange to the Dining Out without apology, and would have made it look damn good. There was no way to say that now without pissing her off. So he walked to her and kissed her forehead. "Not even close to embarrassed. I'm going to have to beat the guys off with a stick."

She laughed at that, her body even more relaxed now. "Well then, should we get the show on the road?" She walked to the door and paused, looking back at him over her shoulder.

God. What a picture she made. That impish little smile peeking over one bare shoulder, curls framing her gorgeous face. Tim's chest tightened in what he wasn't ready to identify yet. Not quite. When he had more time, he'd think about the emotion that was more than pride, more than gratitude, more than lust. But tonight, he had a Dining Out to get through.

Chapter 21

SHE WAS DROWNING. THERE WAS NO OTHER WORD FOR IT. She couldn't breathe. Couldn't think. Couldn't handle the tightness in her chest that had nothing to do with the fit of her dress and everything to do with what her life had come to. What she'd talked herself into.

She was one of a million. Though Beth had tried to convince her that colors were fine, Skye wasn't so sure, and had picked black anyway. Black was universal, right? It was the color people wore when they wanted to show how serious they were. And she was serious about Tim. About making sure that she didn't get in his way, screw up his career, ruin his chances for the future.

Which, inevitably, would ruin their chance for a happy marriage.

But as she looked out among the other dresses, so many in dark colors, but even a few in brighter hues, she just felt depressed. This outfit wasn't her. The dress was nothing she would have picked out on her own. It was lovely. The cut flattered her figure. It was appropriate for the event. And it was all wrong.

The dress wasn't the problem. The dress was, in the most basic and complex way possible, the current symbol of how much she had changed.

How happy could the marriage be if she was unhappy herself?

The thought slammed into Skye like a tank.

Beth walked up behind her and put a hand on her shoulder. "A few of us are over by the tables if you want to come have some girl time before everything begins. Cocktail hour always ends up being cocktail hours. At least two. Things never start on time."

Skye nodded and signaled to Tim where she was walking. Suzanne was a part of the group, as well as a few other women she remembered from the other gatherings.

"You look wonderful," Suzanne said. "I love that dress. I'm surprised you didn't wear something colorful though. I was telling my husband I was looking forward to seeing what you chose!" Several women nodded, another one remarking she'd also been curious to see what Skye would wear.

"You really need to take me shopping one day soon," a third mentioned.

Were they laughing at her? Or was she oversensitive?

"She was staring at this gorgeous turquoise number that I begged her to try on. But she wasn't having it," Beth said.

Skye brushed a hand down the front. "I just wanted to be appropriate."

Beth gave Suzanne a side glance, then said, "Well, you are. You look great."

The women continued talking, but Skye only half listened. She was losing her touch with everything. It was to the point where she couldn't tell if the women were laughing at her, or with her anymore. She was going crazy. That was the only explanation. She'd let paranoia and doubt creep in until it coated every one of her senses. But Skye couldn't escape the feeling of judgment lurking over her like a shadow.

A rustling close behind had her looking over her shoulder.

Oh. Bingo. The source of the judgmental black cloud.

Mrs. Blackwater stood just behind Skye, slightly turned, sipping a drink, her eyes on something in the distance. But Skye knew without a doubt she was tuned into the conversation between the group of women, just waiting for some juicy tidbit, maybe even a word about herself. Though the conversation was benign, who knew what simple comment the woman could take and twist into some bit of untrue gossip. To save anyone from the embarrassment of being overheard, she said in a louder-than-necessary voice, "Mrs. Blackwater! You look lovely tonight!"

The instant hush of the group of women would have been obvious to a deaf man. The older woman turned and smiled, her painted lips pulling tightly over her teeth. Clearly, being outed for eavesdropping wasn't her idea of fun.

"Skye, sweetheart. Nice to see you." Mrs. Blackwater's eyes drifted from Skye's head to toe and back again. "You look... appropriate. I'm very proud of you. I'm sure Timothy is proud as well. He must be so pleased you've decided to take his career seriously."

Because that's just how she would think. Skye's entire existence was wrapped up in her husband's wishes. Only an airheaded cardboard Barbie would set aside what she wanted to...

Oh. Shit. For the first time, Skye stared down at the hated black dress. Without ever meaning to, she'd wrapped her entire self around her husband. Without ever meaning to, she lost herself.

Skye plastered a smile on her face, fighting to remain outwardly calm through the painful self-disappointment. "That's kind of you to say. But I'm not a potty-training puppy. I'm fully capable of behaving however I please, with or without my husband's approval." Without waiting to see or hear the older woman's reaction, Skye turned on her heel and left the group of women, heading toward the door.

She barely reached the coat closet when warm fingers wrapped around her upper arm.

"Where are you going?" Her husband's voice was low in her ear.

"Home," she said quietly. Though the thought hadn't occurred to her, in that instant she knew that's where she needed to be. To restart. Reenergize. Reevaluate just how badly this entire thing could have ended up, and how much of it was her fault.

"Are you sick?" Tim's face morphed instantly from confusion to concern as he rubbed his palms up and down her bare arms, as if to warm her. "Do you need to go to the clinic?"

Skye smiled, taking another long look at him. Soaking in what he looked like in his dress blues, committing the image to a sweet memory. His shiny gold insignia winked in the light, his ribbons marked the achievements he'd gathered through his career. And he had only begun. Despite the loss of self, she loved this man. With his sense of honor and commitment, tenderness and stubbornness... she couldn't deny that. But to give him what he deserved—a whole wife, not just a ghost of one—she needed to take a step back.

"No. Not sick. Just need to go home."

He glanced over his shoulder, then back to her. "I'll take you. Just give me a second to give some excuses."

She tilted her head at him. "You can just come to Texas like that? I would have thought you needed to fill out some form or something first."

"Texas? What the hell are you talking about?"

"Home. Where I grew up," she clarified. "Texas."

"No." He shook his head once, firm. "Home is the townhouse twenty minutes away."

"It's not. Not for me. Time to face that fact. It's your home, and I've been living there."

The hurt that bloomed in his eyes mirrored the pain in her chest, but the truth was the truth. And she couldn't ignore it any longer.

She kissed his cheek. "I'll let you know when I get there."

"How are you—"

"O'Shay! Get your sorry ass back to the bar; you owe the next round before this thing starts!" The call was followed by the deep rumble of masculine laughter. Tim didn't even look, only kept his eyes on her.

"Go." When Tim didn't move, she gave his chest a little push. "Seriously, go."

"How are you getting h—back to the townhouse?" he asked hoarsely.

"Cab. I hear they have those even here in California." The joke fell flat, and Tim didn't crack a smile. "This isn't the end of the world, you know." *We'll figure it out. We have to.*

Tim only shook his head, as if he didn't believe her at all. But he let her go, to walk into the lobby and away from the choking, smothering feel of conformity.

—∼—

She left. Tim stared at the closing lobby door. She honest to God left. And he didn't even have the presence of mind to ask if it was for good, or for now, or for the weekend… He wiped a hand down his face, like he could erase the memory of her sad smile looking up at him. Christ, what the hell was going on?

"O'Shay."

"What!" He spun on his heel, only to come face-to-face with Colonel Blackwater. "Sir, apologies. I thought you were someone else."

"No harm done," the CO said, his lips twitching. "Did I just see your wife leave? I hope she's not feeling poorly."

Fishing. It couldn't be more obvious if he had just hung a sign around his neck saying *Tell me all your dirty secrets*. "Yes, sir. She just needed to head home." There. That was as close to the truth as he could get without lying or sounding like an idiot. An idiot who didn't know if his wife would be his wife any longer.

The Colonel shook his head, a sad sort of smirk on his face. A look that made Tim clench his fists against the unholy desire to remove the smirk permanently. "I hate to say this, especially when it seemed like she had such promise. Leaps and bounds, my wife said. She was really getting there. But to leave you alone so suddenly, and during a formal event like this. Well…" The patronizing smile only grew. "It's just unfortunate. I hate to say I told you so, so I won't." He walked away with that.

"Right, you'll just let me know without a doubt that you did tell me so. Smug bastard," Tim muttered to himself. He glanced at the door again, torn between wanting to run after Skye as fast as he could and stop her. The other part wanting to kick the door in at the frustration of being put in the position of having to choose between her and his job.

She already made her choice. And it wasn't you. Skye clearly didn't need him. Didn't want him. Who left their husband in the middle of a Dining Out, just because?

Your wife does. The woman you love. The spontaneous, outspoken, vibrant woman that you need. Not want. Need. If she left, it wasn't for malicious reasons. It was serious. To her.

"Tim, hey. Come on." Jeremy walked up and waved a hand in front of his face. "They're seating for dinner." He paused and looked around. "Where's Skye?"

Tim gave one final glance at the door. "Gone."

———

Skye let her bags drop on the porch and reached for the front door, knowing it would be unlocked. The small house, one step up from a log cabin, really, was her sanctuary. As a child growing up, it wasn't at all uncommon for the open door policy to be used quite literally for the rest of the commune. Everyone's door stayed unlocked. And if you needed a place to stay, there was always an empty couch. Of course, one never knew when you would be walking in on a group of goddess worshippers, performing some midnight dance in the nude. But those were the risks you took.

Skye walked on tiptoe, not wanting to wake up her parents. Though they were night owls for the most part, she assumed even they would be asleep at two in the morning. She should have pulled over hours ago and spent the night in a motel. But something kept her driving, urged her to press on until she reached the safety of her childhood home. She could sneak into her old bedroom and get some sleep, then talk to her parents in the morning. They would see her car outside and understand.

The house was silent, with only the sounds of her father's snoring to welcome her. She smiled. At least some things never changed. On tiptoe, she walked the same path she had a thousand times up the stairs, skipping the one step that creaked loud enough to wake the neighborhood, and stole into the room that she used for eighteen years, and every visit home since she moved to Vegas for school.

She didn't turn on any lights. Didn't need to. And she was too exhausted to bother changing. She toed her shoes off, found the edge of the bed with her knees, turned around, and fell, ready to be unconscious as soon as her head hit the mattress.

Instead, her head hit something hard as a rock.

"What the hell?"

A shriek louder than a siren split the night, and it wasn't Skye's. Skye scrambled off the bed and across the room, bashing her knee into the desk as she went. The shrieking continued as she limped toward the door. But before she reached it, a blazing light flooded the room, and she had to blink several times before her eyes adjusted.

"Skye Meadow?"

"Dad?" She turned to the voice and was immediately enveloped by strong arms and a stronger chest. The smell of pine and tobacco, her father, filled her nostrils, and despite the erratic crying behind them, Skye felt more at peace than she had in weeks. Nothing could be so wrong in her father's arms.

"Hey, pumpernickel. What are you doing here?"

Two in the morning didn't seem to be the time to get into the long story of her marriage, and her failure, so she just shook her head and burrowed closer, like she was seven again.

"What's going on? Peter?" Skye peeked over his shoulder to see her mother standing in the doorway. Amber's hair stuck out every which way from beneath its wrap, her eyes were wide, and she was clutching a yardstick in both hands with a white-knuckled grip. As if a yardstick would really help against a burglar. "Is Veronica all right?"

"Veronica? Who the hell is Veronica?" Skye pulled away from her father slightly until her mother caught sight of her.

"Skye? Oh, sweetheart, you scared me to death." Amber dropped the yardstick and held one hand to her chest, as if to calm her heart.

"Um, excuse me?" The soft but sure voice came from the bed. And for the first time, Skye remembered they weren't alone in the room. She turned to see someone— presumably the aforementioned Veronica—sitting in her old bed. The covers were pulled up around her chest, her knees were drawn up, and she looked tiny in the double bed. Two braids of dark blond hair draped over each shoulder, and the poor thing's complexion was as white as the sheets she clutched around her like a security blanket.

But even as she watched, Skye saw her straighten her spine, as if willing herself to be more present.

Skye looked expectantly at her parents.

Her mother pushed hair back under her wrap with smooth motions, completely unruffled now that all physical threat was past. "Skye, this is Veronica. Veronica is your cousin. Veronica, this is Skye, our daughter."

"Hey. Nice to meet you." Given the time of night, and the fact that she'd scared about ten years off both their lives, she opted for a wave from a distance instead of a handshake.

Veronica smiled shyly and nodded. "I apologize for..." She waved a hand over the rumpled bedspread.

"No worries. I should have known better than to just assume the bed was free." Her parents picked up another stray. It wasn't uncommon. In fact, if she had been thinking clearly, she would have thought to check before assuming her bed was unoccupied. Anyone needing a place to stay was welcome at Chez McDermott/Gibson. It was only a matter of asking.

Veronica started to stand, then looked down and realized she was still in her pajamas. "Uh, if you just give me a minute, I can be out of your way." Though she still looked a little pale, she wasn't as shaken as before.

Skye glanced around and realized that since her last visit home, her old room was no longer a shrine to her childhood. Things she didn't recognize were scattered over the desk and dresser. A skirt she didn't own was hanging from the closet door. Veronica wasn't here for a one-night stay. That was certain.

Skye waved her off. "No need. I'm the intruder this late. I've got the couch."

Veronica looked like she wanted to argue, but Amber stepped forward.

"Why don't we take this reunion downstairs so Veronica can get back to sleep?" her mother suggested gently, guiding Skye and her father out the door. "Veronica, dear, we'll talk in the morning. Don't worry about a thing. Go back to sleep."

The young woman looked unconvinced, and Skye gave her a quick, bright smile. "We'll catch up tomorrow. I didn't even know I had a cousin."

Veronica breathed deeply, letting out a long, low stream of air, as if relieved. "All right. If you're sure."

"I am. In the morning, though, you and I will talk." She shut the bedroom door behind her, noting that even on the way down, a faint glow came from under the crack of the door. Veronica probably still had her bedside lamp on, perhaps still too startled to fall back asleep. Not a great first impression on a relative she didn't know she had. She'd make it up to her in the morning.

After settling down in the kitchen with a cup of organic herbal tea—her mother's own blend—Skye sighed. "I'm sorry about that. I should have checked before I climbed, or rather, fell, into bed. I hope I didn't jump on someone who's going to be scarred from it or anything."

Her father waved the worry away, as he did all worries. Peter was a man with nothing on his mind but the positives and the future. The past and negatives were nothing to him. Admirable way to think sometimes. But in other instances, it drove Skye nuts. You couldn't always ignore the negatives in life. "She's a tough one; she'll be fine."

"So." Skye blew on her tea. "Cousin, huh?"

"On my side. My brother Ronald's daughter." Her mother spoke like Skye had any clue who this Ronald person was. Like it was a well-known fact that her mother didn't just pop up in a cabbage patch.

Skye wouldn't have a clue. Her mother never spoke of her family. Ever. Interesting. A relative. Something to think about later.

"Did she have an accent?"

Her father patted her hand. "You can find out tomorrow."

"But what about—"

Her mother cleared her throat and arched a brow. "Clearly discussing the family tree is not what drove you to our home in the middle of the night. Care to speak of it?"

"No." Skye knew that would be the end of it. Her parents wouldn't ask again. They believed all things were revealed on their own time, and if they weren't revealed, they weren't meant to be known. Skye agreed… to an extent. But for tonight, knowing she was safe from interrogation was a blessing. "Just needed some home-time." It was a half-truth anyway. She was too exhausted to get into her marriage tonight.

Her father rubbed her back in soothing circles, just the way he did when she was a child. "You've come to the right place then, pumpernickel. Word on the street is this is home for you."

Skye felt her lips curve, but there wasn't much humor to the gesture. She should have been back in California, asleep with Tim, his warm weight behind her, curling around her in subconscious protection.

Instead, she would climb on the sofa bed and sleep alone. Was she absolutely nuts to give that up, simply to take some time apart?

It's not nuts if you need it. And she did. For now, this is what she needed. For once, she could concentrate on her.

Chapter 22

Tim rubbed his eyes with his thumbs, completely lost in his thoughts. The Taliban could have blown the battalion building up by now and he wouldn't have blinked.

He was going to work late. Again. On purpose. The thought of heading home to his empty townhouse disgusted him enough to stay well past the normal quitting hour. What was there to rush home for? An evening alone with a beer and a Hungry Man microwave dinner? God, he missed his wife. Unconventional though she was, the actual life she breathed into his world was a tangible thing. A thing that, without it, made his personal life feel like a big black void. No color. No character. No surprises. Ha. Didn't he used to hate surprises? Yeah, he had. Then he got the best surprise of all, and he let it slip through his fingers.

Other than the brief voice mail Skye had left on his phone saying that she made it to Texas just fine and not to worry, that she'd given her work notice that she was taking vacation, he hadn't heard from her. He tried calling a few times, but the first call rang until her voice mail picked up, and the rest of his calls went straight to voice mail, as if her phone wasn't even on any longer.

He knew that she joked about growing up in a commune, but they had to at least believe in cell phones, right? Who didn't these days?

"Okay, I'm really sick of the 'Woe is me, my wife

took off so now I'm going to mope' bullshit. Pull your head out, O'Shay."

Jeremy's voice pulled him from his thoughts with a snap. He looked up to see Jer standing in the door of his office, blocking all view of the hallway. Jeremy's face and body language screamed, "Pissed off Jarhead comin' at ya."

"Fuck off." It was weak, as far as comebacks were concerned. But he knew an answer was expected.

"Aw, honey. Is that any way to talk to your best friend when he brought you lunch?" He tossed a brown sack on the desk, scattering papers. The logo on the bag told Tim there'd be a hoagie from his favorite sub shop inside.

"Thanks. See ya." Tim turned back to his computer, not even sure what he was looking at.

Jeremy's fists landed on the desk with a thump, rattling Tim's empty coffee mug and scattering papers. "No. The three of us are going to sit down and have lunch together, dammit. And if I have to duct tape your ugly ass in your chair to get you to do it, then I will. So don't make me. It'll only make you look like a shit."

Tim looked around the office. "If you haven't brushed up on your numbers lately, there's only two of us."

Jeremy jerked his head and Tim pushed back in his roll chair. A few clicks of the keyboard later, and Dwayne was waving from Tim's computer screen.

"Damn, took you long enough, Jer!"

"He was resistant." Jeremy grabbed a chair and swung it around to sit behind the desk.

"What the hell is going on?"

"Intervention," Dwayne said through the screen with a small smile.

Tim stared at Jeremy. "You're using Skype to hold an intercontinental intervention?"

"Trust me. If I could kick your ass, I would. So this will have to work." Dwayne's voice was a little hollow, carrying an echo through the speakers, but his frustration was clear all the same.

"I filled him in on the situation this morning over email. Well, morning for us. Early evening for him." Jeremy dug through the bag and tossed Tim a sandwich, pulling one out for himself.

"And what does my deployed therapist have to say?" he said around a bite.

"I'm disappointed." The words were soft but no less intense for their lack of volume.

Tim stared at the desk, picking a chip in the paint to focus on. "So am I."

"No. I'm disappointed in you."

Tim looked out the corner of his eye, but Dwayne had taken the same approach of staring away instead of at the camera. Jeremy, for his part, was retying his bootlaces as if it was the most important thing in the world. "Care to elaborate, Deputy Dwayne?"

Dwayne shook his head, and Tim immediately regretted the swipe. Dwayne was definitely one to prove that though country boys may talk slow, that didn't mean their minds worked at the same pace. "It's been almost a week. I thought for sure by now you'd have asked for some leave time, gone down to Texas, and figured out how to bring Skye back. But you haven't."

Tim didn't have an answer for that. It was the truth. He hadn't requested leave, hadn't made plans to head down to Texas. Other than those calls, he hadn't made the effort at all. He'd been just waiting. Waiting on word from Skye. Waiting on papers from a lawyer. On a smoke signal. Anything. But why should he put forth the effort to chase after a woman who didn't want him?

"Because you love her," Dwayne answered, as if it was the most natural thing in the world to be able to read a person's mind.

"I didn't say anything."

"Didn't have to."

"Shouldn't you be out doing deployment-type things?" Tim asked without any heat.

Dwayne just smiled. "It's my downtime. I'm seven and a half hours ahead of you. I'll be climbing in my rack once we're done kicking your ass."

Tim glanced at Jeremy, who was still focused on his boots. "And what do you think, oh Quiet One?"

Jeremy shrugged and said nothing, but Tim wasn't about to let it slide.

"Put up or shut up, jackass. You were against the marriage from the start. And you sure as hell weren't quiet about your opinions when I first said we were going to make it work. I can't believe you have absolutely nothing to say about the situation now. So speak up."

Jeremy let his boot drop back down to the ground, watched the papers on the floor rustle and settle. Then he looked at Tim, eyes focused and intense. "I just can't believe what a coward you are."

Tim sucked in a breath. *Coward my ass.* He was ready to nail a good right hook, but Dwayne grunted and muttered, "Don't do it."

"Yeah, I was against the marriage. Can you blame

me? You come home from Vegas, and you don't even know you're married. Then some woman shows up with a certificate and some pictures saying you tied the knot. You knew her less than a day, and suddenly you were going to make it work? Sorry for looking out for my friend." Jeremy shook his head. "But I know you're not an idiot. And as much as I wanted your best interest, you were determined. Determined enough, I thought, to see it through. Now shit's gone tits-up and you're diving into the foxhole. You just wait for her to make the next move. That's not you, man. And if I thought you were happy without her, I might let it go. But you're a fucking wreck."

Dwayne scoffed at that. "Dude's right. I'm not even gone a month and everything falls apart. You look like hell. If you feel half as bad as your face says you do, then this plan's not working for you."

Tim couldn't argue.

"So yeah, I'm actually with D on this one. If you're ready to call it quits, then call it quits. Draw up papers. But if you want her so bad—and you act like you do— then fucking do something. Don't sit here and mope around like someone stole your car and ran over your dog, for crissake."

As much as Tim wanted to slug him for the insult, the truth was the truth. "Shit," he murmured.

"Shit," Dwayne and Jeremy echoed. Surround sound from round the world. Great.

He'd messed up. Somehow, things had gone wrong in his marriage. In his life, period. And it was time he stopped sitting back on his heels and watching it fall away. Time for some affirmative action.

Skye's arms ached after carrying the last of the boxes in from the makeshift loading dock. Her parents' little "mom and pop" organic grocery store had grown leaps and bounds since they set up shop over twenty years ago on the commune. They had been successful, providing a healthy, happy, and stable—if a bit unorthodox— childhood for Skye. And if they'd had to live off of what they sold to the community and random passersby alone, they would have been just fine. But although they believed in grass roots and investing in your own community first, her parents weren't idiots. The minute the organic wave hit mainstream America, they set up a serious web presence, shipping organic herbs and spices and other all-natural food items directly from their store to countless homes across the country.

"Mom?" She dusted her palms on her flowing capri pants. "Where are you?"

"In the office."

Skye grabbed her Nalgene from the mini-fridge under the counter and headed back to the office, rubbing the cold material against her neck to cool her off. She stopped in the doorway and just watched while her mother moved around the office, searching for who knew what. Her tank top was wrinkled and stuck to her back thanks to the humidity. The long skirt draped and swished around her ankles, showing off her bare feet. Skye knew the material for the skirt would have been made in the commune, likely by their neighbors, the Vecheks. Whenever physically possible, her parents shopped in-commune.

"What are you looking for?"

Her mother didn't jolt at the sound of her voice. Neither of her parents were ever shocked by anything. As if they had some sort of mysterious, uncanny way of knowing someone or something was behind them at all times. "A tax form. I'm sure I placed it around here somewhere."

"Well, at least it wasn't important," Skye joked and sipped water. Now this was a familiar sight. In her parents' quest to remain carefree, details were often left behind. Swept under some mental rug, not to be dealt with again until physically necessary.

Without turning around, her mother asked, "Are you almost done?"

"Yeah, finished bringing in the last box. It was a heavy one. But everything is in the back, in order. I'll unpack it here in a minute."

She held up a paper, shook her head, and put it back. "No. I mean are you done hiding?"

The question almost had Skye dropping her bottle. "Hiding?"

The file cabinet shut with a metallic scrape that had Skye wanting to cringe. Her mother turned then and sat on the corner of the desk, the form completely forgotten. "Sweetheart, you know your father and I love you to pieces. And you are welcome anytime, as long as you want. But you're not here for a visit. You're here to hide."

"No." Skye took a deep breath. "I'm here to give myself some space. To figure out what I want. To remember who I am." *Please don't push me. I don't want to think about this.*

Her mother sighed, as if the answer was so obviously wrong. "You are who you are. And you always will be. What worries you so much, sweetheart?"

When Skye showed up on her parents' doorstep five days earlier, she had only given the basics of the situation. Her fast marriage with Tim. Their choice to work through it. That she needed a little time to process because of how rapidly things were changing. Her parents didn't press for more—Skye never expected them to. They likely had some theory about the great earth mother or the wind goddess blowing her into their paths or something. Who knew. But she knew she was at least safe from interrogation.

"I'm just worried. I thought that the whole thing was a sign. Fate. That despite our differences, Tim and I were supposed to be together. But I don't think he can be with me as I am. And I can't be the woman he's always needed. It's not in me."

Her mother was silent a moment. "We can only be ourselves in the long run. Everyone can be someone else for a time. Actors have jobs for a reason. But eventually, our true natures win out. You never could have been someone else for long, even if you tried. It would have broken you." A soft hand caressed her cheek. "And you're too special to break." Then her mother stood back up and started shifting through files again. Such was Amber's way. Just like that, the conversation was forgotten. Not because it wasn't important. But because it wasn't in the now.

Skye walked out to the main grocery portion of the store where her father was helping a family load their pickup truck with boxes of something. She brought the last box out to the pickup truck and watched her father give a fond farewell.

"Regulars?" Skye took a seat on the top porch step.

"Yup." Her father sat beside her. "Drive over twice a month from the city for the organic selection."

"Good news for you."

"Hmm." He stared out into the road, dust still settling from the departing truck. "Am I ever going to meet this man you've married?"

Great question. "Soon, Daddy." *If I still have a husband.* "He's got a lot on his plate now with work."

"A Marine." Her father rubbed a toe in the dirt. "I'm not quite sure where we went wrong…"

She sighed. "You didn't go wrong. He's just the man I fell in love with." Saying it out loud, for the first time, only reaffirmed that truth. And strengthened her resolve to face the music and do her best to make things work. And work for them both. They couldn't continue on the way they were, with one pretending to be something she wasn't.

"But he carries a gun, Skye Meadow. And uses intimidation and force to get what he wants."

"In his job. Which protects the right for you to sit here and own this store. He's not some gun-toting mercenary that just runs around scaring people all day to get what he wants, Dad." Wow. Where did *that* come from? She checked her rising anger and forced herself to speak more calmly. "He's my husband. So please, just let that all go?"

Her father nodded but still didn't look at her. She placed a hand on her father's shoulder and stood up, going back inside to the air-conditioned store. Behind her, Peter muttered something about the evils of war and how the human race was one step away from blowing the planet to bits. She let the front door shut tightly behind her.

Veronica stood behind the cash register, thoughtfully quiet as always. Skye was determined to make a friend out of this woman. They were complete opposites. But at the same time, Skye could appreciate how composed she was, sweet and even funny in a shy sort of way. The only problem was she wasn't all that open. Yet. But if her parents and the community had taught Skye anything, it was that a blank sheet was nothing but possibilities waiting to happen.

"Veronica, how are things?"

The woman ducked her head, then as if determined to make eye contact, raised it deliberately. "Fine." Her voice was naturally soft.

"Do you like the area?"

"Yes."

So far, she wasn't much on sharing past the basics. Her parents hadn't given Skye her cousin's background. They wouldn't though. If Veronica wanted Skye to know, she would share. That's the way it worked around the commune. Nobody was obligated to share their past.

"So where did you come from?" Skye hopped up on the counter and grabbed an apple out of the basket by the register. She wiped it on her shirt and took a bite.

"Around."

Skye tried another tactic and said nothing. When Veronica realized she was still waiting, she added, "We moved around often."

"Huh. I grew up here. Didn't really leave until college.

Might have been fun to explore other places. You're my mom's brother's kid. Are there more of you?"

"Just me." Veronica turned away, busying herself with looking for something—likely nothing—behind the counter.

Okay, so no family talk. "Have you met anyone around here? Hung out with anyone in the area? There were some people my age when I grew up here, though they might have all taken off now."

Veronica shook her head, the thick gold braid shaking as it fell between her shoulder blades. For the first time, Skye could appreciate how long the woman's hair really was. It reached past the waistband of her skirt. She could probably sit on it if she tried. That had to be annoying. She took a longer look at her cousin. Plain clothes, slightly baggy. Whether she bought them that way or she'd lost weight, Skye had no clue. Not a hint of makeup. No jewelry either, simple or otherwise.

"Do you like working at the store? If not, I bet my parents could find you another job in the commune. Maybe working at the teashop or the bookstore. I know when I was saving up cash for college I used to grab a few hours of work over at—"

"No." The word was sharp, definite. Skye smiled. So she wasn't entirely a mouse after all. "I like working here. Your parents have been wonderful. I couldn't have hoped for better."

Skye's smile grew. "Yeah. They are pretty great. How old are you?"

Veronica eyed Skye out of the corner of her eye. "Twenty-six."

There was a formal tone to her speech. Sort of like

people who spoke English as a second language. Even more interesting. Skye was determined not to pry, however. "Well, my parents are great to work for, and live with." She hopped down from the counter, ready to head over to the house for a break and some privacy before the town meeting that night.

As much as she loved her parents, loved the commune, and loved revisiting her past, it was time to figure out her future. Tomorrow she'd head home.

—◦◦◦—

Tim followed the GPS as far as it would take him, which wasn't far. Apparently Skye's family lived in the middle of nowhere. Literally. Tim's symbolic little blue car on the GPS screen was driving through nothing. If he hadn't stopped at the last gas station to ask where the infamous commune was located, he would have been lost an hour ago.

Actually, he wasn't entirely sure he wasn't lost now. Hippies, despite their *peace, love, happiness* attitude, apparently liked their solitude.

He didn't have time to roam around the great state of Texas looking for his wife. He had exactly one week to reach Skye, figure out where things went wrong—on both sides—and convince her to come back with him.

If he could find her first.

Chapter 23

ANOTHER FIFTEEN MINUTES AND TIM FELT LIKE SINGING A hallelujah chorus as he saw signs of civilization in the distance. Inching closer, he picked out several buildings that appeared to make a complete circle, with one road that led in. He drove on, heading straight for the opening. If this wasn't it, then he was going to demand a guide like Lewis and fucking Clark to get the rest of the way there.

Tim headed for the first thing that looked like a business—a café of some kind—and parked in their front lot. He got out and walked around to the front of the business, taking in the area. The circle of buildings looked like it was a mile around, with another layer or two of buildings behind the first, sort of laid out in a spiral. The wide sidewalks flanked decent, well-kept roads. And not every building was cookie-cutter perfect, each carrying its own charm. This little town was definitely not built by a mega-millionaire corporation.

He jerked on the door to the café, determined to ask a few questions, but the door didn't budge. On second glance, he saw the *Closed* sign. Sort of an odd time to be closed, being in the middle of dinner. He walked over to the next building, a salon, and found the same. Closed. Then Tim looked around, listened.

Nothing.

No cars driving around the roads, no people walking

from store to store, no radios blaring or kids laughing. It was a ghost town. Or was it a ghost commune?

Someone had to live here. A ghost town didn't stay this well-maintained and preserved. So where the hell was everyone? He wandered down the sidewalk, searching for signs of life, practicing the speech he would give once he finally found his runaway wife.

As Tim rounded the curve, he heard a faint buzzing noise. The first real sign of civilization since he parked. He followed the noise, winding back between a bookstore and a coffee house and then slipping around a house to find an open field full of bodies, a few hundred by his estimate. Some sitting, some standing, some... dancing? Yes, a few were actually swaying to some unheard music. Tim hesitated to call them crazy. His wife would simply say they were free spirits, moving to the beat of their own drummer—literally. But it was impossible to see if Skye was among the crowd.

People of all ages were gathered, from babes in arms to a few with wheelchairs and walkers. Everyone was dressed very Skye-like. Or rather, Skye before she started changing her look. Flowing garments, loose folds, tunics, crazy patterns. Tim glanced ruefully at his own khakis, button-down shirt, and simple dress shoes. For once, he was the one who stood out.

He realized someone was up front, standing on top of a pickup with amplifiers, speaking into a microphone. Though it was difficult to hear, he worked his way around the outside of the crowd until he had a better spot. From the sounds of it, it was a sort of town hall meeting. Business about the community. Updates about a homeschool co-op was next up on the agenda.

"Hi there." A woman, probably in her eighties, with steel-gray hair and a feel of frailty about her, placed a hand on his arm. Chunky bracelets clanked as she moved, and her eyes were kind. "Are you passing through?"

"I don't know." Tim continued scanning the crowd, looking for any hint of Skye. There was so much color, so much light, it almost hurt his eyes to stare at it. Almost nobody wore dark colors, and black didn't exist to these people.

I have to be close.

"Are you searching for something? Enlightenment of some kind?"

"I'm searching for—whoa!" Tim pulled gently against the woman's grip, which tightened on his wrist. The rings covering her gnarled fingers dug into his skin. "Can I help you?"

The woman turned serious eyes to him. "All newcomers should be introduced."

"Oh, there's been a mistake. No introduction necessary." *Please and thank you.*

Watery blue eyes stared back at him. Then, as if she hadn't heard him, she repeated, "All newcomers should be introduced." With that, she started walking toward the front, pulling him behind.

No. Oh hell no. Tim tried digging his feet into the ground, but she managed to continue pulling. He could have jerked his arm away, but the thought of causing the elderly woman to fall or hurt herself was worse than being dragged around like a lost child in an airport. He followed, grudgingly, still scanning the crowd for Skye.

No such luck.

They reached the side of the pickup located at the

front of the crowd, where a bald man in his late fifties, maybe early sixties, was reading about someone's newest little bundle of joy. Tim's captor tugged on the man's flaring capri pants with authority. "Peter, we have a newcomer."

The man looked at Tim, his eyes narrowing a moment. "Yes, we do. Well, come on up, young man. Tell us about yourself."

Tim stared out into the crowd, praying for a glimpse of Skye. Or at least someone to rescue him. Nope. Not his lucky day. He sighed and stepped up, figuring it was easier to go along with the shenanigans than run away. He could easily guess nobody would be overly helpful to the man who knocked down an eighty-year-old woman just to escape saying hi. Besides, why not ask four hundred people at once where Skye was rather than one at a time? It was just more efficient, really.

Yeah. Efficient. That's how he'd mentally file this one. Efficient sounded better than crazy.

Hopping up on the bed of the truck, he waited until the vehicle stopped rocking, then took the mic from the older man. He stared into the sea of faces, some smiling, some skeptical, others lost in their own world, like their minds were tuned to a completely different channel.

"Hi, my name is Tim, and I—"

"Hi, Tim!" The roar of the crowd almost knocked him back. Christ, what was this? Some AA meeting?

"Uh, right. Anyway, I'm not here for enlightenment or anything like that. Or maybe I am. I guess that depends."

There was some mild chatter, and a few brilliant smiles aimed his way. He rubbed the back of his burning neck.

"Ignore that. First things first. I'm looking for my wife. Skye McDermott? I think this is where she grew up."

The crowd, buzzing with welcoming energy, shut down faster than a frat party during a raid. The smiles melted away, the skeptics looked smug. Even those who appeared lost in their own world seemed to shrink back, as if some psychic wavelength told them he was bad news.

What the hell did he say? He's a stranger, and these people don't know him. Right. Of course, a small little commune like this would circle the wagons—or rather, circle the flower power—around one of their own.

He tried again. "She came for a visit, and I was just trying to find her. She's about this high—" he held up his hand to shoulder height, "with long brown hair. Blue-gray eyes? Beautiful? Anyone?"

Silence. Owl stares. Sweat dripped between his shoulder blades.

"Right. Well, if you see her," and he knew they would, "tell her that her husband is looking for her. Tell her... just tell her—"

"Tim? What the hell are you doing?"

He jolted, almost dropping the mic. "Skye?" He turned around, not daring to hope. But there she was. Her hair was pulled back on either side from her face, curls and waves flowing around her shoulders. The sunburst tunic top skimmed over her hips, and her legs were in some bright yellow leggings. Her feet were bare, kicking up dust as she walked toward him.

"What are you doing here?"

His mouth was dry when he tried to speak. She

looked so beautiful, so naturally Skye, that he almost lost his thoughts. "I came. For you."

The shock showed on her face. "Really?"

"Yeah. I didn't come to practice my public speaking skills." Realizing he still held the microphone, he thrust it at the other man and hopped down from the bed of the pickup. In three long strides he reached her but stopped just short of wrapping his arms around her like he wanted. "I'm here to bring you home." Before she could speak he shook his head. His world narrowed until all he saw was her face, all he heard was her breath, growing heavier. "No, I meant that. Home. Our home. I hate that you think you were a roommate. You're my wife. And I want you to be home with me. I don't care if that means you'll burn twelve different incense a day and hang up posters of spirits and leave your socks on the coffee table. Just come home."

She stared at him for a moment, eyes widening. Then she jerked her head to the side and walked back behind the pickup truck, shielding them from a majority of the curious onlookers.

"Why?" Her voice was soft, almost scared.

Thank God. An easy one. "Because I love you. I love you, Skye Meadow McDermott, the way I married you. I don't know what happened, why you thought you had to change completely to make me happy. And I don't know why I ever let you think you needed to. But I want Skye back. You."

Skye closed her eyes, and Tim felt his stomach drop and the blood rush in his ears. He was too late. He didn't move fast enough. And now he was going to suffer because of it.

But then without opening her eyes, Skye launched herself at him, wrapping her arms around his neck and her legs around his waist, taking him completely by surprise. He stepped back a few feet to regain his balance and held her tight. Thank God the side of the pickup was right behind his back or they would have topped into the dirt.

"I love you too," she mumbled into his neck. "I just… I didn't…"

"I know." He stroked her wild hair once, tangled his fingers in the curls. "I know."

Past the roar of his own heartbeat, Tim heard the sound of applause, muffled and distant. As they stood peacefully, soaking each other in, his hearing cleared and the clapping became louder until it was like a tidal wave, crashing over them.

"Uh, Skye, I think—"

"Yeah. They're clapping for us." Her voice held laughter, and he smiled. He'd put up with a lot to hear her that happy again.

Soon—too soon—Skye slid down until her feet touched the ground. "Dad."

The bald man from the truck peeked over the side of the cab, a huge grin on his face. "Yes, pumpernickel?"

"That's your dad?" Tim asked incredulously. When Skye nodded, he turned to the man. "And when I was up there, pouring my heart out about my wife, you didn't think to stop me and say, 'Hey, she's back that way'?"

The man shrugged, completely unapologetic. "Not my decision to make."

"Dad," Skye broke in, laughing. "We're heading to the house for a bit."

"I gotcha." The man winked and turned back to the

crowd, asking them to settle down so he could finish his announcements.

Tim let his head drop to the side of the truck with a thump. "That wasn't awkward or anything."

She grabbed his hand and tugged. "Come on. Everyone here will be busy for at least another hour."

"Say no more."

———※———

Skye pulled the door shut behind them, watching as Tim wandered the living room, soaking in the mementos of her childhood. Pictures, childish crafts, awards were all displayed in random order, scattered throughout the room and the house. She wondered what he would think of the completely mismatched home, with its worn, broken-in furniture and bizarre decor.

"Looks like you," he said after a minute. "I see you in this place." He stopped to grab a framed picture of Skye at seven, holding a trophy for being the homeschool co-op's best peacekeeper. "Cute," he said with a grin.

"So you flew in?"

"Yup. Didn't have a lot of leave time. But since you have your car, we can drive back." He glanced around and saw the suitcases next to the kitchen door. He stared at them, as if he'd never seen luggage before. "Are those packed?"

"Yeah." When he said nothing, just continued to stare at the bags, she went on. "I was leaving tomorrow morning."

"Going where?" he asked, his voice hoarse.

"Home. Back to you." When he finally looked her way, she smiled. "You just beat me to it."

He reached her in two steps and crushed her against his chest. "Don't do this again. Please. Talk to me. Scream at me. Rearrange the furniture or burn the place down. Just… don't leave again," he mumbled into her hair.

Poor Marine. Always so sure of himself at work. Ready to fight wars, take over countries. Solve any problem. And instead, he suddenly looked so… lost. She scratched his scalp lightly with her fingernails until his body started to relax, tension seeping out. "I'm sorry. I just didn't see another way at the time. That was rude of me, to leave during the function. I hope I didn't get you in trouble at work. I know—"

"Fuck work." He held her at arm's length, his face fierce. "I mean don't leave me. Just me. I don't care if you never host another coffee or never go to another function. I want you to, because I love being with you, having you with me. But if you don't, I won't care. Just don't run away from me."

"The coffee wasn't too bad," she murmured as she eased back into his arms. "And I like barbeques."

"I'm sorry too. I didn't see how you were taking things. I should have spoken up sooner, let you know you didn't have to change. But the truth was, I wasn't sure myself how things were going to work. It was so much, so fast and I—"

"Shh. It's okay. We're okay."

His hands stroked over her back, soothing at first. Then he slipped under the tunic, his rough fingertips electrifying the nerves along her back until she shivered.

"Are you making a move on me in my parents' living room, Captain?"

"I sure as hell am." His hands moved around to cup

her breasts, pulling them out the top of her flimsy bra. Skye let her head drop back while he nuzzled her jaw-line. "If you have to ask, I must be doing a piss-poor job of it." And without warning, he bent at the waist until he could lift up with Skye draped over his shoulder. She shrieked, then laughed as he carried her to the sofa and plopped her down. "Is this more obvious?"

His heavy, comforting weight draped over her, and she smiled. "You're nothing if not a perfectionist."

"I aim to please."

Skye let him please her until the meeting was over.

Dinner should have been uncomfortable, eating with his in-laws who he had never met before. Not to mention the numerous not-so-subtle digs about the military and war that Peter kept tossing into the conversation.

But, no surprise, Skye's parents were unconventional and didn't seem to feel any sort of discomfort. They acted like it was a weekly occurrence, having their only daughter's husband show up to claim her, making unin-tentionally public vows of affection and love.

And then there was Veronica, the quiet, tiny girl who was almost silent. No, not girl. Woman. She had to be at least in her mid-twenties. But with her hair in two long braids, and her naturally subservient manner, he couldn't help but think of her as much younger than her real age. Like a pre-teen getting to eat at the adult table. He could tell she wanted to speak, and often. Her hand clenched around her fork repeatedly. But she held back. Skye introduced her simply as her cousin, nothing more. But Tim couldn't help thinking there was far more to the story than that. It just wasn't his place to pry.

Amber placed the last of the vegetables on the table. Next to the other vegetables. And the bread. And more veggies. Ah, the feast of vegans. So he'd have a burger tomorrow on the way home. Surprisingly, the vegetables were delicious.

"What's the seasoning on these potatoes?" he asked between helpings.

Skye's mother smiled. "Family secret. But we sell the mixed seasoning in packets to customers."

It was an odd combination. They lived in a very old-fashioned manner, without a television or computers in the home. No sign of even a radio that he had noticed. And most everything they owned seemed to be made in the commune, from clothing to furniture and everything between. It was almost completely self-reliant, this little community. And nobody was in want. But their business sense was as savvy as any entrepreneur straight out of Harvard. They operated their store with the same family-friendly, local charm as every other place in the commune. But they also had a booming Internet business, as Skye showed him earlier that evening, shipping organic spices and herbs and other food-related items around the country.

"Did your mother tell you about our next trip coming up?" Skye's father asked. To Tim, he added, "We often travel around the country, speaking at smaller conferences about the benefits of homegrown organics and integrating natural foods into the American diet. It's a great way to promote the business."

Skye shook her head. "No. You hadn't said anything." But she didn't look surprised. "When do you leave?"

"Sunday. The Clarks will be watching the store while we're gone."

"Will you be going with them, Veronica?" he asked.

Before the cousin had a chance to answer Tim, Amber said, "We were hoping you might take her with you. Let her experience more of the world while we're gone. We can swing by California and pick her up on the way back."

Skye looked thoughtfully at Veronica before glancing at Tim. "I don't know. What do you think?"

He knew that was her way of saying she wanted to. If she didn't, she would have said so. This was his out. And he wasn't going to take it. "It's fine with me."

Her brilliant smile told him it was the right choice. "Veronica, do you want to come back with us for a bit?"

Tim doubted she was even paying attention, she was focusing so hard on her water glass. But then she nodded. And surprised him by giving more than a one-word answer.

"Yes. I'd like to go. I need to see more. More… everything." Raising her head, almost defiant in the gesture, she looked him straight in the eye. "As long as you don't mind the burden."

"Not a burden. You're my wife's cousin. Family's never a burden."

She nodded once, and her eyes were shining. Gratitude? It was just a trip to California. How little had this woman been given the opportunity to experience if a simple road trip and a week or two of Cali sunshine had her near tears? Well, it made his wife happy. And that was enough for Tim.

—◆—

Veronica watched as Skye and her husband loaded the small car with suitcases. When Tim came to take the one small bag she'd packed, he looked around.

"Got anymore?"

She shook her head and forced herself not to take a step back. Men, even in a platonic sense, were not something she was used to dealing with on a daily basis. But Tim was kind, and her cousin's husband. She trusted Skye, and therefore she trusted Tim.

He smiled and shrugged. "Makes packing the car easier." Then he jogged down the front steps and started working on rearranging the trunk again.

She bit her lip, wanting desperately to call back her bag. Tell him not to pack it. That she changed her mind. That she would stay in her safe little bubble where nobody could hurt her.

No. That's what they *would want you to say. Make your own choice.*

This was why she came to America in the first place. Why she went against everything her parents believed in to experience life. Now here was a chance to take another step in the right direction. The *normal* direction.

He finally managed to squeeze her bag in and shut the trunk. And so, shut the door on any chance to change her mind.

This is good for you. You need this.

"Are you ready to go?" Skye walked up behind her from in the house and placed a soft hand on her shoulder. Veronica barely felt the touch at all. "If you want to stay, I'm sure that—"

"No. I need to go."

Skye said nothing. But her hand squeezed slightly

before it dropped away. A tiny show of support. Of encouragement. It was all she needed. Following Skye, she walked down to the car.

"Ready to roll?" Tim asked Skye.

"Let's do this. I'm ready to head home."

They both climbed in the car, and Veronica opened her back door. With one final glance at the house she'd stayed in the past few months—her baby step into the real world, she thought of it—she blinked against tears. Peter and Amber had been her saviors. And now she was hoping Skye would be half as understanding.

Her cousin looked back, a sweet smile tilting her lips. "You ready?"

With a deep breath, she nodded. "Ready."

***

That night, after unpacking the car and settling Veronica into the guest room of the townhouse, Skye curled against Tim in their bed. The warmth of her body, the softness of her curves had him smiling.

She traced his lips with a fingertip. "Why so happy?"

"I don't know what brought you to me—"

"I told you before. It was Fate," she said smugly.

"I was thinking more like an ace-queen. Vegas, the blackjack table," he explained when she gave him a confused look. Then she chuckled.

"That works."

Sure did.

Duty Calls

Chapter 1

JEREMY PHILLIPS SETTLED THE PROTECTORS OVER HIS EARS, adjusted his glasses more comfortably on the bridge of his nose and took a comfortable stance. Then, at the signal, picked up his Beretta, clicked off the safety and fired fifteen rounds. As the smell of black powder and CPL agent filled his nostrils, he checked his gun, set the safety, then slapped a hand over the switch to draw the paper target forward.

His best friend, and today's shooting partner, Timothy O'Shay ducked his head around the divider and mouthed something.

"What?" Jeremy yelled back.

Tim cocked one eyebrow and tapped a finger to his ear, pointing out the obvious.

Oh. Shit. Right. Jeremy took the protectors off and set them on the ledge in front of him, next to his Beretta. "What?"

"I asked how long you were going to waste bullets when your head's not in the game."

Jeremy gave him a withering look. "I'm not wasting bullets."

Tim's answer was to glance between the two targets—his and Jeremy's—now only a few feet away. Jeremy took a look also.

Tim's dummy showed two tight clusters of bullet holes, so close together they'd ripped large chunks from the paper. Several in the head, the other in the chest. Not a stray hole at all.

His dummy, by comparison, looked like a constellation of wrongness. Half the bullets sprayed over the outline's shoulders, the other half catching the figure in the arm or some other undesirable area.

"You'll have to remind me how you shot expert at the last firearms qual," Tim said casually as he stripped the target down and replaced it with a fresh one.

"Just having an off day." When Tim said nothing, Jeremy glanced over his shoulder. His friend smirked and shook his head. "Bite me, O'Shay."

"You know what Dwayne would say to that." Tim straightened his shoulders in an effort to look taller. "If you were a female, I just might take you up on that one," he said with an exaggerated drawl.

Though he tried to fight it, Jeremy cracked a smile.

Their deployed friend, Dwayne Robertson, always did let his natural drawl thicken up to an almost obscene level when he was telling a joke. Tim nailed it perfectly. He clipped on his own fresh target and sent it back. "Yeah, yeah. When's that big lug coming home, anyway?"

"He just left not that long ago. For all we know, he might get delayed past the original seven. Stuff's shifting over there. Makes for interesting deployments." As he thumbed the last few bullets into his clip, he pushed it in and locked it. "Seriously, what's going on? You've shot for shit all day, and I know you could do better than this blindfolded. What's up?"

Because Tim was holding a loaded weapon, now was absolutely not the time for the truth. So instead he lifted a shoulder and dismissed his friend's concern. "If marriage is gonna turn you into some walking therapy session, I'm not so sure we can be friends anymore."

Tim just laughed and flipped the switch to send his target flying back. "It's not the prison sentence you make it out to be."

"Right."

"No, really. I guess it could be if you were unhappy. But when you've got the right partner, it works out. Pretty damn well, I think." A self-satisfied smile crossed Tim's face as he watched his target settle into place. But the preoccupied look in his eye behind his protective glasses said he wasn't actually seeing the target at all. He was thinking about Skye, his wife.

Jeremy gave a grunt and rolled his shoulders. Tim might be blissful in love and all that, but it wasn't for everyone. At least, not for him. Not right now. He had

shit to do before he thought about settling down. And his
mind wasn't in the dating game. Not when he was too
hung up on one irritating, annoying, always-in-the-way
female who made his teeth grind and his blood fire.

In all the right ways… and wrong ones.

He waited for his own target to settle before readjust-
ing the mufflers over his ears and reloading his weapon.
Deep breath in, then back out. This time he wasn't going
to rush it. Wasn't going to just punch holes through the
paper for the satisfaction of the hit. Concise, precise,
accurate.

He sighted the target, took a calm breath in. Waited
until his heart beats slowed enough to time the trigger
squeeze between them. And on a slow breath out, he
fired one shot.

And his brain exploded in color and sound, light and
movement. Voices. Action. Motivation and intrigue.

Before he even glanced at the target to check his
shot, Jeremy clicked on the safety, set the gun down and
started patting his pockets for a pen. Where the hell did
he put it? Aggravated, he turned in a tight circle around
his cubicle before spotting his pen on the ground by the
bag he used for his ammo. He sifted through the bag
but came up with no paper. Terrified he was about to
lose the scene playing out in his mind, he pushed up the
sleeve of his Henley and started to write across the underside of his arm, from biceps to elbow to wrist. Black
ink smudged but he kept going, knowing he'd have an
interesting time deciphering it later but not caring in the
moment. He had to get the idea down or he'd lose it.

Writer's block was a bitch in heat. And he wasn't
about to let the perfect solution to the corner he'd written

himself into last week slip through his fingers because of a lack of paper.

Distantly, he realized he no longer heard the muffled pops of Tim's gun. Quickly, before his friend could realize what he was doing, he jotted the last few words down across the inside of his wrist and pulled his shirt down.

"Hey, what stopped you?" When Tim glanced around the divide and saw Jeremy squatting on the floor, his brows rose in question. "You okay?"

"Yeah." Standing, stuffing the pen back in his pocket, he shrugged. "Decided you were right. My head's not in the game. No point in wasting bullets."

"I was planning to go a few more, if you don't mind waiting."

Jeremy smiled, feeling more relaxed now than he had in a week. "Sure, maybe I'll go one more round." He waited until Tim was settled, then lined up his own fourteen remaining shots. With a more relaxed breathing rhythm, looser stance, he fired until he came up empty. And when he recalled his paper target this time, he couldn't hold back the satisfied smirk.

Fourteen head shots, one through the chest. The chest shot being his first before he'd started jotting notes. Not a single stray in the bunch. "Not bad," he mumbled to himself.

Then everything in his brain stalled as he caught a whiff of something feminine, something that climbed over the scent of black powder and CLR and made its presence know. A scent he knew too damn well.

"Not bad at all."

And with that light, airy voice from over his shoulder, his mood dipped dangerously low once more.

—◊◊◊—

"Mad, hey." Tim leaned over to give her a hug. Madison hugged back tightly.

"Thanks for letting me know you were out here." She hefted her bag from over her shoulder, taking the stall on the other side of Jeremy. "Empty for a Saturday."

"It's early yet. Lazy people are still in bed." Tim peeked around her arm. "What'd you bring?"

She held up her twenty-two, brand new and ready to be tested.

"Ah. See you broke out the Desert Eagle for this one," he said solemnly, then laughed when she punched him in the arm. Her brother's face twisted in comedic dismay. "Well, hell, Mad. That's a girl gun."

"I *am* a girl, you ass." She kicked at his feet and he shuffled back, laughing all the way to his stall. "And this little sucker fits in almost any purse," she added, then felt stupid for justifying the completely frivolous purchase of the small handgun. It really was a girly gun. But it was so cute…

Not able to avoid it any longer, she glanced at Jeremy's face for the first time since she got to the range.

Thunderclouds would have been a friendlier welcome. His face was a mask of annoyance and frustration. Well, that made two of them. Though God only knew what he was so frustrated about. If he thought she was stalking him, he had a more self-inflated ego than she thought.

But either way, she'd play it cool. "Morning, Jeremy," she said, keeping her voice light and casual.

Acknowledgments

The road to publication is a strange and winding one. But the great part about that is you meet some fantastic people along the way. And I have them all to thank for helping me achieve this dream. First the Divas, for providing me with a place to learn and grow. Then my critique group, who are a fantastic cheerleading team. My one-of-a-kind critique partner, Keri Ford, for her hilarious, insightful editorial notes. My lovely agent, Emmanuelle Morgen, for guiding me and being a great support. My editor, Deb Werksman, for giving me the push to make this book the best it could be.

And then those who have nothing to do with writing, but who matter very much to me. My dog, Clyde, who manages to provide comedic relief during stressful times (as all the best pets do). My mother, who was the one to put my first romance novel in my hand, inspiring my love for the genre. My dad, a girl's number one fan. My sister, who appreciates my own sense of humor. My daughter, who gives the world's best snuggles and always manages to make Mommy's heart melt. And my husband, for being a research assistant, maid, cook, therapist, nanny, and shoulder to lean on when I needed it. You wear a lot of hats, Hubs, but you wear them so darn well.

My people. Couldn't have done it without you.

P.S. Though it may come as a shock, I'm actually

not perfect. (I know, right?) Any and all mistakes made concerning the fine fighting force of the United States Marine Corps were mine and mine alone. There. You're now off the hook, Hubs.

About the Author

Jeanette Murray is a contemporary romance author who spends her days surrounded by hunky alpha heroes… at least in her mind. In real life, she's a one-hero kind of woman, married to her own real-life Marine. When she's not chasing her daughter or their lovable-but-stupid Goldendoodle around the house, she's deep in her own fictional world, building another love story. As a military wife, she would tell you where she lives… but by the time you read this, she'll have already moved. To see what Jeanette is up to next, visit www.jeanettemurray.com.

SEALed Forever

by Mary Margret Daughtridge

—⁓—

He's got a living, breathing dilemma...

In the midst of running an undercover CIA mission, Navy SEAL Lt. Garth Vale finds an abandoned baby, and his superiors sure don't want to know about it. The only person who can help him is the beautiful new doctor in town, but she's got another surprise for him...

She's got a solution... at a price...

Dr. Bronwyn Whitescarver has left the frantic pace of big city ER medicine for a small town medical practice. Her bags aren't even unpacked yet when gorgeous, intense Garth Vale shows up on her doorstep in the middle of the night with a sick baby...

But his story somehow doesn't add up, and Bronwyn isn't quite sure who she's saving—the baby, or the man...

—⁓—

Praise for SEALed Forever:

"Take two strong characters, throw in some humor and a baby and you've got a perfect combination for a heartwarming romance. The suspense subplot is a bonus in this well-written story."—*RT Book Review*, 4.5 stars

For more Mary Margret Daughtridge, visit:

www.sourcebooks.com